THE REBEL
OF SAVANNAH

D1522895

Hayim Tawil
and
Chananya Weissman

with
Mazal Mizrahi

KODESH PRESS

Cover artwork is an image of Savannah in 1734. The proper name is *A View of Savannah As It Stood 29 March 1734*. It is an engraving done by Pierre Fourdrinier (though now his first name is believed to be Paul), one of the most prominent engravers in the eighteenth century. It has also been attributed to James Oglethorpe, the protagonist of *The Rebel of Savannah*, but it seems more likely that it was done by Fourdrinier, who was trained in this discipline. The image has been scaled and cropped to fit the dimensions of the book cover. The original is currently owned by the Toronto Public Library, and it is in the public domain in the United States, Canada, and most countries due to its age.

The Rebel of Savannah was originally published March 2014, and the text has been slightly modified, June 2014.

Published by
Kodesh Press
New York, NY
www.KodeshPress.com

This book is dedicated to the early settlers of Savannah whose spirit of freedom helped Georgia to join the twelve other states of the Union.

Acknowledgements

From Hayim Tawil

I would like to thank heartily the librarians of Yeshiva University: The reference librarian, Zalman Alpert, the loan librarian, Mary Ann Linahan, and especially Zvi Erenyi, the acquisition librarian who provided for the project all the historical and the anthropological material requested. This enabled me to conduct the right research for *The Rebel of Savannah*. Likewise, my thanks to Professor Richard White, Dr. Bob Wolf and Harry Epstein, who read part of the material. My son, Dr. Arye Joseph Tawil, while a student at Atlanta, Georgia, assisted me to visit Savannah and probe and understand the early life of the Jews in Savannah.

Special thanks to my partner in life, Dr. Gloria Silbert, for her relentless support that brought the project into fruition.

From Mazal Mizrahi

A work of literature is never that of a single man alone. Such is the case for this novel. Professor Tawil provided the opportunity and the privilege, and for that I must acknowledge and thank him. Writing a book of historical import is a challenge, but I was not left without the support and encouragement of my dear husband, Eric, and my parents. They demonstrated enthusiasm and concern at every moment, from conception to publication. And most of all, I must acknowledge the miracle G-d has so graciously bestowed upon me: the energy to write pages of this novel when I was beyond exhausted from long days of work and caregiving.

ABOUT THE AUTHORS

HAYIM TAWIL a professor of Comparative Ancient Semitic Languages. He has published numerous articles in Comparative Semitics and Lexicography and he is the author of *An Akkadian Lexical Companion for Biblical Hebrew* (2009). His other books include *The Rose and the Thorns, Operation Esther: Opening the Door for the Last Jews of Yemen,* and he is the co-author of *The Crown of Aleppo: The Mystery of the Oldest Hebrew Bible Codex.* In 2001, Tawil was nominated for the Eleanor Roosevelt Award for Human Rights for his work in Yemen (www.hayimtawil.com).

CHANANYA WEISSMAN is the author of five books, including the recently published *EndTheMadness Guide to the Shidduch World* and *Tovim Ha-Shenayim: A Study of the Role and Nature of Man and Woman,* as well as numerous articles. He is also the founder of EndTheMadness (www.endthemadness.org).

MAZAL ALOUF-MIZRAHI graduated from Brooklyn College with a M.A. in English Literature. She worked as an instructor in educational institutions and lectured on a variety of literary topics. She is the author of *The Silent Sister: The Diary of Margot Frank* (www.thesilentsister.com).

TABLE OF CONTENTS

PART I: 1733-1765

Part II: 1765-1791

PART I: 1733-1765

GALES AND SAILS

THE RODENTS WERE THE FIRST to sense the coming upheaval. Next, the hens. They ceased laying their eggs, and the roosters began crowing, quite uncharacteristically.

The wind brought respite from the stale odor of dried sweat and roasted pork loin. Captain Hanson took to his bottle of rum and headed to the stern to meet Hannah, the obliging matron who boarded the *William and Sarah* at the fair exchange of providing respite from the toil of the seas for the chance at new-found liberty. Hoping to settle in the newly founded colony of Georgia (so named to honor His Royal Majesty King George II), a group of Jews had hired Hanson behind the trustees' back. The trustees, the designated men who saw to the allotment of tickets to the newfound land, shared with Hanson a distinct aversion to the Judas syndrome of below-deck dealings; nevertheless, Captain Hanson was all ears—particularly when he saw that Hannah would board as well. The woman had a fine mane of chestnut curls, and most of her teeth; her gown, if one could call it that, was poorly stitched from harsh linen and a bit of brownish cotton. It was completely ragged by the hem, as though rodents had gnawed it. He knew she was a fallen woman by her demeanor. So far, their agreement had panned out well enough. On those nights, Hannah imbibed ale to ease her already fallen soul into a state of numbed stupor. An escaped convict, she conceived of her situation as mildly enviable, save for the disgrace of satisfying a flea-ridden and rusty captain with three missing teeth. (The British curse, no doubt.) On the masthead, Tommy kept careful watch, using his telescope to monitor his superior's activities with Hannah, stifling a guffaw when the captain nearly fell overboard and a gush of seawater bathed the amorous couple. Tommy felt the violent tug of the vessel and gripped the splintered mast, focusing once more on the captain—only to discover that the two were no longer there.

Lightning erupted almost at the same moment as thunder caused the hens to holler below. Captain Hanson, who had spent years at sea, knew the incline of the vessel spelled trouble. He quickly fondled Hannah one last time, whispered, "Don't think you're done with!" and ran to the main mast, yanked the step ladder and bellowed, "Tommy, get down, you fool!"

The ship's panting, only slight hours before, began to increase. As if an angry ancient wind sought to eradicate the debauchery, Tommy could have sworn he was partly to blame for the tumult at sea, a lesson he never forgot—Jonah and the wrath of God at sea. Since they first began their journey with those strange people, Tommy had ceased praying and sought to catch glimpses of humans in the most intimate of activities. He cursed his stupidity, recalling a priest's admonition that all sin catches up to a man, and in the harshest way. Hell itself could not tame the fires of earth, if God so decreed.

The sudden lurch of the seas was a blessing for Hannah. She considered herself relieved of duty and fortunate, for the deceased nuns of her childhood parish were surely watching her, God bless their souls. She detested Captain Hanson's lust. Just as she gathered her skirts to make her escape, Captain Hanson snatched her stained waist-sash and gruffly spitted—

"No you don't, girl. Go help Tommy there down all sails!"

Hannah thought the captain had lost his senses. She stifled a giggle. It was well known that women lacked the musculature to succeed in such missions. She ran past him to the fractured steps. The sorry cabins of the Jews (and some Scottish crewmembers) were three flights down. She was hoping to find Dr. Nunez awake, a sturdy man despite his age. The kind doctor helped stave off hours of nausea and unease. He even sought to guide her wretched soul. Why, he had served as chief physician to the Spanish Emperor! She did not resort to thievery with *him*. He kept offering her different goods, particularly cotton handkerchiefs, which he had in ample supply. He sought to make a better woman of her, and deep down, she appreciated the gesture. Hannah found him, in fetal position, quietly resting his head on a medical tome wrapped in silk garments.

"Dr. Nunez, a storm is a-coming. Wake up! Please, sir!"

But he could not hear her. He was ensconced in another world, harking to a long-gone voice. She shook him and banged a wooden spoon on the thinning planks by his ear. His wide forehead felt a bit clammy, and his dark, mostly curly hair was tightly cocooned in a purple sleeping cap.

Não olhe. Never look into their eyes. They'll know, Caríssimos. And then we are all done for. Never piss in public, little boy. They'll see. Then we'll regret it all, the Conversos, the pork-lovers, but secret, filthy, Jews. Don't think the English will treat you any better, bela. They all pray to the same Mariah. A stretch of a limb, my poor filha endured. Gracia with the olive skin of lizard almost condemned to the burning of the flesh. Ah Clara. So long ago it all happened.... How they say she screeched when the flames blinded her. For Mariah. All this for their Mariah.

Dr. Nunez wished he could silence the insistent voice of *Avo*. Grandmother spun tales of Spain and the bounty of her father's family. How she threatened his sleep when he most needs to escape the terrors of day. Her cane, of splintered Portuguese Oak, agitated him, with its rhythmic thumping—*especialmente* when his ears yearned for silence. *Avo*, who never loved the rabbis as much as she detested the monks of her small Portuguese town, with the church bells rousing the populace every morning—infidels and believers alike—to Matins.

Hannah searched for a harsher utensil; she found a bell and a medical mortar. She rang the bell inside the mortar, by the physician's ear, in her attempts to disturb his slumber. She noticed that his ears were well groomed, unlike Captain Hanson's, which she was certain she could water, and sprouts would surely grow. As though on a different plane, Dr. Nunez's heavy lids bobbed with the ship's upheaval. Hannah could detect his eye balls drifting back and forth, until he finally awoke to her honey-dipped eyes. She stared at his dilated pupils.

"Doctor, Please! They need able-bodied men above. Do you not sense the tides, sir?"

In his daze, Dr. Nunez thought his own dear Gracia had transformed into a younger woman, but for the stench of alcohol on Hannah's breath. His poor wife, she had never, despite her earnest efforts, managed to attain proficiency in the British tongue. How this Hannah differed from his wife, mother of his many children. How Gracia languished in the dungeon beneath the Lisbon cathedral! Dr. Nunez believed her Portuguese, so florid and beauteous, would mask her Jewishness. Indeed, it may have been to her great avail as a closet Jew, but nakedly useless for deception during the "question"—the ordeal only the Church could have instituted. Had this Hannah come to him at night to inform him that there was no refuge in the Bright New Land? He reached out, touching her face,

"Hannah—whatever is the matter, my *criança*?"

The physician rose and took her arm. He removed the cap, and lit the way with his lantern. She apprised him of the ferocious winds and upcoming storm. She did not mention that she disregarded his injunction to remain "far from captain"; feeling paternal, he seated the young woman, and handed her a copy of the New Testament.

"Remain here, dear *criança*. Pray to your Lord."

Hannah laughed bitterly. "Sir, I do not think he would wish want to hear from the likes of me!"

"Nonsense, my child."

He asked Hannah to turn around, swiftly dressed, and rushed three cabins down, ignoring the chafing of the untied shoe buckles on his ankles.

He peered into Benjamin Sheftall's compartment, more of a cargo closet than the so-promised "respectable accommodations" he had been promised. They were Ashkenazim and probably not as well off as he. Even before entering the cabin, he realized the husband and wife were awake. They conversed in a harsh and guttural Germanic tongue, vastly different from his own.

"What in Heaven's name are we to do if Oglethorpe closes the doors on us? I cannot possibly endure another six months of this torment!"

13

Benjamin held Perla's hands, noticing they were slightly dry. He then entwined his fingers round her luscious hair, usually hidden from other men's peering eyes, now uncovered for his own delight. Perla leaned back, and when Benjamin heard a knock on his cabin door, she quickly buttoned her gown and covered her head with the lambs' wool scarf.

Dr. Nunez entered, ill at ease. "Shalom," he said in the Semitic language common to Eastern and Western Jews—the language of the Bible. Benjamin rose and shook the doctor's hand. They conversed in broken English when the Hebrew words seemed to fail. Although both Jews, they practiced very different versions of the same religion. Benjamin Sheftall spoke German and some Jewish German, but Dr. Nunez never uttered a word of such. Dr. Nunez informed Benjamin of the sudden turbulence, the precariousness of their position. Benjamin gave up on falling asleep after praying to the One God of Abraham. Instead, he grabbed his crocheted hat, only to drop it and snatch his cowhide cap.

"Yes, it is most likely raining—heavily," Nunez concurred.

Perla, Benjamin's pregnant wife, modestly covered her long, dark-walnut colored tresses with the fabulously woven covers, one of her few remaining trousseau treasures.

"Benjamin?"

"Perla, please rest." She held her belly, looking pleadingly at her husband.

"The baby is unsettled tonight. Do you suppose it's a sign?" she asked in a whisper.

Benjamin bent down, kissing his wife gently on the forehead.

"Pray to the *Aibishter*, my dove. It is all in His grand hands. And remain calm. Your tears are not good for the baby."

Perla held her husband's hand, closed her eyes, and nodded.

"Go with God."

Both men, seized by the boat's sudden and sporadic charge against unpredictable waves, lurched toward the staircase, holding on one another and the mildewed walls in fear. The boat reversed its trajectory, sending all three in the opposite direction. Perla screamed, holding her womb as though the anchor of the world lay within her. The waves, however, remained steady, and the men quickly climbed the stairs, refusing to look back.

They lifted their heads and raised their hands as temporary shields against the torrents. Unable to see clearly, they relied on their hearing. As they neared the bow, the roll of the vessel churned their innards. Dr. Nunez thought of Sheftall's wife, wondering if the movement would unduly harm the fetus.

"Man overboard!"

A seaman, a rugged fellow whose blouse was swept off revealing an odd growth on his left ear lobe, shouted for assistance.

"It's Tommy, Captain!"

Without hesitation, Captain Hanson reached for the sturdy rope and hurled it toward the boy.

"Tommy," he insisted with a bark, "hold onto the rope, you hear?"

Tommy, still underwater, could not make out any sound, save for the calmness of the underwater seas, disturbed only by the crashing waves above. Treading rapidly, his legs working without conscious effort, he struggled to remain afloat among the undulating and strident ripples. He made out the lights where the sorry Jews kept vigil and envied their position—safely stowed away, it now seemed to him; he could have sworn he caught sight of a child waving goodbye, as though he were departing on some coveted journey. All those Jews, (some indigent, most hoping to escape poverty and unemployment), now headed without him, toward their destination.

Tommy was jostled out of his reverie by a resounding smack—a man whose words he could barely make out shouted:

"Wake up lad! Grab on to this."

Tommy was quickly losing consciousness. He felt the grip of the man's strength bearing him aloft as the crew members struggled to heave them aboard the *William and Sarah*. Tommy recognized the man, the bolts of lightning revealing his Semitic features in spurts. He recognized the small eyes and beard. This is the same man who prayed on the deck with his fellow Hebrews, asking for the compass to determine east over west. Yes. *To pray toward Jerusalem.* He remembered the way he mumbled surreptitiously every evening, particularly Friday nights, to candles no less. And the man wouldn't share his grape juice, not even for some coveted currency. He kept muttering some strange phrase, in some Germanic tongue he could not identify. The rippled tides crashed over their heads, and the Jew nearly lost sight of Tommy. As if his God were testing his reserve, a crash of thunder further disoriented Benjamin. But the man had an iron will; he grabbed Tommy once more and tied the rope around their waists.

Dr. Nunez, by the prow, gathered the men. Jacob Yowell, another Ashkenazi, as well as Mr. Minis assisted the efforts. The physician noticed the Jews were unaccustomed to such labor. Thankfully, a Negro supported the group, and more Portuguese Jews joined the endeavor.

"Lift!" yelled Dr. Nunez, at the head of the rope, "Don't cease—they are nearly above the sea!" He repeated his refrain in Portuguese, and the other men repeated, "Don't stop!" to one another.

Their hands began to bleed, and the rope showed signs of tearing. Just as Dr. Nunez made eye contact with Benjamin, the vessel, contradicting the human effort, rocked Tommy and Benjamin sideways, forcing more and more crewmembers to assist in the rescue. Tommy began to hurl some of the seawater he inevitably swallowed and felt his strength return. He softly swore to the good lord Jesus Christ that henceforth he would shelter his eyes from the pleasures of the flesh and wickedness from hence— if he could but touch his feet upon the deck.

Both men landed on the boat's fractured planks, soaked, cold, and relieved. Tommy vomited more, onto the planks, and a bit on his trousers. He held Benjamin's shoulders, and whispered, "Thank you." Benjamin nodded, and looked upwards. Dr. Nunez held a warm blanket and rushed to cover them. He encouraged them to undress quickly so that they would regain their normal body heat.

And just as it had begun, the fervent tremors of the sea ceased with the calls of the morning cock. The sins of the night as though forgiven with daybreak.

Perla's stiffened lips formed the words *The Lord is my Shepherd, I shall not want* throughout the perilous eve. Perla clutched her belly in agony most of the time. Although not very far advanced in her pregnancy, she had begun to detect the baby's movements. She opened the Torah scroll at one frightful moment, and beseeched God to have mercy on His displaced nation. Hannah, only two doors down, recited Hail Mary's with fervor. (Captain Hanson was all epithets, regrettably.) Dr. Nunez and Sheftall at one pointed even murmured their last *viddui*—remonstrance for penance and succor before Almighty God—with a hastily assembled quorum of Jews. One or two Scottish oarsmen looked on, holding their breath. The babies cried; the children wet their linen trousers; the women in fear folded their arms across their chests. It had surely seemed as though they were all in the great whale's belly—as if they all were the very embodiment of Jonah. To have touched the depths of sheer mortality—only to awake to an ordinary morning—was a miracle indeed. The three Ashkenazi families shook hands with their Spanish-Portuguese counterparts. God must have intervened, they all agreed.

Early the following morning, Benjamin slipped once again under the woolen covers. His soaked trousers dripped into a bucket, and some light entered through the hallway. He was too excited to sleep, but he knew he had to keep warm. Beside him Perla lay, ashen and spent.

"The baby is at rest—after too many blows," she whispered ever so softly.

"Rest, dearest. Soon we'll certainly see great sights. Just imagine! Georgia awaits us. If ever we were to perish, certainly the Lord granted us life!"

Perla clutched her book of Psalms, kissed the torn pages, now moist with her tears, and placed it beneath her hay-filled pillow.

"Certainly. But you should not have risked your life. What would I have done as a pregnant widow?"

"I could not allow that boy to perish whilst I still had energy in my bones."

Perla shook her head from side to side, expressing her discontent. Too tired to argue with her husband, she shifted her position on the floor mattress, now quite rumpled. The sound of the water hitting the bucket soothed her, and she eventually drifted into slumber. Sheftall gazed at Perla's fine features, her slender

17

neck, chiseled brows, and silken skin. How pale she was, and how utterly unaware of the spell she continuously cast upon him! He held her hands, and kissed each palm. The ring he had bestowed was a bit loose on her delicate finger. It had been his mother's, a bright emerald stone in yellow gold. It was not flamboyant, but it was a token of his heartfelt feelings. She had been selected by a very astute matchmaker back in his Prussian town. They had met only twice before the nuptials: once in her home, and in her grandparents' house, for the engagement. Closing his eyes, he recalled the perfume she had worn that evening, a lavender mint, and how she initially refused to meet his gaze. But he had found favor in her eyes, and she began to smile when he told her his favorite joke of a fat man and his misplaced *cholent* pot. Perla's parents raised her as though she were a rare butterfly; her body bore not a single mark of hard labor. On their wedding eve, he noticed her hips were slender, a child's despite her twenty-two years. He felt all the more protective of her. When they traveled to London, they hoped to find an excellent doctor to guide Perla's health. She had yet to sustain a pregnancy, and they believed the Sephardic Congregation Bevis Marks would help, hopefully, fund her nutritive needs, which required heavy amounts of meats and poultry. The Sephardic community was indeed quite generous, and they even insisted they join a group of Sephardic Jews to the New World where they promised "all the best sort of cattle and fowls are multiplied without number and therefore without price." Land was to be had, and the weather in "winter is regular and short." He re-read the pamphlet *A New and Accurate Account of the Provinces of South Carolina and Georgia* as though it were a secret chapter of the Bible itself. He believed, wholeheartedly, that Georgia would help Perla and perhaps make him a wealthy man. He inhaled the covers; the lavender mint still clung to their bed sheets. He kissed Perla's ring and arose to join the men for early prayer above deck.

The sun warmed the crewmembers, drenched and half-naked, as if to whet their senses. Opposite the men stood the three devout Ashkenazim, with some Portuguese brethren standing, waiting to be told when to answer "Amen." Tommy lay beside Little Beauty, the deformed cat that had survived scurvy, famine, and the chills on the voyages of years past. The ugly feline jumped at the sight of the rodents who had escaped their cramped quarters in search of victuals. The smallest rat, dubbed White Babe for its soft, white hide, found refuge inside Tommy's breast-pocket. Edward Bell, the dimwit, lurched at Tommy with a witch's broom, hollering, "Out you, White Babe," forcing Tommy to awake, quite unexpectedly, to blows on his head.

Captain Hanson grabbed the lice-infested broom from Edward's burly grasp and lifted his rum bottle, boat-brewed, in midair, and he declared, "Let's hear it for poor Tommy, here. And to his great Captain!"

The men stared at the ship, destroyed by the winds of the previous evening. The Jews, who had just begun their services, looked across at the captain, waiting for him to continue rambling, as he was wont. The boat was in poor shape when they had departed from London. Indeed, they had to repair it right after setting sail. The six-month voyage had been hellish. Gale after gale. Splintered wood littered the deck. And now it had nearly capsized off the coast of North Carolina, one of the North American colonies. Miraculously, it was safely en route to a great new land. They had not felt Captain Hanson was to be congratulated, despite his efforts, and they were increasingly anxious to place their feet on dry land. Benjamin Sheftall continued his prayers and thought of the unity he had felt the night before, the closeness he experienced with his fellow Jews.

During the voyage, Sheftall had felt slightly alienated from the others, mostly because of their different cultural and economic backgrounds. Dr. Nunez, the wealthy Sephardic Jew with his well-worn accoutrements (signifying his status as a previous court physician), represented the great divide between Spanish-Portuguese Jews and their Northeastern European counterparts. Most of the Jews on board were indeed of Levantine descent. They spoke a strange language, a mixture of Portuguese, Spanish, and Hebrew, called Ladino. Their mannerisms markedly differed from the three families of German Jewish descent; they kept to themselves; some even looked askance at the three Ashkenazi families, trying to make sense of the Diaspora's effects on Jewry. Did they all descend from the same great Jacob? The Portuguese men barely prayed to the One God. Their women did not cover their hair as was the custom. Indeed, many wore glaringly immodest dress—of taffeta and lace, with abundant décolletage for all to view. Perhaps the most unfortunate of all was their blatant lack of adherence to some basic laws of *kashrut*. Prayer was almost entirely abandoned. The Ashkenazi men had to convince the Sephardim to join forces for prayers, as they desired to pray with a quorum of ten men. But that night somehow erased the differences, even if for a brief moment, when all faced their mortality and the sword's edge. Benjamin Sheftall kissed the phylacteries in his possession and began unraveling them. He placed one leather-bound box on his forehead and another by his arm, just as he had learned on the day of his *bar mitzvah*. The phylacteries at first had sent a shiver of fear down Captain Hanson's spine; it smelled of witchcraft to him. But time will undo many a fear, he learned. Captain Hanson turned for a brief moment to stare at the Jews, wondering what it would take to prevent the Hebrews from partaking in their strange rituals.

Dr. Nunez heard Captain Hanson's self-rewarding toast and thought it best to place honor where it rightly belonged.

"Hail to Benjamin Sheftall, who saved the poor lad from meeting his Maker too soon!" he enthusiastically cheered. Benjamin Sheftall was surprised, and then gratified. He shook Dr. Nunez's hand. The crewmembers, Edward the dimwit with Little Beauty, and the sea-worn Jews, relieved to escape death and destruction, gathered round the young Ashkenazi who had demonstrated valor, despite his white skin, his peculiar skull cap, and his strange accent.

They took turns congratulating Benjamin, "Prosper, and may you live long."

"Continued strength."

"You sanctified God's name. A true honor."

Even Edward the dimwit offered Little Beauty as a gift, which Sheftall naturally declined. Tommy took the bottle of rum from Captain Hanson's hand, and raised it high above his tousled head, "To safe tides and clear skies!"

Hannah, no longer hiding in Dr. Nunez's compartment, nudged Tommy, stole the cup, took a quick swig, and proclaimed, "Amen!"

The rest of the Portuguese crew lifted their heads from the stairs, and Tommy and Captain Hanson made their way to the helm where the coast of Georgia and the clear beaches of Savannah suddenly stood in sharp relief. Benjamin continued praying, and swayed together with the boat. He stared eastward to where the Georgia coast met the vast Atlantic Ocean. He removed his phylacteries, kissed them with reverence, and allowed himself to exhale and shed a tear of optimism. The *William and Sarah* softly rocked, and the crewmembers unfurled the sails, ready to enter the harbor of the new American frontier.

ROACHES &
ENCROACHES

TOMOCHICHI NAILED THE FOUR SCALPS that had been dangling from his breechcloths above the hearth. He immersed the tomahawk in a bucket of water to prevent the blood from congealing. The Yamacraw chief scowled at Mary Musgrove, the half-blood, once Princess Coosaponakeesa, who married a white man. She sat, balanced on her knees, four feet from the hearth. She smelled of mint, a white man's odor. He didn't have much patience that day, although most of the time he was rather congenial. His darkened skin itched, and he removed the beadwork around his thick neck. He glanced at his nephew, Tooanabey, a boy of tender years with feathers around his loincloth and asked him to fetch some water. Mary wore the clothes of the white people. He recalled the days she was not ashamed of the hide dresses and wide deerskins of his women. But Johnny, the British officer, obliterated the remnants of her Creek heritage, and now she arbitrated for the European settlers of his great ancestral land.

The British made fools of many Indians before him, he sadly noted, but he did not want to feel at odds with the white men. It was for this reason he was particularly displeased to learn that James Oglethorpe, a British officer, with the blessing of the South Carolina colony, was founding a colony in the heart of Savannah. This was a direct insult, an incursion, far beyond the agreed-upon borders. The South Carolina Treaty did not permit this expansion. How was he to explain the illegitimacy of Oglethorpe's plan to his clansmen?

Land was not up for grabs, the way the white men envisioned. It was challenging enough to maintain order among his nation, to settle disputes, organize the crop trade, without all the political upheaval the colonists aroused. He was not entirely opposed to the notion of more settlers; it could very well spell prosperity for his Creeks, but it was the gall of Oglethorpe's stealth and secrecy that riled him. And the extension of borders was a touchy topic for all Creeks. But yet again, the white man settled in land as he deemed fit, without taking into consideration the Creeks.

Mary stared at the dusty floor, waiting for the chief to begin. He crouched by the hearth as well, his back to Mary.

"Doubtless you are here to speak on their behalf. I sense fear in the nostrils of a once well-bred Creek."

Mary gritted her front teeth. It had become a ritual; he had to remind her of the true origins of her bloodline before each encounter. She found her life as a mongrel frustrating—she was a betrayer of her people either way. Her uncle arranged the marriage as part of a goodwill treaty some years ago, but she had fallen in love with Johnny long before. He was probably the only man who would have accepted her hand this side of Savannah anyway, since he was a half-blood as well. She gazed at the silver wedding band, then turned it slightly, nervously.

"Chief of Yamacraw, I ask you to please look upon me favorably. I come to you in peace. The British mean no impertinence. As great leader of the Creeks, perhaps you can look beyond their breach—"

"The great English man forgot his courtesy? In all his books he cannot recall the law of the land? I shall hear no more of this, Mary."

"Please, Tomochichi. Reconsider your position. Living in harmony with the neighbor will bring great honor to the Creek. I beseech you, great one, to be forgiving, as you are wont."

Mary knew how to persuade Tomochichi. His greatest desire was to maintain Mother Earth and peace on Her land. The British colonists and the other Europeans before them tested his resolve. The Natives were a dogged nation; they would not accept sole arbitration from Tomochichi. A consensus would have to be reached, a meeting arranged. Tomochichi feared this new British man whose surname that sounded both monstrous and strange to his ears would prove proud and maybe even contentious. Mary would no doubt try to negotiate on his behalf. He glanced at her and detected uneasiness, perhaps even shame; she sensed the dishonor in the British ways after all. She had inclined her head, and her dark hair trailed on the floor. She was studying her nails, noting she should file them, rotating the wedding band bought by her Johnny with baskets of corn. His ire tapered off, and he touched Mary's shoulder gently.

"Send word to Oglethorpe that I extend warm greetings. Invite him and his people to my village in one month, on the eve of the full moon. A holiday shall be pronounced for his arrival in four-moon's time. I want you to don a deer dress in honor of your people. I shall meet this English man on my own."

Mary's eyes widened and her lips parted, revealing strong white teeth. She was surprised the old chief, whose skin surprisingly remained taut by his jowl, should evince such a rapid shift in demeanor. How strange! She expected him to growl disapproval, perhaps even strike his tomahawk in frustration. But wisdom and many suns had tamed the chief. He learned it is not wise to remain bitter foes of the white man. Mary nodded her head. She stood on her muscular legs, covered by an English dress of fine spun linen. Unlike the fashion of the day, her bodice hung loosely; Mary preferred some agility. She dusted off her dress, and bowed slightly.

"I believe you will approve of this man. He is regarded as a gentleman."

Tomochichi disliked the word "gentleman." He did not see what the white man's ways had achieved. They pillaged the Earth and harvested more than was necessary of its bounty. They did not respect holy treaties. But he did not want to argue with Mary Musgrove on this topic; the blood of the white ones surged within her. Did she ever smell the spirits? Did she commune with the great rivers? He sensed the tides gurgling presages of war years prior, and blood soon drenched the banks during the vicious

Creek raids on the Spanish. An odd sensation filled him today as well, one of promise, but with an ominous streak. Mary's confident air did not dispel, entirely, the worry he harbored. But the moon dance should disperse the ashes of demons, and the meeting with Oglethorpe, the white man, should presage a promising beginning, with the help of Mother Earth.

Mary departed Tomochichi's stacked hut, nimbly clambering down the wooden stairs to the mud-encrusted road. She mounted her mare and rode back to her plantation near the Savannah River, towards the land that would become the state of Georgia.

She glanced at the verdant fields, rich with foliage and majestic vegetation on both banks of the river, and wondered what the new settlers would bring with them. She rode by Creeks gathering twigs and leaves, berries and some worms. It was rather warm for January, she thought. Neither the men nor the women feared her presence. They greeted her softly, and she returned their greetings. She descended the steed, removed her worn moccasins, and walked across the river until she was ankle-deep in clear waters. She cupped her hands and washed her sweaty face. She glanced at the sky and noticed a hawk undulating, slowly tracing its prey. She looked down at her feet, and noticed orange fish were circling her ankles. Nature speaks, she thought, but few can translate her language.

*

James Oglethorpe sighed heavily. The muggy Georgian air did little to assuage his tension. His wig clogged his hair follicles. He threw it on the dusty ottoman. He leaned on the mantle of the hearth, never lit since his arrival in January, and muttered under his breath, "Damned committee!" His long, aristocratic nose, aquiline and tapered by the nostrils, gave James an air of upper-class dignity. He stood erect, his large hazel eyes shifting across the room. Good God! It was a blessing he was not married to a genteel woman; she never would have agreed to live in such conditions! He was living in the same squalid conditions as all the settlers these past five months—in huts made sloppily of bushels gathered by the wayside. The outdoors reeked of dried urine, and many settlers refused to bathe by the river, fearing Indian reprisal. The furniture, shipped from London, was at odds with the primitive housing. Suddenly, he felt as though he were roasting; he removed his Hacking jacket, heavy boots, and folded the sleeves of his wide-shouldered blouse, leaving the collar open and wide. He shooed away a mosquito, the pest that spread grave disease. The bug persisted; James grabbed his shoe and rammed it on the fly, splattering its contents onto the sole, which was finely stitched in France. He had conceived of this entire operation, the colony of Georgia, but did not foresee the political troubles the strange Natives of this land would stir. Only one old chief had greeted him upon his arrival, a Tomochichi. Johnny Musgrove, a British warrior who allegedly sacked the Spaniards in Florida with fierce barbarism, accompanied the half-naked man. A war-crazed Indian they called this Johnny. But he spoke with the cool precision of a true British officer that morning; congratulating him; speaking on Tomochichi's behalf, "We welcome in peace all men who seek peace." Half-weary from sucking on limes to prevent scurvy during the long voyage and glad to sense solid ground, Oglethorpe did not conceive of the difficulties he would soon face. The Georgian colony sat upon land belonging to these barbaric people. Their women did not cover their breasts, and the boys wore loincloths of the most hideous shape and color. They had some type of treaty the trustees had neglected to mention. He only discovered the news this afternoon.

To make matters worse, the colonists refused to live up to James's standard of behavior: no rum. That blasted drink caused all sorts of debauchery. Most of his able-bodied men were not fit for duty the next morning, and the marauding Spaniards had a nose for their weakest moments. James believed some of the prostitutes were working for the Spaniards. He needed his men to stand guard by the bastions before his own hut was up and ready. He didn't want the men to purchase Negros either. Detestable. Once they were free from their Floridian owners they should remain so. But those British debtors were constantly looking to avoid hard labor. And the women were no better. They're the ones who poured all that rum down their husbands' greedy throats. They needed a respectable vintner to rid the Georgian colony of its drunkenness—then only the rich would be able to afford expensive red wines. And the lazy mornings would cease.

James heard boots stumbling up the stair case. His white skin was beginning to redden from the heat.

"Yes? What is it?" James asked, a bit flustered.

"It's me. Cox, sir."

James let Dr. William Cox into his hut. Cox was the colony's sole physician. Oglethorpe pleaded with the trustees in London to enlist more than one expert in the field of medicine. But they denied his request. "There are plenty of doctors in Charleston," they argued. "We need strong men to break the ground, to plant and sow!" James had proposed sending all those impoverished prisoners to America in the hopes they would be able to make good use of themselves instead of languishing in debtor's prison. But he did not have much say as to who would embark on this fine journey; he had liberated them from prison, but the trustees were the ones who authorized the trip. No longer adjudicating in Parliament, James realized he had to rely on his own judgment. While working in London, he had grown accustomed to working with others and coming to sound judgments based on a consensus. Here, he was judge *and* jury—to a certain extent. He could not rattle those in London too much; after all, those back home still held the purse strings to the entire venture in Georgia.

Dr. Cox entered the hut, waving his angled hat of fine velvet. He failed to cool himself despite the effort. The man, of middle age, boasted a well-rounded belly and liver spots on his left cheek. He had sailed from Gravesend with the other one hundred twenty colonists with sheer determination to begin a new practice in the New World. But he could not understand what James Oglethorpe had to gain by the entire enterprise of founding a new colony. The tenth son of a well-to-do Englishman, Oglethorpe could have remained in his comfortable and accommodating household. He could have settled down with a fine English wife, travel occasionally to Bath, and spend his time in Parliament, gathering prestige and renown. But he had chosen to find his future in the colonies. Cox had found James a congenial companion and a well-informed conversationalist on the long, arduous voyage from Britain, most unlike the arrogant Parliamentarians of London's upper-class. Cox felt indebted to Oglethorpe; after all, he would still be rotting in debtor's prison if not for Oglethorpe's proposal to send them all to America. His Majesty's kingdom will prosper, if only the poor prisoners were given a fair chance, Oglethorpe successfully argued. But what had Oglethorpe to gain from this venture?

"Sit down, Dr. Cox." James cleared the papers and myriad books from the ottoman and placed them on the table, by the door. His hut was in shambles, but somewhat still livable. James's cot, by the far end of the hut, was covered with a finely embroidered quilt, of salmon orange and lavender lilies. Cox imagined his mother or sisters carefully stitched the quilt, picturing their poor son and brother cold and lonely in a remote land. James sat beside Dr. Cox. The timepiece on the table read forty-five past noon. James shook the doctor's outstretched palm. Dr. Cox noted Oglethorpe's slender, soft hands were beginning to toughen. "What can I do for you? I hope all is well."

"As well as circumstances permit. I would like to inform you that the wells are in operation, but the people of the colony continue to leave pots outside their homes, hoping the rain will fill them with water. It is unhealthful and perhaps dangerous to the colonists, especially if the rains cease and the mosquitoes gather there. Furthermore, they need to be wary of leaving dung by the roadside; it is extraordinarily unhygienic."

Oglethorpe knew the physician's concerns were well-founded. Dr. Cox's beard, graying only on the bottom half, reminded James of his schoolteacher, Mr. Cornwall. He too had been cautious of disease, always holding a handkerchief in his left hand. The Savannah swamps were problematic, but Oglethorpe had little time to worry over the colonist's water-gathering habits. He thanked Dr. Cox, who truly demonstrated gentility despite the ravages of Georgia's climate, and walked him out. Dr. Cox was fond of James, but wondered what the founder would do to help prevent any outbreak of disease. The physician removed a handkerchief from his breast pocket, wiped his half-bald pate, and summarily left Oglethorpe's dwellings.

Dr. Cox returned to his hut, and found Rose dusting the planks with a hand-made broom of twigs. She was bent over, half her height, trying to clear the debris. The broom handle was short, and the dust particles flew around the room. The broom fell apart at times, and now partial twigs got caught in the planks, and Rose bent to her knees trying to pluck them off. She turned around, noticing Dr. Cox did not greet her. He had purchased Rose for a pittance in Charleston. Her previous owner, a widow, had died. The widow's next of kin had no use for Rose, who was well over forty-nine and quite worn by years of labor. They refused to set her free; they didn't want to abandon her to traders; and they didn't want to defray the costs of a private auction. He found her with a sign on her chest, "for sale," in the marketplace, and immediately purchased Rose, who was somewhat relieved that Cox was a gentleman. At least she had a roof over her sorry head, she figured. He tended to greet her upon arriving from the outdoors, unlike her previous owner (who was also deaf). But today he seemed preoccupied.

Both Rose and Dr. Cox raised their brows, as a sudden clamor at the door rather frightened them both. John Musgrove entered, without waiting for Rose to announce his arrival. He wore the traditional dress of the colonists, with few garish embellishments as was the fashion in London. His hair was uncombed, mud clung to his breeches, and his sleeves revealed brown skin, with slight dark curls alongside the forearms. Rose stared at Johnny's brow; it protruded, making him appear pugnacious and frightful. Her previous owner's son, she refused to utter his name, had a similar forehead. His eyes too were deep, like Johnny's, and he was utterly untamable. She wondered if John Musgrove beat his slaves.

He held his cap, surprisingly starched clean, and stated officially, "I hear you're a doctor. I gather you can assist me and then lead me to Oglethorpe's hut, which appears similar to yours. I heard the two of you are friends of sorts. I'm sure you'll oblige."

Dr. Cox nodded in agreement. Johnny undressed, unabashedly. He smelled of musk and sweat for working in the fields all season. He removed all, save for his breeches. Johnny stood well above Dr. Cox, with broad shoulders and a well-defined waist. A scar, from a tomahawk most likely, wrapped his lower abdomen. His back was full of hives, red and bleeding from incessant scratching.

"My wife realized I had these reddish dots last night, sir. It burns more than it itches. This might sound odd, but the mutton had a strange taste, and my throat hurts."

"Fetch this man some water, Rose. He's burning!"

Rose colored a bit, thinking of his wife undressing her husband, but Johnny did not think much of it. Dr. Cox had some experience with hives, but was unsure if Johnny's back would be healed with the tonic he usually prescribed. It looked quite a bit like the pox, but it was centered in the back, with a minor streak toward the belly. Johnny's lymph nodes were swollen by the throat, and his head was burning. Dr. Cox truly did not think he had any medication or ointment that would cure Johnny's condition. But he knew patients wanted some type of medicine, or else they would feel he was inept, or worse, unknowledgeable. He excused himself, and searched his cabinet for an anti-burn ointment, made from aloe vera. It relieved burned skin quite well, and maybe it would be of some use to poor Johnny. He handed Johnny the medicine, and explained the importance of washing up, before meals and before bed. Johnny was half-listening. He wondered why he bothered visiting Dr. Cox when the Indian superior Mother would know how to heal far more efficiently. At least she would burn incense, calm the spirits and ease his pain with some type of ancestral potion, concocted from rare herbs. Johnny drank the water thirstily, nodding at Rose. So Dr. Cox already has a Negro, he thought.

"I recommend you remain in your quarters, while your body heals. It shall take time, so perhaps it is wise to meet Oglethorpe a different time. You are quite ill." Dr. Cox washed his hands in the basin, fearing contamination. He instructed Rose to clean the floor with lye, particularly where Johnny stood. Johnny handed the physician a couple of coins, which Dr. Cox gladly pocketed.

"I have an important message for Oglethorpe. Let us stroll outdoors. I don't have the time to rest right now." Johnny winced as he wore his shirt, this time leaving it unbuttoned. His chest appeared a slightly swollen as well, and his eyelids drooped a bit. He swore to visit the sage doctor of the Creeks, Soft Paw, after his business with James Oglethorpe was done with.

*

Oglethorpe stretched out on his cot by late afternoon, enjoying the bits of breezy air finally wafting from the seaside. He left the books on law and philosophy to keep the door ajar; he had little use for them now. He lay with both palms supporting his heavy head, elbows and arms in perfect triangles. He removed his socks and wondered how he had fallen to idleness while he castigated some of the men for the same crime. He closed his eyes, and Lady Elizabeth Wright suddenly burst in his mind's expanse. He had completely forgotten her! With ringlets, blonde and cherubic, cascading down her back, as promising as a lady in one of the paintings by the great da Vinci. Her eyes were the palest green, with fluttering blonde lashes that looked more like silken strands than hair. So wispy. He often thought of the bountiful arms she revealed on Christmas Eve, in a gown of green velvet and a bonnet of lace. It had seemed to him that her arms were softer than the butter he spread on his biscuits that morning, if she would but let him touch her. Of course she would never oblige, and he wouldn't dare try; it wasn't genteel. His mother approved of her as well, but he could not pursue the matter. America held him spellbound. A woman would have to wait, despite the pain. He heard Dr. Cox's familiar voice, in the common British dialect and accent together with a very American version of the proper language. Both voices neared James's entry way, and he immediately stood to greet his visitors.

"Yes. Dr. Cox, once again, greetings. And Johnny Musgrove, yes?"

Dr. Cox nodded, and Johnny entered the room. Johnny rummaged in his pocket for a pipe made of beech tree. He looked around Oglethorpe's hut for a candle or urn. He needed to smoke some of the tobacco leaves. He asked James for a flame to start his pipe. James stared at the man's chest, wondering how it became well-defined and taut, as though he were a Roman athlete or a great Greek god. Johnny seemed a bit tired, ragged, and his hands were clenched. He was ill, perhaps, or simply vexed. It was unclear until he spoke. He first sucked on his pipe, releasing an odor of wet trees and fresh tobacco, warm and inviting.

"James Oglethorpe. You'll have to excuse me. I am truly ill." He puffed on his pipe again, somehow relieved. He continued, "The Creek headmen are willing to negotiate a new treaty with you. You'll have to excuse the abruptness of my speech, sir. Either my wife Mary or I will interpret. They prefer the full moon. A holiday was ordained when you arrived on this day. Perhaps it is fitting that a treaty will ensue as well." Dense smoke filled the hut, but the wind dispersed the vapors.

Oglethorpe's mood improved dramatically. His hopes for the colony's success were not fictitious after all. With enough wit and tact, he may procure peaceful dealings with the Natives.

John neared Oglethorpe and spoke in a subdued tone, "I hate to spoil the celebration, James, but this matter with the Indians is far from settled. I received word from Coweta that some of the headmen are distressed, greatly so, by your settling on the side of the river. Treaties are sacred bonds to the Creeks." John cleared his throat. He felt his palate dry up. Where was this man's hospitality, he thought. I could use some ale or liquor. Ignoring the burning sensation on his back he stated emphatically, "They don't view minor infractions as a technicality. To them, it's treachery. And your settlement violated the South Carolina treaty, James, no matter how your people would like to present it. Trust me, it's a good sign they came to me first. It could be much worse."

Dr. Cox appeared uneasy. Oglethorpe's initial jubilation now ebbed to a sense of optimism. His face appeared pasty. Although he suspected a problem, he had to somehow justify the trustees, and of course, himself.

"There must be a mistake. I was informed the treaty was supposed to be a mere formality. The South Carolina assembly assured me all was taken care of."

Johnny sighed. How many times was he going to explain to these fresh-from-the-boat English people the damage they incur each time they assume something "was taken care of"? The South Carolinians don't want to bother with the Indians, and those back in London don't even consider the natives in all their scheming. And then the boats moor in the bay, and the people march out expecting easygoing natives, bowing and offering their thanks. This was ridiculous, and he was tired.

Oglethorpe sat on the ottoman by the table. This is far worse than he had initially thought. Not all Creeks were like the first Indian man he met, the Tomochichi with the feathers in his gathered hair. Of course they would differ. So Tomochichi was slightly more accommodating than the rest of his clan. It could be his age; maybe he was wise not to pick a fight? But what about the others? He looked at John with a hint of shame, "This is outrageous. I am truly sorry. Please send word to Coweta of my sincerest apologies—for the misunderstandings, yes? Please inform them that I wish to meet with their leaders as soon as possible to settle this matter. We will try to accommodate their best interests." Oglethorpe rose, and he held a hand to Dr. Cox and then to John. John refused to touch the founder.

John nodded and summarily left, clenching his fists in severe pain. He had done his duty. He hoped the Creeks would settle the dispute hastily, so he could rest his aching back.

James Oglethorpe motioned for Dr. Cox to sit beside him. He whispered to Cox, "Let's pray we don't have a war between the heathens and our people." Dr. Cox noted Oglethorpe took offense at Johnny's refusal to shake hands. Cox thought it best to describe John's medical condition before more animosity stirred between the inhabitants of Georgia.

That night Oglethorpe awoke to memories of Lady Elizabeth. This time he dreamed of her in the pink gown that illuminated her fine brow. Damn this desert! Where was he to find repose for his mind and body in this place? He immediately recalled John Musgrove's ominous tidings, and felt the stress of the day bearing down on his aching limbs. The cot was so damn uncomfortable, and the whizzing mosquitoes and rats disturbed his sleepy ears. It then occurred to him that Tomochichi should host the meeting in Yamacraw. This would demonstrate Oglethorpe's diffidence and deference to the Indian chief. He rested his head that night, hoping the Indian with red paint on his chest would come through for him.

Tomochichi rested his head that same evening with plans quite different from Oglethorpe's. Tomochichi was going to insist Oglethorpe play host to the Creek delegation. By the crowing of the morning cocks, eight Creek headmen will arrive in Savannah from the Lower Towns, including Youhowlakee, mico of Coweta, and others. This will mark the beginning of the new moon, and the following evening the holiday he prophesied five moons ago will take place: a meeting of all the great Creek leaders and the new white man with supple fingers—the English man who violated the treaty his brethren agreed to. His wife lay beside him; long buffalo hide covered the couple. The old man no longer longed for her, but was rather glad she provided his limbs with warmth, as he realized more and more that old age brought cold shivers in the blood. She lay, asleep, her braided hair a mixture of black and gray. His own hair had been coal black until a few years ago, but turned gray when her strength waned. Soft Paw insisted he drink garlic juice, and she informed him that corn oil slathered in goat's milk should be of some use to his wife. He thanked her for the remedies, and used them for some time, until worries kept him awake at night.

*

The children marched before the great leaders. Bare-chested and wigwagging ancient chants, the little boys proceeded with dignified commotion to the tent where Oglethorpe, John, and Mary Musgrove were patiently waiting. One boy held a strange-looking tambourine, with stones and beads attached. Another had two white stripes painted across his loincloth and almost all had feathered necklaces. They parted, and the headmen, led by Tomochichi and Youhowlakee, advanced toward Oglethorpe. Candle-lit lamps decorated the tents and provided warmth and direction for all. The unmistaken aroma of roasted pork as well as fresh squash whetted their glands. The Indian women and Mary Musgrove prepared the feast—a gesture of unity. Oglethorpe proudly donned a bold blue collarless coat with deep cuffs. His long waistcoat, of a maroon color but lined in sky blue, matched his breeches, which were cropped by the lower knee, revealing black shoes with square buckles and long, ribbed socks. The fashion had a touch of the Dutch influence, a style Oglethorpe found quite befitting authentic gentlemen. He washed with the buckets of water Dr. Cox disapproved of and a lavender French-milled soap his mother stashed between his handkerchiefs. He was perspiring; he was wary of breaking a code of behavior or perhaps gesturing in a way the Indians might, erroneously, perceive as offensive. He was mildly amused at the children's antics, but was worried a smile might be misperceived as mockery or disdain. He nearly fainted when the ladies in waiting marched with red, long strands of trinkets adorning their torso. Yellow and white paint outlined their necks, and their hair was finely braided, revealing a bare back. The men, too, were bare-chested. Chief Youhowlakee boasted a bone-pierced nose and left ear. Tomochichi walked upright, with a cane made of oak and wrapped crocodile skin. He dyed his nails oxblood to signify the sacrifice of his people, and Oglethorpe then took note that the old chief was missing a third toe.

Oglethorpe regretted pasting the wig on his head. He felt the grey curls graze his cheeks, a sensation he rather detested. Mary stood beside him, looking straight into his eyes. She wore a deer-skinned dress with thin fringes made of the same material. The dress was a beautiful cognac color in the lamplight. He noticed she too was sweating. Her triceps were taut, and she held both palms across her belly. John Musgrove couldn't have appeared more nonchalant, smoking his reed pipe. Soft Paw's remedy of creamy crocodile dung and rabbit droppings healed his wounds. If it wasn't for the primeval recipe she learned, he might as well have burned all the way through the spring, he thought. All of a sudden, the commotion ceased and Youhowlakee stared Oglethorpe straight in the eye. The English founder noticed a bit of mucus gathering around the Indian's pierced nose, slathering down the bone lodged within it. He mustered a tremendous amount of reserve, and addressed the Natives, "Welcome to Savannah, honored guests." He bowed, gallantly, and smiled. Mary nodded and proceeded to translate. Tomochichi took a step forward, stood ram-rod straight and began speaking, rapidly, in Creek Indian. He spoke for quite some time. Johnny nodded his head, spewing tobacco into the air. The muggy air kept the vapors within the tent. Oglethorpe became a bit anxious. What in heaven's name is he muttering, he thought. Be patient, he almost heard his mother whisper in his ear. Give him a chance to speak. Tomochichi held a necklace made of buffalo molars and hawk's feathers and placed it over Oglethorpe's head. Oglethorpe raised an eyebrow, rather taken aback. Tomochichi bowed and returned to the head of the line.

"He says he is honored to share this abundant land with such dignified neighbors. He blesses you all with health and success in your endeavors. He hopes your homes are filled with bounty and grace. He prays you accept his gift of brotherhood and friendship. He also wishes to complete the treaty quickly; he has become rather impatient in his old age."

Oglethorpe laughed, clapping his hands in amusement. And all this time I suspected him of maliciousness, he thought. Relieved, he said, "Let's not keep you waiting." Oglethorpe gestured for the Creek headmen to follow him to the negotiating tables, surrounded by an oblong table bearing refreshments— ale, smoked beef, and apple cider. Mary sat to Oglethorpe's right, almost touching his elbow. She was not ashamed of being the only woman in attendance. Tomochichi's eyes radiated warmth. He rather liked the English gentleman. He had very fine round eyes, almost like a doe. And his hands no longer appeared untouched, a sign he had communed with the Earth. His thighs were thick, indicating a healthy male. He smiled, with most of his front teeth, displaying an open-hearted nature. Even his skin no longer appeared as wan as on that first day back in January.

Tomochichi pointed to Oglethorpe's wig and asked, "Aren't you too young to wear gray hair?" Mary stifled a giggle and told the chief, "I do not want to offend him!" Oglethorpe understood Tomochichi and laughed. "It's a British custom. It's the fashion, similar to your hair style. It's our way of showing dignity." Tomochichi nodded in content agreement. Youhowlakee stared at Oglethorpe. He suspected the smiling Englishman of conspiring against him. He heard many stories of smiling white men who hid treacherous schemes behind friendly veneers. They always did what they wanted in the end, what they planned all along. "What happens if we deny your permission to settle here?" Youhowlakee asked contemptuously. Mary translated, hesitating to speak the words as harshly as Youhowlakee. Oglethorpe blanched. He had sensed this man's hostility, but was rather surprised by his belligerence. He drew in his breath, unsure how to respond. It was true. He intended to build Georgia. John placed his pipe on his lap, and looked at Tomochichi. Finally, the old man stood, indignantly.

"Why do you seek to dishonor a hero? He has come to this land to help his people. I have known this man from the moment he arrived on our land in the winter months, and I attest to his kindness and peaceable intentions. He seeks to build. He has agreed to protect our holdings. Why must we speak as though he is an enemy when he came here to seal our friendship?" Tomochichi pointed to Oglethorpe with his cane, and met the eyes of the other chiefs with strength of mind. They looked away, ashamed.

Oglethorpe asked Mary, "What did he say?"

She shook her head from side to side. "He says you are a friend and a hero. He's upset they dishonored you."

Oglethorpe whispered into Mary's ear, "Tell them we will not interfere in their lives; we do not intend to dominate them in any way."

Mary looked at the chieftains and decided to add a bit of her own logic instead. "What great Tomochichi says is true. You would be wise to consider the economic benefits these white people can bring you. They do not know this land like you. Think of the new markets and the competition you will now enjoy between South Carolina and Georgia!"

Tomochichi returned to his chair, and the Creeks grunted in agreement. They began to vociferously debate the amount of trade that has been limited to the South Carolina colony, and now the opportunities for greater routes, even to the south of Georgia. Within the hour, the men settled their disagreements. That May afternoon, in the year 1733 of His Majesty's throne, James signed the Treaty of Savannah in the Creek capital of Coweta. The harmony was maintained; tomahawks remained in the grass huts, and the children did not fear learning too soon of the fate that awaits them all. They continued to squeal, well into the late May evening, in the sultry days of Georgia's infancy.

Outside the tents the children played stick games; the older ones joined the women in shinny. The young girls decorated the sticks and balls used in shinny with turquoise beads the previous afternoon. They hit the ball with a curved stick, hoping the opposing team would be unable to return the ball past the goal line. Sometimes, a few beads would break loose, and one caught Tomochichi in the knee. Oglethorpe was impressed—*this game was similar to the ones played back home.*

James approached Tomochichi and pulled the aging chief to the side. He motioned for John to come join their conversation, "Tell Tomochichi, 'I am greatly in your debt,' John." Tomochichi smiled. "I am obligated to treat my friend with honor."

This man has the manners of a refined gentleman, Oglethorpe noted. "I shall take leave and travel to England. I must ratify the treaty before Parliament and the King. I would like you to accompany me as my guest."

Tomochichi grinned at James, and joked, "Shall I make it across the treacherous seas, an old man such as myself?"

James shook Tomochichi's hand, "You are strong. I insist!"

Tomochichi led James to the tent. He walked with the white man until they both stood by the fire-lit lamp, "I have one request. Let me dance for your queen in tribute to your great people. That shall be *my* honor." James smiled and gently nodded his head.

James walked steadily to the small English settlement near Yamacraw he now referred to as "home." His tent, pitched near the bank of the Savannah River, boasted steep steps. His wooden hut now seemed strangely inviting. He thought of the women back home and the beautiful brick buildings in London and wondered how he was going to convince any lady back in London to settle in his little village. He yawned and wondered how in sweet Mary's name he was going to convince more Brits to settle near a muddy waterway, completely unaware a boat filled with Jews was heading his way.

*

Chief Tomochichi raised his arms, quickly alternating his feet. He glanced directly at the great Queen Caroline. His dark falcon-like eyes pierced at King George II; the regent was taken aback. He inhaled. He sat on his magnificent throne surrounded by sentries. His crown, bejeweled with sapphires and rubies, was held firmly in place.

"Is this heathen mad?" He whispered to his wife. Queen Caroline encouraged Tomochichi with a faint smile, ignoring her husband. She always wanted to visit the colonies, and this creature was oddly entertaining. The feathers in Tomochichi's ears bobbed. He gesticulated fervently. He had waited for this opportunity. After all those sick months at sea, the sheer vastness tried his patience. Oglethorpe insisted he wear a silk robe to cover his nakedness, to honor the throne. The English did not expose their bodies, save for the women he noticed, whose décolletage was generously in full view. Instead, they covered all their flesh with expensive threads Tomochichi's people did not weave. Tomochichi smiled faintly at Oglethorpe and removed the silken robe, revealing a fabulously painted chest. Tomochichi's wife chose bright yellow paint—symbolizing the joy of their agreement, and each nipple boasted a tiger's eye—to symbolize fierce brotherhood. She weaved his hair into two intricate, long braids, with a few silver strands of English beads, a token of gratitude embedded within his hair. In a sudden burst, Tomochichi lay on his arms and somersaulted, landing near the sentries to the left. He began to make loud war noises, slightly frightening the ladies' gentle graces. Queen Caroline put a gloved hand to her mouth, excited for a moment. Tomochichi bowed as he moved his feat rapidly. He imagined the beat of drums, the call of flutes. He danced, swaying his backside and arms, before Her Majesty the Queen, flailing his fingers to the beat only he could hear. The King became a bit incensed when the old chief nearly revealed his thighs. Tomochichi then took two dried roaches from his necklace and placed them in his hair. He tied twine around the insects, as his feet nearly twisted, like an old tree trunk. Sweat began accumulating on his chest and upper back, melting away the paint. His breechcloths clung to his thighs, and the fringes on the moccasins vibrated.

James Oglethorpe held his parliamentary cap in his right hand, a gesture of diffidence to the Indian. He was worried the Queen would castigate him for allowing the heathen to dance, but she seemed amused. Some of the ladies turned the other way; sometimes his loins were indecently exposed. Tomochichi bowed, quite suddenly, and handed a roach to the Queen, a symbol of eternity. Tomochichi placed the insect in the sentry's hand, and then Caroline clapped her hands, "Well done!" The ladies followed the queen's ovation, out of honor to the queen, and the men stood erect, quite stunned.

Am I my brother's keeper?

"Am I my brother's keeper?"

OF TRUST AND TRUSTEES

"I'M NOT ONE OF YOUR damned Indian friends, James. Stop calling me by my title, and tell me the truth. How are things *really* going in Georgia?"

Oglethorpe detested Sir John Perceval, Earl of Egmont. He was the President of the trustees, and if James didn't put a fruity spin on Georgia, all the funds would dry up. James stood, holding his velvet cap and placing it gently on his wig.

"Sir, I have a previous engagement; I do apologize. Everything is quite swell in the colonies, truly—as well as can be expected. We set sail in a week's time. Hopefully, we will meet once again before my departure."

Sir Perceval was not satisfied with Oglethorpe's response. The Earl lit a cigarette. He knew things couldn't be as easy as Oglethorpe painted. He heard horrendous stories of murderous natives, with speared arrows, and of barbaric Spaniards ambushing poor Englishmen in the middle of the night. He was hoping to hear some good news about the harvests, hopefully of lush vineyards. But instead, James held out his palm and smiled warmly.

The Board of trustees didn't reveal all of its dealings with Oglethorpe either. James, and many of the members, desired Georgia to become a colony for the oppressed, and of course to open its doors to all sorts of people. The trustees didn't necessarily agree—particularly when it came to Jews. James made his voice clear, but he wasn't present at every meeting, so he wasn't privy to the committee's every whim. James thought it best to follow their tendency towards selective silence as well.

He hurried past Sir Perceval's open gates and hailed a chaise. London was just as busy and foggy as he remembered. The Thames was murky, and the poor huddled around the numerous shops, begging for alms. The meeting with the Queen and the trustees went exceedingly well, with Tomochichi shocking all the fine ladies at court. James smiled while sitting beside a merchant in fine silk stockings and a fine beard. (He must be a Jew, James reasoned.) James recalled how his wife Senauki practiced painting the chief's chest the evening before, and how that silly steward Luther walked in on the old couple. She too was naked, save for a loincloth around her pelvis. Luther yelped, and Oglethorpe ran to Tomochichi's room, three doors down the corridor. On the day of the meeting, Tomochichi bowed and John Musgrove interpreted. Tomochichi suddenly began dancing provocatively, swirling his hands while Senauki clapped her hands. Oglethorpe had to convene John Musgrove. Tomochichi promised to wear silk garments, to honor England's dignitaries. Thankfully, he wore breechcloths when he danced on that fine morning.

James recalled Tomochichi's words, "I come in my old days. Although I cannot live to see the fruits of future days, I shall rest in peace knowing the Creeks shall be instructed in the knowledge of the English." Tomochichi must have been impressed by the culture and civilization in London, no doubt. It was a far cry from Georgia. But James began to miss his new homeland.

He informed the driver to halt the horses. He summarily left and rang the bell of Elizabeth Wright at Abingdon Street at Westminster. She did not know he was in town. He believed young women rather liked surprises. He was thirty-five. Perhaps Elizabeth, who was twenty-eight, would see his age as an asset, and not as a detriment as his friends imagined. He had been enamored of her for so long, and living in America heightened his loneliness.

James stood in the wet street, impatient. His dainty shoes were beginning to soak up the rain, and his knee-stockings were beginning to drop from their weight. A chamber-maid finally opened the gates. She was in the last trimester, her bulge appearing before her small face. Oglethorpe wondered how women did not capsize when they were so heavily with child.

"Lady Wright and Sir Wright are not in town, sir."

James was confused. "I am here for Elizabeth, miss. Is she disinclined or perhaps on holiday as well?" The chamber-maid stared at the tall man with hazel eyes. She did not recognize him. He seemed agitated, and his fine lashes were wet with rain. She ushered him in. He seemed like a gentleman. Once inside, the finely-painted blue walls a welcome respite from the rainfall, James was able to sit on the divan in the foyer. This was the first time he called on Elizabeth like this, unannounced. The chamber-maid wobbled with a towel in her hands. James nodded and thanked the woman. He removed his cap and wig. He dried his face, particularly his forehead.

"Sir, Elizabeth is in town with her sister, Lady Martin."

James looked up at the woman and whispered, "Who is Sir Wright, then?"

"He is Elizabeth's suitor, a cousin of the family."

James nodded his head, sadly. "Do you perchance know if the two are engaged to be married?" The maid felt a false contraction, and had to sit down near Oglethorpe to regain her composure. She pitied the British officer. He looked like a fine man.

"I do not know, but there are rumors of such, sir."

Oglethorpe nodded, sadly assessing his options. "When is she to return, do you know, madam?"

"Aye, in a good hour's time. She left before the sun disappeared."

James was hoping he could remain indoors. The chamber-maid read his mind, thankfully.

"You can remain in the parlor, until her arrival, if you will. It is warm there." James stood and slightly bowed. He handed her his thick waistcoat—now wet and quite heavy. Before leaving him to ruminate, she said, "My name is Mary, and please don't hesitate to call if you should like your tea before four, sir."

"I would like that very much." She nodded politely and left.

James entered the parlor and took in the room. What am I doing here, he thought. How can I bring her to my wooden hut? How can I even entertain the notion? This room boasts porcelain and finely woven rugs, not to mention gold-rimmed sofa beds. The hearth is so large! Just look at those busts. Ah. This must be a painting of Elizabeth. Just look at those soft hands, the dainty smile. The lace rosettes on her shoulder nearly the same color as the iris of her eyes. And the ceilings are quite high—the molding's design is superior by far. What am I to say? How can I convince such a fine lady to marry a frontiersman such as myself?

Mary left the tea in fine English fashion to cool. She placed the sugar cubes beside the saucer.

"Anything else, sir?"

James turned around; he forgot about the tea. "No, thank you." He continued to stare at a silhouette painting; he was sure it was of Elizabeth as well. Her nose was thin and slightly curvaceous, and the dark figure pictured such as well. He sighed heavily. He heard commotion by the entryway and immediately looked out the window. He saw a steward holding open the doors of a fine chaise, and a lady he did not recognize came out. She wore a large bonnet on her head, of royal blue velvet, and her gown must have cost a fortune. The taffeta and silk skirt was bounteous. She was corseted as well, her waist cinched in. Her gloves were turquoise, with orange trimming. She walked quickly, revealing long, black boots. Another woman exited the coach—and James recognized Elizabeth immediately. Suddenly feeling his palate dry up, he quickly placed the wig on his head. He fixed his cravat, which was a bit damp. He wasn't sure if he should remain standing or if he should sit down. He sat. Then he stood. Then he sat again. He heard voices nearing the parlor door. He recognized Elizabeth's in an instant. "And the latest fashions are utterly magnificent, with all that lace and muslin. I especially—"

Elizabeth's pink gown shone, and her crimson cheeks appeared fresh, as though she walked for a good hour in the park.

Her eyes were just as green as he remembered, but her lashes were slightly more brown than blonde. Ringlets fell on her cheeks, her intricate up do slightly undone by the winds. She bowed leisurely, and smiled.

"Mr. James Oglethorpe. What a pleasant surprise! To what end have you arrived in London?! How is America! What a surprise!" She held her hands by her midsection, and looked at her sister, the Lady Martin with conviviality. James, encouraged by her warm greetings, neared the ladies and bowed.

"I have come to convene with the King; I had to ratify an important treaty, and I must say, the beautiful Lady Wright never left me, even when our ship nearly tore to pieces in the middle of the great ocean. Dear Elizabeth, how have you been these months?"

Lady Martin felt as though she were intruding. She excused herself on the account of the sleeping children, and left the two to converse. Elizabeth felt her heart beat rapidly. James was as grand as ever, even more than she recalled. His eyes were large and inviting, unlike Sir Wright, whose eyes were always darting across the room at all the voluptuous women, no doubt.

"There is all this commotion about a dancing Indian! We heard all about it. It must have been quite alarming. One woman said he was clad in breeches that were missing pieces!" She grinned and blushed at the same time. James found her decency and gentility breathtaking. Every finger was covered in lace and her brows were so finely arched, every blonde hair in place like a perfect link on a duchess's necklace. It must have been so long since he sat in such company. The vessel he sailed was constantly wobbly; his cabin a sorry excuse for accommodations. The Natives were clad, thankfully, due to the winds. The sea captain hurled epithets, and the Scottish men by the masts chewed rat bones. John Musgrove kept to himself, smoking his pipe during all hours. Tomochichi was a pleasant old man, but mystifying. He chanted interesting tunes, to which Oglethorpe attached his own imaginative interpretation. James stared at Elizabeth remembering all those dark nights of loneliness and deprivation.

He wanted to hold her small hands, but instead admired them before speaking. "Elizabeth, I can speak to you for hours at end, and I know I can listen to you for eternity. But I must ask you in all earnestness, if you will answer me, just once, I will know if I can rest peacefully at night. Please, tell me if your heart is not pledged to another? I know I have no right. I have not even written a single correspondence during my long journey across seas, but please, answer me."

Elizabeth began to cry, almost as soon as he mentioned her heart. What had she ever known about her heart? Since she was a child, her parents insisted she must wed her cousin, Sir Wright. The matter was settled simply because he was her senior by five years, and her sister older than he. She successfully married Mr. Martin, who was introduced to the family by a gracious aunt. But what had Elizabeth known all these years? How could she answer this man, a man who made her feel alive, who breathed such interesting tales of adventure and who assisted so many poor Englishmen, the same debtors who made Elizabeth feel so guilty about her own uneventful but magnificently lavish life. What could she say? Her heart ached inside, and she felt a strange pain in her womb. It was as though her ladyhead, her womb, cried out. She wondered if this was desire. She had read about it, in the library, when her sisters were all asleep. The French verses sometimes awakening emotions she had repressed since she became a maiden. Twenty-eight years, and still waiting for love to capture her. She looked longingly at James and wondered why she had to be the one to break someone's heart as well as her own.

James sat, beckoning her with his eyes. Pleading. He wondered why she was crying profusely. What could possibly be the cause of her tears? He could barely stand the sight of her like this. This must presage something terrible. Why would a lady cry like this?

Elizabeth began apologizing. James nodded, waiting for her to answer his question. Suddenly, he felt over-heated. He loosened his cravat. Elizabeth kept fumbling her fingers. Finally, she glanced at him and said, in a barely audible, monotonous tone, "I don't know what to say. I too have thought of you, and I wondered why you had not corresponded. We always seem to get along so nicely, wouldn't you say? But I can't just follow my whims, like you James. You can dream this idea of settling in America; you can even convince Parliament! And I, I am barely in control of my own heart." She then began to cry again.

James was confounded. She was dodging the question, and hinting at its answer at the same time. Perhaps I should make this easier on the woman, he thought.

"Elizabeth, I know I cannot ask you this, since you are by far the most genteel woman I have ever come across. But I must wonder if you would leave all this splendor for a chance to settle in a land far, far removed from such luxuries—"

Quite suddenly, Elizabeth stood and walked to the hearth. Her back was to James, and he felt bewildered. Her gown, which was decorated with small buttons all across the back, was all he saw. Despite her agitation, he imagined loosening each button, slowly. Her lovely figure a painting, but her eyes were turned to the wall. He patiently waited. He stood as well and walked to her. He whispered in her ear, "Are you engaged to your cousin, Sir Wright?"

Elizabeth blushed, and turned to look directly at James, "No, not officially, but I have been destined to be his mate since I was a child of two or three years." She sobbed once again, into her gloves. James suddenly felt a pang of compassion for the poor girl. How long has she waited for this cousin of hers to propose? How did she feel about him? Was the estate entitled in Sir Wright's name? How long has she been subject to this intended engagement? James held her, overcome by passion and sadness. She sobbed onto his cravat, and he stood perfectly still, caressing her hair with his little finger, as though she were his child.

"Would you reconsider the arrangement, on my behalf? Is it even possible to request such? Tell me, Elizabeth, is this even a possibility, however remote?" She finally looked up, and before she could utter a sound in response, he kissed her passionately. Elizabeth's heart beat rapidly, as though she were feeling something profoundly forbidden. She felt her head spin, and she held James by the shoulders.

And then she pulled away.

"Oh, James. You are so lovely and kind. I hope you can see that this matter is not entirely up to me. I am mad for saying this, I know I am, but I will still love you even if I am to marry Sir Wright."

"Then it is forbidden for you to do so! You cannot split your soul in this manner!"

Encouraged by her avowal, he grabbed her once again, and tried to kiss her again. This time, she turned her cheek, and he kissed her neck. She began to moan, slightly. And then she began to cry. She gathered her pink skirt with a swoop, and ran out of the room, with her right hand covering her mouth.

"You damn fool, you," James muttered to himself under his breath. Always looking for shortcuts to a woman's heart! He shouldn't have done that. It wasn't fair. But he could barely resist. He had been so lonely for so long in that shack of a hut in Georgia with gnats and flies buzzing all night and all those dreams, and her absolutely enchanting spell on his sorry old soul; whatever shall become of him and his wretched plans for a colony that was just as barren as his heart was now—the Lord only knew.

Mortified, James looked around the room one last time and saw a pin of ivory beads and pearls on the floor. He knelt, and with his thumb he snatched it from the rug. It was so delicate and fine, just like Elizabeth. He placed it in the pocket of his breeches and summarily left the house, nearly forgetting his waistcoat by the foyer.

The rain came down heavily; James felt as though the heavens were punishing him for his ambition. James thought of all those ladies who had been eagerly presented by dignitaries and well-meaning relatives. All those ladies would have been honored to accept his hand in marriage, but he had to be fixated on the one woman he couldn't have. So Sir Wright was her prearranged soul-mate, as it were. James turned onto the main street and looked earnestly for a pub. He wanted to drain the memory of Elizabeth's soft neck from his mind. He held the pin in his hand one last time, and opened the large mahogany door to the Gentlemen's Saloon, hoping to forget the entire affair.

Elizabeth refused to come down for supper. Lady Martin guessed her sister was ill-disposed, and that British Officer probably the cause. He was a very imposing figure, and his big eyes quite arresting. The Lady Martin missed those days when men would speak to her, making her feel desirable and pretty. Her husband was running business matters most of the day, and he did not pay much attention to her during the long winter nights as much as she would have preferred. Her sister was lovelier than she had been at twenty-eight; well, Elizabeth never bore any children. Elizabeth's blonde ringlets did not have any shades of grey, and her cheeks had a natural peach tint. James Oglethorpe wasn't the only man poor Elizabeth rejected. In fact, there must have been at least five other gentleman who desired her beautiful sister. No doubt it was because of their father's fortune, or maybe because Elizabeth resembled a graceful Madonna in a da Vinci. Whatever the case, her sister was likely to forget the entire matter by next week when Sir Wright would return from holiday. It was just too bad, though. All that mutton gone to waste.

*

Lord Perceval paced across the room. He had expected to learn of good news in Georgia. The colony was an investment, after all, despite the honorable intentions of its founder. A well-functioning town meant a new market for British goods, particularly those that are hard to come by in the New World. But they had to be careful; they didn't want the colony to become another town overrun by rich Jews. Thomas Coram, a Trustee member no one truly liked, lived in Massachusetts for a portion of the year. He vociferously spoke against permitting Jews to settle in the new colony.

"It would be shocking!" He commenced his argument by including a prediction that Jews would ruin the entire enterprise. Georgia would become "a Jewish colony," and all Christian colonists would most certainly "fall off and desert it, as leaves from a tree in autumn." But Jewish commissioners had requested permission for settlement. This caused much ruckus. Those afraid to dissent with Coram kept their mouths shut. Those that spoke up, and they were the majority, tended to agree with him. The Jewish commissioners were ordered to surrender their requests. James Oglethorpe had not been apprised of the matter. And Mr. Martyn, the secretary of the trustees, was somewhat inclined to delay important matters. Perhaps he was opposed to their rants against the Jews; but the politics didn't matter to Lord Perceval all that much. He just wanted to ensure that the trustees would benefit financially from Georgia. Lord Perceval nearly coughed when he remembered the Indian chief dancing before the queen. That must have been the most revolting dance! But Queen Caroline was gracious as ever. What did she say? Yes. "You represent your people well." How did Oglethorpe manage to live with such barbarians as neighbors? The trustees were counting on Oglethorpe. Lord Perceval just wasn't sure how much James could be trusted.

*

James sipped his brew of London ale with a pensive brow. He should have guessed. "The lady doth protest too much." Isn't that what Shakespeare had in mind? Who was this Sir Wright anyway? James stood and looked around the room. He spotted Lord Perceval entering the saloon. James wanted to avoid him. He would probably want to learn more about the situation in the colonies. James moved farther across the room. He placed his knee on a footstool and peered out the large window, which was slightly clouded by a mist. James took his index finger and cleared it. He saw a boy of eight or nine holding wet newspapers, holding another child's hand. James wondered how parents could allow their children to fend for themselves in a brutal world. He continued to stare out the window, and he immediately recalled the breeze of his wooden hut in Georgia. The compendium of law holding the door ajar. All those colonists waiting for a word from him. The Natives offering him goods and services. The young men gathering a militia to protect their lands. And the children swimming in the banks of the river. James placed the unfinished glass on the marble table, glanced longingly at a beautiful woman who resembled Elizabeth on his way out, and decided to bid farewell to England on the following morning. He had to set sail as soon as possible. At least his heart was sealed in its love for the unknowns in America than the prosaic ways of London life.

50

*

Tomochichi rested, half awake, in his plush bed, compliments of the Mother Queen of the White Man. She had lovely eyes, like the Savannah River. Clear and blue, reflecting the sky's hue. And her King had glowing jewels on his head, finer than all the beads he had ever worn in all his life. Senauki chanted an Indian tune. They will remain in England for a hero's tour. So far, they have seen the most beautiful buildings, so tall and strong. He had to feel every monument, touch the work of man. The White Man must be very powerful if he mastered the earth and seas so well. Their food was another matter. Both Tomochichi and Senauki suffered from indigestion. The English do not consume maize; they eat breads and biscuits. Tomochichi had a hard time chewing their food. They missed their grass hut. But they will set sail in a week's time, without James Oglethorpe. He apologized—but he had to leave tomorrow. Tomochichi prayed for James's safe arrival in the homeland. The seas were always angry this time of year. Tomochichi wondered why the gentle man who had previously exuded confidence and poise appeared beaten and empty. James's eyes, it seemed to the Indian chief, had a misty appearance, as though he had been drinking too much or crying in his sleep.

*

"Those damned Jews set sail behind our backs! Have you heard, Mr. Perceval?" Thomas Coram entered the private room in Winchester, holding a letter in his hand. Coram raised both brows, and then furiously paced around the room.

He looked directly at Mr. Martyn, addressing the secretary in third person, "Didn't the secretary specifically instruct the Jewish commissioners to recall their requests? Always thinking they can get away with duplicity. Bloody perfidious, I say. What are we to do?"

Mr. Martyn shifted uneasily in his chair. He had not sent the Hebrew commissioners the detailed reports that the trustees would not permit Jews to enter Savannah's ports. The land was equally available to a privileged few. That was the consensus. It was his duty, but he neglected to speak with Da Costa and Suasso, the Sephardic Jews with Italian mustaches, who collected funds from their own kind. They were truly eager to settle in Georgia. He even visited the Bevis Marks Synagogue where he met some of the Portugese Jews, from a distance, of course. And they provided the funds themselves. But now his dereliction would cost him. Had he neglected his duties out of sheer compassion or financial common sense? Even Martyn didn't know. And perhaps it didn't matter. Now Coram would make them all wish they had assigned *him* as the secretary, despite the fact that he was not a permanent resident of the English countryside.

"Where's Oglethorpe?" Lord Perceval loudly replied, nettled that this boat of Jews was an issue at all. Goodness knows money flows where the Jew goes, or so the saying goes. "I could have sworn I had seen him not too long ago. Why—it must have been at the Gentlemen's Saloon, the bastard. Always carries himself as though he is better than his fellow—"

"That's enough aspersions on the man, Lord. We are not here to discuss Oglethorpe's private matters. His whereabouts is all we need to know!"

Lord Perceval's nostrils flared minutely when Coram spoke. Thomas was a dreadful man, his poor wife suffered no doubt. Perceval shrugged his shoulders. "How should I know? How does the saying go—'Am I my brother's keeper?'" Perceval poked Mr. Martyn aggressively, on the shoulder, trying to elicit a chortle.

Thomas rolled his eyes. A steward just then entered the room with another letter. Coram had a feeling it was of grave importance.

He opened it, and read the contents aloud, "Oglethorpe here states he has 'set sail, so fare you well.' I am surrounded by bloody poets!"

Lord Perceval stood. "Then that settles it, Coram. There is nothing you can do but write a letter to the chap. I'll see you all in a month's time." He grabbed his hat and set off for the saloon on Main Street—the one where the loose women can be found at a pretty pence—leaving Coram bent over, muttering "damn Judas trick every time."

*

James finally docked in the Savannah ports after a surprisingly quick journey. A few more British, a few Scots and even some Germans accompanied James. He tried to play cards with the other crewmembers, and he even learned how to operate the mast. He read the Bible, but skipped most of Genesis; there were too many romantic accounts. He preferred the segments of rebuke in Deuteronomy. It made him feel as though love is altogether a messy affair. He tried to ignore some of the indecent noises he heard every now and then; doubtless the Germans were not the most refined, but they would make good militiamen when the time called for it, no doubt. A child caught his fancy, a little girl with yellow hair. He held her hand around deck when her parents entered frays with their dirty neighbors.

James was glad to step on dry land. A man with discolored skin greeted James. He smelled like rotten eggs. James nearly forgot his manners.

"Good God!" he exclaimed. He teetered back, a couple of feet, instinctively. The man had sores all over his mouth. James wondered what happened to him. "I see you have not heard, Sir. The rain has ceased for some time now." James wondered why the porter chose to tell him this seemingly irrelevant piece of information. Was that truly an excuse for poor hygiene? Oglethorpe took a complete and full view of the coastline. The sky seemed a bit greyer than he recalled. The beaches were deserted. James continued walking; the porter following him. He looked around and he noticed heaps of dung by the main road. Mosquitoes were buzzing between the piles of human and horse excrement. Buckets of rainwater were half-turned, half-empty. A few bugs lay in puddles, dead. James walked up the side road leading to his wooden house, and turned to the porter.

"You should see Dr. Cox about those sores of yours; I'm sure he has a tonic of some kind. Do you know where he lives? I can show you the way, if you need assistance."

James turned and looked the porter straight in the eyes; he couldn't bear to look at his dreadful sores. He noticed they were yellowish.

"Have you not heard, Sir? Cox is dead."

"Mysterious ways."

Of Cabin & Yellow Fever

PERLA'S BABY DIED. SHE SAT in her cabin crying. It happened the next day. The storm tore her innards, and the baby was severed from its placenta. Blood trickled down her thighs, and then the cramps became unbearable. Dr. Nunez eased her pain with a strong brew of willow leaves, and he promised that her womb will become especially fertile in one moon's time. That terrible night sealed her child's fate. But her pain was somewhat more bearable when she recalled Abigail's dead baby, buried in waters, to be eaten by eels. At least her child did not have a face. Or name. And at least she did not have to mourn for a week, a month, a lifetime.

Benjamin could not sleep on the same cot as his wife. She was impure; he had to borrow a cot from the Minises, an affluent Portuguese family who were glad to assist the poor Ashkenazi family. Perla wondered if she had sinned terribly. Was it because she slept with her husband during the day? Why was this happening? How will she become pure again? Will she be able to maintain another pregnancy? Hungry, she walked towards the dining hall only to find rotten turnips and half-cooked potatoes. They were going to starve because the British wouldn't allow them to dock. They were trapped, and she was barren again. She began to cry. She lost her appetite.

Benjamin Sheftall was speaking rapidly, in German, to Jacob Yowell, the single man with a grey complexion and a hunched back from learning many long hours. Benjamin didn't want to alarm his wife, but he needed to speak to someone from his hometown, in a language they both shared. They finally docked by the Savannah ports, but they were denied entry. Jews. It was a problem. The trustees forbade them to enter American shores. They were stuck. Provisions were running low. Benjamin's wife lost her glow; the Jews were to be cast off. Jacob Yowell kept giving away his bread portions to the children. Abigail's baby died from an unknown disease, and now it seemed they were all doomed to a similar fate. They set sail hoping for the best. Their naiveté—lost at a heavy price.

"Soon we'll all starve! How in heaven's name are we to provide for our loved ones if the provisions are nearly gone and the colonists won't let us step on their land? Eh? How are we to make it back to London? Did they even consider that—or the Jews just don't matter!?" Benjamin held both hands, palms up and open, leaning toward Jacob. Jacob had often wondered why the *goyim* treated them like a sub-species. Jacob's palate was parched. He simply nodded at Sheftall and looked at his beaten shoes.

"So, what else is new, tell me? If they are kind to you, it's only because they hope you'll convert. You know the second coming is dependent upon converting all the Jews; I don't need to tell you that. It is written in their book, in a chapter called 'Revelations.' *Nu?* You see the problem? How can they tend to their ladies and to their businesses if they have to convert all the Jews? They would rather we just perished—easier for them, you see."

Benjamin gazed at Jacob and wondered how the man slept at night. Surely what he said wasn't entirely true.

Just then, a few Spanish-Portuguese walked up, across the planks, in sheer linen undergarments. The sun was terribly intense, burning their already darkened flesh. In quick succession, they began arranging a plan—to trade with the Indian natives, who were eager for gold and beads. Dr. Nunez had many gold coins, which he could easily sell for victuals. The Lady Minis offered her emerald brooch. Abigail sadly parted from her baby's golden talisman (to ward off the evil eye). Captain Hanson would be with Hannah tonight. It was the perfect time to meet with the heathens who might just be the only civilized people on this land. The natives curiously greeted them, by the shore, balancing sacks of strange vegetables and other foods on their heads. They had no way to communicate with the Indians; they were heathens who did not even cover their legs. Just the groin. But they were wearing gleaming jewels, particularly hammered gold necklaces. Gold was valuable, and the international language they all understood—currency for food. They had to barter or die. They spoke in broken English. Even a word or two of Spanish; the natives trade with the Spaniards in Florida, it seemed. A word here, a gesture there. The meeting was set.

Benjamin saw the Portuguese crowd eagerly communicating with one another, pointing fingers at one another. They were planning something, but it wasn't entirely clear. He couldn't understand a single word. Frustrated, he walked up to Dr. Nunez and asked him in English, "What is going on? I sense something of importance."

Dr. Nunez placed his index finger by his mouth. "It is too hot in the cabins. We cannot speak down there, you understand? The captain doesn't speak our Ladino, heh?" He began to whisper in English, "We plan to trade with the Indians. They will come again at night as they always do, to watch us. They are curious, you see. We have been here for more than three days, sitting like sorry, neglected children."

Benjamin Sheftall thought of Perla and wondered what he could barter. He removed the gold pendant his mother gave him when he turned thirteen.

"Take this, and please buy food for my Perla. Potatoes or anything the natives have. If there's a hen, that would be wonderful. My wife needs poultry; she is suffering. Please help me in this!"

Dr. Nunez refused to take the pendant. He shook Benjamin's hand and promised to do his best, but Benjamin would need that pendant for a later time, no doubt. There's no telling what this strange place shall bring.

Benjamin peered at the Savannah port wondering how they could write those promising things in the pamphlet he eagerly read every night. The grass and wooden huts were breaking apart, and even from the ship's prow he could see the lack of irrigation.

The river wasn't far off in the distance, but it seemed eerily quiet. He had seen one or two white men and one woman walk across the road, darting quickly from one hut to another. He saw a female Negro in a worn-out dress holding a small broom made of twigs darting with the man, from hut to hut. Mosquitoes were constantly buzzing around the deck, particularly around the rotten food supply. Every morning now for six months the Scottish crew members would dump the fetid contents of their "chamber pots" into the ocean, laughing at all the poor fish, telling crude jokes, offending the graces of all the ladies who were educated enough to understand their strange accent. He noticed that now they joked about dead mosquitoes in their pots. ("You've got some killer shit there, Tommy son!" and the likes.)

There were few farms in sight. He noticed many trees were brutally cut down, their jagged stumps hazardous; one hut had a cross dangling from its roof, slightly lopsided. Protestants. It was well-known that Georgia was to become a bastion for "poor but respectable Protestants." They didn't fit the description. Jews. Some rich, some, well, not so rich. But Jews. Where was James Oglethorpe? He heard he was a very compassionate fellow. Why wasn't he allowing them to step foot on his precious colony? Captain Hanson left the boat every evening with Hannah, leaving them all moored, abandoned. How were they to make it back to England now? They were nearly out of funds. The children were sickly, and poor Jacob looked as though he ate too many carrots. The men were sick of fishing for food, and Benjamin didn't want to witness his brethren eating pork anymore. He wanted to live in a quiet corner with Perla, thinking all Jews ate kosher and blessed the Lord before and after meals. He could barely handle the sights of his counterparts smoking reed pipes on the Sabbath and even behaving immodestly before the Scottish men. It was all a disgrace—but they were Jews nonetheless. It was a sad measure of the Portuguese and Spanish Inquisition, generations after Jews feigned conversion. It was as though what they had simulated in fear became their practicing religion in times of relative peace, here in the corner of a new, unadulterated world.

Benjamin sighed. He desperately wanted to jump into the sea. He couldn't maintain his sanity in the heat. The lower decks were well over ninety degrees. The wooden walls exacerbated the grave intensity of pure fiery heat. His feet were developing boils. But he couldn't remove his shoes. Then his feet would burn. The ladies on deck were half-clothed. No one seemed to care anymore. Families gathered on deck, and their mattresses decorated the planks, all across the stern up to the main mast. Stockings and garters, breeches and waistcoats became temporary shields against the sun. Tommy removed one of the sails and made a sailor's tent for his men. But they could leave. Benjamin heard the rabble-rousing of Hannah and the men well into their first night in Savannah wondering if he settled in a land where the only rules to follow were the impetuous whims of a man's heart.

Disheartened, he sat near the Minises, the friendly Sephardim. They thought Benjamin would pray for them, if they needed assistance from the Lord. They would cross their hearts before a storm, or when they saw Abigail's baby all wrapped in a makeshift shroud. Benjamin would shudder, wondering how long it would take to turn all the Jews into unrecognizable *conversos* or *morranos*—the secret Jews, the ignorant half-Christianized Jews.

They hadn't bathed decently for months. The ladies were beginning to reek; and the perfumes couldn't mask the unmistakable odor of accumulated sweat. The water supply was dangerously low, and some of the children began to faint in the heat. Dr. Nunez was especially busy during the day. Dr. Nunez simply didn't know how he could forestall a terrible tragedy, with no wind to cool them off, and the heat of midsummer threatening to consume them all.

Some of the couples copulated at night, above deck, to the disapproval of Jacob and Benjamin. It was a disgrace—what will the Scots think of the Jews? And all Captain Hanson needs is another excuse to brand them "dregs." Most of the Portuguese Jews didn't know precisely what the word meant, but they had a strong intuitive belief that it was malicious. They tried to tip-toe around the Captain, fearing he would go off on one of his rants. The sun slowly started to descend, and its rays waned in strength. Orange hues spilled on the expanse of the vast Atlantic. Night descended and the men took to the rear of the boat.

Captain Hanson returned that night earlier than expected from the Savannah pubs. "All them people afraid of spreading the plague! Yellow fever. All that vomit! This place is a curse, I tell you. Damn this country. Stuck with these wretched dregs because no one wants Jews in their land. Now how in bloody Mary's name am I going to get me back to London?" Benjamin overheard Hanson's inebriated rants and ran toward the Portuguese men who intended to barter with the naked men. Jacob was there too. He volunteered, it seemed. He slowly climbed down the vessel's exterior planks. His four-cornered garment, the *tzitzit*, got caught in a loose nail. It tore off and remained on the wooden splinters. Jacob didn't take notice. He landed safely on the canoe.

The Indians were clad in loincloths, sweating onto their exposed toes. Lamps made of animal fats burned at each corner of the canoe. A man with a bone pierced through his nose and left ear approached Jacob Yowell. He motioned with his hands and said, "Money."

Jacob said, "First food." The native reached for the tomahawk attached to his loins, in the wrap of his pelvis. Jacob pretended to eat. "Food," he repeated, hoping the Indian would understand his gesture. The native took the tomahawk and held it near his neck, "Money." Jacob began to fear for his life. Was this barbarian threatening him? What should he do? What if he took the money, ran off, killed him, and then left all those poor, starving Portuguese children? Benjamin saw the entire exchange and yelled at Jacob in their common tongue, "Do not give him the gold, Jacob! It's a trap!" The native did not understand a word, but he sensed the urgency in Benjamin's voice and immediately threw the tomahawk in Benjamin's direction. Benjamin barely ducked in time; he felt his left ear burning. He touched his ear, and his hand was as red as the Egyptian Nile of the cursed Pharaoh. Jacob, an assiduous student, found himself completely incapable of defending himself.

Out of sheer instinct, he jumped into the water, trying to swim underwater, where the Indians would not be able to detect him. The other Portuguese Jews began gathering round when they heard Benjamin's urgent plea. They yelled for assistance, desperate to save their friend and their gold. Just then Captain Hanson stumbled on board, cursing his fate.

Out of sheer luck, the Indians became frightened when they heard Hanson's inebriated tirades. He gesticulated and stomped his feet, altogether yelling into the heavens. The Indian with the pierced ear stiffened. And then he froze—the white man summoned the demon of the crescent moon. ("You're all Delilahs, you!") He searched one last time for Jacob, hoping to kill him with an arrow and carry his body back to his camp, sure that the gold was tucked in one of his pockets. "You sniveling, mucky cheats! You all owe me four hundred pounds, you hear!" Captain Hanson repeated this refrain, tripping over the coiled ropes and rum barrels. He lifted his pistol and shot three times into the air. "Next time that's going to be in your heads!"

The Indian regained his quick senses. He searched the vicinity, but could not find him. He shot a couple of quick arrows into the water, and headed towards the shore, angry that he missed the chance of deceiving the white man just as he and his people had been deceived. Terrorizing them would make them turn around and set sail straight away. As the native pulled his canoe back on shore, he shuddered at the outburst of rage, "Get you out of here!" Captain Hanson meant the Jews.

Benjamin quickly darted to the opposite side of the *William and Sarah*. Yowell came around, but was groaning. He had a strange protrusion on his upper arm, by his triceps. A spear the length of two men's arms was firmly attached to his flesh. Benjamin muttered under his breath a quick *Shema Yisrael*, and assisted his beleaguered friend. Jacob didn't have much strength to carry his own weight, but somehow managed to climb back on board. Jacob was wounded, wet, and bleeding. Benjamin carried his friend out of the water. This time Tommy assisted, knowing full well how

Jacob felt. Dr. Nunez rushed to Jacob's aid. The men on board cursed the natives and the women screeched and crossed their hearts, murmuring *Ave Maria* under their breaths.

"Don't touch the spear! Do not remove it!" Nunez ordered the Portuguese males, who were eager to save Jacob.

Jacob looked at the black sky and all the stars and wondered just how the sons of Abraham would be like all the stars if they are murdered and executed and burned in every generation. Jacob thought of all those tractates of Talmud he mulled over... his mind stopped at Jacob's ladder. What does Rashi say? Ascending for years upon years. The many exiles the Jews must face—Assyria. Up the ladder—Babylonia. Go up, Jacob. He still has Persia. Greece. Rome. *Edom*. And then for ten months—Ishmael. Up Jacob must go. When will Jacob come back down and redeem this sorry nation of Jews? Was he to die before witnessing a redeemer? Jacob sighed. There was still a chance for that—if he believed in the waking of the dead. Or maybe like the secret texts illuminate—he would return, reincarnated. Jacob's mind churned these thoughts. And then images of his hometown in Prussia flashed before his eyes. He was screaming—but inside he was thinking of his mother's *cholent* and of all the days he spent in the *cheder* reciting the prayer with his index finger pointed at the beautiful Hebrew letters. And then his mind went blank. Was it truly time for the final valediction to this tangible universe?

Jacob's eyes rolled; he began to convulse.

"Poison," Nunez whispered. "The arrow is poisoned!" He quickly removed the spear, causing Jacob to scream like a laboring mother. Dr. Nunez held Jacob's skull; he was violently shaking, uncontrollably. And then he went limp. Dr. Nunez touched Jacob's wrist, and felt a very weak pulse. He placed his ear by Jacob's chest and listened carefully for signs of life. Orange liquid spurted out of the wound, and Nunez rushed to place a rag on the torn flesh. The toxic blood was capable of poisoning anyone who had an open wound. One woman rushed to see Jacob, holding a little girl in her hand. She fell to the floor, stricken by the sight of the young man who risked his life so her daughter wouldn't starve—and for what? Now he lay on the floor, blood leaking from his nose, ears, and eyes. The little girl cried and then her mother fainted. Benjamin recited prayers for his friend, hoping Jacob would be received well in heaven. Benjamin prayed all evening. Dr. Nunez left the two Prussian Jews alone. Benjamin kept swaying to some ancient Hebrew verse, and didn't stop until daybreak.

Jacob was dead before sunrise.

*

Oglethorpe paced across his hut. He wasn't permitted to leave. He immediately sent for John Gale, a member of the militia, to call on Dr. Winthrop of Charleston. He needed a physician, desperately. What were those trustees thinking, sending only one man with any inkling of medicine to settle in Georgia? Colonists were dying like cattle stranded in the Sahara. One by one. He shouldn't have left—but then maybe he would be like Cox. Dead. The natives were dying too. This plague was impartial, attacking the Protestants, the Creeks. God, it didn't matter. The cemetery was accumulating gravestones. And to make matters worse, a boat full of Jews was docked by the river. What in sweet Jesus' name was he to do about those Jews? The trustees never informed him of this Jew boat, but even if they did, Oglethorpe intuitively reasoned, they most likely would have forbidden them entry. It was tacit Georgia would be a proprietary colony mainly for Christians seeking a better life… refuge… a second chance. And the debtors were mostly Christian as well. Rose, the Negro woman who worked briefly for Dr. Cox, fell ill the previous morning. By nightfall she was dead. God, how he hated to see any slave working for a white man. It was a disgrace—and now she had no one to bury her. But she was a good woman, and she believed in Jesus. Oglethorpe threw his walking stick across the room. Someone had to give that Negro woman a Christian burial. Ignoring the warning to remain indoors, James quickly left his hut and walked to the makeshift morgue that was previously Dr. Cox's home. He would take a chance; some things had to be done.

Oglethorpe neared the house and noticed an overbearingly fetid odor. He placed a handkerchief across his mouth and nose;

his governess once told him it helped to ward off disease. At this point, Oglethorpe had to prevent more outbreaks. Burying the dead was crucial. Fear of contagion lurked behind doors, and the inhabitants distrusted one another. Sarah Parker's girl died. She was only a lass of thirteen. And many able-bodied men fell to yellow fever—to Oglethorpe's tremendous chagrin. He desperately needed a militia. Those Spaniards down south were notoriously violent, beating the women into submission and raiding their stocks of fowl and swine. They must have ravished a number of their women, and his men only recently learned how to defend the colony from their guerilla tactics. The Creeks were generally peaceful, thanks in large part to Tomochichi's influence. The old man was still at sea. The old man was fortunate indeed.

James nearly keeled over when he entered Cox's hut—there were well over twenty bodies lying side by side, bloated. The stench was overwhelming, and he stood, retching, immobilized. His eyes caught sight of a doll tucked in a baby's blanket. And then he saw her—with the broom: Rose was in the corner, next to another Negro. A boy of about fifteen with flies hovering over his toes and ears. It was an impossible feat. How could one man bury all these cadavers? He expected to see Rose, alone, hopefully covered in a shroud. But this was simply inhumane. No one wanted to bury the Negros. They were useless once they became sick, and not a single soul bothered to care for them once they fell ill.

Enraged, James ran to the church and began yelling well before he entered the nave, "You call yourselves Christians? You purchase your Negroes and then leave them to die and neglect to bury them! Are they not God's creatures? You call yourselves God's messengers? Right now I order you all in the name of the King and the Lord Almighty to follow me. Tonight you will bury those poor Negros, so help me God!"

A group of seven or eight missionaries, mostly middle-aged men, mumbled. One stood. "We don't want to contaminate our families. And we don't want to touch those dead bodies, sir. There's evil in it."

"I will deport you all to England if you refuse to do your duty! Do you hear? Each household member shall reclaim his maidservant, and shall bury the Negro man, woman, or child. No one shall remain in that house by sunrise. Dr. Cox's house shall be extinguished. Now. Go!"

The men gathered their belongings and did James's bidding, begrudgingly. They had been told the yellow fever would remain with the dead so long as the bodies remain together, but no one wanted to bury them. Not yet. They were waiting for the plague to stop, and then they would burn the house down. But James wanted those Negroes to have a Christian burial, and who could argue with James? James fed them when they had no food, slept in their dilapidated vessel when he had a luxury craft. He even spent large sums from his own coffers to fund the colony and its people. James, who left his palace, who swore like a real man, and who assuaged the women when it stormed at sea. They owed him. But they feared their sense of gratitude may just cost them their lives.

*

Perla hugged her knees that night. She could begin counting her clean days soon. The bleeding ceased. But her heart ached. Not only for her dead hopes, but for her husband's warmth. Her frangible spirit nearly spent, she yearned for another child. Benjamin was awake the entire night, praying for the emaciated Jew, Jacob. Perla knew his family. They were indigent and very pious. Jacob's father fasted every Monday and Thursday for eons. To mourn the Temple. And his mother recited psalms between customers in the corner of the small goods store that sold near-spoiled milk. They barely eked out a living—because the entire town's poor bought on credit, and who could pay that sum by the time the New Year rolled its head? Jacob's father would just nod, cluck his tongue, and accept a bartered pot, rusty but functional instead. And still they called them all money-hungry. It didn't matter, Perla thought. Because at the end of the day, they *all* were hungry. Not only for food, but for all that money could truly buy.

They buried him at sea. It was a ceremony that began with gravity. The *Kaddish*. Benjamin crying and eulogizing. But suddenly, Salvi Costa rammed Benjamin and yelled, "Where's the gold? You cheating Ashkenazi! I know you have it! Give it over, before I dump you with your friend into the ocean!"

Salvi's breath had the distinctive odor of a man who had not eaten properly for days on end. Atrabilious and half-naked, Salvi demanded an answer. The other Portuguese men nodded their heads. They have not forgotten about their gold. The Ashkenazi with the dark skull cap must have it! They began shoving Benjamin, sticking their hands into his pockets. Benjamin, stunned, moved away, pushing their hands away. The other Jews barely understood him.

"Stop!" He said in English. It mattered little. The men imitated him, now rolling Benjamin onto his back, rummaging in his back pockets, in between his legs.

Salvi had enough. He remembered how Benjamin stood watch over Jacob, how he wanted to know what was going on that morning, how he spoke to Dr. Nunez. It was clear this Jew had nothing but treacherous plans up his dirty sleeve. Should have figured. Righteous on the outside, rotten in the core. The way he always stared at his lady's brooches. And then pretending he didn't stare at her breasts! Sure. It was all clear now.

Salvi held Benjamin by the throat, and pulled him up.

"Where is it?" He asked in Spanish. Benjamin stood erect. He moved his head from side to side, opening his palms. Salvi suddenly loosened his grip and staggered to the corpse. He removed the shroud and began probing the dead body for the purple pouch of golden coins. His pelf; their pelf. Not the Ashkenazi's hard-earned gold! Benjamin held his hands to his head, nearly howling in deep grief and horror.

"You can't do that! That's a desecration!" he yelled in Yiddish.

Angered by the violation, Benjamin tore at Salvi's back, tearing the Portuguese man off of his deceased friend. He punched

Salvi square in the jaw, sending the desecrator reeling, holding his lips, bleeding unto his palm.

Benjamin's tears clouded his eyes. He quickly placed the shroud over Jacob's body.

"It is better that you had died than witness this, my dear brother," Benjamin whispered. Salvi removed a small dagger from the inner side of his breeches.

"He's going to join that friend of his before he cheats me," Salvi thought.

"*¿Qué es esto por todas partes? No toca le!*" (What is this all about? Don't touch him!)

Dr. Nunez bellowed at Salvi, rapidly moving toward the crowd. He had seen from far the glittering silver. The dagger. He had been dozing, exhausted from the previous evening, administering compresses to the ailing children. He awoke to a nudge. His son reminded him. The dead Jew. They meant to bury him this morning.

Salvi ignored Dr. Nunez, too enraged to halt his impetuosity. Salvi's saliva, previously stuck to his palate, now drizzled unto the musty planks. Salvi gaped and roared; he held his arm above his head. "*Ladron!* Thief!"

Benjamin dumped Jacob's body into the Atlantic. He turned his head, and saw the sun's rays reflecting off a sharp, silvery poniard. Benjamin remained in place. His ears stopped ringing. Instead, he counted Salvi's advance. One. Two. He will be right here by three.

Benjamin ducked and grabbed Salvi by the ankles, throwing the Portuguese man, drunk with rage, overboard.

Salvi's cronies, men whose wives were starving too, ran towards Salvi, peering at the ocean floor, looking for their friend. Salvi came up, gulping for oxygen. Dr. Nunez yelled, "Why would you do this?"

Senor Minises whispered a few words to the physician. The doctor's eyes began to water. His face blanched.

"You fools! I have the pouch right here!"

*

Hale made his way to James's hut by nightfall. Winthrop refused to leave Charleston. It was useless. Hale handed Winthrop's letter to James. James collapsed, falling to the floor, defeated; the plague would continue, and there was little Winthrop could do. Contagion was a greater possibility than any effective treatment. Try compresses. Control nose bleeding with head elevation. Once a person begins to hallucinate, quarantine him. He will die in a matter of days. There is no cure. Just pray it is over, soon. And once the eyes become yellow—expect the worst. Make sure all ill colonists are housed under one roof. Wash hands. Keep children safe—remove any dead people immediately. Pray. There is nothing that can be done. This is Satan's work.

James sat on the floor, his face buried in his palms. This disease was a *bete noir*, and the only doctor he knew became just as contemptible. Some doctor.

Hale addressed Oglethorpe, "Sir. I have another letter."

James barely registered Hale's presence. His head began to ache, and he felt slightly nauseous. Georgia was going to die in its infancy, and there was nothing he could do. Cox warned him. He had the vatic fear that one day Georgia just might succumb to some terrible outbreak. Cox saw it coming, and he was the first to fall into the clutches of death's ugly claws. James began to weep, imagining all the children who would die and the young jolly fellows who would never have the chance to build a new home. How had he not foreseen this eventuality! Falling short of provisions, yes. Arming a militia—certainly. But hellish disease?

Hale nudged Oglethorpe, "Sir—a correspondence from London. Marked urgent."

James's large eyes, now luminous and red, frightened Hale. Hale could have sworn the sick colonists had those same reddish eyes. He summarily left the hut, running toward the church. James barely noticed. He read—

Dear Sir,

I confirm with utmost certainty that a group of Jews have set sail without tacit agreement from the trustees. Alvaro Lopez Suasso, Francis Salvador, and Anthony Da Costa assisted them greatly in this operation. They refused to account for the funds collected from the Jewish community, despite our severe insistence on the matter. They shall be removed post haste from their positions. We have concluded (despite some dissent) that the Jews shall be denied entry. Compliance on your part is urged upon. Forbid them from disembarking. The very safety and sanctity of the colony of Georgia is at stake.

Any speculation about the Jew boat ceased with the arrival of Sir Perceval's letter. Slaves were forbidden. Papists too. And now the Jews. James was conflicted. Their motto had been *Non sibi, Sed Aliis*, "Not for ourselves, but for others." Except for the Jews. As if they died any differently! The trustees wanted to keep things in Georgia "sanctified." Little did they know of the ale-houses and the whores who settled in rented rooms, profiting from the lack of female supply. And he never informed Sir Perceval of the midnight carousels. James thought of Noah. God had eradicated the entire world, only to have Noah's son, Ham, molest Noah in a stupor, drunk. The old world carried into the new. And didn't Ecclesiastes declare, "There is nothing new under the sun"? James threw the letter into the wooden basket by the door, which was closed now. He opened a tome on British law, read a few words, and then flung it too. It was useless. His colony was falling apart due to yellow fever. They had buried too many men. What in bloody hell was he to do? James, flummoxed and unsure of his next step, rummaged through the trash and picked up Sir Perceval's letter. He straightened the parchment and noticed Sir Perceval listed all the Jews on board in a fine cursive hand. James gave a cursory glance, pointing his middle finger at each name. De Lyon, Henriques, Minises, Nunez (physician), Sheftall.

"That's it!"

This Jew boat may be a godsend just yet, James thought.

*

"Sit here, Benjamin. Forget the whole affair. You'll become ill. Please. It is not worth your health. Isn't that what you always tell me?"

Benjamin peered into his wife's soft eyes. How could he control himself at such a moment? He desperately wanted to hold her. But Jewish law forbade such. He excitedly awaited the moment they could reunite. He felt guilty for conjuring thoughts of passion when his friend was doubtless suffering. He wanted to forget the entire incident, but he couldn't stop imagining poor Jacob, crying from the ocean's depths, *"Why am I to suffer without a proper burial ground? Why will my death be meaningless? Was my life that way too? Who shall remember me? Am I to become fodder for halibuts and bass? Where is your compassion?"*

"Benjamin. Do you hear me? Please. I implore you! There is nothing you can do now. Those Sephardic men will never learn to be decent. They have no moral guide—they abandoned that long ago just so they could live in their precious palaces. Well, now I guess we're all paying the price for that."

"Please, Perla. I don't want to speak ill of those men. What will change? It's Jacob I'm worried about."

"Thank God I wasn't there. That poor Jacob! They had no right to tear apart his shroud, exposing him like that! It was so indecent—"

"Perla, please."

"I'm sorry. I'm so sorry. But Jacob isn't suffering anymore. Poor man. Never married. Never had children…."

Perla began to take notice that Benjamin needed to be alone. What more could she do? She wanted him to stop crying, but she didn't know what to say to make him stop. And she couldn't hold his hand! She sighed.

"Benjamin. I can tell you that you truly tried your best. There's nothing you could have done differently."

"I could have given him a proper burial, Perla. Instead,—"

"What do you mean? Is it your fault the British refuse to let us out of this hellish boat? Are you really to blame for that?!"

Benjamin wiped his nose on a dirty tablecloth. He said nothing.

Benjamin realized his wife would probably never understand his deep fears. They were based on all he had learned in *yeshiva*. Women didn't learn about the teachings as did the men. What happens to the soul post-mortem…. What awaits the deceased—the morbidity of the soul, crying to reunite with its previous owner. And now Jacob's spirit would hover over the boat, over all of Savannah, looking for respite. With no grave, Jacob would suffer. And Jacob was the only one who would have understood his deep despondency. And now he was dead.

Perla left him; she walked up the decks to the dining hall, most probably. Her dress hung on her, her flesh thinning with hunger. It was useless. This entire enterprise was a mistake. His mother always warned him, "Don't believe anything that sounds too good." Georgia. A land of milk and honey. How could he have been so blind? He looked at his nails and began crying again. They were wretchedly dirty, and soon it would be the Sabbath. How could he greet the holiest day looking worse than the dirtiest urchin in all of London?

Benjamin abruptly removed his shawl. He would dip in the ocean. That would cleanse him. He refused to remain in filth. He wore loose linens and began making his way to the upper deck. It was still somewhat bright out. An hour before candle-lighting. He maneuvered around the Portuguese children who pointed their fingers at his four-stringed garment. "*Locos,*" they would giggle. Benjamin found a quiet corner and began to undress. He wished he had a bar of soap. He lowered himself using the same rope he had used that terrible night. It was Tommy's destiny to live, and Jacob's to die. He wore short breeches, making sure his lower region was still covered. Clutching the rope, he decided to jump into the water, remembering the eerie noise Jacob's shroud-covered body produced just as it hit the water. Perhaps Divine Dispensation willed all those terrible blows; perhaps it was a punishment. Or a message. Jacob's body would suffer now, and so should he. Benjamin began to pray, reciting whichever words first came to mind. Forgive me Father in heaven. Shall I not be cleansed, like King David, of my sins? *I swear to you God Almighty I shall undo this wrong. Just give me the chance!* Benjamin felt at peace, quite suddenly. And then he decided to swim. He needed to feel alive.

James Oglethorpe could have sworn he saw a naked man jump into the sea from the stern of the *William and Sarah*. He read the vessel's name from afar. How strange. Should this man drown, James would feel remiss. James began to row his dinghy with urgency. The man's head did not reappear. James feared the man was suicidal. James remembered the madness of those who hadn't stepped on land for a long time. It was this feverish insanity that afflicted all, even the most level-headed. James began counting in his mind. That's twenty seconds. James nearly reached fifteen yards from the boat when he thought he saw an arm. And then a head. Was it the same person?

James neared the stern and began to yell, "Are you all right? Was that you who jumped into the ocean moments prior?" Benjamin's heart skipped a beat. He had been discovered. He began to head towards the boat, reaching for the rope that was floating near its edge. He had not realized that his anatomy was jutting; his breeches were transparent and falling towards his thighs. In fear, Benjamin began climbing up, carrying all his weight and wincing with each splinter, frantically making his way onto the vessel.

"A Jew," James muttered. He had never seen a circumcised male before—not even in paintings. The man had a very large torso, with strong capable legs. He was hairless. And he was fierce. James realized this Jew would be an excellent replacement for all those dead militia, now buried; but then again these Jews were forbidden entry. Blasted trustees, James thought. I'm low on officers. How can I keep those belligerent Spaniards out of my land?

Benjamin ran to his cabin, causing a stir.

"Perla! Perla!"

"What is it? Oh my! You are all drenched! What's happened? Did they throw you overboard? Did they?"

"No. No. God forbid. Listen, Perla. I think I saw James Oglethorpe approaching the boat. It had to be him. He was wearing a bright red waistcoat with army insignia all across his lapel, like this, you see? His accent was distinctly British."

"Oh, Benjamin. What do you think this means?"

"I don't know, but we should go up as soon as I'm dressed. I must find out."

Perla nodded her head and searched for a clean pair of breeches for her spouse. She found one with a stain, but it would be covered by a longer jacket. She found a skull-cap and long, ribbed socks. She handed them to her husband.

"Go upstairs. Wait for me. I'm coming."

Perla nearly forgot it was Friday evening. They had no more candles. They had no wine. But they saved their bread. She walked toward the stern, and saw an unusual sight: a tall man with a long nose and bright, big eyes was pointing at all the Portuguese men and repeating, "Doctor?"

Just then Captain Hanson appeared, no doubt with Hannah by his side, gesticulating at all the men to make way. The Portuguese listened, as though trained, and parted slightly.

"So you think, don't you, that this boat is yours! Did you even consider that this vessel is *my* property? Who are you and why should I allow you to board, sir? Eh?" He smacked Hannah in the behind, and walked to Oglethorpe, standing only a couple of inches from James. "Just who are you?"

James was unaccustomed to such brutishness. But the stench on Hanson's breath calmed Oglethorpe's initial ire. The curse of rum.

"My apologies, sir. James Oglethorpe." He bowed, slightly, keeping his eyes steady. Captain Hanson began to laugh.

"Well, you could have said that, sir!" He looked for Hannah. Perhaps this fine gentleman will solve his problem. He hated America. He detested the Jews. And he missed London ale. Something *had* to be done.

"This is an urgent matter. I need an English-speaking gentleman to translate. I have something of great import to inquire."

"Well, Jamesy, don't look at me. I can't understand a word of their gibberish. There's this one Jew who might know a word or two. He's this fancy fellow, with a fine gold brooch, wouldn't you say, Hannah? Speaks all Portuguese, he does. Big fellow. Why, there he is—"

Dr. Nunez was conversing with Benjamin. Perla stood to her husband's right, brows furrowed, mien hunched. Benjamin kept silent. James recognized him. He seemed less imposing with all those strange clothes. He reminded James of the downtrodden Jews of London's poorer streets. Oglethorpe took a step forward. The man speaking to the swimmer was dignified indeed. Of course. He was probably the famed court physician. Fancy he should settle in Georgia, James mused.

Benjamin stared at Oglethorpe's imperial posture. It was clear Oglethorpe had never been assailed. I wonder if I would appear so proud and secure had I been a gentile, Benjamin subconsciously thought.

"Dr. Nunez?"

"*Sí.* Yes. How do you do, sir?"

Oglethorpe bowed as did Nunez. Benjamin wondered what the famed officer and founder of Georgia sought from the derelict crew of pathetic and dirty Jews. Certainly they had little money. Benjamin counted only fifteen coins in Jacob's purple pouch. But one never truly knew the intentions of gentiles. It was safer to be cautious than to be optimistic and naïve. It was clear this English gentleman never saw any true warfare. The dirty work is always left to the lesser kinds—the Negroes. The Jews. His hands were too clean. Benjamin thought of all his ancestors who bowed to men like Oglethorpe, begging for rights, only to be thrown in ghettoes, putrid dwellings, with gates. Shut out. A money-lender his great Uncle Mordechai became, only to be called a greedy Jew.

"A word with you?"

Nunez followed Oglethorpe to the prow. Tommy was drinking a bit of ale, but was lucid enough to depart the vicinity. Oglethorpe didn't mince any words. It was urgent: Georgia was in a state of crisis. There is only one doctor for miles around. His assistance is a moral imperative, but still, a request of his services is quite necessary. It would be remiss to neglect the current situation. He had a wealth of knowledge—certainly he owed a debt of gratitude to the Throne. Would Nunez agree, take the risk, perhaps save the colony from imminent destruction? Sixty dead. More dying.

Nunez followed Oglethorpe's every word. He listened. And he realized he had the power to refuse. Up until now this British man let them all waste away on the wretched ship. He didn't even apologize for their misery!

"We have been here waiting, suffering. My people are hungry and tired, dirty—"

Oglethorpe had not expected a lecture from the doctor. For Christ's sake! These Jewish men and women ignored the trustees' direct orders, and now they dare to blame him?

"I am sorry to hear that, doctor. Truly, I am."

The Portuguese crowd began to convene. Silva pushed through and accosted James.

"What you want?" Silva muttered.

Dr. Nunez immediately turned to Silva and spoke in rapid Portuguese—"I won't have you interfere in these matters. Go back to your wife and family and let me take care of this—"

Silva turned to the other men and pointed at Nunez. "He thinks he can speak to the English gentleman without our consent. He thinks because he once worked for a king that he now *is* a king! I'll tell you what, Nunez, don't give that stinky English man anything! Anything, you hear? He left us like this, he deserves nothing. Nothing!"

Benjamin had enough of that lowlife Silva. Although he had not understood a word of their sing-song tongue, their body language was enough. He approached Silva and whispered in his ear, "Nunez might be able to negotiate a deal with the Englishman! Why all this fuss?"

Silva's nostrils flared three times in rapid succession, very much like an ox before goring his prey. Nunez overheard Benjamin. *Negotiate.*

Nunez calmly walked over to James and said, rather imperially, "I don't see how we can work anything out, as you can see my people are rather contrary, ah, rather disappointed."

Oglethorpe cursed the day the trustees agreed to a no Catholic, no Jew policy. Some of the women began to crowd around Silva. He was gesticulating at Benjamin, accusing him of being an appeasing, worthless *Ashkenazi*. James assessed and reassessed. This was time for negotiation. Money. Yes.

"I will reimburse you the amount to re-sail to England."

Benjamin looked over his shoulder and noticed Nunez's eyebrows and overall demeanor. The doctor seemed mystified. What was crossing his mind? What did Oglethorpe just say? He pushed Silva away and joined the doctor. Oglethorpe took note of Benjamin's skull-cap and side locks, which were prominent, although not too long. The Jew's dark eyes were unafraid to meet his. A mark of conceit in many royal circles. But Benjamin's glare had more intensity than pride. Oglethorpe recalled his muscular hamstrings and for a second wondered if he had any practice in archery.

Nunez turned to Benjamin and whispered, "What should I do? He promises to compensate me for my services—and he will defray to send us back to England!"

"Absolutely not, Nunez! Even if he does pay you, no one here wants to return."

"That's what I thought, but I wasn't certain. Tell me, what should I do?"

Benjamin whispered into Nunez's ears and then went to deal with Silva, who had begun to curse and bawl at Captain Hanson and Oglethorpe, defining them all as "white drunks."

Nunez immediately realized that he had to take a tremendous risk. He searched James's eyes for a glimmer of compassion and humanity. Nunez knew very well that many gentiles can indeed be kind or cruel. His poor wife would have agreed. Perhaps this man is not born of Satan, just maybe he has a thread of kin and kindness.

"I do not want a fee, sir. I do not lack for funds. It is freedom from tyranny we seek." Oglethorpe breathed a sigh of relief. He had been running low of means, and the trustees would quibble for every penny. Perhaps this Jew was not as greedy as Shakespeare had surely depicted. The doctor paused. He ignored Silva's rants. And then he said, slowly, "I will only administer to the ill on one condition."

Oglethorpe raised his eyebrows. A Jew—always expect to haggle, he nearly said aloud.

"In lieu of any compensation, I would beg of you, Oglethorpe, admission into Georgia."

Oglethorpe was taken aback. He had not expected this. If anything, a hefty price. In pounds. But ignoring the trustees' adamant directive? Allowing the Jews to get away with backhanded dealings? How would he convince the trustees to dispense with their own anti-Semitic stance? Bloody hell! He was in a predicament, and this doctor was the only way out. He *had* to bend some rules. He had to make an exception.

"Only for you and your family." Nunez thought of his sons— did he truly have responsibility for all those Portuguese Jews? Ashamed of even entertaining the thought, Nunez immediately replied, "I will not accept that. All the Jews must disembark. *All* Jews."

A *stiff-necked* people. Isn't that what they are called? Oglethorpe looked at Nunez in the eyes. He had not seen desperation on the one hand and doggedness on the other so strangely inter-mixed. The *wandering Jew*. Isn't that how they're known? Their country sacked eons ago by strangers. First Nebuchadnezzar. Then Titus. Then the darkness of dead oligarchs and monarchs, from Byzantium to Rome to the Turks. To hell with this. The trustees aren't here. They can't possibly understand the situation. If this Jew, this supposed magician of medicine, doesn't do something to stop this plague the trustees might as well bite their own toes and kick themselves in the shins.

"You have my word—your services for their admittance."

Nunez shook James's hand and placed the other on the officer's shoulder.

"God bless you. Let me get my valise."

Nunez nearly clapped his hands and thanked his *Avo* for convincing his own dear mama that "Samuel must become a doctor. No other profession will suffice." She had saved his life well before his life needed to be saved. It was as though she knew one day his knowledge would buy his freedom. The doctor made eye contact with Benjamin Sheftall and smiled ever-so-slightly. Benjamin nodded and calmed the Jews. Some of the men were rather disappointed with the doctor for even negotiating with the dreadful Englishman who had ignored their needs up until *he* needed one of their own. Some others didn't care. They were just relieved that perhaps America would become a land for their own kind. They continued to argue amongst themselves. Benjamin walked over to Perla and looked into her eyes. She glimmered with hope. "Next week we'll celebrate *Shabbos* on land," he said in Yiddish.

Perla smiled and said, "God works in mysterious ways."

Survival and Revival

A ROVING DOG WHINED IN the dark. A few huts were twinkling with candle-light. The cross by the church dangled silently. The crickets penetrated the mist, and the few remaining clotheslines undulated, bare and bereft. Oglethorpe held a lantern in his right hand, trying to discern the fifth house from Cox's burnt-down mausoleum. Nunez followed, clutching his valise, looking for signs of life. The earth was dry, and his legs were beginning to tire. It had been a long time since he had ventured into the countryside. The distinct odor of filthy swine and oxen harkened memories of his childhood. As much as the boat's fetid stench caused him to retch, this odd town induced waves of nausea of greater intensity. But he had to continue marching. Oglethorpe finally said, "Tis here. The Joneses."

Dr. Nunez stared at the wooden hut, thinking he had surely landed in a backwards country. The primitive hut stood in sharp contrast to his Portuguese palace, and even the London homes were far more structurally advanced. Oglethorpe walked in, without waiting for an answer. Tim Jones's wife died the week before. She took their only child with her. Now Tim was certain the plague would claim his sorry soul too. The Indian witch doctor probably harkened their deaths, with her strange incantations and potions. Soft Paw. Rhubarb. Diascordium. And a rabbit's foot tied to the bed. Tim figured he got what he deserved for putting his faith in a barbaric infidel.

Nunez followed Oglethorpe to the backroom. A child's wooden chair lay in an awkward position, quite as though the child had just sat in it and decided to run off to play outdoors. Corn husks filled the kitchen floor, and a bucket of water was half-filled with a brownish substance. Acorns littered the hearth, and a wooden bowl with stalks of rhubarb jutted between peeled potatoes. A hen clucked from the coop. A few eggs were neatly piled in a basket of fine, chestnut-colored twine.

"I won't have you sitting around all lazy now, Timmy! You go help your papa now, I say. Wait. No you don't. You sit here now, you will. I say that poor mamma of yours suffered for nothing if you don't eat your porridge, sonny."

Nunez looked around and saw an orange-haired man gesticulating. He was naked.

"I won't have you disobeying your papa, young man. You get yourself right here before I count to three. Two! Three!"

He was slapping his own hand, raving. He was completely hairless. Blankets fell to the floor, and his hair was drenched in a sweat days old. A rabbit's foot was tied to the bed, and a ladies bright-colored dress hung by the post. The man began to stand up, only to sit back down. He then fell into his bed, crying.

"I won't hurt you again, I promise, sonny boy. I won't again. You'll see. You'll behave and then all will be better. I promise."

Nunez immediately rummaged through his valise and arranged his most potent medications on the dusty dresser. He noticed a wedding band of silver and a brooch. He placed a bottle of clear liquid near the ring. He then took out a small jar and handed it to Oglethorpe.

"You must calm him down, and then he must drink the contents."

Oglethorpe had seen men fall in battle and cry for their wretched mothers before dying. He had caused a couple of grown men to weep and moan, but he had never witnessed as sorry a sight as Tim Jones. How the battlefield could pale in comparison to the horrors of civilian life, he sadly thought. It filled him with horror. And then with fear. How was he to calm Tim?

"Tim. It's James. James Oglethorpe. I have a doctor with me. He wants you to drink this. It will help ease your pain."

Tim felt someone touch his right arm. He began to screech. Nunez walked up and smacked Tim in the face, hard. Tim jolted and looked Oglethorpe in the eyes, "James?"

James managed to soothe Tim. Nunez insisted Tim drink all the contents with food. A few dry pieces of bread were sufficient. The doctor dabbed a strong-smelling ointment in random parts— the chest, the groin, under the arms.

"He must bathe. He is ridden in filth. You must swab his chest with this ointment three times a day and administer the tonic twice a day—until his fever subsides. But he must not sleep in this bed. It is ridden with dirt."

Oglethorpe nodded. He would take care of Tim.

"You must instruct all your townspeople to wash before meals and before bed. It is imperative that you do this. I shall return. You must let me see another patient before sunrise. Please tell me where I am to go before this terrible plague strikes another in the same violent manner!"

Oglethorpe thought of Tim's wife. She could have been alive had he ignored the trustees earlier. And their little daughter, she would have been the first Georgian-born settler. Time would tell if Tim would be grateful at all for being alive while his family lay cold, underground.

James rushed Nunez to Anne's place. Her brother Isaiah was notorious for walking around town without breeches. The men would laugh, of course, never bothering to help the child. Charisse, the Negro somehow in charge of child and abode, was left to fetch him hours after he had disappeared. Oglethorpe remembered poor Anne—a beautiful child with golden curls, very much like his love Elizabeth—giggling on the boat playing with her younger brother Marcus. The Hines family. Most community members had little to do with them once they discovered the mother was a Catholic.

Dr. Nunez walked into the hut and scanned the area. Layers of filth and human waste lay between stacks of hay and empty bottles of rum. Oglethorpe's people were suffering—not from disease. No. From ignorance, Nunez thought. Cattle shared residence with colonists. Outhouses were clogged and the hens left to cluck between pots and wooden spoons. Rats scurried between foodstuff—particularly around the cheese curd or rotten potatoes. Nunez wondered how Oglethorpe would go about teaching the fundamentals of hygiene.

"Who are you?" a boy of about ten asked Nunez. He was poorly clad, with grimy fingertips.

Nunez turned, but realized Oglethorpe had left him to attend to Anne.

"I am a doctor. I am looking for your sick sister. Where is she?"

"Mama said we have to leave her alone. No one is allowed near her. We will die if we touch her."

Nunez bent down to look the boy in the eyes.

"Where is she?"

Marcus pointed to the corner. He then ran out the house.

Anne was prostrate, drooling onto a smock—she had been quarantined three days prior and left to die, alone. Nunez placed a cotton cloth by his mouth, to protect himself. The poor girl relieved herself while lying in bed, as though she were a child, a newborn babe whose mother would see to her care.

Anne was glistening, her mass of curls glued to her forehead and chin. Freckles adorned her cheeks and ran across her nose. Three flies buzzed—one by her left ear, another by the ridge of her chin and yet another by her right brow, which was gossamer, tinged with orange. She had been a healthy young woman, no more than thirteen, up until the plague. She was glistening. And Nunez knew there was little he could do.

He felt her pulse—slight. Her temperature—extraordinarily high. He lifted each lid. The eyes were as yellow as the corn on the fields.

This was no way to die.

Alone, dirty, wretched, and unconscious.

Nunez called for Charisse, the only Negro woman still working for her master, the mother of the poor child. Charisse had fallen ill too. But unlike Anne, the Negro had the constitution of an ox.

81

"Bathe this child. And tell her family she is no longer contagious. She should die in dignity—not like this. It is a sin to allow a child to die like a forsaken animal."

Charisse began to tear. "There is nothing you can do, sir?"

Nunez looked at his hands.

"No miss. She's almost gone. But so long as she is alive, she must not depart like this, you see? Alone and in filth."

Nunez departed the house, leaving a strong tonic to relieve the burning fever, knowing death's door shouldn't appear unwelcome—as it may yet prove otherwise. Samuel was not a religious man, in the traditional sense, but he believed a world of splendor must await all those who suffer silently in this wretched one.

Years later Marcus would remember the funny-looking doctor who told him it was safe to say goodbye to his dying sister. He took solace knowing Anne did not die alone, but was holding his small hands just as she departed.

*

James ran about town searching for the Portuguese doctor. Tim had recovered after many cooling drinks and cold baths. But now a couple of Negroes were terribly ill and their masters had abandoned them. James recalled poor Rose following Dr. Cox around town not long ago. She had administered to the ill, but not a single soul bothered to assist in her time of need. How he detested the entire institution! He forbade slaves, but settlers insisted on purchasing them, "to compete with the northern colonies," they argued. Afraid of another catastrophe, and feeling terrible remorse at not preventing the deaths of all those Negroes only weeks prior, James continued to march about the town, until he spotted Charisse chasing after that terribly ill-mannered boy, Isaiah. She wore a white kerchief on her head, and her dress was fraying by the sleeves.

"Charisse! You must help me find the doctor. It is quite urgent!"

The black woman held the boy in her strong arms, and followed James. She had seen the worst of this plague and was tired of listening to white men. Her friends were dying like sick dogs, and not a single soul cared. Her master, Mr. Hines, beat her whenever he was tired of kicking his wife. Charisse had a strong feeling the Portuguese doctor would have preferred Mr. Hines died of the yellow plague, rather than his sweet daughter. But life wasn't very fair. Especially for her type. They were going to die either way. From a white disease or a white hand. James stopped suddenly and gesticulated, "Go to the boat, maybe he went back there to fetch something."

Charisse nodded and headed toward the boat. Sure enough the doctor had fallen asleep, exhausted. Dr. Nunez, urged by Tommy, awoke to find a black woman standing on the shore, holding a child of about three in her arms. Nunez recognized her and wondered what she wanted. The Jews were rather astounded to see such a dark-skinned person with a Christian child. They overheard slavery was forbidden in Georgia, and from what they understood whites were particular with their children. Back in London no such thing would occur, most certainly. Her forehead was sweating profusely, but she did not bother to wipe it. Instead, she sang the child a soft melody. The child was barefooted. After a while she let him run around on the shore. Dr. Nunez joined them, followed Charisse, and eventually made way to Oglethorpe's hut, where two sick Negroes were sitting side by side, leaning on one another. Charisse began to wail. It was Jeremiah, her sister's son. And Cain—the able-bodied man who had escaped his previous owner, a Mr. Jenkins.

Dr. Nunez exhorted Charisse to leave the vicinity; he feared contagion. But Charisse refused to leave her nephew with the white man, no matter how wise he was. Nunez did not wish to argue, recalling her strong constitution. Together they lifted and placed them on two separate cots. He removed their clothes, save for their undergarments and marveled at their beautifully structured muscles.

"They should not die," he said aloud. He proceeded to cool their bodies, with tonics and baths. Afraid they should shiver too much, he began to ask them if they were hungry. Both nodded their heads in unison. Charisse began to cry and departed after some time. Mr. Hines wouldn't spare the rod if he found her out of the house for too long.

Nunez found James sitting outside his tent, holding his head in his palms.

"I am terribly sorry. Those men should have been taken care of long before today. I don't know how to remedy this situation with the Negroes. It is most distressing to me. What can I do for them, doctor?"

Nunez nodded his head. It was most certainly detestable. Were not his people slaves in Egypt? Is this America a land for free people or for people who are free to find others to free them of hard work and difficult labor? These men were certainly God's creatures, yet they had been neglected. Nunez lamented in his heart, but had to focus on the men's health.

"Please have a woman cook a warm broth for these men. Preferably with meat. They must regain their strength."

Nunez returned to Oglethorpe's hut and saw a Bible on the bed table. He kissed it and then felt the palms of both Jeremiah and Cain. They were both half-asleep. Their temperature moderated, Nunez placed a light blanket on them. He shooed a fly. He noticed the boy's nails were very long. He trimmed the nails and combed the boy's hair, which had a rough texture. The older Negro, with extraordinary lashes, began to lift his brows in recognition and gratitude. Nunez hushed him. Shh. Sleep. But they were both awake. Nunez thought of his own sons, who also had large, brown eyes. "But these Negroes have a very white iris because of their skin, so I can't help but look into their eyes," he suddenly thought. And then Nunez stared into their large eyes a bit more, and he knew he saw the image of God.

Who will bemoan the loss of these Negroes when they die? Who were their parents? Nunez recalled Abigail Henriques' terrible cries at night, bemoaning the loss of her little baby. Where's the compassion for these men? Nunez continued to think such thoughts throughout the long week of tending to the sick inhabitants of Savannah. He had succeeded to treat a sixty-year-old grandmother only to witness her crying a few days later when her two grandchildren, John and Sarah died of illness, the tragedy of having been saved. The grandmother didn't last too long after that tragedy. Nunez sighed. He knew all too well what losing a loved one felt like. His beautiful wife lay in England, buried in a strange land. Those left behind must pick up the pieces, he often mused. He would see some of his previous patients while walking along the beautified city squares years later, and he would recall the emotional turmoil of those early days, and particularly his concern for the ill and dying; Nunez wondered what type of life the two Negro men would lead once they fully recovered. The value of life was of supreme importance, but Nunez couldn't help but wonder what their lives had in store once they were at the mercy of the world.

Weeks later Nunez would see Cain picking cotton, and the black man would stop, smile and bow. The little boy, Jeremiah, hugged him on many occasions. It was then that Nunez entertained the notion that perhaps Georgia would become like Pennsylvania one day—slave-free. Certainly that's what God wanted for all his creations; otherwise, why would He have redeemed the Hebrew slaves? Were not humans to imitate the Lord?

*

Perla anticipated the sunset with a secret eagerness. Tonight she would cleanse her body from the impurity of blood and the death that occurred within her. Her womb had shed its toxicity, together with her unborn child, and had now sufficiently recovered its fecundity. Her promising fertility would surely ensue. Thanks to Nunez, she and her husband had been able to move inland, into a safe hut, together with hearth and furnishings. The boat's inferior cabin forever banished from her memory, Perla wondered what life in Georgia would bring. The oppressive heat simmered down in the past couple of days—and the rains began. The yellow fever now under control and the church door open to all. Sunset would hearken a new day.

Perla gathered her hygienic utensils and began to cleanse herself. Her nails were dirty; she cleaned them well with a dab of cotton cloth and warm water. She removed her long, white tunic and stood naked in the middle of her new home. She poured the kettle of warm water into a bucket and lathered her body with a loofah soaked in lavender soap—a rare luxury—a welcoming gift from the big-eyed gentile, Oglethorpe. Her skin soaked in the lavender, and her spirit revived. She continued to cleanse her belly, hips, lower back, and thighs. She wrapped herself in a warm, clean cotton robe, around her lean figure. She ensued to wash her feet. Perla made sure her feet weren't touching the planks—she wanted to keep them clean. She then bent down, and dipped her hair in the bucket, pouring some more water onto her head. She straightened away the knots. She wondered what it would feel like to have her husband touch her hair again. Benjamin loved the nape of her neck and usually stroked her head very softly.

The sun was beginning to set. Benjamin would watch her as she dipped in the ocean. She was ready. She brushed out her hair and placed a linen robe of pink and red stripes over her head, fastening the back with a round button. She belted her garment, revealing a thin waist.

Benjamin waited for his wife outdoors. Impatient, he planned on consummating their love as soon as she was permitted to him. He had been anticipating this evening for a while. His wife had been impure for longer than usual due to the unfortunate miscarriage. The only available *mikveh*, a purification source, was the vast Atlantic. The great Atlantic became their new vista and would now provide Perla's purification.

The two locked eyes as they walked, a few good feet apart, toward the bay. Few men or women were out at that hour. No one would comprehend their actions. Indeed, they would interpret Perla's dipping in the ocean as immodest. But in this heathen country, it mattered little, Benjamin believed. Maintaining their traditions was of supreme importance.

They reached the shore, and both Benjamin and Perla treaded in the water. The sky was an ashen gray, and the gulls flew overhead. Husband and wife searched for any voyeurs—thankfully, the shore was vacant.

Benjamin stood behind Perla, watching as the water revealed her form. He stared at her body, realizing she had retained her form, despite the pregnancy. He felt a sudden emptiness. His lost child a memory he had repressed but had now surfaced. Perla turned and smiled at Benjamin. This was the first time she had gone with her husband to any purifying bath. It was usually a private affair. But she liked the intimacy. She stood waist-deep in water. A wave gushed at her, wetting her hair. She let out a squeal. She looked at her husband once again, and then turned her back.

She removed the robe slowly, beginning with the edge of the garment, bending down to catch the hem. She steadily undressed, removing the robe over head. She was naked. She nearly dunked, but stopped.

"First say the blessing!" Her husband urged.

She nodded and smiled sheepishly. She recited the proper blessing. Benjamin answered, "Amen," and watched as his wife dunked completely, submerged in water.

Perla felt the waves gush overhead and held her breath. She unclenched her fists and lifted her feet slightly off the ground.

She thought of all the women who had predated her, who fulfilled this mysterious commandment of purification. She wondered if they too felt the mystical powers of the waters. Healing, rejuvenation, and utter serenity enveloped her each time she dipped. She often pretended to be in her mother's womb; the sound of water clouding her ears often reminded her of something she had thought she would never recall.

Life was so peaceful beneath the deep waters. She felt revived. She emerged and recalled she was in a new country, with a new home, and a husband who eagerly covered her with her wet tunic, ready to submerge himself in her pristine body.

*

The sun set at its usual pace that late afternoon. Even Silva found a way to be agreeable, particularly to Abraham de Lyon, a rather quiet man who traveled alone but whose opinions every Jew seemed to honor. Silva had good reason to be genial—

Oglethorpe had deeded land to the experienced vintner. Raised and born in Portugal, Abraham was an expert in a potentially fiscally productive enterprise. (Most of the other colonists were not experts, and England was eager for a new market of wines; the Americans despised the exorbitant rates of imported French cabernet sauvignon.) Abraham paid him little attention.

The Indians from Coweta and other provinces marched into Savannah to celebrate the town's complete recovery from the yellow plague that had nearly decimated the settlement. Tomochichi recovered from his lengthy trip and rather enjoyed a cocktail and pleasant stroll. He did not usually imbibe the English beverages, but this one was very tasty. John Hale, a very brutish fellow in Tomochichi's opinion, laughed when he observed Oglethorpe's obvious scorn for the beverage. Tomochichi later discovered the name of the delicious cognac-colored drink: rum. Tomochichi realized long before Hale's brazen disregard for his superior's caveats that not all the inhabitants of the colony respected Oglethorpe. Tomochichi had his enemies and allies as well. He imagined all leaders shared similar experiences. But it was too bad in the old man's view. The tall man with an important-sounding name became one of Tomochichi's few friends in old age. Many of the Coweta Indians disappointed him. They began to question their heritage, and there were rumors of Indian girls conceiving in the harems called "bars." This was a place the white man found the woman, but not to share a Teepee. The offspring of such unions were never fully accepted by the Indian communities. And to add to the bitter juices, the white man never supported these "mongrels" as they were called. Luckily, one small contingent did not mingle much: the Jews. (The ones with the white skin, not so much the dark-skinned ones.) Those interesting people refuse to buy Indian products because, as the rumors go, they fear it is a work of idol-worship. His women weave baskets, but they refuse to buy them, even at a reduced fee. The Christians don't seem to object. As much as Tomochichi rather disliked how religions draw people apart, he was impressed with the doctor whose charms and tricks outdid those of Soft Paw. Soft Paw refused to honor the doctor from the Portuguese; she masked her shame with a self-inflicted rash (which required rabbit dung to undo). She reminded Tomochichi of his own duty to the Jew—for Dr. Nunez averted a catastrophe in the Indian camps. It was a well-established occurrence for some time that the English bring certain diseases from the oceans or the winds, diseases from which the natives have little protection. The spirits of the English countryside, and all those European cities, hovered only on land. The sea destroyed any immunity. It was a miracle of some mystery that this stranger was able to summon the spirits of the Portuguese town and heal all those poor colonists who nearly became spirits themselves. He finished his drink and felt a warm sensation in his belly. Perhaps he will dance tonight.

Oglethorpe had decided on a celebratory dinner for Dr. Nunez and the doctor's beloved family, and the entire town for that matter—Christians and Jews alike. Even men from outlying areas attended: Abercorn, Thunderbolt, and Hampstead—all neighboring settlements converged on Savannah for the festival. James did not feel guilty for overriding the trustees' direct command to "Allot no land to the Jews, pay Dr. Nunez for his service." (Granted he had already deeded land long before he received the letter in the two months it took for the letters to reach American shores.) His militia was nearly decimated by that blasted disease! The Jewish men were potential soldiers as far as he was concerned. The Spaniards down south now had the persecuted Jews to contend with, and the Spanish-Portuguese men were certainly capable and quite eager to protect themselves from the children and grandchildren of the Inquisition. Oglethorpe didn't care so much *what* inspired the soldiers—so long as his borders were calm and safe. James reasoned the Prussian Jew, who had extraordinarily large calves and hind legs, should become the first lieutenant of his militia. Perla wasn't too enthused with the arrangement, but Benjamin said he was duty-bound to take part in the development and protection of their new homeland, even if at grave risk. Benjamin donned his red corned cap with pride and rather liked the feel of a deadly weapon in his hands.

John Hale despised Benjamin and thought Oglethorpe had lost his wits. Who the hell lets Jews have so much influence? He spat on the floor as Benjamin Sheftall walked across the decorated huts. Why didn't James give him the title of first lieutenant? For all they knew these Jews would secretly collude with the Spaniards and ravish their white women. They spoke some strange language, and they seemed too eager to intermix with the townspeople. Come to think of it, it sounded a great deal like the language those down south spoke.

Oglethorpe had too many liberal ideas, that's what. And to add more bitter salts to a festering wound, that man had no gratitude! Who was around long before these Jews came along? Where's the respect? The seniority rights? Who goes deeding land to males who were not supposed to step foot in this country altogether? John knew he wasn't alone.

John muttered, "Georgia's meant to be a safe haven for Christians. Let them go back to wherever they come from, I say." Mrs. Hines agreed with John, and her husband for once nodded in approval. It was a disgrace. One man helped with the plague, Hale granted them that… but deeding them land? What did the trustees have to say about all this?

John wanted to march to Oglethorpe's hut and tell him off once and for all. Jew-lovers smell bad. Everyone knew that. Now Oglethorpe was a Negro-lover too. Forbidding Negroes from working on the farm. The man was a lunatic, that's what. Who the hell gives a lying Judas-Jew Jesus-killer a title of first lieutenant? John looked at his boots and suddenly felt a strong urge to settle his stomach with rum, because if that Benjamin Jew walked by and his stomach was all in knots, Jesus only knew what he would do.

The Portuguese Jews had no problem sharing all that wine and pork with the Christians. Back home they had often intermingled with the townspeople, regardless of creed. For years now they had lived a double life, and by this time they had not thought twice about the precepts and laws of their religion; indeed, they were entirely ignorant. Benjamin, even after months of sharing close quarters with the Sephardim at sea, could not witness the desecration of God's laws. The Christians read the Bible—they surely knew of the prohibitions. Who knows what they think of us, he wondered, nearly tripping on a white man's foot. Benjamin looked up and nearly froze. The cold stare of John Hale ripped through his spine. Benjamin was familiar with that look. Benjamin unconsciously held his skull cap tightly, and he quickly made his way to James, who had been merrily conversing with a pretty Portuguese woman, Mariah. Nunez was holding onto his mother's arm, Zipporah, and led her to a bench made of dilapidated wood. His three children followed, each son wearing a starched white shirt with ruffles all along the collar, neckline, and by the edges. Their red coats were in the London fashion of the previous year, and their white socks had been dirtied when they marched by the wet fields. The boys were rather taken by the Indian children who were completely naked save for a loincloth. Nunez's sons continued to stare at the natives for most of the evening, wondering how their mothers could allow them to romp so freely outdoors.

The dignified doctor didn't feel entirely at ease. He detested parties. They reminded him of those dark days of hiding his faith in Portugal, forcing pork down his throat to prove his fealty to the Church. And then the escape from Portugal took place at night, when festivities were in full blast in his palace. All the Portuguese Christians were welcome to his palace, but *he* was never welcome in their country. His beautiful wife rotted in prison only months prior to their escape. Oh Gracia. Gracia. Her hair was always bound in lace, and a large emerald cross hung loosely by her long neck. But little did they care. The Christian monks had no problem tormenting his wife in a cold dungeon for days. And now he was supposed to smile and be merry around these Christians? But these were the same men and women whom he had loyally served and healed these past few weeks, and he *was* rather fond of them. In this new American land perhaps the old animosities will fade? Marcus Hines walked by Dr. Nunez and pulled the regal-looking long, blue jacket. Dr. Nunez looked into Marcus's eyes and recalled Anne's: both were of the same crystal blue with dark, bold lashes. He rummaged in his pocket for a treat, and handed Marcus two—one for Isaiah, Nunez said. Most of these Christians are Protestants, anyway, Nunez reasoned.

Benjamin looked around and did not see much of a distinction between the Christians back home and these English-speaking *goyim*. Both were cut from the same cloth. Did Perla see that look on John Hale's face? You would think a pig passed him by or a disease-carrying rat. Despicable. A Jew saves their flesh and they can't even show the proper gratitude to his counterpart and friend. Should have realized I would only see more of the same. But these Indians, Benjamin nearly gasped, these Indians are entirely another matter. By God in Heaven—what woman doesn't cover her breasts? This is insane. Why are these heathens here? If I should just see that hideous man who killed Jacob I, by almighty God, will simply leave this party, no matter how much I am obliged to Dr. Nunez, God bless his soul. And who is this half-Indian half-white woman? Her dress is exceedingly form-fitting; fringes of leather and an open bodice, for goodness sake, is there no shame in this new country? How could Oglethorpe permit such immodesty? Oh good. Here comes Oglethorpe. I would like to return home. Let me show my face and get back to the Talmud I left for this celebratory event that is causing my heart to suffer more than I would care to admit.

James Oglethorpe wondered if Mariah would dance with him—he was fond of dancing. Of course he had to rely on the talents of the town fiddler, who had picked up the trade somewhat by force—he was trained in the military to entertain his superiors. It will have to do, James admitted. Oglethorpe caught sight of Tomochichi sitting calmly, hands folded by his lap and over his loincloth. His wife, sitting beside him, listened to the fiddler with much interest. Oglethorpe would have preferred to dance a jig with the old man. Tomochichi had received the Jews very well, sending the doctor a basket of corn and beads. (The basket Benjamin insisted should be returned.) Oglethorpe smiled and bowed at

Tomochichi, put aside all notions of geniality, and walked to the podium which was stationed in the center of the field. Lighted by strong fires set up by Mary's friends, James appeared regal and intense. He cleared his throat and commenced to speak, in an unusual tenor pitch:

"Ladies and Gentlemen! Thank you for attending this feast. I am much obliged to Mary Musgrove for extending her generous hand this evening. The pork loins are particularly sumptuous—feel most welcome to indulge. We are gathered to celebrate on this most auspicious eve, and we are all well aware as to whom we owe our sincerest gratitude. From the people of Savannah, Georgia, I, James Oglethorpe, by virtue of the Lord Jesus Christ and our King, George the Second, hereby grant you and your family a deed of land—and may we all live together in harmony."

The townspeople clapped their moist hands. Most were still eating the pork; it was so very delicious. They wiped their hands to clap, to signify their appreciation, but few didn't bother. They didn't agree with Oglethorpe's deeding policy. It was too generous. The doctor was to receive acres and acres of land. Knowing they had little say in these matters, most just continued to enjoy the meal and took note there was no rum. John Hale had brought his own, which he only shared with a pretty Indian girl and the Old Chief, Tomochichi.

Oglethorpe shook Samuel Nunez's hand and returned to the podium.

He continued, "I do recall, when I had visited those awful jail houses in London, that a great many Jews were unfortunately imprisoned as well. Up until today, only Christians have been permitted entry. However, as we were all created in the image of God, as the Old Testament so states, I, James Oglethorpe, have opened doors to all peoples of all creeds and races. As such, I forbid slavery in this colony, as those born of flesh and blood must not suffer for their perceived inferiority, under God and State."

Charisse let out a deep sigh. She had believed she would never find a white man so vested with truth and integrity—but here was this strange Oglethorpe promising her freedom in a society that relied on her very enslavement. How wonderful to imagine the Georgian colony as magnanimous as God. She entertained the thought for a brief moment, looked over at her nephew, and wondered, "what if?"

Most of the townspeople, among them the newcomers, were a bit astounded that Oglethorpe could be so out of touch with the economic necessities of the colony. By George! How would they subsist without the due diligence of their most productive workforce—and all without paying them a fee! Where would they find such ideal conditions in the Old world? And didn't the Bible declare that Ham's decedents would be enslaved? Truly. This Oglethorpe had the Bible all wrong, he did. Mr. Hines grumbled and shook his head in disbelief. Someone had got to explain to this rich man that money doesn't come by inheritance for most people.

The Indians at this point walked up to the podium and placed gifts for the Jewish doctor, rather haphazardly. They had desired to do so earlier, but had not understood the main significance of James's earlier call for gratitude and commendation. Their people did not clap hands for this purpose. Now, when he had somewhat completed his speech, so they thought, it was best to shower the bounty upon the Hebrew. The women and children layered fruit baskets, beads, and corn, as well as batches of deer skins and woven garments in a beautiful display. Each child hooted, and the mothers proudly marched behind their male sons.

Nunez was taken by the spectacle, and said immediately, "Thank you." He must have repeated it nearly a dozen times. Oglethorpe appreciated the distraction, since he noticed most of his fellow colonists weren't too happy with his regulations. Upon the dais, in the beautified Robert Wright square (so named after the Governor of Carolina), Oglethorpe had a vision of a country united despite religion and color. He noticed the black woman who took care of that churlish boy Isaiah rather taken by what he had said. He knew his father would have been proud, may he rest in peace.

Tomochichi stood, and James stood still. Mary Musgrove stood as well, ready to translate.

Her skin glistened with a musk Soft Paw secretly concocted from deer and buffalo males. Her hair was woven in two very long braids, black as the sea at night. Some of the men shifted in their seats; Mary subconsciously believed she had much sway over the males and enjoyed the attention. Mary turned to her husband, just to ensure that she "acknowledged" his "acquiescence": it was not customary to speak in public without the husband's approval. Johnny Musgrove subtly nodded his head. Mary translated as Tomochichi gestured and wigwagged his cane:

"Doctor from the Portuguese whose wind-power can overcome the sea-power, we humbly thank you and bless you for your service. May you see many winters in tranquility and summers in peace. May there only be concord between your people and mine."

Dr. Nunez rose, bowed, and sat. The colonists clapped, this time enthusiastically.

Oglethorpe smiled at the old chief. He truly did know how to calm the atmosphere. Oglethorpe decided to move the evening along; he cleared his throat:

"We must give thanks to God for providing us with Dr. Nunez. Our ranks have thinned, as we all know. For that reason, ladies and gentlemen, please pay careful attention, I have allowed all males to enlist in the militia, and position of first lieutenant belongs to Dr. Nunez's good friend and able-bodied man, Mr. Benjamin Sheftall."

John Hale spit near his own two feet. Oglethorpe did not take note, but Benjamin did. Benjamin figured the Christian was unfit for duty—otherwise, James would have certainly appointed him. As far as Benjamin could tell, the blond man with a beak-like nose and a slightly pock-marked forehead was nearly one foot taller and three years his senior. It was also rumored that Hale had connections with the outlaws by the bayside. But either way, Benjamin knew he had with whom to contend. Perla nudged Benjamin to rise and take a bow. He immediately complied, but no one truly cheered or hailed his succession to the coveted position in the militia. Maybe his predecessor had been immensely popular, and certainly, beyond a doubt, he was a Christian. Benjamin fell short on both accounts. But he was still grateful; Benjamin tried to suppress these thoughts, and instead, concentrated on Oglethorpe's grand speech:

"However, as much as we can assume a strong militia can protect us from the Spaniards down south, I must profess that there is one plague still amongst us! And this plague a God-fearing doctor cannot cure! The curse of rum has been the cause of much suffering and debauchery in this colony. By the power vested in me by the Great King of England and the trustees of this colony, I hereby forbid the consumption of rum."

At this point, Hale, and his cronies, particularly Thomas Christie who subsisted largely on the sale of alcoholic beverages, stormed out of the huts and toward their inns, disgusted and tired of this white-handed rich boy who thought he owned their bodies and souls because some damned powerful people in England decided to give him a title. They were thankful for all James had done, but there was a limit to their magnanimity. Enough was certainly enough. A man was allowed to drink in his own tavern, and there was little this Jamsey boy could do.

James imagined such would be the response of Christie, but he was surprised by Hale. Hale was one of his best. He heard rumors. He knew the Christie preferred the Indian women, but this was absurd. And John Hale was a trusted officer not too long ago. Overwhelmed, James began to raise his voice in agitation—

"And anyone caught violating this order will be taken into custody and flogged under the jurisdiction of the constable of his district!"

For good measure, Oglethorpe pounded the podium and lifted his hands—

"The deaths have ceased, but they may spring upon us once more if we are not vigilant! Rum spreads disease, as you all know my intent, and may you all be wise to hearken my call for sobriety. Now enjoy the festivities, and may we know many happy occasions together! Thank you."

The Indians began hooting and began a competitive ball game that appeared quite violent in Perla's eye. She had never seen men holding sticks and running after balls with such fierce enthusiasm. She imagined they won much honor in such a display of utter aggression. She looked up at Benjamin and wondered why he appeared wan. Before Perla gathered the right words to approach her husband, Tomochichi approached them, with his half-dressed wife. Perla was disgusted by the brazen display of flesh: old age is not becoming, she thought. But the chief was congenial, despite his strange outfit of feathers and (what appeared to be) Buffalo molars. The old lady had strings of beads woven into her hair and turtle shells tied together, a necklace Perla assumed. The old lady's eyes were barely detectable; her lids were puffed and black paint covered what remained of her brow bone. Both Tomochichi and his wife were incapable of communicating with Perla, but they smiled and pointed to their hearts.

Perla smiled weakly and nodded her head, "Thank you." She thought this was the best response in most situations.

Tomochichi said, "Thank you" as well, and revealed three teeth in an otherwise toothless mouth. Perla gasped, and the old man laughed. He thought she was more child-like than his beloved nephew—even he no longer feared the old man's gums. They stared at one another for a few seconds more, and then the aged couple plodded along to the children, who were squealing from innocent delight.

Soon thereafter, they followed a quiet path to their humble home, still quite hungry and thirsty. Neither had eaten a crumb at the festivities. The air had a thickness to it, and down the road they overheard the jolly guffaws of Savannah's ruffians. Some dried leaves rustled, a sound Perla unconsciously feared. She imagined demons whispered blasphemous words that most humans can no longer detect. The land was not holy, and the people, although Christians, behaved, in her estimation, in a godless manner. The echo of laughter did not fade as she trudged along. The Christians were generally harmless, but Perla didn't like to imagine what happened when the rum traveled to their nether regions. Perla was raised with terrible anecdotes of pogroms and midnight madness throughout Christendom. America may be a new country, but the people Perla feared were very much the same. Maybe they too will pilfer and awake to murderous rage as her mother so often reported. Perla shivered, but the night was warm and dry. Perla's shoes treaded the soft path, and she tried to engage her husband in conversation, but he was uncharacteristically reticent. They finally reached the front door, and Perla was hoping her husband would lift her again—they way he did that first day. But his eyes were glued to the floor. Perla walked in first, tired and simply famished. She left her husband by the door. "He just needs some time alone," she thought.

Benjamin, preoccupied with his thoughts, nearly forgot to kiss the *mezuzah* he placed on the right side of his front-door that particular evening.

And John Hale remained awake that long night pondering how much money Benjamin Sheftall paid Oglethorpe for the position of first lieutenant in the militia of Georgia, the king's colony for Christian folk.

DIVISION OF LABOR

OGLETHORPE STRETCHED HIS ACHING HIND legs. Keeping the town safe from those marauders down south was taking a toll on his aching back. By this time he once hoped to procure a wife to soothe his feet, or at least to entertain him at night. He removed his muddy boots and lay on his bed. His hut had taken on far better proportions. Mary Musgrove took care of the furnishings of his home out of the goodness of her heart. She also introduced him to Florence, a dark-skinned girl of mixed heritage who offered to warm his bed. Being that he had not found a suitable mate, and that his departure for England was yet to be determined, Oglethorpe secretly indulged in a practice which his mother would not entirely approve. Elizabeth's engagement was the talk of London's upper echelon for quite some time—and of all people to relate the matter—Sir Perceval himself noted such in an aside months ago. Since then, James perceived sensual delights as a prerogative he had earned. Florence was most obliging. And she *was* most pleasant. James was, however, worried of a possible heir, in which he wasn't entirely interested. Perhaps it was best to desist in indulgences for now, he begrudgingly thought.

It had been a very busy time since the Salzburgers arrived. They were finally settled in Ebenezer, but that took quite some time! A whole group of German-speaking people, Austrian Lutherans, who could barely speak a word of English, landed just as, the winter's storm became milder. Oglethorpe picked up a couple of phrases while a soldier in the King's army, but these people required a translator. James once again felt a tremendous amount of gratitude for what he viewed as God's intervention that fateful summer—the boat of wandering Jews. Among them two German-speaking Jews: Benjamin and Perla. Those two were now expecting a child. At the time, Benjamin had assisted him in speaking with the men and finding suitable, arable land. They traversed for a good day's journey, until the Lutherans decided it best to settle twenty-two miles from Savannah. Benjamin's wife cooked rice soup for all the men and women on the day of their arrival. James tasted some and didn't see what was so unique about kosher food.

Benjamin was a hard worker, and James couldn't find a reason to replace the Jew with Hale, who had become notorious for anti-Semitic rants at the underground rum bars. First Lieutenant was a position most enviable, but also requiring responsibility. Hale disappointed him. It was a shame. And now with the contingents of Jews following the *William and Sarah*, Hale had only more fodder for his scurrilous diatribes. James wondered if Hale knew about Benjamin's long trek in the heat of spring. He returned nearly famished and weakened by the sun. It had been an error on his wife's part, but like the gentleman he ensured restitution: Perla accidently took a whole crown from Mrs. Smit, who believed she had in her possession a half-crown. It was a matter of conscience. He travelled, by foot, the twenty-two miles to Ebenezer, and returned the half-crown rightfully due to Mrs. Smit. It was a deed done in silence, but Mrs. Smit did not stop speaking of the matter until James overheard it from Florence. What did Benjamin say? Ah yes.

"God should keep him from unjust property in his house since it could not bring any blessing." At one point Reverend Quincy in his Anglican parish mentioned this anecdote in one of his long sermons—to contrast Benjamin's behavior with the behavior of those terribly iniquitous Sodomites. Perhaps the reverend was hoping Benjamin Sheftall would overhear the praise and begin attending the sermons, but that didn't seem likely. James laughed. Actually, if anyone wanted to convert the Sheftalls, it would have to be Revered Boltzius—the Lutheran minister and leader of the Salzburgers. The man was mad, in James's estimation.

For goodness sake! These Jews obstinately clung to their faith. Why would they sign conversion tracts? They never ate a single morsel of food, save for an uncut apple or uncooked corn. They baked their own bread, and some residents whispered that the woman, Perla, dipped *naked* in the sea. The men congregated in Sheftall's home, and rumor has it they have a Torah scroll in their home. They remained at home on their Sabbath, refusing to carry a single item from one home to another. Once, the coals no longer burned on one of their holidays—the Feast of the Tabernacles, James believed. (The Sheftalls assembled a makeshift hut, tent-like in appearance. They slept, ate, and sang in it for nearly a week, and even decorated it with fruits of the season, hanging on vines.) They hinted to their neighbor, Mr. Kensington, "Please. My food is no longer warm. Can you help?" This was permitted, since the holidays, Benjamin explained, were not similar to the Sabbath in certain stringencies. James believed all religions had their beliefs and laws, and unless one is part of that religion, it surely sounds bizarre from the outside!

Oglethorpe reached for a sparkling glass and filled it with cider. He enjoyed the dearth of company on nights such as these. He had dealt enough with the Yamacraws, although he certainly enjoyed Tomochichi's company. The old man had strange wits about him—signaling with his hands and even his feet. Once translated, the old man faithfully demonstrated wisdom, and he offered his guidance, which Oglethorpe had sorely lacked from a young age with his father's passing. His mother informed him of Elizabeth's soirees; her dinners had become the epitome of upper-class finery. Her dishes gleamed. Supposedly, and this is a rumor circulated by the chamber maid, her pillows were bedecked with gold threads from the far, far east. Oglethorpe kicked the divan by his bed and removed his riding boots. He recalled her white skin and cursed that dreadful relative of hers who had bought his way into Elizabeth's life. James slowly removed his cravat and trousers, and he realized it was time to replace his linens with light-weight cotton sheets. He touched his pillow and wondered if

Elizabeth even thought of him at all on those cold, London nights. James prided himself on many things—and he eagerly fantasized Elizabeth's expression when she would one day meet him again, not just as James Oglethorpe, but as the founder of one of the King's colonies. Certain titles, James thought as he drifted off to sleep, one must earn with the sweat of one's brow.

*

Perla held her breath. The pain was oddly familiar—but this time she smiled knowing her fetus was a healthy, rambunctious entity waiting to greet her. Benjamin swore by the fat hens he force-fed her. Nine months of anticipation and hope, and now it seemed that all those fine chicken tenders weren't enough to satisfy the baby; he (it had to be a *he*) wanted to taste his mother's milk—the sooner, the better.

Perla winced once more. The pain radiated from her womb and caused her already swollen belly to tighten. Perla began to sweat; she ran to the outhouse. As she squatted in relief, she felt a different tremor; Benjamin had yet to procure a cradle, and the Sabbath would begin in a few hours. Perhaps the baby could wait a little longer, she thought. She decided to rest her head. Maybe if she fell asleep, the pain would disappear.

The incredibly painful contractions continually harassed Perla for three weeks now. There's really no reason to fret, she silently muttered. She had placed the soup on the coals; the bread was freshly baked, and the aroma filled the hut, the street, the neighborhood. Even the Salzburgers, who lived in Ebenezer, claimed Perla's *challah* smelled divine, and they were *Christians*.

Perla sighed. She was tired of feeling uncomfortable at night, shifting from side to side. Benjamin forbade his wife from carrying any heavy pots or barrels. He fed her in bed and refused to listen to her objections. Oglethorpe sent a basket of eggs for Hanukkah—and Benjamin cooked two each morning (one for Perla, and one for the baby, he insisted). It seemed that Benjamin's waist thickened as well. At night he complained of swollen feet and heartburn. He attributed his toe sores to the many miles of patrol and the hours of labor on the farm. Perla shifted her position on the cot. The hut was now her home, and the bare walls testament to their simple, unadorned lifestyle. Savannah's environs were lush, verdant, and inviting. She had traversed the leafy woods with her husband on those wonderful Sabbath days, as well as on Sundays, which Perla found somewhat relaxing as well. There was no ghetto in the New World, and she and her husband attained a home of their own. London's precipitation and fog conformed well with Perla's melancholy disposition, and there was no doubt her responsibilities were manifold in this strange, new land. She remained at home, knitting her husband's mittens for winter, crocheting a blanket for the new creature about to surprise her in myriad ways, and darning fine silk hosiery from the Old World and her dear husband's socks.

Perla was content. The protracted pregnancy gave her the chance to consider the ways in which her newborn would irrevocably alter the course of her life. She wasn't sure, of course, whether she was carrying a male or female child—so she prepared for the eventuality of either gender. (Soft Paw had predicted a boy. Perla feared for her life when the Indian woman touched her belly. But that was a while ago.) If it were a boy, she figured, she would knit him socks of navy and pink yarn, preferably of the softest texture. A girl—she would have to purchase a bonnet from Mrs. Burgher who was an expert in children's wear.

Her husband had been attentive to her needs throughout the pregnancy, caressing her belly at night and singing songs on the Sabbath to their unborn child. Benjamin's attention compensated for the loneliness in her heart. Perla had been ever so lonely since she last departed her Prussian hometown. Her Mamma would have been quite helpful now, teaching Perla how to nurse, feed, care, and deliver the baby.

Perla let out a primordial yell. The pain was far more severe than she had experienced in past days. And the sharp pain continued for some time. Perla buried her head in the pillow, turning in fetal position, moaning slowly, slowly. She held her breath, unconsciously trying to control the pain. She opened her mouth and meditatively breathed out the painful sensations. Finally, the searing throb subsided, and Perla couldn't grasp how a beautiful child could cause his dear mother such life-altering agony. All those failed attempts at a viable pregnancy, and the anxiety and fear of the first few months, now faded into the past; the contractions held her bound. Eve's sin, she thought. This was the curse of her sex.

Once the aches subsided, Perla gathered her strength: she must inform Benjamin. She battled with her bulge, and slowly pealed herself off the cot. She had to make her way to the Minis household, where her husband was praying that Friday night. Since they had begun their life in a new exile, Benjamin, who had brought a Torah scroll and prayer book along with his phylacteries and Psalms, dedicated their home for the daily services. This week was somewhat different; out of all the weeks and months of prayer, Mr. Minis had fallen ill and was temporarily unable to leave his home. Just as she needed Benjamin most—he was far from reach.

Perla donned her robe, made of fine ivory cotton, and commenced to trudge along the patches toward the Minises. The roads were parched and the fields lay fallow. Thankfully, the neighbors obeyed Oglethorpe's direct exhortation to place all rubbish materials in a centralized receptacle. A few households refused to comply, mostly the poorer ones, Perla noted. The sky was still a brilliant azure; it was an hour or so before sundown. Her slippers were a bit tight—her thickened ankles, swollen and utterly painful to the squeeze, prevented a proper fit. They fell off a couple of times. Perla turned suddenly: a child let out a screech not far from her. Each time she heard children cry or scream she inadvertently became quite agitated. This time she was too focused on her own pain to feel the suffering of others. The baby pressured his mother's womb erratically. His head, now centered between Perla's thighs, seemed to etch closer and closer, as though primed for departure with a single forceful thrust on his mother's part. She froze. What if the baby were to emerge in the middle of Savannah? Should she sit? Perla instinctively crouched and somehow felt relieved, more at ease. She resumed her pace, this time hurriedly, afraid of another attack.

Benjamin prayed to the One God of Abraham with careful concentration. He thought of the Sabbath as a day, not only of rest, but also of contemplation: this week he would deliver a brief sermon, *dvar Torah*, on the week's portion. He figured Deuteronomy was rife with remonstrance and warning—particularly with regards to idol-worship. Reminders were always apropos when living amongst Christians, whose vision of God was blasphemous anthropomorphism. Constant pressures were placed on many of the newcomer Jews—especially the Sephardim and non-affiliated Ashkenazim who were the new human shipments from the Old World. *Shabbos* keeps the Jews, he thought, more than the other way around. With these running thoughts, Benjamin was wont to forget himself. De Lyon tapped him again—

"Benjamin! Your wife is in the parlor. Over there—see?"

Benjamin didn't wait for an explanation. He had seen enough in one glance. Perla was in active labor.

The time had come.

The hour was late, and the baby had yet to be born. Each contraction riveted through Perla's fibers; her sinews screeched. A midwife was called in, a Christian woman related to John Hale, the infamous anti-Semite of their small town. She anointed Perla's feet and placed a washcloth by Perla's temples. But the pain was all Perla's. Just as her pleasure had been hers the night of the baby's conception, so too was the pain on the day of his birth. Perla's every instinct was to yell. But she refrained for Benjamin's sake. The child was still inside and Shabbos nearly over. The child, boring through her narrow walls, stubbornly attached himself to her innards. Susan insisted Perla open her legs wide, but Perla simply couldn't. The midwife insisted she needed to feel if Perla was ready to push, but Perla was afraid to push. Susan insisted pushing out the baby would actually feel *good,* but Perla didn't see how that was possible. Susan tried all methods to convince the young woman.

Susan Hale knew her brother would disapprove, but she had to do her Christian duties—it was a matter of conscience. The Jewess Perla was a fine woman, but she was too frail in Susan's estimation. For an entire fortnight Perla had groused of incredible aches in her abdomen, yet she had not even begun her laboring contractions in earnest! It was quite clear to Susan that Perla was raised in *too* fine a manner. Benjamin often required assistance around the barn. As far as Susan knew, chores were shared by husband *and* wife. Perla's husband took on more responsibilities than fashionable in Savannah. The house was tidy; Perla's cooking was quite satisfactory. But her constitution wasn't hardy. Susan wondered how Perla would fare during the most critical hours of her pregnancy—the delivery.

So far, Susan's predictions were accurate. For hours Perla was sprawled on the bed, surrounded by delicate embroidery with Jewish symbols (a menorah and Star of David), bent over, barely able to breathe calmly between contractions. Susan kept count: a mere ten minutes apart they were. Susan knew they would only increase—but so far, Perla refused to spread her legs. Fear gripped the young mother-to-be, and Susan was entirely helpless. The man of the house, the one with the large eyes and somewhat long nose, prayed before the Hebrew God. He too was nearly sprawled on the floor. In a strange German tongue (similar to the Salzburgers') he gesticulated and swayed. Back and forth. Spurts of phrases, exotic sounding, echoed in the large room: *El, Rachum, Ana, Elohim....*

Benjamin felt at a loss. His poor wife! How long can a woman labor without delivering a child? The Christian woman was of little help. Should he call Mrs. Minis at this late hour? He prayed one last time and ran out. Perla imagined her husband had enough of her tears. Susan wondered if the Jews, too, ran off to bars while their wives labored in excessive pain. Feeling abandoned, Perla realized her only course of action was to cease her inaction. Perhaps the Christian midwife was right. Maybe it would feel *great* to have this baby out of her body.

"I think I'm ready now," Perla whispered.

Susan had nearly given up hope, but a renewed sense of urgency helped Susan regain confidence.

"Lift your pelvis a bit, Perla. I am going to check how open you are on the inside. Breathe if you feel any pain, but don't move."

Perla winced: she hated the idea of another person touching or seeing her intimate parts. Ever since she was a child, modesty in dress and behavior had been not only a guiding principle, but also a way of life. Perla recalled how she kept covering her breasts the first night she was intimate with Benjamin. He did not have the same reserve as she. But this intrusion, this woman placing her hands inside her during her hours of vulnerability and pain, was overwhelming. Her mother had not mentioned any of this during her virginal years. After long consideration, Perla could not recall a single conversation regarding a woman's most critical hours— her entry into marital contact, the pain of initial intercourse, and now this—delivery.

Susan breathed a sigh of relief. The baby's head was in proper position, and Perla's cervix was open and ready.

"All you need to do now is push when you feel a strong and painful ache."

"That's all?"

"Yes, Perla."

"And are you not to assist?"

"What do you mean?"

"Will you not take out the baby?"

Susan laughed out loud, unintentionally insulting poor Perla.

"Child—it is called 'labor' for a reason! And that is the mother's job!"

Perla understood immediately that all the work was hers and hers alone. Once again, she had been completely ill-prepared for this eventuality. But the baby would certainly help her along, by pressing and pressing, urging Perla to push and push. Perla breathed deeply and imitated the breaths of Susan Hale with ridiculous accuracy. If Perla turned red in the face, Susan tapped her abdomen: this was a reminder for Perla.

"Child. You must push as though you are constipated. You must push as though you must use the outhouse! Do you understand?"

Perla nodded her head time and time again. By this time, Benjamin returned with Mrs. Minis, and Susan felt a bit relieved.

Perhaps this Jewish mother of numerous children can tell Perla something that she had not thought of as of yet.

Perla started to cry.

"Benjamin. I don't want you here right now! Please leave!"

Perla didn't want her husband to see her canal or the blood and gore that began to protrude from her body. Ashamed and embarrassed by her own body, she did not want her husband to view her as a laboring animal. Benjamin could not comprehend his wife's demands but he respected them nonetheless.

"Perla," he whispered, "I had brought Mrs. Minis. I will be outside; please keep up your strength."

Perla no longer had the strength to suffer in silence. She let out a primordial yell. Mrs. Minis held her hand and encouraged Perla. Poor child, she thought. So beautiful and so pale. Her mother so far off, and not even her husband can be with her now. It was forbidden for him to see her in this situation. And of course he couldn't touch her, not in her state. Perla's brows were clammy and her mouth excessively dry. Perla begged for water and Mrs. Minis ran to fetch some. Perla's head scarf long fell off her head and luscious curls revealed themselves. Her eyes were glistening, and Mrs. Minis detected a bit of grey mixed in with the green. Her brows captured the sweat that had gathered. Yet she did not reek. Even Susan Hale's bloody hands did not have an odor. It was as though Perla was as pristine as her name intimated—a purity Mrs. Minis secretly admired. Perla's legs were just as white and silken ivory as a Christian woman's. Although well with child, Perla's form was still evidently proportionate and beautiful. But poor woman; she was too weak to sip the ladle Mrs. Minis offered. Childbirth had taken a toll, and the child had yet to demand his due on Perla's strength and disposition.

Perla placed all her concentration on her pelvic floor muscles; she felt a tear and a strange protrusion. It felt enormously painful and pleasurable to finally eject this powerful force from within her. Her groin protruded a bit, and Perla let out a feeble screech. What was this she was feeling? Goodness! What was trickling from between her legs?

"Very good! Perla! We see the baby's head. He has a lot of hair! Continue, continue to push! Don't stop! One more! One more push, child!"

Perla imagined her baby's hair, hopefully dark like Benjamin's. She began to feel an elation she had never experienced before. Nine months of darkness to be revealed in a moment of utter pain and utter excitement was so very new. Mrs. Minis kept saying, "Only one more!" Over and over. Encouraged, Perla did not stop pushing until the two women screeched from joy, and the child's screams filled the room.

Benjamin swore to the Almighty that he would raise the child in the ways of his forebears, but just that he should emerge! Before Benjamin tore at his every inner fiber and beseeched God once more, Susan Hale, the good Christian woman who was nothing like her brother, turned to him and said, "It's a boy. Come and see this angel. He is a true beauty."

Oglethorpe received an invitation to a circumcision. The father of the child, Benjamin Sheftall, was to perform the ceremony. Oglethorpe subconsciously winced and thought of his precious organ. He was quite curious; how was this Jewish ritual performed? He understood from Tomochichi that the Indian was welcome as well. The Yamacraw village was not too far off; the old man would attend. Word got out that John Hale no longer permitted his sister, Susan, to lodge in their shared home.

"No Jew-loving sister of mine enters this home," he hollered. The sheriff was called in, to no avail. Oglethorpe settled the matter by threatening Hale—deportation. That settled the matter. The Trustees had finally agreed to rescind their initial anti-Semitic stance amid reconsideration; the Jews seemed to have contributed fairly well, enough for the readjustment. Oglethorpe put his feather down. He had jotted down enough in his journal for today. He stretched his arms above his head, let out a rather frightening sound, and rummaged for a silver-encased whiskey holder. Up until recently he had not given in to temptation. But word got to him, from his mother, that Elizabeth was now the proud mother of a beautiful daughter. Many praised the daughter's graces; the doll entertained many women at court. Even the Queen was fond of her. The child's name assisted in that regard—Anne. Oglethorpe choked on his whiskey, and spit out whatever was left into the wooden bowl by his bedside. Images of Elizabeth with that husband of hers was anathema to James. It was simply more than he cared to endure. He bent his head so that he stared straight at the ceiling above and finished the contents of the whiskey-holder. He wiped his hand on his sleeve, stained from imported snuff and collapsed on his bed, with his riding boots still tied and fastened.

Benjamin held his son proudly. This was the day of the child's spiritual birth, and he, the father, was to initiate his son's entry into the Nation of Israel. Benjamin was delighted at the mass of gatherers: Oglethorpe. Tomochichi. The Minises. Dr. Nunez. And even his Christian neighbors. Benjamin thought of his grandparents in his old German town and delighted in the *mitzvah*. The Covenant of Abraham. Poor Perla! Weakened from birth, she could barely think of her precious son in a vulnerable situation. But Benjamin was confident. He had been well-trained to perform the *bris*. His family boasted many learned men, and the rite of circumcision was not a neglected area of expertise. Indeed, he learned *shechitah*—ritual slaughter—as well. His education paid off, he gladly noted. His table was replete with poultry, seasonal fruits, and even alcoholic beverages, to the chagrin of Oglethorpe. (To James's favor, drinking publicly was not outlawed, and James shut his eyes during occasions such as this.) A separate table of *rugelach* and *heimish* baked goods was especially delectable, a gift from the newcomer Ashkenazim.

Perla camped in a small room close to the barn. Her husband took care of the arrangements—from the guests, to the chairs, and even to the very frock the newborn now wore. The child was constantly hungry; he desired her breasts every two hours. Perla felt her energy slowly drain. And she still bled heavily. Mrs. Minis said this was very typical, but Perla couldn't remember a time she had felt as exhausted as the first week of motherhood. Preparations for the *bris* took precedence, and she was too nervous to sleep at night, even when the as of yet unnamed infant lay somnolent beside her. Oglethorpe was kind enough to send a cradle upon hearing of the child's birth; this proved very thoughtful, since her husband had yet to build one. The baby began to fidget. Perhaps he was hungry again? For such a small creature, Perla thought, he has a mighty appetite.

Benjamin insisted she feed the child after the *bris*—to help soothe the baby and help lull him into slumber after the procedure. Perla's knees buckled and she immediately returned to a seated position. She truly could not think too much about the *bris*. Of course it was natural for her people to perform this tremendous *mitzvah*, but as a mother she could not help but worry about her child undergoing pain in his first week of life. She soothed herself by thinking of all the men who never recollected their own *bris*, and the small organ, she reasoned, surely did not have the same sensation as a grown man's; it was just too small! She was rather surprised at its shape when she first saw her son. The organ looked lopsided; despite the pain of the reverse contractions, Perla laughed. That will irrevocably change today.

Perla wore an ivory gown with lace inlets all across the side. Her belly was still swollen as though she was four months pregnant. Her figure was fuller now, and her breasts were heavy with milk. The gown she borrowed from Mrs. Minis, who happily provided for Perla's needs. Mrs. Minis said the trick was to take attention away from a protruding post-partum belly with details on the side or back of a gown. Perla generally cared for fashion, but she did not feel up to thinking about her appearance so soon after the birth. Perla's eyes were now more grey than green, and she was usually faint. Dr. Nunez insisted she eat chopped liver and spinach, kale and beef of any kind. She had to regain the color in her skin and stamina. Perla sighed. She never realized child-birth would drain her every fiber.

Benjamin walked into the room just as Perla pinned her hair into a fine chignon and placed a bonnet on her head. Perla's ears were bare, but she wore a delicate brooch of pearls.

"You are lovely today, Perla! Just as a bride!"

Perla blushed. Her husband had been incredibly gay since the baby's birth. He remained awake at night and even hired Susan as a caretaker in the interim. He looked quite handsome in his breeches, and his cravat was finely starched.

"Is the child ready? The guests have arrived, and it is past eight in the morning. The services will end momentarily and the *bris* will begin. Did you delay the feeding as I requested, Perla?"

Perla nodded and swallowed. Her mouth was dry. Benjamin knew his wife's sensitivity surely fell on the baby's pain.

"Don't worry my love. He will feel very little pain. I will perform the *bris* quickly. You need not be in the room when this happens. Mrs. Minis will bring the baby. You shall remain here. I'll have Susan fetch a beverage and some fruit. I want you to eat. You look quite pale."

Perla nodded. "As you wish, Benjamin. The child should be hungry soon."

Both mother and father stood for a moment, facing one another. Perla placed the infant on the soft cot, and both mother and father stared at their creation: the baby's eyes slowly opened, and he yawned. White foam gathered a bit on his tongue—the residue of many feedings. His skin had a pinkish sheen, and his eyebrows were barely detectable. The lower lip protruded a bit, and the baby revealed his tongue. His hands were incredibly formed, and he held them in a grip. The bonnet on his head was loose, and it covered his left eye a bit. Benjamin bent over and held his son; he smelled of Perla's skin and of milk. He took in a deep breath, the scent of heaven he imagined.

Benjamin let out a deep breath. This was not going to be as simple as he imagined.

Oglethorpe marveled at the precise movements of Benjamin's hand; with a swift slice, the father removed the foreskin of the eight-day-old infant. The poor thing cried, but only for a brief moment. The father then recited a blessing and named his son—Sheftall Sheftall. Needless to say the entire crowd, both gentile and Jew, found the name a bit awkward, but the parents seemed to know what they were up to, so after a brief interlude of bewilderment, the *bris* continued and the men gathered around a hearty-looking meal and enjoyed the festivities. Oglethorpe had yet to congratulate the mother; she was nursing the baby he was told. Motley crowd, he subconsciously thought. He sat beside Old Tomochichi and bit into a *rugelach*. Tasty bit of pastry, he mused. Tomochichi placed a glass of cider in James's hand.

"Drink," the hoary chief gestured. James nodded and watered his dry palate. From the corner of his eye he detected Perla; her gown was elaborate and slimming. How odd this woman appears as though she had never carried a child, he nearly repeated. But her lids were heavy, and a halo of tiredness emanated from her. Perla made her way to James and slightly bowed in deference. She nearly whispered, "Thank you dear sir for coming. The cradle is very useful—"

And she fell to the floor. James caught Perla before she harmed her head, and carried her to an ottoman by the side of the cabin. Mrs. Minis ran to Perla's side and a general stir disoriented the guests. Benjamin's heart skipped a beat; and he rushed to care for her. Dr. Nunez detected her pulse; it was weak.

"Fetch juice! Quick! Water!"

Perla felt a flow of blood oozing from her womb; the cotton cloths would not be able to absorb it all and her gown would ruin. Fearful of mortification, Perla insisted she was feeling, "Much better, I thank you all, please don't fuss," and she devised a way to return to her room. Dr. Nunez whispered into Benjamin's ear, "If you don't see to it that she fully recovers, she may be too weak to care for your child. Do you understand, Benjamin?!"

Sheftall proved to be more rambunctious outside the womb than within. He quickly sucked his mother dry, and Benjamin had to purchase goat's milk to satisfy his son. Perla's strength did not gather enough momentum, and eventually a nurse was hired, Ms. Morgan. Benjamin could barely conclude his work in the field, in the militia and in the home. without nearly collapsing by his wife's side at night. Sheftall Sheftall, or "Shefy" as they fondly called their first-born son, refused to sleep much at night. Ms. Morgan insisted he needed to be fed "heartier meals" despite his tender age. During *Shabbos* meals, he would squeal in his cradle. Ms. Morgan insisted the baby "wants to taste adult meals." Shefy was a mere three months of age; Perla dismissed Ms. Morgan's assertions, believing they were premature.

Perla was frightened of another delivery. But she was warned that if her milk did not come in, she was susceptible to another pregnancy. There wasn't much she could do; her religion proscribed contraception—Perla simply didn't know how to go about it. She was too ashamed to speak to Mrs. Minis regarding the issue, and she couldn't broach the subject with Dr. Nunez, who was a man—and worse, he might question her religiosity. Perla castigated herself for even entertaining the thought of visiting Soft Paw; the woman was a witch and idol-worshiper. If Perla were to take any illicit drugs from Soft Paw perhaps Perla will come to sin other ways, G-d forbid. Maybe she will have inappropriate thoughts or become lax in certain stringencies set forth from the Rabbis. No. Perla refused to take any chances. But she was torn at the same time; she still recalled the fervent pains of labor. Maybe another curse women must bear is the fear of childbirth too.

Benjamin knew his home could not remain the makeshift *shul* indefinitely. Perla had little privacy during those hours, and now that the baby was born, walking around the house during the morning hours was a necessity; warming the milk, washing the child, calming him, pacing around the cottage, and entertaining him was a constant operation.

Tensions began to run high in the *minyan* lately. Granted the mishaps on the boat increased the distrust of the Sephardim and Ashkenazim from the onset of their entry into Georgia, but the proposal for a *shul* tore the *minyan* into partisan groups: the mildly religious Sephardim and the observant Ashkenazim. Benjamin petitioned the Georgia Trustees only to discover dissent within his own ranks—particularly the Sephardim. Benjamin was certain the virulent anti-Semitic posture of the Trustees would cool, and he was right to a certain degree. (Benjamin didn't want to suspect any one particular Sephardic counterpart, but he was sure Silva had something to do with it.) Fundamentally, the Sephardim had no objection to sharing the synagogue with the Ashkenazim, but since the funds were largely contributed by the wealthier Spanish-Portuguese Jews, they insisted it was only in their right to set the religious structure of the synagogue. Benjamin chortled bitterly—the lax observers wished to set the tone in a house of worship. It was a matter of religious principle, and the Ashkenazim agreed wholeheartedly with Benjamin's stance. But the Spanish-Portuguese Jews, and the most prominent among them were *not* an exception, conceived of the entire matter as a business acquisition—and he with the most input had the greatest influence. Benjamin sighed. This synagogue was tearing them apart, the opposite of what he hoped to achieve in America. After all, the Jews, regardless of creed, are all perceived as "JEWS" by the gentiles.

And in America, the Jews have to form a strong bond or the bonds will dissipate—or worse.

LITTLE AND LATE

THOMAS CHRISTIE STARED AT MARY Musgrove's delectable display of hearty Indian food. It was quite some time one of her Indian friends served him his early supper; he had starved all day, tending to duties Oglethorpe had left in his hands. He looked out the dirty windows and sighed; the Savannah River in February dazzled him. The midday sun nearly blinded him, and this year there was even some ice and snow to pain the eyes. Mary's trading post was the most convenient stop and a preferred retreat from Georgia. It was a thankless job, this "scribe of Georgia" post Oglethorpe graciously bequeathed to Christie. Mary's Indian girl finally came by with corn chowder soup and some dry corn bread dipped in garlic sauce. Rumor has it Oglethorpe had his pickings with her too. That scoundrel. Outlawing rum on the account of decent folk like Christie. Christie noticed the woman's deerskin dress was tighter around the hips than usual. Mary's trading post served as a pub. It was a well-known fact among the half-breeds that Mary did as she pleased. But the rum warmed them all and drowned their memories. Not that it mattered much right now— Oglethorpe was away in London.

Christie saw Thomas Causton outside the pub, tying his black horse, Blackbird, to the post. Causton sauntered into the room without so much as a glance of recognition. Causton's riding boots were impeccably shined and the rim a cognac hue only the finest gentlemen wore. His breeches, unusually starched, boasted taut thighs. He wore a velvet gabardine that must have taken hours to properly stitch. Oglethorpe's deputy. The man was in charge of all Georgia proper until James's return from England. It was no secret Causton couldn't care a fiddler's thumb for James's ban on rum. Christie stood and shook Causton's hand. Christie noticed Causton's dry, wrinkled hand. Causton's mustache and crisp blue eyes glossed over Christie with apparent disdain: Indian fornicators were not much respected this part of town. Christie knew all those men were really just hiding the truth—when it came to women, few men were saints. Both Causton and Oglethorpe sauntered around as though they never mingled—and more—with the reds. And Causton had his share of brawls in the past too. Just everyone was willing to overlook James's defaults because of his impeccable mannerisms. Christie spit on the floor, paid his bills, and left Mary's pub. *Once them men get the title, their self-regard swells like a blister. Everyone knows what's inside.*

*

Oglethorpe sat beside his mother and Queen Anne's ladies in waiting. They listened, quite captivated by his descriptions of Indian chiefs, Spanish marauders, and of plague and disease. Oglethorpe's eyes shimmered as he recalled Savannah's foliage, and his eyes protruded with each description. Of course Elizabeth sat beside her mother; she barely ate a morsel. Instead, she stared at her wedding ring and admired James without saying much. His life seemed adventurous and exciting. Even the way he described the Jews was fascinating. To think that in the New World men and women of all color and creeds, not to mention different denominations and religions, intermingled! Tomochichi created a stir last year, which she recalled. But it seemed so much has happened since she last saw James. He had gained a few pounds around his waist, and his face was full around the neck and cheeks. But he was still handsome, and his voice melodious and calm, just as she remembered. His wig suited him well, and his long waistcoat was tailored with intricate buttons that gleamed in the candle-lit room. His shoes boasted brass buckles, a design her husband detested. Indeed, her husband detested one too many fashions—

117

he hated the white breeches, and his preference for navy overruled his hatred of "low-class" colors, such as black and gray. Really, Elizabeth did not see how color and class were connected, but her dear husband seemed to have formulated an opinion which he now assumed was fact. James continued to entertain the ladies:

"And, suddenly, the entire colony was at risk of imminent demise but for a Jewish doctor, by the name of Dr. Samuel Nunez. It was Providence, I tell you. I, my dear ladies, would not be sitting here with you today were it not for this man."

"But truly, James, you don't mean to inform me that a *Jewish* man should treat *genteel* men and women as if he were a welcome *Christian*! It is absurd!"

"Indeed, mother, it is not. The Spanish-Portuguese Jews are quite diligent. I dare say they have contributed a great deal more than many a colonist, who, unfortunately, has fallen into ill-repute. I need not tell you of a shipment of ex-convicts and the situation with our prisons, madam."

An awkward hush filled the room. Elizabeth cleared her throat—

"Sir. Did not the Trustees forbid the entry of Jews into America?"

"Yes, Elizabeth. But they have rescinded their initial stance since then. Indeed, I have their letter of withdrawal with me should you like to read it."

Elizabeth blushed. His eyes penetrated through Elizabeth's. It was as if he was staring straight into a part of her that she had herself to recognize. James's mother stood—

"Let us toast my dear son, my youngest child, upon his grand success in the King's colony, and let us hope he decides to remain here with his dear and lonely mother; although I do fear he is wont to return to the American country!"

"Hear, hear!"

*

Benjamin had enough of Causton's burly mannerisms. As lieutenant of the militia, Benjamin believed it was in his right to dictate orders to his inferiors. While it was true James did not specify

Benjamin's precise duties during James's absence, Benjamin believed he should do as he deemed fit. Causton flouted the ban on rum, and he constantly besmirched Oglethorpe's name. Rumor had it an Indian girl was carrying James's child; but Benjamin dismissed malicious rumors. If Causton had anything to do with this, perhaps it was *he* who had begun the terrible story. With title of deputy, Causton took liberalities with the rum, the women, and now with Benjamin's militia men—ordering them around, and deviating from Oglethorpe's initial operations. To make matters worse, his wife was extraordinarily weak from the labor and barely functioning. She slept well into the morning hours. The baby kept her awake at night. Nurse Morgan insisted the baby's teeth were coming in and a teething device was of great import. Benjamin asked Perla to see to the baby's needs.

Benjamin brought in the hay to feed the cows. He was lucky his livestock did not catch any disease. His neighbor's cattle were sluggish; some didn't produce enough milk. Benjamin stood in the barn and fed the hens. He collected the eggs and placed a stool by the cow's udders. He milked each cow, sometimes twice a day. His wife churned the butter, with Shefy in tow. His son usually napped in a wrapped blanket, neatly tied round Perla's shoulder and upper torso. Lately, he noticed his wife was thinner than usual; the nursing depleted her completely. It was a shame. Perla was still young. All of the fatty deposits from the pregnancy now lay in their son. Shefy reminded Benjamin of his father: the boy smiled with his hearty soul when tickled. Benjamin recalled his father's wide, welcoming smile. It was a shame the child could not meet his grandparents. Back home, a family unit solidified a marriage, and each successive child became part of a larger group. Here in America, Benjamin and Perla had to rely on one another. The Minises were pleasant, but their children were older in age, and Perla did not socialize with the other townswomen very often. She wrote to her mother, sang Shefy lovely songs, and she even knitted blankets and a warm one-piece winter ensemble from blue and yellow yarn. Shefy's cheeks were ruddy, and many times Ms.

Morgan insisted the baby needed a bath. His heavenly eyes were now a dark green, and some professed he shared his mother's fine eyes and complexion. But his mother always placed a bonnet on his head, so poor boy, not too many people could see the lovely hair on his head—dark, like Benjamin's—with curls along the edges. The texture was finer than silken threads.

Benjamin heard a horse's pounding thump and left the stall. It was pastor Boltzius. Since Benjamin assisted the Ebenezer Lutherans, originally form Salzburg, their pastor, Johann Martin Boltzius, conducted affairs with the Sheftalls. Lately, Benjamin began to feel uneasy around the pastor. They conversed in their natural German tongue, which felt quite nice. But their discussions focused on the trinity, the power of the saints, and even the crucifixion. How could he and his wife speak about the Christian faith without recalling how their poor grandparents suffered? Was it not because of Constantine's strange visions and the philosophy of the Church that the Jewish nation suffered every generation? Be it persecution or inquisition, conversion or intermarriage, the numbers of the stars God promised to Abraham diminished considerably. It was a shame and a disgrace to God's very name, but how was he supposed to convey this to Boltzius? The man was convinced Benjamin's jolly nature and good-heartedness and general desire to live in peace even with those who had been enemies in the old world was nothing more than a pretense for conversion to Christianity. No doubt Boltzius had another tome on Christian rites and moral teachings to "lend." Benjamin had to come up with all these strange excuses, sometimes even lying, just to avoid brining blasphemous works into his kosher home. "My poor wife needs my every assistance at home. I truly do not have time to read for leisure, good priest." That went very well. But how long could it last? Benjamin preferred to help the Ebenezer crew in financial dealings, agricultural needs; he preferred to leave religious matters where they belonged: in *synagogues* and *churches*, respectively.

"Good Benjamin! I have excellent tidings!"

"Yes! Won't you come in, good priest?"

"I am afraid I do not have much time to remain in Georgia. Our friends in South Carolina will be required to obtain Georgia licenses to trade with the Indians!"

Benjamin immediately understood the implications; the South Carolinians may not barter or conduct business now that a license may be necessary. Indeed, those in Georgia have the upper hand with relation to the Indians. Those in Ebenezer would surely benefit—simply due to their proximity to the Indian tribes in the South.

"I am very glad, Boltzius. Greetings to Mrs. Smit and all the lovely children."

"Most certainly. Good day!"

Benjamin heaved a sigh of relief. The good pastor did not accost him this time about Christ or church. Benjamin returned to his duties, somewhat uplifted.

Ms. Morgan noticed the Lutheran pastor made his way to the Sheftalls again. It was a matter of conscience to let Perla know of the man's true intentions. Ms. Morgan detested the man. She believed those missionary types were foul. To each his own, her mother would say. Of course her father was of a different opinion; he called all Jews bloody Shylocks and all the Catholics boy-lovers. There really was no way to appease the old man anyhow. Her brother inherited her father's scurrilous mouth; no wonder her mother passed on before forty years of age. The nurse rather liked her employers. Both Perla and Benjamin saw to it that she had enough to eat. Perla apologized if her son was a bit edgy or otherwise difficult to care for. And she had the added benefit of resting on Saturday as well as on Sunday. Her father would have her neck if he discovered she rested on a Jew-day. But she had very little to do with him since she began working for the Sheftalls.

Ms. Morgan lifted Shefy from his mother's arms.

"He's mighty heavy now, Perla. Won't you say?"

"I am afraid so. My hips hurt too!"

"They are bent to the side?" the nurse playfully asked.

Perla smiled.

"Soon they'll most likely be if the lad doesn't learn how to walk."

"Ah. Don't you worry, Perla. The child will grow too fast for all of us, I can promise you that."

Perla sighed. She was told to enjoy her baby. Poor Mrs. Hines. She lost her daughter Anne during the plague, and she often exhorted Perla to enjoy the little ones.

Perla began to worry: her monthly cycle resumed. She had not bled monthly since her pregnancy. Nursing warded the menses as well. But now this meant she could conceive at any moment. How could she possibly run the household, care for the child, and be heavy with child? She sighed. She silently prayed to her lord that He would bestow strength onto his humble servant, Perla Sheftall.

*

Elizabeth stood in the parlor of the Oglethorpe estate. The furnishings were beautiful, but not as grand as the Wright's. One could not compare the workmanship of the divan, for instance. The trimmings were most certainly burnished, not inlaid. Furthermore, the draperies were a bit dusty, a sign of neglect. It has been a mark of distinction in the Wright's household that all drapes and linens were customarily laundered on the first and fourteenth of every month. Sadly, this was not the custom in the Oglethorpe home. Well, so be it. The cook was well-versed in mutton dishes and the manners of the crew—polished. Elizabeth walked around the room, touching with the rim of her fingers the oak mantle and crystal vases. She stood erect and stared at her reflection in the glass mirror, which was finely decorated with gold and silver loops of fleur-de-lis. Her brows were finely arched, as she preferred from a young age, and her lips were still a crimson hue. Her intricate up-do in the latest fashion, with pearls in her hair and a gossamer lace handkerchief covering the top of her head, so the first quarter of her forehead was covered in lace. It was rather ethereal in her estimation. Her gown shone beautifully, and the light-blue satin nicely complimented her eyes, which appeared blue-green in tint. Her eye-lashes were slightly curled; a trick the hairdresser taught her. Her daughter, little Anne, was even more of a beauty, Elizabeth gladly noted. This is one of a woman's greatest assets, she mused.

"How do you find the estate, Elizabeth?" Oglethorpe had been examining her every gesture and was rather amused at how Elizabeth stared at herself. Women tend to stop and readjust when they pass a glass, he gleefully thought. Elizabeth is no different.

"Oh. You startled me. It is quite handsome. The furnishings are—"

"To your liking, I hope?"

"Yes. Most certainly."

"Very well. I shall hope to hear that you and your child visit as often as you like while I am abroad."

"So you shall return to America, then?"

"Yes. Of course. I have urgent business. The colony is still in need of leadership."

Elizabeth stared into the space between Oglethorpe and the edge of the room. It had been only some time ago that he had stolen an embrace from her. Yet she had been reliving that moment ever since. Her husband was not very warm toward her, and many weeks of the year she had shared her bed with no one but her daughter, little Anne, whose hands were so tender and whose eyes so deep. The baby has been a consolation during those long nights. And her husband preferred to sleep in his own wing, even a year after their marriage. She lifted a finger to whisk away a strand of hair from her eyes. James really did appear quite handsome in his ensemble, despite the rugged appearance of his hair. But he had changed. There was no doubt. Perhaps there was even a tinge of bitterness between his brows. His smile had not that wide openness as before. The colonies were harsh, and James was evidence of such.

James neared Elizabeth, and stood face to face.

"How do you get along these days, Elizabeth?"

Elizabeth immediately looked down at her fingertips. She did not have the wherewithal to admit her loneliness. It was a matter of modesty and even decorum to put on the necessary airs of a satisfied wife.

"Very well. I can assure you."

James searched her eyes for a bit of sadness or regret, but he only detected evasion. She had answered quickly, but her eyes only met his momentarily.

"James. Will you show the guests out to the gardens?"

"Excuse me, Elizabeth. Yes, Mother. I am coming."

"As I said, Elizabeth. Please visit as often as you desire."

She nodded her head and sat down on the beige couch, noticing the cushion was a bit too hard.

*

Benjamin knew Thomas Causton was behind the rumors. One couldn't walk around the market without nuances of "Oglethorpe's secret lover" being some half-breed friend of Mary Musgrove. Now she's pregnant, supposedly, and Oglethorpe out of town to "prove" it. The girl *was* attractive, despite her heritage. She had very long black braids, and her deerskin dress was ill-fitting due to her heavy pregnancy. Unlike Mary Musgrove, Florence's skin was more yellowish in tone, and her height less than average. She was known to work in the clandestine pub Mary Musgrove kept. Some say for extra pay, she may provide certain services, which Benjamin knew were debauched. Thomas Causton was one of the regulars of the now not-so-secret bar up at Mary's. The *goyish* ways persist, no matter which part of the globe any Jew will reside. Back in his hometown, there was the well-known *shiksa* who afforded favors to the men of the town. The good wives would spit at her, but she was all smiles. Seems this Florence is headed in the same direction, Benjamin sadly noted.

Benjamin continued on his rounds. Causton had neglected to mention if he should continue to check the northern entrance to Savannah as Benjamin was wont every Monday and Thursday. Perla has been very pale lately. She lost her appetite and refused to eat poultry, even though it was his specialty. The child began eating solids, which sustained the lad longer than the bottles of milk. The nurse, Ms. Morgan, was less than satisfactory in his opinion: she slept in the afternoon and chatted with the neighbors too much. She also ate more than her fair share, but Benjamin never dared open his mouth. He took pity on the woman, having heard her family was impoverished. So long as her gentlemen suitors remained far from his house, he did not see any reason to speak to Perla about Ms. Morgan's derelictions.

Perla saw Benjamin from the backdoor window. He seemed heavy-hearted. She wondered if the Deputy in charge of Savannah during James's stay in England was taunting her husband again. Benjamin bore it all, but Perla knew Causton called Benjamin foul names, albeit with a smile.

"Hey. First Jew of the militia. Your company will not remain in the outskirts tonight. I don't have the men or the monies. Is that understood?" Something of that kind. Either way, Benjamin feared an incursion from the Spaniards. They would most certainly attack from the southern borders—Benjamin's route of responsibility. Here he comes now, she thought.

Benjamin walked through the backdoor and smiled. Perla's hair was uncovered and very nicely braided. Her hair had streaks of blonde, and she applied a bit of rouge to her cheeks as well.

"Benjamin, I thought you would like to know…."

Benjamin at first was a bit confused. He placed his arm on her shoulder, pulling her in.

"What is it, Perla?"

"I am with child," she whispered.

Perla recalled the afternoon. She had deduced her situation as though caught in the whirlwind of pure logic. What had taken so long for her to realize? To think it all started with her breasts: They were tender again. Her belly was sore. She had not bled in more than two months. She sat down, holding her head. She was pregnant again. All the blame could not fall *only* on Benjamin. That wouldn't be entirely just. She got carried away on some nights too; but later the toll would fall on her in ways that she believed exceeded the pleasures of those nights. The delivery. The aches of the reverse contractions. The sore nipples, the sleepless nights. The terrible fears, the nightmares, the dread of an unhealthy baby. It was all overwhelming. Why wasn't she smiling, glad to hold another beautiful baby? Perhaps this time a girl? Why wasn't she thinking of all those giggles and precious seconds of glory? How could she be so dark? Surely her husband provided for her. And certainly little Shefy was too sweet, an angel? And didn't he need a sibling to play with? Hadn't she prayed with all her heart for a family?

"Are you certain, Perla?"

Perla recounted her fitful afternoon, the realization. Benjamin stood, listening, hugging her. She seemed very tired, not unhappy, just apprehensive. Yes. She had tender breasts, even her voice changed. But was she truly prepared for this pregnancy? She *did* seem exhausted to him. Was she prepared for the new child? Worried, suddenly, Benjamin asked:

"How do you feel, Perla?"

"A bit shocked. I wasn't trying this time for a child. I thought it might take long, as the first."

"Yes. We did wait for Shefy for quite some time."

"Yes. I do recall."

"You must rest. Come. I'll care for Shefy tonight. I want you to sleep early, my dove."

Perla rested her head and didn't think or dream of a thing until early morning.

*

"Must you leave so soon, dear son?"

James leaned in and kissed his mother's drooping cheek.

"Yes, Mother. I am afraid so."

"My dear son, when will you settle down? Start a family of your own?"

"Oh, Mother, when I'm ready, you can be sure."

"Yes, I suppose so. You always had your way, even as a child. Goodness knows you even tried to parent me! Very well, then, be well and take care of yourself dear boy."

James stood in his mother's parlor, waistcoat in hand and anxious to catch the next vessel to the Americas. His dealings with the trustees were over with; Elizabeth seemed quite satisfied with her lot, and the London air began to irk him again. The trustees began to suspect that Oglethorpe had "too much confidence and desire to spend and not enough incentive to generate funds," as Sir Perceval put is so eloquently. The others did not try to defend James's purposes; indeed, they remained silent. James had quite enough of those men who never bothered to feed themselves or bathe themselves. This was absurd! It was very a simple matter for them to smoke rare cigars in their London mansions while he toiled away in Georgia, facing expenditures and near-debt. If his mother knew of his personal losses, the pecuniary risks that he knew, deep down, would not yield much gain, she would surely lose many hours of sleep. It was too late now; he had begun a journey overseas, and he had betrothed himself to its advance.

His love for Elizabeth subsided, but only slightly. There was no point in staring at a married woman. She was not of the type to carry on a clandestine friendship with another man. Nor would Oglethorpe have her so reduce her circumstances. James had a strong feeling, however, that she was not very content. She was just too fine to admit it, he lamented.

*

Florence knocked on James's door. She had waited nearly six months to see James. He had a right to know, she believed. The baby was most certainly his. She had not taken the prescribed treatment Soft Paw had kindly administered: a bull's eye boiled in a cauldron for three days. It was meant to ward off any "mistakes." But Florence believed James may marry her if she produced a child. He *had* to love her. He stroked her hair very gently and spoke kindly to her. He even gave her a nice gift of soaps from his country. Florence spoke the English language but she could not read; nevertheless, he read to her from his library on some occasions. But now she wasn't sure of much, especially his feelings. He had kindly asked her to leave two weeks before she discovered "the way of women" ceased. Frightened, she was sure James would never return. Those men by Mary's eyed her. Somehow too many townspeople knew—particularly that Causton. But it would not end. If James would not wed her, she would be known as "one of Mary's kind," and there would be no turning back.

Florence knocked again, sweating in the late summer heat. Savannah was blistering hot during the day, and the night offered little repose. She felt a stinging sensation; the child pressed on her bladder. She began to pant, afraid of an accident. Quickly, she ran to the outhouse and breathed a sigh of relief.

"Yes? Who's there?"

Florence gathered her skirts and ran to greet James. She ran to him and tried to hug him, pleased to see him after so long a separation.

"Oh my! Come in, Florence."

James could not suppress his surprise. He had not seen the woman since his departure. No wonder the people in town looked at him in that odd manner. But who's to say this child was *his*? He returned Florence's greeting, but was anxious to speak to her.

"Come inside. Let me fetch you a drink."

Florence grabbed his arm, "No, James. I have to speak with you. Please sit."

James swallowed. He feared this all along, and now it was too late.

"The child is yours, James. My time will come before the moon is full again. What shall I do?" Florence began to cry, realizing James would not marry her, a half-breed, even if he did share strong feelings for her. And what would be done? With whom would she live? She can't raise a child in Mary's pub. It was out of the question.

"Tell me you love me James, that you will take care of the child, that you will serve me right. Tell me you care for me!" She began to kiss him and tousle his hair, running her hand on his back, holding his arms tightly.

James, overcome with compassion, suddenly held Florence and whispered, "Girl, I cannot deny you. I will take care of you. Of course I care for you. Please, don't work yourself into a frenzy. You want this baby don't you?"

Florence nodded her head.

"Then you shall have him."

"Will you marry me, James?"

James winced at the mention of the word. Of course he wouldn't. He couldn't. But he would care for her, and that would have to be enough. James slowly moved his head to the side. Florence cried once more, whimpered, stood holding James for a while, and then said, "Is it because you love someone else, James? Or is it because you are a gentleman?"

"Please do not work yourself up!"

Afraid she upset him, Florence began to hug him again, and the two re-united, in the bitter-sweet way Florence feared would not last.

*

Soft Paw stood in her hut holding aloe and stone. She had to concoct the salve for Florence. It was her time. Poor girl was resting on the floor. Like a whimpering cat, screeching every now and then, Florence crawled on all floors, begging her ancestors to stop the pain. Soft Paw rubbed the girl's back, pushing aside her long braids. Florence did not reveal the father, but Soft Paw believed it was a white man's. She will find out soon enough, she knew.

"Oh! Soft Paw. This baby. I feel as though he won't budge. I want him out! I can't bear it anymore!"

"Then you must begin to push him out, dear child. He cannot remain inside forever. Come on. Push him out!"

Florence began yelling, afraid of pushing, and afraid of keeping him inside. Soft Paw began to remove Florence's dress, until she lay completely naked. Warning Florence not to move, Soft Paw began to rub foul-smelling dung and crushed herbs on her swollen belly. She then washed it off with scalding water.

"Sit in this tub now."

Filled with hot water, the tub relieved Florence's aches, and she suddenly relaxed. Her abdomen was so far stretched; she could not see her lower region. Suddenly, Florence felt the urge to expel, and just as she pushed the baby out, an incredible wave of pain filled her and she froze. Soft Paw ran to see if the baby emerged, but instead, the old woman saw the baby's buttocks come out first. The cord was wrapped around his poor throat, which was all blue, and not a sign of life remained in the child. It was a boy, and white. With very large hands and a long torso.

It belonged to the White Man.

*

Benjamin was disappointed in James; he thought Oglethorpe would have been a bit different from the other countrymen. Flor-

129

ence lay cold and buried near her son, who was more alive while in his mother's womb than he ever was in the world. The poor woman bled for hours until her soul departed. For goodness sake! Who delivers a child in a witch's home?! Of course the woman died. She was probably poisoned by some potion. James didn't seem himself for a while, walking around town with a walking stick, head bent down. He was a pitiable sight; even Causton no longer opened his mouth. James's beard grew in, very much like the custom of the Jewish mourner, come to think of it. Mary Musgrove went to visit him, and rumors began that she offered another female companion but he refused. At least he learned his lesson.

"Fancy seeing you here, Benjamin!"

Benjamin lifted his brows and recognized the pastor, Boltzius.

"I heard your wife is expecting a child. My blessings."

Relieved the priest had sincere intentions, Benjamin smiled apprehensively, thanked the man, and summarily continued his rounds, eager to return home to Perla.

Perla had been asleep that afternoon. Nurse Morgan held Shefy most of the morning but for a brief period. The child had been yelling most of the afternoon, in spurts: his teeth. His gums swelled and his breath was rank. Drivel filled the boy's apron, and he refused to take his breakfast meal of oatmeal and honey. Instead, he bit Morgan's fingers for most of the morning. Even his forehead felt warm to the touch. Morgan didn't know what to do, so she went for a walk. The child had begun crawling and was now quite good at it. She rested by a tree and saw dried acorns on the ground. Shefy crawled as she rested her aching arms and legs. He slowly crouched and selected an acorn from nearby. It wasn't very large, so he was able to hold it well. Immediately, he took a bite of the acorn and seemed quite pleased.

Morgan studied the child and thought, "Wouldn't this be fine for the child! I'll wash it at home and give it to the poor boy!" She scooped Shefy, allowed him to chew on her finger, and gathered a few acorns and placed them into her apron.

"Grand idea. This child is a wonder!" She kissed his wet cheek and marveled at his beautiful eyes.

Everyone whispered when they saw little Shefy, "Beautiful boy. Have you seen such a bonny boy? His eyes are large, like his mother. And his skin is perfectly white. The picture of a perfect Christian—but for the hair...." Perhaps it was his extraordinary charm that helped Morgan during the long, arduous days of caring for the child. He really was the picture. She passed John Hale as she trekked to Perla's house, frightened by the man's malice. It was well-known in Savannah that John Hale detested Benjamin Sheftall. Morgan also knew Hale fathered an illegitimate child who was rather neglected and often ill. Instinctively, Morgan averted Hale's malicious gaze, and held Shefy close, covering the baby's face with her free hand. Hale made a lewd gesture, and Morgan began running toward the house. Shefy squealed; he loved the feeling of the wind in his face. He winced and smiled.

"A tooth!" Morgan lifted Shefy above her head and kissed his forehead. "How did I miss this? So it must be his other teeth that hurt. I better rush to clean the acorns." Fastidious with the child's needs, Morgan quickly rubbed off the dirt from the acorns. Surprisingly, they were not too filthy. She placed Shefy by the hearth, on top of a rug, and noticed Perla was still asleep. It was half past four in the afternoon. The master would be home, she thought. She took the acorns from the drying rack, and scattered them near Shefy's voluptuous frame. She bent down and kissed each thigh; he was truly scrumptious, she marveled. She sat down near Shefy, and calmly watched him gnaw the acorns. He eagerly turned each acorn round and round, looking for the perfect angle to soothe his gums. Morgan lay down on the floor, propping her head with her hand. Tired, she rested her head on her forearm, and without truly intending, drifted off to sleep. It was not more than five minutes, but it was long enough. Shefy, with the aid of his top tooth, managed to break a piece off the acorn. He chewed it for a good half minute, just as Morgan realized she had fallen asleep. Suddenly, Shefy began making choking sounds. Frightened, Morgan awoke, her heart pounding; she began to scream. Shefy was blue in the face, and his eyes were rolling back. Morgan froze.

She screamed and screamed. Oh God. God. What have I done? Shefy! She turned him around, pounding his back. Please wake up. Please child. Please breathe. His arms flailed; his back arched. He struggled. His skin was no longer beautiful nor white. Please! Shefy! Oh God. This child! Please help me! But his body no longer responded. Morgan began to cry, her entire body shaking with intense grief and guilt. Shefy, she whispered. Shefy.

Perla awoke to the image of her son, who lay listless and lifeless in his nurse's arms. Perla stood, screamed with intense fright, and fell to the floor.

Benjamin walked in that afternoon with the solemn greeting of Dr. Nunez. No one else could break the news of the boy's death but the doctor—who had been called too late to do too little.

Why must angels die?

BRIEF CANDLE

"PERLA. PLEASE. COME OUT OF the room with the child. We must bury him before it is dark out. I beg of you. Please. *Please.*"

She had been in the room with little Shefy's body the entire night and into the following day. Holding her son comforted her. How could she possibly inter the child in the cold ground? It was so cruel! And no Jewish burial ground... and why must her son be the first to die? Of all the Jews in Georgia, why had *her* son died? His eyes. What did they look like again? Shefy. Please. If I rub you, will you come to life again? She asked. Bitterly, she cried, forgetting herself. She had not washed or eaten a scrap since the previous morning. Shefy. My child. Please. Why must this be your end? Beautiful child. An angel. Why must angels die?

"Perla. I have secured burial ground. Please! I beg of you. Open the door and let us do this service to the child!"

Broken, Benjamin lay on the floor, weeping. His wife must have gone mad. She cried for an entire day and refused to part from their son. When she awoke from her collapse, she ran in search of the boy. When she saw his chubby body wrapped in linen, she screamed, uncovered him, picked him up, held him to her chest, and rocked him. She then ran to her room and secluded herself since. At first she sang him songs and then she burst into a torrent of screams. She now began to whimper like a dying cat. It was too much for Benjamin. Dr. Nunez had remained with them since that fateful afternoon, administering to Benjamin, running errands on his behalf, tying to secure a proper burial ground for the first Jewish fatality. Poor nurse! The woman ran into the Atlantic and drowned herself. They say she loved the child, but had somehow been neglectful of duty. Some say the baby was cursed by that Hale. The one who cursed Benjamin night and day in his depraved way... some say it was a test of God. Dr. Nunez only knew one thing for certain: it was a hell to bear.

"Perla, think of the child's soul. It is not in peace until his body is buried. *Please! Woman!*"

Perla held her child and sang him one last song. She cried, unlocked the door, and peered through. The sight of her dear husband on the floor, the weakness from fasting, was too overwhelming for her: she nearly collapsed.

Dr. Nunez held her, and Benjamin gently held his son, blessing him, "My son, may you rest in peace by the seat of the great Master of the Universe. *Baruch dayan emes.*" And tears ensued until the poor child's burial.

Perla did not attend, but some have sworn they saw John Hale by the gravesite, appearing rather numb and perhaps a bit stupefied. Perhaps his tongue won't wag as much, now that God had refused to reveal his mercy on Benjamin Sheftall's household.

*

It was a cursed business, it was. Oglethorpe stared at Benjamin Sheftall's back as the Jewish militiaman bent down to place his son's tiny body in a wooden box. It was too small. Soft Paw buried his son too, but without ceremony. His son had been dead at birth, so he had never learned to love him. Florence was another matter. The poor woman would not stop hemorrhaging; why didn't they call in Dr. Nunez? Maybe the Portuguese Jew could have prevented another senseless death? Oglethorpe stared at the dirt, the mound near the burial site, and recalled Florence's curves, the way her hair fell on his arms. He must have loved her. It was wrong of him to have taken her in an unchristian manner. God had rebuked him; he lowered his head. But Benjamin Sheftall. He did not sin as I had. Mysterious are Thy ways, James thought. He removed his cap and held Benjamin's arms. He had seen enough parents bury their

134

children in his day. Perhaps he too had been guilty of killing such children, during his many battles, but had never considered the pain of his victims' loved ones. It was all a rotten business, it was.

"I am sorry, Benjamin." Oglethorpe whispered, shedding a tear for all the parents who never had, nor ever shall, see their children grow.

Dr. Nunez lit a cigar. Perla was due any day and had buried her son only the month prior. She had eaten very little during this pregnancy, carried on like some waif in a half-dazed universe, and had still managed to swell. Her belly was quite large, but her face was thinner than he had recalled. Her arms were like two branches from an olive-tree. He often wondered if she refused to eat or if she had simply lost her appetite. Benjamin resolved to care for the house, and he resumed to host the *minyan*. His home once again became a vibrant makeshift synagogue. After Benjamin's loss, the Jews of the town lessened their ire against the shared synagogue. He made sure to speak words of the holy Torah every day after services, not only after the *Shabbat* prayers. He dedicated his words to his son's *neshamah*—soul—so that it may rise higher and higher in the heavenly spheres. His wife rarely left her room, locked into her bed. Talks had resumed: who shall begin collecting for the synagogue? Who shall dedicate the prayer-books? Where shall they build? Who shall become the architect? The discussions were lively, and most of the Jews began to warm somewhat to the idea of a shared *shul*, where the Ashkenazim and the Sephardim would be able to congregate. Benjamin rarely spoke. He just went on learning, praying the psalms, and tending to his household. Dr. Nunez thought of little Shefy's last words to him: "Hi! Candy?" the boy had begun speaking few words, but somehow learned about sweets and candies. His mother had stitched a fine skull-cap for the child, but he never tolerated anything on his head. Even at nearly two years of age, his mother refused to cut his hair. Long curls cascaded from the child's forehead, almost like the vines on ripe grapes. Dr. Nunez was a cerebral man, but he believed in the powers of the evil eye. The child should have worn a charm. It was the custom of his people, the Sephardim, to ward off the evil eye. There was no harm in a little extra precaution, no matter how strange it sounded. It was too late now.

Susan Hale was summoned again. This time around Perla knew precisely what to expect. Still mourning and numb from her loss, she had nearly forgotten another child was to be born. As she began feeling the first contractions, Perla awoke from her slumber. *Tehillim.* I must pray, she repeated to herself. I must beseech God. I don't have the strength to do this on my own. How is this child so hardy? How has he subsisted these last months? Fears mounted in Perla's mind, and she began to cry.

Benjamin had been patrolling the borders again, thinking of his wife. Perla was in need of help, he knew it. Quickly, he grabbed his musket. Off he went to see to his wife's needs. Running quickly, he entered the house panting, calling, "Perla! Perla!" only to find her crouched by the bed, whimpering.

He ran to the hearth, heated water, and returned to his wife.

"Perla, please, *sheifelah.* You mustn't sit on the floor. Please. Did you call for Susan?"

Perla, pale and weak, shook her head and squeezed her husband's hand.

"You must tell her not to tarry. He's quick! I feel him!"

Nervous his wife should deliver the child on the floor, Benjamin hastened to prop his wife on the bed. He had spoken with Dr. Nunez. If the baby were to give Perla a difficult time, he would call for the Portuguese Jew, despite Perla's uneasiness with a male delivering her child. She had been very stubborn with Shefy's delivery, but this time he didn't want to run any risks with her health.

Susan, recalling Perla's first delivery very well, was surprised to find Perla holding onto the bedpost, ready to push at any moment. Susan didn't forgive her brother for all of his malicious gossip. These poor people never truly harmed anyone, she thought. Immediately, she commenced cleansing Perla's opening, massaging the small area. It was as though she had never given birth before. Her legs were thinner and her belly was not as

136

large. This time Perla seemed dazed, as though she was not truly present. She muttered strange Hebrew words and fell silent during contractions. Without much ado, the second child began encroaching toward Susan's hands, which were open and ready to capture the newborn. Benjamin sat in the other room, with *sefer Torah* open to the birth of Isaac. Crying, he swore to raise the new baby in *derech Hashem* even in *galus*. The child will become a *gadol*. He will bring a *Kiddush Hashem*. Just have *rachmanus*.

Let the child live a long and meaningful life. Please good God in Heaven, Host of Hosts, do not let my labor go to waste. Have mercy on your servant, and may I merit to see this child grow in good deeds and Torah. Please! For your sake, Elohim. Have mercy on Perla, my dear wife. She has suffered enormous pains to fulfill the mitzvah of "be fruitful and multiply."

Susan's hands grabbed hold of the little boy's newborn bloody head, gripped his body as it slithered right through his mother's fortress and whispered, "Blessed Mary! He is the very coinage of the first!" Perla held the child in her arms and cried tears of relief and grief, joy and profound sorrow as the newborn babe's insistent cries filled the Sheftall home.

*

What the first had taught poor Perla was beneficial for the second: the newborn was hungry, tired, and very active at night. Shefy's little face fading with the autumnal winds, the second-born slowly replaced the first. But the pain inflicted weakness—so Shefy's presence lingered in the effects: Perla. She was incapable of caring for the second child, no matter how much she held him. Susan said it was too much for the "poor lass. The li'l one resembles the first. It is such a mystery, it is!" Even their voices were eerily similar—high pitched and delicate. Benjamin was delighted with the second-born, but celebrated his *bris* with only the necessary quorum of Jews. This time, he held a low profile. It was for the benefit of the child. Too much ostentation breeds evil demons' jealousy. At least that is what Mr. Minis and Dr. Nunez argued. The night before the bris, during the *Zohar* reading, Mrs. Minis pinned a *chamsah* on the child's undergarment.

"To ward off the evil eye. It is a tradition. The demons are very, very envious of the beautiful souls inside these precious gems. Oh! Look how he's trying to suck his thumb. What an angel!" She kissed the child and whispered to her husband, "I truly hope they don't give this child the same name as the first who died. That is an ill-omen." Mr. Minis nodded his head. "That would be unwise. But I don't feel it is my place to inform him, you understand."

"Of course!" she answered, almost shedding a tear for Shefy. How frightened he must have been, poor child. Only a baby when he died. And that nurse. She was too young to die too. God bless their souls.

*

So they named the second child after a biblical figure this time, James thought. Very apropos. Mordechai Sheftall. Second yet first. The year: 1735. The day: the second of December. A surprisingly mild morning, if I do recall, he thought. What else occurred on that day? What else should I list in this report? Ah! Yes. The news of a synagogue. Well. That is not a bad idea at all, he thought. That should certainly aggravate Boltzius. But the funds... well, the Portuguese Jews had enough between them, he supposed. Well. What else... Yes! Hope of bottles of Georgia-brewed wine! That should please all those back in London. James felt a sharp pain in his temple. He placed the quill near the diary and massaged his temple. He opened the drawer and uncapped a very inconspicuous flask, partly covered with a fine, supple leather. Elizabeth. Ever since Florence died, her image kept reappearing in his dreams. At first he saw only glimpses of smiles. Then her hair, falling on her cheeks, and a mysterious smile. And then, of course, his dreams became more and more intense. Drat! How much more of this torment could he take? He rummaged for another flask. Both were nearly empty. Ever since he returned with the official Negro Act and Rum Act, more and more Georgians were leaving town. Farmers complained they couldn't sow or reap without the Negroes. They were tired of any restrictions, particularly rum— their only vice according to the indignant masses. He had to rid his army of Causton. That dreadful man. How does Shakespeare put it? "There's no art / To find the mind's construction in the face." He built an absolute trust in Causton, and now half his armed men look askance at me, he miserably thought. Even Hale would have been a better choice—at least his bitterness was a product of loyalty. The position Oglethorpe bestowed on Causton was a "borrowed robe" that did not sit well. Oglethorpe suspected Causton wanted to keep what was meant to be returned. There was no real way to determine loyalties. Oglethorpe simply had to go with his gut. Where's my pipe? Annoyed with his own needs, Oglethorpe stood, grabbed his waistcoat, and summoned his coach—this time he would initiate talks with the Creeks. All my yesterdays, he thought, should add up this time.

*

"Benjamin, take the child please. I need to bathe a bit. I am feeling very warm. The milk is coming out profusely and my breasts hurt a great deal."

Crouched in pain, Perla removed her robe and sat in the warm tub. Poor Benjamin. Relegated to the barn so she could bathe in privacy. At least it was warm in the house. Perla lifted her arms and lathered her belly, all deflated now. The baby was a charm. His eagerness for life a reminder for Perla to embrace life too. The only problem was that she couldn't feel the eagerness. She could only feel remorse, regret, and tremendous guilt. She wondered what was wrong with her, why she couldn't smile like Mrs. Minis even though G-d had certainly repaid her loss with a beautiful son. The baby's name was Mordechai, or Mordy or Mordcha, whatever her mood suited her. But on more than one occasion she thought of the newborn as "Shefy," and her heart filled with tremendous sadness. If she touched Mordechai's tiny hand, she was immediately transported into the past. Only half of her was there with Mordechai. If she heard Mordechai cry at night, for an instant she thought perhaps it was Shefy after all who had simply aged in reverse from that fateful day. And to think I had relegated all that time to the nurse. I lost out in the end, she thought. This time, only I'll care for Mordechai. No matter what Nunez says. I won't take any chances this time, she ruminated. She stood, all clean and slightly refreshed.

*

Thomas Causton spit on the wooden planks. Corruption and gross negligence. Too bad that dead half-breed couldn't accuse Oglethorpe of the same. Ever since James arrived from London a new wave of authoritative decrees have been drafted—and all overseas! The ban on Negroes was now official, with a stamp of approval from the Trustees sitting in their pretty lawns. That Jew who lost his baby, beyond all doubt, spread rumors like the pestilence. The Jew tried to cover it up, of course. "Cordially invited to circumcision," the invitation read. And not long after Thomas's demotion. Over his corpse on St. Nicholas' day would he step foot in that dirty Jews' house—if only the man's horns would gore him first!

"Another draught of ale, Mary, is what I need, if you please," James said, rather lethargically.

Causton nearly regurgitated the half-decent ale. "Well, what do you know. The master general himself in all his regalia—and speaking to Mary again. *Should have figured he's the type to remain single and woo the women, married or not*," he thought. James recognized Causton's back; he hunched, revealing a wedge of skin on the back of his neck. James did not deem it necessary to address the man. During James's absence, his militia had nearly starved; his men had no ammunition at times and their families subsisted on charity—or worse. Poor judgment, his mother said, is an ill few can afford. Who was it that stated mothers know best?

Mary Musgrove had been helpful in the past, and James required her assistance with the Creeks down south of the Georgian border. He had not frequented her pub in a while, but he now had reason to do so. Their patrol of the border now a necessity begot by malfeasance: Causton had embezzled money, appropriated sums from the town, leaving James in yet another pecuniary quandary. Too many men defected, and now the official declaration of the Spanish throne threatened neighboring colonies.

140

A new issue arose, one that Oglethorpe had initially foreseen, but perhaps not to this extent. Slaves deserting English colonies were offered protection in Spanish Florida, and the governor, Don Manuel de Montiano guaranteed their safety. Countless Negroes have escaped from South Carolina towards Florida. Many by sea, a considerable amount by land. Legally, Georgia forbade Negroes from enslavement. But the poor slaves weren't safe in Georgia. Too many South Carolinians had "friends" in the Georgian territories. During James's absence, many Negroes managed to escape successfully, in part due to the lax attitude of Causton's charge, and in part due to the lack of men on the field. Either way, James was now pressed to secure the borders. But those who remained in James's militia did not suffice, not even by a thin margin. They weren't enough. The Creeks would have to fill the gap. Tomochichi was ill, but perhaps he could still arbitrate on behalf of Oglethorpe. Mary was the key to solving his debacle: she solved his language barrier once, and he was hoping for a repeat.

*

"Benjamin—why do you suppose James Oglethorpe arrived with all those soldiers?"

Perla lay in bed, nursing little Mordechai. She was wearing a pink lace cap that matched the tone of her skin quite nicely. She had bathed earlier, and her hair was still damp. Her lips were light pink, reflecting the color of her chemise, which was a light ballerina pink cotton lace. Two pearl earrings lightly shone in the room, outlining the luminescence of her iris. Benjamin looked up for a moment and rejoiced. He stared at his wife for a moment and wondered how she came to be so beautiful. Perla felt as though her husband had not heard her question. She repeated herself.

"Seven hundred to be exact, Perla. There are rumors England will declare war."

Perla gasped. The baby lost traction of her nipple. Perla assisted the baby, and he continued to suck.

"War!"

"Yes…."

141

"Over what?"

"Florida. The Spanish wish to spread North. Georgia is their first target."

"My gracious! *Riboneh shel olam!* Perhaps that is the reason all those Negroes are running off... my goodness, what are we to do?"

"The British won't allow the Spanish to overtake their colonies. I assure you, they will defend the country."

"Do you know when it shall be declared?"

"No, my love, but from what I've heard, Oglethorpe is amassing an army of Creeks and South Carolinians."

Perla breathed a sigh of relief. *Then he's not interested in Benjamin.*

"What about Georgians?" she asked.

"Too many Georgians are bitter. They don't trust him or forgive him for placing Causton in power."

"Oh yes. I heard of the charges."

Benjamin did not want Perla to worry over a war that had yet to be finalized.

"Darling, go to sleep. These matters shouldn't rob you of sleep."

Truth be told, Perla was too exhausted to worry about political situations. Feeling entirely spent, Perla had been eager to fall asleep. The baby took his last belly full of milk for the evening, and Perla drifted quite quickly into deep sleep. Benjamin peered at his wife and noticed her gaunt visage; no matter how much he tried to coax her, she refused to eat his poultry dishes. She claimed the scent of chicken caused either nausea or vertigo—it all depended on her mood.

The baby flourished, and it was mostly due to Perla's labor. To Benjamin's chagrin, Perla refused a nanny, and afraid of conjuring overwhelming emotions, Benjamin declined to speak to her on the matter. And now with war looming, he was fearful he wouldn't be reliable on the home front. But his fears were premature. So long as Oglethorpe had not specified the nature of the tension between Spain and England, Benjamin could dole out his worries one day at a time.

*

Caríssimos. We are all done for. Did you piss in public, little boy? Even the English will kill you if they see. No one loves the pork-eating filthy Jews. Even if you are no longer a secret Jew. Marranos. Don't think the English will treat you any better, bela. They all pray to the same Mariah. What will you do my beautiful boy? Will you listen to your dear grandmother? Your poor Gracia died, but she is too ashamed, you see. They do not recognize her in heaven. They say pork-eaters can't see the spheres. What will you do to help poor Gracia?

Nunez awoke, startled. His grandmother had not visited him in his dark dreams since that stormy night. *The same night we nearly drowned.* He recalled how he made his way to Benjamin Sheftall's compartment, finding the man's accommodations entirely unlivable. The poor woman's frightened expression, and the ensuing storm above deck. The Jews of Georgia have certainly come a long way since then. His poor wife never made it to the promised land. Gracia. Was she not in heaven? Did she not suffer enough in that dreadful prison in Lisbon, beneath the cathedral walls? She clamored, how did Shakespeare put it? "The live-long night." The night that would never end. All his jewels didn't suffice the blood-hounds of his town. And what a beauty compared to Georgia! Lisbon of white-walled castles, cathedrals from years past and edifices of awe: lost to him. And his beautiful palace, now a papal dormitory. But it had to be done. He had no choice. It was the perfect pretense. *A party for all the delighted guests aboard ships. The obscure night lending dark shadows the ability to escape undetected. Family aboard the ghost ship; escape to London. It had to be done. Beds undone. Lamps still lit. And a future yet unforeseen.*

Nunez removed his pocket watch, a remnant of his opulent past. He squinted in the darkness. He shifted his round, gold watch to catch a glimpse of light and read the time. He was late. Perla would need his attention tonight. The frost was long gone, but a chill filled the air. He grabbed his waistcoat and walked briskly towards Perla's modest home.

Perla gazed at Nunez's compassionate eyes. They were a dark Semitic color, with grayish bags beneath each tender glance. She recognized the concern in his expression.

He stepped aside, into the parlor, and whispered to Perla's husband, "I'm afraid she doesn't fare well, Benjamin. Her blood pressure is extremely low and she appears too wan. Liver. You must force her to eat as much as possible. She healed from the delivery, but not from the anxiety; do you comprehend my concerns?"

Benjamin held little Mordechai in his arms. The baby fidgeted a bit. Dr. Nunez placated the child in his arms. He rubbed his belly, the underside, with his palm. He was just as beautiful as little Shefy had been: bold eyes, pale skin, and luscious red lips. Nunez imagined Perla kissing each finger, each toe, and his lips. They were so tender and delightful. Dr. Nunez paced the room as Benjamin consoled his wife. The house was immaculate. Every pot had been neatly stored; the bins were empty; the pantry clear of crumbs; the floor was smooth; and no cooking oils or residues were evident near the hearth. Perla was extending herself. Benjamin reappeared and thanked Nunez for calming the baby.

"Hire a hand to keep the house tidy. Perla needs her strength."

Benjamin sighed. Perla's health was the reason he embarked on the arduous journey, and now he feared it was all an error of judgment on his part. While America certainly proved an abundant land, his wife's delicate disposition did not necessarily fare better. Back in Prussia, his dear mother could have helped Perla—instead of a strange woman. Benjamin was certain that perhaps a family member would have been more vigilant with little Shefy. Perhaps a rotation of caretakers would have been best. Perla's mother, her siblings, his mother... a whole town. The *shtetl...* But now, that did not matter much.

Dr. Nunez left, after a hearty handshake, and Benjamin was left alone, standing in his parlor with little Mordechai fast asleep.

*

James spoke brusquely, "I need extra assistance, Benjamin, and I'm short of hands. I'm aware of the precarious situation at home, but I beseech you to consider my request. It's a matter of days. I'm certain of it now."

Benjamin nodded his head. He felt beholden to Oglethorpe. After all, James had deeded land to Jews—a rare sign of mutual respect. Benjamin recalled his first impression of James. Benjamin believed the British soldier was a pampered man who had never dealt with dilemmas or devastation. Measuring a man by adversity, Benjamin had little regard for those who never met with misfortune. But James had proven himself a strong man indeed; however, at the same time, Benjamin had yet to see James's mettle during battle. It would be an interesting prospect, to imagine James in battle. Any British man, who cares for propriety, is a spectacle in battle, Benjamin mused. Perla didn't need to know of this... James spoke in confidence.

Benjamin shook James's hand.

James's grin was only *slightly* detectable.

"Then it's settled."

*

Causton wondered what detained Captain Richard Williamson. Mary eyed Causton with her usual suspicion. She disliked the man simply for trying to destroy James. Of all the gentlemen with whom she had contact, it was James who had never tried to stir an immoral act. Causton was beyond reproach. Poor Florence had been *her* recommendation. And now James would not take another girl. It wasn't out of loyalty, Mary believed, but out of experience gained by harsh realities. Florence would tell her about James's darker side: his melancholy and brooding tendency. Florence swore he whispered some strange woman's name in his sleep. She rummaged through his things, without finding so much as a hairpin. At one point, Mary believed he liked the Jewess Mariah, the woman with bold eyes and dark hair. But she had been less than a passing fancy. Instead, James remained cocooned in his home, busy with taking charge of affairs. Florence had been a diversion. Although Florence believed, whole-heartedly, that James could have been hers were he not smitten with an image or a fancy of another woman. *But this Causton. Why does he keep coming to my pub, she wondered. He is heartily disliked by his own townspeople. I wish he would go to Hale's place. At least there he will find like-minded company*, Mary thought.

Richard finally walked down the planks of stairs, holding his waistcoat behind his back. A woman with tousled hair waved goodbye and squealed up the stairs to her room. Mary handed Richard a bottle of his favorite London-brewed ale with two large glasses. Musgrove's place proves beneficial in subverting James in more than one way, Causton thought. Now all this place needs is a Negro to tidy the place and James will surely collapse! This Richard Williamson, Causton carefully measured, is a thorn in James's royal rear, a far more irritating one than I had ever been. Causton stood, shook Richard's hand, and got to business.

*

Perla lay on her back, contemplating the past five years. Since her marriage to Benjamin, she had known many joys, but her sorrows had been far more overwhelming.

Her family. She had forgotten the scent of her mother's lemon verbena. Her mother could not tolerate any other perfume. Lemon Verbena. Who knows when she is likely to be seen again?

Her brother. He married not long ago, and her little sister was now of marriageable age. Perhaps she too will learn of the harsh ways of women. Perhaps God will be kinder to her.

Her father. He fell ill to tuberculosis but had recovered after a long and debilitating illness.

The family's business shattered, and now her mother was forced to work as a seamstress for one of the wealthier Frankfurt families. Benjamin sent some money now and then to her parents, but it was a source of shame for her father to accept money from his son-in-law.

And that terrible boat ride that ended in near starvation? Who could forget that terrible boat? The stench? The fetid smell of half-rotted flesh amidst the nauseating rocking? She believed she would never be sane again.

Her pregnancies weighed her down, the deliveries a form of indescribable torture. Just the thought of the pain sent shivers of terror down her delicate frame. She began to cry.

Shefy. Convulsing. Shefy. Little, poor, beautiful boy. My Shefy.

146

Never to be seen again, buried before his time.

Barely learned to run. Could hardly speak. Little boy. A babe.

And what if Mordechai should die too? And what if the child were to contract some terrible disease?

What would be then? My life shall be plunged into an abyss, an abysmal grave.

She continued to weep, over and over, imagining poor Shefy crying in his underground cave, and then imagining a lifeless Mordechai, choking, his eyes rolling, his lungs gasping for air.

And then she cried more, envisioning the pain of more and more loss.

Perla fell asleep and awoke with a terrible cough. Shivering, she warmed a pot of water. I need some tea, she thought. Tea always helps, her mother taught her. For fever, for chills, for heartache. Tea.

Mordechai began shifting in his little bassinet, the same cradle James had bought for little Shefy. She opened the cupboard, poured some honey into a wooden bowl, placed the boiling water into it, and began sipping slowly. She tasted the honey and recalled *Rosh Hashanah*. A year full of hope. Of blessing. Of promise.

"May we be full of *mitzvot* like the pomegranate. May we merit good deeds." Honey.

Mordechai's whimpers became more insistent. Perla deliberately walked to the crib, but before she could lift the child, she saw yellow stars darting around in magical swirls, first to her left, then to the center, and then all went mysteriously black.

LOVE AMONG THE RUINS

PERLA SHEFTALL. ANOTHER VICTORY FOR dusty death, James thought. Poor Benjamin and his cemetery. Two occupants in less than a year. James recalled Perla's frightened expression when they first met, aboard the *William and Sarah* back in '73. She had the fear of God in her eyes. He felt like a brute when he considered the source of her fears. She had been utterly surprised when he handed her the fine lavender soap as a gift. She averted his gaze, in modesty. Poor woman. Perhaps she was happier with her first son. She collapsed in the middle of the night, near her infant son's crib. Some say she was tormented by the child's screams; the two infants had an eerie similarity about them. Particularly the voice. Others say she was too weak for the Americas, which required a hardy body and a sturdy mind. Now Benjamin had an orphan to care for, his son Mordechai.

"*Itgadal v'itkadash shmeh rabah....*" Benjamin uttered the *Kaddish*. James listened in silence to the Aramaic words. He stared at his boots. He echoed "Amen" with the Jews. Dr. Nunez held Benjamin throughout the ceremony. A single white rose adorned her casket. Susan Hale placed it there. The Jews placed stones by her casket as they left, one by one. Benjamin eulogized his own wife, wailing between half-English half-Yiddish phrases. *Eyshes chayil. Davened* with *kavana. Tzneyoos. Ahavas haTorah.* Her gravestone was marked with Hebrew words. Boltzius attended, honoring his friend. The pastor had been saddened by Benjamin's loss. And far off in the distance, James swore he caught sight of John Hale, whom some have said had repented for his foul ways. Mrs. Minis helped the quorum of Jews take care of the corpse the previous night, purifying Perla for her burial. Mrs. Minis swore Perla's body was pristine like a virgin, pure in death as in life. Few had seen her dipping naked in the ocean on more than one occasion. It seems that was a purification process the Jews adhered to as well. James understood little of the Jews' custom, but he respected their adherence to the Law. They spoke of the Jews by the Musgroves, commenting on the peculiar behavior of the Jewish folk, the ones who kept strict dietary laws, ritual cleansing laws, and *shechitah*— the slaughtering rites. Perla had adhered very carefully to the *Shabbos*: she was never seen carrying a single book, fan, or carry-all during the day of rest. What did King Solomon state? What did Bolzius say? "Greater than a rare pearl is the worth of a valorous woman." Yes. How rare indeed are the precious women of our lives. Some men only seem to possess these women in passing, and some others only view them from afar.

Benjamin tore his blouse, and began mourning in earnest. His tears fell to the ground, watering the fresh overturned earth. Susan was crying too, mourning for the mother who lost a son. Tomochichi sent his nephew to respect the dead. He bowed his head in recognition of their loss. It seemed the entire town felt sorry for the Jew. Men from the militia stood ramrod straight, with muskets in hand. They rather felt sorry for the wandering Jew who seemed to suffer as Job. Benjamin's sobs increased as the Portuguese Jews gathered round him. He repeated Perla's name. Perla. Perla. Why, my love? Why? Feeling enormously guilty, Benjamin crouched down, touching the casket with his hands, somewhat shaking it. Why? I tried. God knows I tried. And then all this Yiddish. *Riboneh shel Olam.* His side locks seemed longer, as they fell and covered his face. He placed his hands over his face, allowing the mucus to stream free. Dr. Nunez offered a handkerchief, and had to wipe Benjamin's face.

Slowly, the townspeople began to leave, barely capable of witnessing the poor man's pain; it reminded them of their own loss. Many of the Georgians had buried their loved ones during the dark plague in that fateful Yellow Fever of 1733. Many were buried in a mass grave. Some were burned, and the ashes of their dead ones fortified the earth of Georgia. Perhaps a peach was laden with the nutrients of their dead. It was hard to know. But it was a part of their history many had decided to bury. Benjamin's raw display of emotion was not for the faint-hearted. Susan gathered little Mordechai in her arms and made her way to Sheftall's home. Mrs. Minis prepared the meal of lentil and eggs—to symbolize the circle of life: from dust thou art made and to dust thou shalt return. Mrs. Minis warmed the soup and set the table. A number of Jews would gather by Benjamin for the next seven days; reciting psalms, *davening*, praying, and comforting he who seemed inconsolable.

Benjamin would have to find a suitable wife, Mrs. Minis realized. But it was too early to broach the subject. Perhaps in a year or two she will try to maneuver a *shidduch* for the poor man. In the meantime, he must be able to grieve and come to realize he must find a second wife all on his own. And that poor child? She will help raise him for now.

*

Oglethorpe frowned. "You know I wish to drive Montiano into the Atlantic, just as much as you, but—we can't rush into war. England must declare it."

William Bull rolled his eyes in frustration. The lieutenant governor of South Carolina didn't understand why his good friend bothered with scruples and protocol. Since 1733, the two had been mutual allies, friends, and soon comrades in arms. But James was adamant: we must wait for orders to attack Florida. No surprises. No guerilla tactics. Bull didn't share James's sentiments or his moral regard for counter-intuitive rules of engagement.

"Negroes are escaping as we speak, James. These desertions are crippling our economy."

Oglethorpe sighed heavily. Depending on Negroes was an error of all those South Carolinians farmers. Relying on slave labor—and what of it? Now that the Negroes found a bastion in Florida, the farmers have been raging mad. Who will till the earth?

Who in bloody Mary's name will plant and sow? There were ugly rumors farmers caught up with "their hands" and brutalized them. The women fared just as bad: rape, molestation, and unwanted babies bred from rancor. The situation could only worsen once war was declared. Mutiny may occur from within the ranks—Negroes were likely to join forces with the Spaniards—Bull's greatest fear, though as of yet unmentioned or perhaps not entirely realized.

James stood. "Bull, I've tightened the border as much as possible. My men have returned droves of Negroes in the past weeks. There's nothing more I can do."

William Bull, with his searing eyes and Roman profile, turned askance and stood face to face with James.

"My planters and farmers, even my women, want blood James. They crave it. That's all they're clamoring for. And I believe they won't discriminate!"

"Bull. You'll have to—"

William Bull left James's parlor for the first time since 1733 dejected and disappointed. Deeply so. His friend's inability to break certain rules of conduct, just every now and then, to secure his fellow countrymen's financial security, was a deficiency Bull could barely stand to contemplate.

*

James needed more hands. This wasn't going to do. Homesick English warriors who hadn't seen battle in months kvetched their tedious hours away. Mary's women placed notices throughout town for men in arms, but few signed up. His militia dwindled since Causton's abuses. What in heaven's name was he to do? How could he call Benjamin Sheftall after his near collapse? James was no longer sure Benjamin was the best man for the job. It was too early. The man was still mourning, and war was imminent. James knew it. He was awaiting orders from London at any day. But his army was a pathetic amalgamation of desperate men, some Creeks who were far better with their tomahawks than with the muskets, who preferred bows and arrows for Christ sake. And those South Carolinians who spoke of Negro blood just as much as Spaniard blood, sickening James to the core. This was all a bloody mess. If

Georgia fell, the rest of the colonies would be next. The Spanish were eager for the Americas.

But the Jews. The Portuguese Jews. *They* were eager to fend off the Spaniards. Blood shall have blood. Still bitter and utterly fearful of the Inquisitors, the Portuguese Jews signed up immediately. Dr. Nunez. His sons. De Lyon. Minis. And the others. Even that Silva signed up. Many of the Jews also spoke Ladino, quite similar to the Spanish of the Floridians. The problem was the Negroes. They escaped by sea with precious information. The Spaniards couldn't care a pin's fee for their freedom. They just knew it would weaken the American colonies. Damn them. What was James to do? Mary Musgrove offered to become a spy. She swore her Creek men could help carry her across the border. She was dark enough to pass for a Spaniard and white enough to escape detection too. James knew Bull was right. But he had to await the orders. But what if the declaration came too late and the Spanish jumped the gun? What then? He would lose men before the battle was begun. No. That couldn't happen. Perhaps Bull was onto something. Forty-eight hours and then the battle would begin. With his own men serving as informants. And now, he had to speak to his men.

Oglethorpe searched his closet for the red waistcoat his father had bequeathed him. It was a family heirloom. Attached to the lapel were signs of valor in battle, which all the men of his family proudly earned fighting for the great English throne. The Spanish were a formidable force, but waning in power. Still, war was war, and the thrill of battle surged through his blood. James was bred for war. His mother perhaps sadly noted she had sacrificed her family for England, but she was surely just as proud as any proper English mother. The Spaniards were a menace. From the start of his campaign in Georgia, he had to battle those pests. Oglethorpe donned the waistcoat, and found a matching red hat. The Redcoats. Yes. Just the uniform instilled fear in the eyes of their enemies. James found his wig, dusted it with some powder, and placed it neatly on his head. James stared at his image in the glass mirror and saw a replica of his dead father. The eyes, large and expressive, and the long, aristocratic nose made an impression. Yes.

James practiced his salute and began singing, "Praise to the King, our great George. And to Mother Queen, Anne! We march to thy flag, to honor thee!"

He continued to hum as he mounted his horse, Fleance. Banquo's son in *Macbeth*, the son who managed to escape death and beget a throng of kings. Very fitting, James thought. To call a horse by the name of a Shakespearean character who barely speaks but who symbolizes continuity and victory.

James commanded the combined forces of Georgia and South Carolina, but many of the South Carolinians were utterly offended by being *subservient* to a Georgian. James had yet to fully grasp their reluctance to follow orders. His own British soldiers were homesick and utterly filthy. The Indians were undisciplined and preferred their own methods. Regardless, James rode hurriedly through the marshland and up the hill towards the main fortification, Saint Andrew. He stopped at the main gate, and the men stood at attention. James recognized John Hale. Hale bowed his head, and James slightly gestured as well. James had never seen many of the men, particularly the South Carolinians. Most were smoking or drinking; some were cleaning their muskets. They all remained quiet as James spoke. He stood on a slight hill, by a slender but sturdy birch. His elegant waistcoat framed James's figure, and the metals by the upper chest blinded some of the men. James removed his hat, placed his long spear comfortably in its holster, and began:

"Soldiers of the Crown. We stand today in a pivotal moment in history. America is in its infancy and must fight for her survival! The Spanish hope to spread North. The serpents down below wish to begin their poisonous route in Georgia. But we won't allow them! We will stop them!"

James was disappointed. The men had not caught on to the fury in his voice. A haggard soldier in the middle of the crowd made a motion to speak.

"The General is surely aware that his loyal soldiers are nearly starving. We receive no wages, sir, and we cannot continue to survive, let alone fight, without adequate provisions."

James had not anticipated their dissatisfaction. A rumble of approval ensued from many of the bystanders. Some thumped their muskets in agreement, some hollered, and others mumbled curses. Oglethorpe was agitated. *Don't show what the heart doth know.*

The men gathered round, edging in closer and closer. The men began to spread out behind him, cornering him. James raised his hand. Silence.

"I am indeed sorry and I sympathize with you. I have advanced a large sum of my personal estate to finance our military campaign. Your wages shall be paid in due time. You shall receive what you deserve—and most importantly, if you fight, you will preserve your right to return to your homes! What good is it if you give up all you have *now* to lose it *later*? The Spanish will be at our throats, and if we don't gather strength and—"

A shot filled the void. The slender birch tree shook. Three birds flapped their wings. James fell to the ground. His head hit the earth, and he touched his arm. *It's as though a knife is being thrust into my arm over and over.* James stared at his white-gloved hands. Blood.

All of a sudden James replayed a scene he had witnessed the previous week. Mary's. In a whirlwind of discovery, it all dawned on him.

Causton. Sitting by the bar. Spitting on the planks. The gallant Richard Williamson, marching down the stairs with a wry expression. The brutal and power-hungry gather to dine and to plot. The scheming Judases! Should have known that Causton would return to bite. In the guise of another snake!

Oglethorpe realized he had not been severely injured. Enraged, he tried to find that bastard Williamson, who should be stationed at Frederica but with God's certainty he was sure he would be in Fort Saint Andrew. Another bullet whizzed by him, barely grazing him. Several soldiers were reaching for their guns, but the look in James's eyes shook them. Blood spurted past Oglethorpe's head again, as the bullet struck James's shoulder. *There!* Before Williamson could fire another shot, Oglethorpe pounced on him like a starving piranha. Oglethorpe kicked Williamson in the shins, then in the groin, wrestled the musket away from him and knocked Williamson to the ground. Placing his bloody forearm to Williamson's throat, James hollered, with spittle flying in the air, glancing upward, "Where are you, Causton!? You bastard! You dung-eating coward! Come here and face me like a man!"

Hale saw Causton darting for his horse, Firebird. As though a gale of Prometheus had infused him, John Hale scampered after the scum, Causton. Causton tried to fire at Hale, but couldn't gather enough precision. Swiftly, Hale punched Causton to the ground, grinding Causton's face in a pile of dirt and fresh urine. "Eat that, you swine."

Men gathered round James, helping him up and tying Williamson down, by the birch tree, together with Causton, who looked like a pig in a sty. *Filthy piece of swine*. Hale thought.

James held his arm, stooping a bit, but still full of vigor.

"This failed attempt at mutiny is over. You. Stand them up together."

Oglethorpe walked round Williamson and Causton, marching slowly, deliberating. Silence.

"You men are guilty of treason."

He then turned to the crowd of soldiers and pointed in each direction, with nostrils flaring. His eyes bulged. *Great God*, Hale thought. *I have never seen him like this.*

"And each and every one of you who failed to come to my defense, as far as I am concerned, you are too!"

The men lowered their heads. Seems James was onto something. Hale wondered how he had not caught wind of the mutiny.

"Your faces betray you!"

There was no fight left in a single soldier. Ashamed and utterly shaken by Oglethorpe, the men began to fear for their lives. James knew he could not afford to dismiss them all.

The benevolent tyrant is loved far more than the cruel diplomat.

"All soldiers who reaffirm loyalty to his Majesty King George and to his cause shall be pardoned. All those who fail to comply with my demands shall face discharge without compensation. Williamson and Causton shall await their fate in prison. Let London decide with you. And you, John Hale. I now place you as first lieutenant of Fort Frederica in place of Williamson. Dismissed!"

*

Benjamin stared at his son. Who would watch him as he joined the men? Mrs. Minis. She was his only resort. Benjamin couldn't sit in his house while his friends risked their very lives. It had to be done. The mourning period would soon end, and a life without a woman would ensue. But there was no future for him or his son if those dreadful Spaniards took over Georgia. Then his entire plan, of moving to the New World, would truly have been in vain. A waste, and perhaps he would be in far greater jeopardy with the Inquisition mongrels in control of Georgian territory. He owed it to Mordechai and to any future child, if he would merit one. But to whom did he bear responsibility today? Right now—it was his poor motherless son that was his greatest concern. He could barely think of it, but he knew his son could not remain without the warmth of a woman for all his life. Staring at his own two hands, Benjamin swore to aid his son first, and then to take care of larger matters.

*

Dr. Nunez rolled his sleeves and inserted a cauterized needle deep into James's fascia: the bullet did not penetrate deeply. He was a fortunate fellow, Nunez thought. James winced. Hale held his right arm as Nunez extracted the bullet. The tweezers filled with blood revolted Hale. A thud on the door.

"Who is it?" James asked, sweating onto his open blouse.

"Bull!"

James glanced at his friend and witnessed genuine concern. Too bad Bull had not been there. He would have aided in my defense, surely, James thought.

"James! My apologies. I am terribly sorry. This is a wretched business. But we must speak. The Yamassee! They are carrying British skulls by the barrels! You just won't believe it! You must check your ranks for traitors!"

156

"Only the Creeks, Bull, joined our ranks. For God's sake, just look at *me*. You know who did this?"

"The yellows?"

"No, Bull. Causton. And Williamson. The whites. If you prefer color precision."

Bull accepted the rebuke. But his main cause for visiting James was not entirely for that purpose alone.

"James. We *must* invade Florida! This is provocation!"

James nodded his head.

"We will respond. Gather my men. Tomorrow before dawn we will begin our attack."

*

How am I to manage in this wildness that is Savannah without a helpmate? Mordechai had grown from a suckling infant to a toddler with endless spurts of energy. Mrs. Minis meant well, but how much longer can he rely on the loving kindness of others? The war effort had not begun in full earnest, not just yet, but the constant calls to the border weighed heavily on Benjamin. The baby cried for many hours, "mama... mama... mama." Benjamin could barely withstand the pain of a double loss. Goat's milk sufficed, but the child needed plenty of other nutritional meals. Cooking had been a pastime, but now it became a vocation. He had to feed the child, as he fed his hens and other livestock. Gathering water from the well was arduous once Mordechai became too heavy for the sack. Sometimes, Benjamin left Mordechai asleep in his basinet while he ran to fetch some clean water. Cleaning the pots and the modest home was a task he didn't wish on the devil's mother. The baby's clothing had to be laundered every day. And how was he to earn a living? Not even a year after Perla's death, and Benjamin felt as though he were drowning. *But where are all the eligible Jewish women? Certainly none here in Savannah as far as I can see.* Benjamin realized he would have to write a brief column in the papers, both in Georgia and Pennsylvania where Jews resided. Perhaps his luck will be in a different colony, he thought. He quickly jotted down his proposal on a piece of fine parchment:

157

Seeking Jewish woman who is willing to become a helpmate
to a widower of two-year-old child.
Please respond.

Benjamin Sheftall
Savannah, Georgia

Benjamin had been quite patient. Between running the
minyan in his quarters and administering to the child, he had
nearly forgotten about the advertisement in the paper. Mrs. Minis
offered to arrange a *shidduch* previously, but he was reluctant to
ask for more help from the woman. Of course she had been most
salutary, there was no doubt. But on these matters, Benjamin
wished to resort to his own devices. Eventually, a letter arrived
from Pennsylvania, in a lucid hand:

Dear Mr. Benjamin Sheftall,

I am responding to an advertisement in the community
paper, here in Pennsylvania. As you well know, Jewish
men are exceedingly hard to meet in America. My name
is Hannah Solomons, and while I am not entirely at ease
writing this letter (indeed, it took me some months to do
so), I am responding in the hopes that you may express an
interest in perhaps visiting my home in Pennsylvania. While
it is customary for a *shadchan* to see to these matters, I am
afraid in our time we must be able to become independent
of the ways of the *shtetl* and manage entirely on our own
resources and considerable wit.

Signed,
Hannah Solomons

Well! Thought Benjamin. Truly this woman is interesting. To
think that months must go by before she decided to pick up her
pen? No matter. From the looks of it, she is probably traditional, if
not Orthodox. Mention of the *shtetl* is certainly evidence of that,
he assumed. Hannah seemed interesting, a far better cry than the

haggard Mrs. Cohen who, five years his senior, seemed too tired to care for a child.... But a trip? Benjamin realized the trip would take a significant effort on his part. He was not willing to do so before he asked this woman some pertinent questions:

Dear Hannah Solomons,

I am very pleased to learn that you decided to correspond, despite the initial consternation, which is customary in our modest Jewish women. However, I noticed you had not revealed too many bits of information about your age and other important matters. Allow me to relate a bit about myself first, to ease your way undoubtedly to do quite the same:

I am a widower for the past year and a half now. My wife, may she rest in peace, passed away in the year 1736. My son was not a year old at the time. Perla's death was an immeasurable blow. I had not seen it forthcoming, and, indeed, I had been overwhelmed by my first-born's death at the time, Sheftall Sheftall, may he rest in peace. My wife and I married in Prussia but eventually made our way to Georgia hoping for a better life in the American continent. God has blessed me with a second child, Mordechai Sheftall, may he live a long and prosperous life, and a warm home in Savannah, where I reside. The generous governor of this town, James Oglethorpe, deeded land to me and to others upon our arrival in the year 1733. My home is warm, but in need of a woman's guidance and touch.

I work many long hours in the barn and yard, as well as in Oglethorpe's militia. Despite the heavy burden of my lot, I have been managing to care for my son. I would like to continue building a future for my child, but without a proper helpmate, I don't see how that will be possible. Have you also been previously married? Do you have children of your own?

I am looking forward to hearing from you, Hannah. And please let me know when, if you please, will be a proper time for a visit.

Signed,
Benjamin Sheftall

Hannah Solomons reached for a pen. She felt immensely curious about this man, Benjamin Sheftall. He had accused her of withholding information, but he had *not* revealed his age or any detail regarding his exact income or level of religious observance! Surely, such details were exceedingly important. Doesn't he want his child to be raised by a mother who knows the *kashrus* laws? Originally from Holland, Hannah spoke a bit of Yiddish, a considerable amount of English thanks to her mother's guidance, and Dutch. From her grandparents, Hannah spoke Ladino as well, as her family originated from the Sephardic countries of Portugal and Spain. If Sheftall was an Ashkenazi, he certainly seemed to keep that to himself. But how picky could she be? She *was* thirty-nine years of age! When would she bear a child? Goodness knows she escaped Holland from all the rumors circulating about and all the *ineligible* men. Most of the men in her town weren't interested in her anyway. Past her prime by more than a decade, perhaps even two if she were truly honest with herself, Hannah had become a woman of desperate measures. How she loathed to think of herself as the spinster she had sworn she would never become! Now, her beauty long consumed by the withering effects of time, Hannah knew romantic notions were no longer a consideration. Alone in America, a governess to a well-to-do Jewish family in Pennsylvania, Hannah had nearly given up hope of having a life of her own, a home and husband. Perhaps she should respond to this man. How bad could he be? Perhaps he was younger than she! Wouldn't *that* be charming, she thought.

Dear Benjamin Sheftall:

I would be very glad to meet your acquaintance at any time. I reside in Pennsylvania and do not intend to move back to my hometown in Holland. I have remained unattached up until this day. I see to the education of my sponsor family's children. I am also an expert seamstress. I enjoy cooking *Shabbos* meals, and I am looking forward to meeting you soon,

Hannah

Benjamin opened the letter and read Hannah's response with a mixture of excitement and aggravation. How old is she? So she is an observant woman. She cooks for *Shabbos*, another indication. But why is a woman of her age still single? What defect does she possess that she is unwilling to reveal? Why did she immigrate to America? How exasperating! So be it. I will surprise this woman with a brief visit in the upcoming week, he gleefully thought.

*

Hannah stood by her boudoir, debating between a lace collar and a shawl. Dinners by the Abrams were formal. The children wore their fine clothing, and Mrs. Abrams spent an hour in her powder room before she deigned climb down the oak staircase. Hannah enjoyed her life in America. She could even bear the winter, which the Spanish-Portuguese Jews bitterly complained of. Even the children were sweet, but she longed for more. Always the late bloomer, it had taken the death of both her mother and father to finally move away from home. Notices were placed in the synagogue promising a new life in America, for women and men who sought an atmosphere of independence. Hannah felt as though Holland held too many memories and lost opportunities. Mr. Shlomo, who had expressed an interest in her hand when she was but sixteen, was now a grandfather. Her best friends, Betty and Florence, mothers to a breed of children, and all the others who had managed to touch her life and then disappear, lived fruitful lives. The town spinster, every man stared at her with pity. The women nearly gave up on finding her a suitable mate, and the town *shadchan* long stopped posting letters to France, England, or Poland for prospective husbands. No one was interested in an old maid. Her mother warned her. "Too picky and you'll end up with nothing! What do you think? Prince Charming is real? There's a reason why it's called *fairy* tales! Open your eyes. Falling in love is for the heroes of a novel. Put those books down and look *around* you. Choose wisely—but choose! *Nu!* How much longer do you want your poor father to wait? Look at your sisters! So their husbands aren't Greek models, but they are *good* men.

Menchen. They all know how to *shecht*—but they still skin the chickens! Eh? Is that considered love in those fancy books of yours? Is that why you know how to read Dutch? For this sake? Is that why I taught you proper languages? So you should languish in literature all day? Go to the market. Maybe Shlomo's brother will be there and have pity on you. Go. *Nu?*" When a romance had begun to sprout between the Baker, a gentile Dutch with kind eyes, and Hannah, the town nearly exploded with vicious gossip. None of it was true. But without a mother and a father to return to in the evening, wild tales emerged. The looks in the *shul* were tantamount to the guillotine. Poor Paul. He had sworn to convert to Judaism. But Hannah never really wanted him. She was only flattered that a man would express an interest in her. It was so different from the meetings in her father's parlor. The dim light in the parlor of her home barely allowed the evening sun to warm her features. Men of all colors, somehow all Jewish and in want of a wife, would sit and wait. They were forbidden to touch, but that was not a problem at all. Both her parents would sit nearby and smile, encouraging her to see the virtues of the fabulous *bachurim.* Although she was certain they merited her parents' regard, she could not imagine herself romantically involved with any one of her suitors. Before her mother had the chance to persuade her otherwise, the prospective husbands would lose patience or interest, and move along their paths to their soul mates. Hannah settled on the lace, and pinned the collar to her long dress, which slightly grazed the floor.

The maidservant, Agnes, knocked on her door.

"A gentleman caller is asking by your name, Hannah. He says you're expecting him. Shall I call him into the antechamber?"

Hannah seemed a bit dazed. She hadn't expected any visitors at this hour. "Yes. Let him in. And please set some tea for him, Agnes. It is quite cold out still, even now. And please make sure the missus knows about this visitor. You know how she is about supper." Agnes nodded and left Hannah.

Hannah stared at herself in the glass mirror. She sighed. Even though she had never undergone the brutal changes of pregnancy, she no longer had the elongated figure of her youth. Granted she was still slim, but not the same. She had always thought that if she never bore a child then she would remain the same, but womanhood is a mystery and childbirth only one element in its many guises. She slowly climbed down the stairs, holding onto the railing with her delicate hand, covered with a crocheted glove she had bought in Amsterdam. The aroma of beef stew filled the home, and she felt her stomach rumble. What an embarrassing noise, she thought. I better eat soon. She deliberately walked to the guest parlor, and saw a man with a walking stick and long waistcoat sitting, ankles crossed. His hat was on the table, and his arm on the edge of the damask couch.

When he saw Hannah, he immediately stood, placed the hat on his head, and said, "Benjamin Sheftall." He slightly bowed, and smiled. "You are quite lovely. A fact you neglected to mention in all your correspondence!"

Taken aback by his comfortable manner, Hannah couldn't help but feel a smile crawl up her lip.

"It is not for me to judge. But I will take your word for it!"

Benjamin rather liked Hannah's wit. He knew she was an intelligent woman from her response. Her eyes were dark and large. Her skin was light, with a tinge of an olive tone. It was clear she had Spanish-Portuguese blood running through her veins. Her hair had more brown that auburn, a mark of mixed heritage. Few creases marked her face, but it was clear she was no longer a youth. But Benjamin wasn't particularly interested in a young girl. Perla was his young love. He had known Perla from his youth, and her memory was forever frozen, as though a snapshot of the past remained ingrained in his imagination. Hannah was different. She had boldness, a fierceness that Perla lacked.

"I take it you enjoyed your trip to Pennsylvania? We've seen too many Georgians in this part of town, unfortunately."

"Yes. I gather you've heard of our terrible luck with the neighbors down south."

"The Spanish can't concede to a British America. Haven't they learned from the Armada? Let them leave peacefully before the British make fools of them all!"

Benjamin was rather shocked to learn Hannah had such strong political opinions. Usually, he spoke of such matters with his men. He was fascinated. She seemed to know a bit about history as well.

"How do you enjoy your employment as a governess?"

Hannah smiled and looked at her hands.

"Let us say the nights are a true pleasure."

Benjamin laughed, but felt a bit worried. Was she disinclined to like children?

Hannah noticed Benjamin seemed a bit at unease.

"Don't fret, Mr. Sheftall. I love the children dearly. But I must be to them more than just a governess, if you understand my meaning."

Benjamin stood once more, as Mrs. Abrams walked in. She appeared stern, but kind.

Hannah introduced him, and smiled at Mrs. Abrams.

"Would you like to join us for supper, Mr. Sheftall?"

Benjamin was delighted. He had been hungry and could not find kosher meals on his way.

"You need not worry, Mr. Sheftall," Hannah said, nearly taking his arm, "This house eats strictly kosher food! Sephardic style."

Benjamin smiled. So Hannah knew Sephardim are more stringent when it comes to certain laws.

Benjamin felt a warm sensation, as though angels in heaven were guiding him into the warm home of Hannah Solomons.

"Yes, of course. I hope you enjoy *gefilte* fish or *kichel*?" Benjamin joked.

Mrs. Abrams smiled, "By us, a meal without rice is not a meal at all."

RETREATS AND DEFEATS

THE WAR HAD BEGUN, OFFICIALLY, in September 1739. (Skirmishes existed previously.) James had gathered men and strength to meet the challenges of the upcoming years.

James sat upright, lifting his sorry head. He decided to chronicle his every thought. He opened to the last page:

"The year of 1739 chronicles a year of defeats. Those bastardly Yamassee skinned scores of our men instigating the invasion of Florida of the same year. We began an advance in the thickest hour of the night quite successfully at first. But that damned Don Manuel trained his men well, and we were forced to retreat to Georgia. Lost over twenty men on that first assault. Hale was wounded, but recovered. Sheftall temporarily took position of first lieutenant. Civilian population of Georgia diminished, a paltry remnant of better days. Five hundred inhabitants, including women and children. Thankfully, the two hundred men and boys who are capable of bearing arms have no intention of surrendering to the bloody Spaniards. Parliament is brutally unsympathetic, ignoring entreaties for monies and men. South Carolina is nothing more than a stock of greedy men, full of empty promises. The fools up north do not sense their own jeopardy. Tomochichi died one month after declaration of war. Tooanabey joined militia, to honor his uncle. He proves an asset, being entirely fluent in the Yamassee dialect. Instrumental in communications with Creeks and reconnaissance. For five weeks my men held onto Montiano's greatest strongholds, St. Augustine and Castillo de San Marcos. But that blasted yellow fever ravaged my men. The Spaniards and their damned cannons prevented any advance on further Spanish soil. My South Carolinian soldiers began to complain. The Portuguese Jews tried to remain steadfast, but they worried for their families back home. On the fifth week, I myself contracted the blasted disease. Wrecked by my malady, I was attacked with yet another ailment: my disorderly men. I was accused of many failings—chief among them my lack of leadership and courage in the face of my enemies. I had no choice in the matter—we withdrew to Georgia where we are now encamped. Dr. Nunez was truly instrumental in salvaging my men, as well as myself, from desperation. I did not lose as many men as prophesied. Again, the man proved a godsend."

James stretched, placing his quill by the journal. He lit a cigar and smoked as he paced across the room. The yellow fever weakened his system, but his desire to fortify and protect his colony took precedence over any physical debility.

The young orphaned child must fight, James repeated. There is no room for frailty. James prayed the time was not out of joint for the young colony.

*

1742: Georgia

James took up his pen:

"It has been three long years of near devastation for Georgia. For three years my men, no more than nine hundred, have manned the forts of St. Andrew and Fort William. Both forts are located on Cumberland Island. Surrounded by sea, yet secured by the intricate landscape. It is the first line of defense against the Spanish invasion. The main garrison is still located, thankfully, on St. Simons Island, home to Fort St. Simons *and* Fort Frederica. Our lines are buttressed by local Highlander militiamen and trusted Creek warriors eager to kill the swine down south. That bastard D. Manuel d. Montiano, may he reel in his own blood, has more than two thousand soldiers. His fellow fiend in Cuba (a most malicious fellow in my estimation)—the Governor-General Juan Francisco de Guemes—delivered over thirteen hundred armed men with the exact stipulation that Montiano conquer the Carolinas once Georgia is done for. The bastard responded, 'I require neither persuasion nor encouragement.' Georgia is in utter decline as I write. Many women and children have retreated for safer colonies—north of Georgia, including the Carolinas and even farther north. The days are long, the heat nearly unbearable. This date in early July is truly one of the warmest yet. The city lies dormant, its inhabitants too weary to take up muskets and barrels of gunpowder. My coffers are nearly spent, and the British throne is sending direct orders to hold the lines with minimum expense. My hair has no longer a strand of dark, burnished brown. Indeed, white curls of wigs are no longer necessary. Georgia may never see her youthful years blossom into robustness. I fear Montiano will rupture the fortifications, and my men have yet to see a battle of true blood."

James cracked his knuckles. He heard a faint shot in the air. The cannons? Located on Fort St. Simons, James knew the distant sound foreboded evil. James ran to the main garrison walls, where Hale had been keeping close watch for the night.

"Sir! I see ships in the distance."

Peering from a high wall, fortified by his men the previous years, James took the binoculars from Hale and searched the distance for the ships. Another cannon was shot in the distance, emitting a fire ball into the sea. James quickly maneuvered his hands in the same direction as the booming sound and peered into the dark landscape. He counted ships. Many ships.

"My God. Hale. Those ships are going to dock on this island within the hour if our men don't prevent them!"

"But our men will devastate their forces, sir! It is our cannons you hear, is it not?"

"Yes of course our cannons are shooting at the ships, but notice the location of those vessels!"

Just as James pointed to the north, another booming sound echoed into the darkness.

"Indeed, sir. You are most certainly right! But how did they realize this superior position?"

"Right now it is pointless to presume any notion. We must follow only one course."

Hale looked into James's eyes, finding none of the fierceness he had perceived on that fateful day in the forest, the day Hale had somehow regained the respect of his superior officer. James's expression was mellower than Hale had expected.

"We must fight to our deaths!" Hale exclaimed.

"No, Hale. We must not. Gather the men. We have less than twenty-four hours to gather all munitions and escape from the south. We must; it is our only way to defeat them in battle."

Hale knew better than to defy James. Immediately, the fort began a retreat all the while battling the ships at sea. By daybreak, it had become clear that thirty-six ships managed to avert the booming cannons of Fort St. Simons. Seemingly keeping a fight at sea, James ordered his men to stack ships with every last vestige of gunpowder, ammunition, and provisions. The little that the men had was not to be left for the enemy. James cleared his room, making sure to empty his chest of any important paraphernalia. Men ate their last meal hurriedly, taking turns manning the cannons against the Spanish fleet. *How the hell did they learn of that superior offensive position?* The fort shook the day long, with fierce retaliation on both sides. *I'm going to lose my men!* James thought. *But I don't want to start a battle. Not a single shot. Not here. The ships will carry my men across to safety. We still have our fortifications in Frederica. Under the soft skirts of darkness, my ships and my men will steer from danger.*

James lamented and scribbled in his journal, buoyed by his vessel, laden with weary men and half-rotten viands, "My Georgia surrendered Fort St. Simons without a solitary shot on this eve, July 5, 1742. May the Good Lord aid us in this, our time of need." James thanked the dark veil for masking his shame and wept silent tears of defeat.

Alexander Parris marched the ramparts of Fort St. Simon with muskets aimed at his left and right alternatively. Termed a "turncoat" or "Rotten Scoundrel," Parris knew his moment of glory was soon to come. The fleet of Spaniards advancing behind him slowly followed the eager defector.

An eerie stillness frightened the men. A few birds chirped in the distance, a mantra ignored by the men. Where were all the *Americanos?* Parris defected months ago anticipating *this* moment. But surely they were headed into a surprise guerrilla attack! Montiano remained behind on the main vessel, the *Isabella*. A long-time admirer of the Inquisition, Montiano named his beautiful ship in honor of the great queen who convinced the king of Spain to rid his country of Jews before she deigned wed him. She must have been a charming woman, of unsurpassed quality, surely, to have persuaded a king to dispense of his profitable subjects, Montiano thought on many occasions. Today was not such a time. Parris had received ample reward for his secret alliance with Montiano: gold and fertile land. Montiano wanted to make sure this Parris wasn't another American opportunist. The gold he received, but the land was on condition of success. Parris had no qualms committing himself to Montiano. Parris had been a long-time adversary of the South Carolinian colony. Corruption on every level. A man had to work excessively to spread a little lard on his bread. Negroes for those with land. Few vocations besides for farming. Laws benefitting the yellows. Forced to sail across the seas for a few farthings. Dangerous missions across seas, to gather all kinds of cretins to the Americas, sometimes with nothing but scurvy to boast of. Poor and wretched prisoners on his boats sailed. Never owning a piece of land; always at the bidding of the English Crown. Now, Florida was a whole *new* prospect: land, and all the honor of aiding the war against the greedy north. But all his fantasies seemed a crude departure from the reality which faced him: Fort St. Simons was deserted. Not a single blasted soul.

Parris placed his musket on James's bed and peered around the dim-lit room. His nostrils, brown and wide, flared. His eyes, a dark brown bordering on black, dilated in the dark. His long hair, grown like a barbarian, grazed his shoulders. His boots, blackened and wet, stained the dirty floor. The cot was all disheveled—and stained in more than one area. The desk, of cheap and mostly chipped oak, was filled with ash and smears of dried coffee. Empty snuff-boxes were strewn on the floor. Dirty British, Parris thought. *I won't take this glorious defeat!*

He took his musket, and in a rage rammed it on the desk, filling the room with ash. Parris coughed. Damn this Oglethorpe! He *knew* this would be worse than battle. Enraged, Parris lifted James's cot, threw it across the room and nearly reeled when the cot bounced off. Somewhat relieved but not entirely spent, he found a glass, half-filled with rum, and hurled it at the hanging glass mirror; both shattered across the walls.

Parris's men heard the commotion and stepped aside until their captain emerged, smeared with black sweat.

James thought of writing to Elizabeth. Really, who could prophesy the future? He had such bright hopes for Georgia! His soldiers joked he married the colony, and now what? Would he be denied the joy of seeing his marriage find fruition? Are all my yesterdays going to end tomorrow? James thought. Nonsense! He heard his mother whisper. Surrender is a gambit, my dear. A temporary loss for a greater gain. Who is this Montiano, anyway? Surely he did not train with the great *British* officers! Over and over, James heard his mother whisper in his ears. James considered his position. He knew the Spaniards were unfamiliar with Frederica's marshy, circuitous terrain. Bogged by moss-filled marches, sloughs of alligator-filled waters and pits of salamander coves, Frederica was a formidable obstacle for any trained officer. Months of manning the intricate hedges of the fort, James and his men knew terrain would prove absolutely crucial. Montiano would soon encroach on their land—there was no doubt on that score.

*

Lachlan McIntosh, a tall man with a bright complexion, clear eyes and a delicate mouth, was scouting the main garrison. Hale's junior officer, McIntosh trained as a solicitor in Manchester before sailing to the New World. Too many class restrictions and rigid customs of his hometown prevented what McIntosh perceived as the proper milieu for his advancement. McIntosh did not train for the military, but rather for the Law. All those law books proved useless in his situation. Rules and regulations, clear instructions for behavior, even during wartime, was a British staple. *But the rules of warring must depart from conventional warfare if we are to survive this scourge*. No lines to be held, nor droves of cavalry marching to the mechanized beat of drums. The cannons would have to be placed in strategic areas, concealed by brush; men would *have* to dig underground and find temporary "lodgings"! McIntosh looked up, and his brownish yellowish hair glistened in the afternoon sun, lending him a boyish look. Yes. He thought. Some trees seem conducive for far-range shooting. McIntosh continued to march along the main trail until he reached the edge of the island. Ah. The marshes. Bloody Marsh closest to the surrendered fort was especially foggy. They were beneficial too: key barriers. There was another element to their advantage as well: the Creeks. Oh! Their tomahawks could slaughter any man, from thirty feet or more at times. McIntosh once saw Tooanabey launch a tomahawk from twenty feet away, hitting a Spaniard right between the eyes. The Indians knew this land long before the likes of him arrived in this new land. McIntosh bent down and gathered some rocks. He flung them into the waters. *Perhaps it is best to wade?* McIntosh began to undress, revealing robust shoulder muscles and taut pectorals. His scalp was itchy, and sweat accumulated by the small of his back. He left his clothes by the strand, noting the mud on his boots. Slowly, he began to swim into the rivers, noticing the depth began to increase. Not very salutary for humans. Bodes well, he mused. Oglethorpe will be relieved. Now, when will this bloody battle begin? He wondered.

*

James stood shirtless in his makeshift hut. The sweltering July heat burned his scalp and depleted him of all his energy. The intense heat robbed him of an appetite; he craved pure water—but that was extraordinarily rare in Frederica. The wells had been overused by his men, and the rainfall ceased early this past year. Mosquitoes were swarming all around, and James feared another plague of Yellow Fever. Nunez had taken leave for Georgia, but was to return any day now; he had few well-trained doctors in his militia. Just as James was about to fall into a state of agitation, McIntosh appeared, wet and well-worn.

"Sir. A word."

"Of course. What is it, McIntosh?"

"If I may. Montiano has no choice but to divide his camp to scout the terrain. If we sit and wait here like schoolchildren—why! Only an act of God will save us. Sir. If we intercept them in the forest—the advantage will be ours."

James listened carefully to McIntosh. Of course the officer was right. James had considered the possibility of having to resort to guerilla tactics. James was a man of etiquette, but even *he* knew when to break from protocol.

"Lead a patrol of men into the forest immediately. Take Hale. And fifty others. Make sure the Creeks come along as well. Let Bull know I am remaining here. I count on him as my second man. Should you encounter the enemy, your orders are to return and relay their exact whereabouts. Fire only if in absolute danger."

McIntosh saluted and left at once.

James wondered when his supply of muskets would arrive. Abraham Minis was James's main supplier. He had shuttled weapons and victuals from Savannah to Frederica in the past. Now, during the Spanish siege, James needed Minis's supplies. Bull had been aiding the effort as well. The Carolinas had no choice, so Bull had supplemented from his own supply—food and foot soldiers. Bull had been steadfast, grateful for Oglethorpe's fierce opposition. Bull's wife had given birth to twin boys, and since then Oglethorpe felt responsible for keeping his friend alive. The South Carolinians preferred Bull to Oglethorpe, initially, but soon enough, even the Indians mingled with those from the Carolinas. The Jews kept to themselves, mostly. Except for Nunez. Stationed by the infirmary, the doctor saw to the men's wounds, carefully treating all patients as though they were his only ones. McIntosh was a big help, Oglethorpe wryly noted. The man had fierce blue eyes and a delicate mouth—not the warring type. Nevertheless, he was courageous. Perhaps Oglethorpe was reminded of himself as he once was, in his youth, all idealistic, and full of promise. McIntosh had a wide forehead, with a thin line running across the middle of his forehead—a sign of a deep thinker. Broad-shouldered and well-built, many of the young women back in Savannah hoped he would look their way. McIntosh's brows were brown, but his lashes were light. This lent an airy look to his visage, one that was captivating. Oglethorpe hoped McIntosh's suggestion would prove successful. Not a particularly spiritual man, Oglethorpe believed perhaps it was time to pray.

Bull stared at McIntosh's profile. How old is this boy? Bull thought. McIntosh seems to know where he's headed. The Creeks followed behind them. A patrol of the terrain earlier in the day guaranteed positioning of firearms by midday. Now it was nearing the late afternoon, and the two other groups—one led by Hale and another by a queer gentleman, Captain Raymond Demere—were following rather deliberately. The Creeks spoke in their native tongue, aggravating Bull. Although the Creeks were sworn enemies of the Yamassee, Bull had a hard time trusting any red. It was their language, and their expressions were difficult to determine. Tooanabey spoke some English, so the two somewhat got along. Mostly inspired by Tomochichi, Tooanabey believed in the spirit of ancestors aiding in battle as well as in peace. So Bull had to put up with a great deal of muttering and paint splattering. The one saving grace, Bull thought, is that Tooanabey easily diced wood, rabbit, and ugly Spaniards with beautiful precision. A true Hail Mary.

"Captain Bull—do you hear that?"

Bull motioned for the men to settle down. Instinctively, McIntosh began a slow, slithering crawl on his belly. Bull was taken by the young man's initiative. Cautiously, McIntosh peered through the underbrush pointing his rifle directly in front of him. McIntosh couldn't believe their ill luck—Indian Yamassee. Maybe two hundred men, with fierce red paint and fringed tunics bouncing in the wind. Tomahawks stowed in belts. Muskets in hand. Feathers in hair and a few strands in loose braids. Behind them the Spaniards. Boots of mud and sweaty mustaches sticking to their faces. Maybe fifty or so. A mile and a half away, the enemy looked fierce. Damn! They found the trail! McIntosh was eager to relay the information to Bull. He calculated the enemy had not made visual of his presence, and hurriedly crouched on his knees toward his men. And then shots filled the air. The Yamassee had the sixth sense—they detected fear. Immediately, Bull returned fire, covering McIntosh. The men began a retreat toward Oglethorpe's tent, some remaining in the underbrush and yet others to man the hidden cannons. McIntosh began to sweat profusely; his musket was hard to maneuver in the intense heat. He yelled like a madman each time a Yamassee fell to the floor. McIntosh turned to his right and aimed at a Spaniard whose gun had jammed. He then ran to a bare tree for cover and reloaded his musket. The musket balls were hard to grasp, so he had to remain focused. For an instant, McIntosh thought of the pretty girl, Rebecca Shires, and her small cottage in Savannah. He really didn't know much of her, only that she was pretty. Thinking of her helped calm his nerves. Again, he took aim. This time, McIntosh's attention was on his friend, Bull. The Captain was the impatient type, but benevolent. McIntosh rather liked the chap. From a distance, an Indian with an ugly scar across his cheek began to take aim at Bull and the surrounding men. McIntosh immediately fired, missing the ugly Indian, but sending him reeling off balance.

"Watch that man! Bull. The Indian with the scar! He was taking aim at you!" Bull could hardly hear McIntosh.

"What? Keep running you fool. Go. I'll remain here. Hurry!"

McIntosh had no interest in running to Oglethorpe or to the cannons. Enough men were there. McIntosh began to run uphill, dodging bullets. A bit on high ground, McIntosh had an advantage. Crouching behind a thick brush, McIntosh realized he could aim the musket at the Indian. He fired. He then ran across to another bush and realized there were two other British officers hiding in a makeshift dugout. Firing ensued, with Bull retreating slightly. They had reached Gully Hole Creek. Where was Oglethorpe?

Then, from the rear, Tooanabey hollered a sickening shriek. With his tomahawk, he aimed at the scarred Yamassee with dreadful accuracy. For a moment, McIntosh thought all the soldiers, on both sides, heard the sickening thud of a skull cracking in half. Wedged between the ugly Indian's head lay Tooanabey's tomahawk. Then a barrage of bullets. Left and right. The gunpowder filled the thicket brush and the humid air. McIntosh turned and saw Redcoats. Hale had returned with Oglethorpe. Oglethorpe dismounted his horse and jumped to Tooanabey who had been shot just as he released his tomahawk. Tooanabey, unshaken, nodded his head. He wasn't mortally wounded. Oglethorpe patted his trusted soldier, and took aim at a fat Spaniard languishing in the front lines. A torrent of bullets followed, and Oglethorpe's men retreated half a mile upon command. The Spaniards, particularly Alexander Parris, began to feel secure in their immediate victory. It appeared the English had retreated with considerable speed at least a good distance from the marsh. Alligators remained underwater as the men slowly began to emerge, trying to make sense of the scene before them. Alexander decided to quickly mount his horse, where he could better observe from a distance. How odd, he thought. I don't see anyone. Smiling, he thought of James and imagined him cursing and perhaps crying in defeat. His hatred for James had grown slowly at first—but when he was dragged and imprisoned for excessive drinking while at sea and for alleged rape, Parris had had enough of the fancy man's laws. Deeding land to filthy Jews—the very same who had killed Jesus—and *he* wasn't a very religious man. What's this I see, he thought. Not a soul in sight.

James ran swiftly, panting by the time he reached the first hidden cannons. The men stood and immediately got to work. Like clockwork, the men loaded the cannon, igniting it with a mixture of awe and fear.

James bellowed, "Load! Stand back. FIRE!"

Cannon balls ripped Indians apart, flinging body parts into the trees and into the creek. Oglethorpe mounted his horse and saw, to his amazement, the Spaniards retreating rapidly back south. Most of the men standing in the front had been blown to pieces by the cannon fire, and a man with a long beard fell off his horse. James, invigorated by the blasts, had to subdue Fleance for a brief moment and then yelled, "Hale! Have the men cease the cannon fire! Men! Capture the enemy at once!"

Immediately, Oglethorpe gave chase. Most of his men ran toward the center of the battle scene, where the Indians lay strewn all across the ground, some muttering, others moaning from fatal wounds. Most were silent. Blood filled the crevices of Hale's boots, and the mud created a thick paste of congealed guts and blood. James's men had seen battle wounds, but the faces blown to pieces, and the innards of the reds and the Spaniards, caused a few to wretch. De Lyon was one. And James too had to overcome the urge. James turned toward McIntosh—

"They're retreating toward Fort St. Simons!" McIntosh bellowed. "Should we follow them all the way there, sir?"

Oglethorpe put a stop to his horse and glanced at the marshes and the dead men.

"No. Take the men prisoners."

Hale ran toward Oglethorpe, his musket beating his back with each step.

"Sir. Both captains of the advance force have been captured. Bull says we are to execute them. What say you?"

"Keep all prisoners alive! We shall need their precious knowledge."

Oglethorpe surveyed Gulley Hole Creek and held his breath. Bloody Mary. This was a hell of a battle. Bodies and parts of bodies scattered the terrain. A stench of blood and guts filled the air. Wretched Yamassee. We'll see what happens tomorrow.

"Leave their remains as is. Let their friends find them like this. Perhaps this will serve as a message."

Oglethorpe lifted his chin. War was an ugly thing.

*

Hannah Solomons slipped into her long, ivory gown. She had been awake for too long. Benjamin Sheftall had regaled her with countless stories of near shipwreck and debauched captains at sea. Could he have truly saved the Christian boy Tommy from certain death? A brave man always stirred her maiden heart. Indeed, at

176

heart she deemed herself a young woman upon hearing of such fantastic tales. And to think the British did not authorize their departure! What gall and what risk! And the account of his wife's miscarriage. What sadness. But he did not focus on his loss. Instead, he held his hat and moved his arms far and wide, gesticulating as he described his mighty adventures. James Oglethorpe seemed like a true English gentleman. She would like to meet him sometime. And although Benjamin's countenance did not necessarily inspire beauty when first glanced upon, Hannah felt herself warming up to Benjamin. In the darkness, with the dim lights of a candelabrum warming their eyes, Hannah detected Benjamin's elongated nose, his strongest feature, and his smallish eyes twinkling every now and then. His skin had begun to wither, but held its own: visible laugh lines, crow's feet, and a strong jaw, slightly well-padded by one too many delicious meals. Hannah wondered how he had made love to his wife, Perla, but quickly dispelled such thoughts. She was certain he loved her, even if she were dead. Hannah knew the heart can beat for another, even if the beloved's heart is long dead and can never return love's intensity. A widower is better than a divorcee, her mother once told her. At least a widower, hopefully, had been able to demonstrate love at one point in time. Oddly, Hannah didn't feel entirely comforted by her mother's opinions. (Her mother had also said that the Dutch gentiles hated the Jews. That certainly wasn't true about Paul!) Hannah had made up her mind; she just wasn't entirely sure of her decision. Not just yet. There was a single one little person upon whose temperament her decision would be weighted upon—little Mordechai.

Hannah gathered her bags the following week, departed from her hostess, who had been rather disappointed Hannah should seek employment elsewhere and was sure the Ashkenazi had something to do with Hannah's sudden leave, begrudgingly kissed Hannah on the cheek and promised to write about the children's developments.

"You'll have to promise me that all the children will remember my name when I visit one day, Mrs. Abrams! Please! Remind them of my labors; I would truly appreciate your doing so!"

"As you wish, Hannah. But promise me you won't enter into a fruitless marriage. My mother always said an empty nest is better than a dreadful one. You understand my intention?"

Hannah nodded and kissed her hostess once more on both cheeks. A chaise had been patiently standing outside, the horse kicking its hind legs in protest. Mr. Abrams helped Hannah along, placing her heavy wooden valise into the overhead compartment. "Shalom," was his last word.

*

Captain Raymond Demere was tired of following orders, marching in the insufferable heat, panting along, feeling faint, and having to piss every half hour from overdrinking. His men, numbering sixty, belonged to the forty-second regiment, and if God had not said "let there be light" on the first day of creation, then his name wasn't Demere. He had enough. He decided to march along by Bloody Marsh (so called because of a bloody skull found there upon their arrival) toward the relative safety of Frederica. Demere desperately pined to become just a bit wounded, so he may manage the cooks. That would include barking orders and at least eating something. The trail was beginning to thin out; men could only get through the thick underbrush marching single file. Suddenly, Demere, the first in line, detected Spaniards up ahead, hiding in the dense brushwood. A heavy mist filled the area, clogging his tear ducts. He motioned for silence. Damn! The Spaniards had been anticipating an ambush! The bog, covered in moss and alligators, separated Demere from Frederica. Just ahead of them the Spaniards lay covered, sweating onto the tall grass. Frogs leaped in midair, and a few indigenous creatures lurked near the waters. It was enormously difficult to see; the air seemed impenetrable. Demere cursed the Spaniards in his head as he concocted the only available course of action: retreat. Just as he was about to motion to his second officer, a loud deafening shot filled the air; Demere returned fire instinctively and began booming, "Run! Retreat! We're surrounded!" Most of the men in the back of the line began running back, headed in the direction of Gulley Hole. But Demere and about forty others remained, fending for their lives. Gunfire. Shoot! Hide in the underbrush! Gunfire! We're down two men, Demere. A fusillade of return fire. Demere tried to reload his musket, but failed in his crouched position. He had to use gravity a bit. He stood and took cover behind one of his men. Shots filled the air. A few more men began to crawl out of view, then quickly bolted the hell out of Bloody Marsh where they swore Satan held communion. As they ran toward Gulley Hole, they immediately halted.

"What is the meaning of this?" demanded Oglethorpe. "Where is your captain?"

"The battle is lost. We retreated."

"Nonsense! Do you not hear? Listen!"

Oglethorpe pointed to de Lyon and Minis. "Quickly inform more reinforcements. This is no time for cowardice!" He dismounted Fleance and allowed Minis to relay the information to Bull. "If something were to happen—Bull takes the command. These are my orders. Go!"

Minis galloped, fearful that Oglethorpe would succumb to the ambush. Just as Oglethorpe marched with some twenty-six men toward Bloody Marsh, a one lily-livered Silva ran, undetected by Oglethorpe. It was enough his family survived the Inquisition. Perhaps this war had not been intended for him; the taste of death was too much for some.

Demere counted three mortally wounded and less than fifty still shooting. Three times their number surrounded them—and like a foolish idiot his first command had been to his greater disadvantage. Oglethorpe heard the fusillade from the Spaniards. Tricking them into believing more Britons were there was the only way out of this deadly ambush. James quickly gathered five men:

"Each one of you must gather a group of five men. In a succession of fire, I want each group to fire together, allowing the second group to fire as you reload. This shall be repeated as many times as possible. Do you hear? We need to confuse the hell out of them! Go!"

McIntosh had been designated as well as Hale, and to the surprise of James and all the men, Benjamin Sheftall. Freshly joined, after a brief leave to visit some woman in Pennsylvania, Benjamin had joined the ranks once again. Benjamin immediately understood James's intention, and gathered four other men. Upon Oglethorpe's command, each group took quick aim and fired. Blast! They took cover and reloaded as another group of five did the same. Bewildered, the Spaniards began cursing, unaware of their numerical advantage. Most of the Spaniards, mercenaries, withdrew when they believed their luck was lost. As James neared the head of the lines, he recognized Alexander Parris—the turncoat! Bastard! James thought. Enraged that a British citizen would turn against his King. It was despicable! James motioned for McIntosh.

"Listen McIntosh. I need you to cover me, you understand? Fire when I say, and each time I take cover, fire once again. Do you hear?"

McIntosh nodded his head, a bit anxious and excited, "Why, sir?"

"I'm going after the bastard who put us in this bloody condition, that's what."

Bullets surrounded James, as some of the Spaniards remained in the underbrush, behind the marsh. The sun shone in all of its intensity, burning James's flesh and nearly blinding him. James placed the bayonet onto the musket. He touched the edge. It was perfectly honed. McIntosh placed his hand to block the sun's rays and carefully watched for James.

James kissed a musket ball he had been saving for a special occasion, made from the bullet of the blasted Causton and Williamson on that fateful day—a sign he had yet to fulfill some destiny. He placed the musket inside the barrel of his musket, clicking it into place. James motioned for cover, and began running, in a zigzag fashion, toward the marsh, an instinctive movement. A barrage flew by; he sunk to the ground. McIntosh instantly fired, and Benjamin had as well. He had overheard the exchange between McIntosh and James and felt it wise to confuse the enemy all the more. Slowly, the entire regiment began to pick up on James's plan, although not all were entirely aware of his goal. What could his target be?

Alexander Parris searched around him and noted many Spaniards deserted. Cowards! He yelled in Spanish. Don't you see! We have this entire area covered! Why are they leaving? He asked aloud. Few had what to answer—for they too wished to flee. Enraged, Parris began to yell. The Portuguese Jews knew what he was saying—it sounded like "impenetrable dogs" and "stupid asses" in their native tongue as well. The voice of Alexander Parris sent a cold shiver down Benjamin's spine. How utterly familiar and alien—all at once! And to hear such words… De Lyon held his own, recalling the epithets of the Spanish Inquisitors. The Jews, too, had been called such—and worse. James marched forward and took a quick aim at Parris. Alexander turned around and recognized Oglethorpe. But it had come a little too late—the trusted bullet lodged deep in his right lung, and then another, fired by Benjamin, passed through his abdomen. Alexander fell back, just a bit, and curled his lip.

"You English swine!" He removed a long spear that had been dangling by his side and began to charge at James. James allowed Alexander to rush at him; James fixated on Parris's deadly arm. Just as Parris tried to thrust his spear at James, a loud single shot filled the air, and Parris reeled backwards. The spear fell back, but only his arm was slightly grazed by the bullet. Alexander didn't miss a single beat and picked up his spear once again. James stood as well, moving backward toward his men, forcing Alexander to exert himself all the more. Finally, just as Alexander turned to drive his sword, Oglethorpe jumped and sliced off Alexander's arm with a swift movement. Alexander's arm went flying over the underbrush and got caught in between two footmen who had been crouching by the side. Blood spurting from his abdomen, and all his muscles splattered and slashed, Alexander fell back first onto the ground. The artery spurted forth blood in gushes. Still conscious, Alexander stared at James with a contemptuous and poisonous stare.

Barely able to speak up, Alexander spit at James. "Let's see you finish a job, like the barbarian that you are, you filthy—"

James bent down and squeezed Alexander's mouth shut. "You listen to me, you worthless piece of swine. Right before you die, I want you to hear a song you'll detest. This song, Captain Hanson, is sung by all proper British regents upon witnessing the King and Queen."

In a splendid voice and as Captain Hanson's eyes shed its last tears, James sang with gusto and pride—altogether grand. In his mind he envisioned Elizabeth singing along with him, proud of his conquest. A traitor to the King must die knowing the King shall long live after the blasphemous traitor had long turned to ash. A sepulcher of hemlock for the ugly captain of the *William and Sarah*, James thought.

Benjamin lifted his eye and stared at Captain Hanson. He had known the man to be dissolute, but what had motivated the man to become a turncoat, for goodness sake! The Portuguese Jews gathered round the man, afraid to look into his eyes as he died. He had been the one who brought them to America, after all. Perhaps they should leave James to deal with the Captain. How changed he was! With a long beard and dark hair, he completely lost the blubber that weighed him down. Jewels decked his remaining fingers, and he wore hand-made boots with a slight curl by the heel. Benjamin turned aside, and wondered how it came to be that a man who had nearly killed James had once been a shipmaster at sea. Fearing the Inquisitors and the Inquisition now seemed multiplied by the fear of one's own kind—the enemies within. Many of his Sephardic brethren had taken vows of Christianity to remain alive—only to witness Christian fighting Christian. De Lyon was moved by Captain Hanson's tears and by James's gentle yet profound voice. The Sephardim gathered round James, holding their hats in their hands. They wanted no more of the blood and warfare of Savannah. A faceless enemy was one thing—a familiar face another. This must come to an end somehow. Captain Hanson slowly perished as his previous crew members gaped at his misshapen soul. Hanson remained on the ground, his blood all drained from his muscular body. James left him there and turned around. Bloody Marsh reinitiated its title of blood and gore.

In utter stillness, the remaining forty-second regiment gathered the deceased, the dying, and the wounded toward the infirmary, where Samuel Nunez awaited their arrival. The venom had drained from their bodies, depleting them—utterly. Few men had what to say, and their thoughts had never been so still. Weighed down by the fruitlessness of war and the venom of rage, the men broke loose into the night. Benjamin prayed, alone, bowing a few times toward the direction of Jerusalem. He fervently beseeched God to return to Zion; for how could America prove the bastion of true hope? Had they not brought animosity and rancor from the Old Country to the New World? Would his son have to fight wretched men, turned upside down in their loyalties? And how could it be the Jews sympathized with an enemy? After all, he had cursed their own kind on numerous occasions, accused them of thievery, called their women whores and ridiculed their ways. But still. To see his body ruptured, torn asunder by James's sheer strength. Benjamin prayed fervently for a time of peace and prosperity, an end to the long war between Spain and England, and a rebirth of true Enlightenment on the new continent.

James sat in his tent, spent and wet from sweat and blood, and thought of Captain Hanson's last moments of life. He had revealed their position to de Montiano, a true mercenary. But what had Oglethorpe done to deserve such wretched hatred from the man? Had he truly represented all of England to the man? Had he been deranged? Undoubtedly de Montiano compensated the mad captain well. James opened his hand and polished the emerald ring with his red waistcoat. It was a gem of wondrous luster. Surrounded by a yellow gold band, the emerald must have been worth four horses perhaps. It was a keepsake James one day hoped to make good use of. James wondered what may have been adorning the left hand—the one he tore off. No sense in wondering now, James thought. Let me write to Parliament one more time beseeching them for assistance.

Just then, Benjamin had been swiftly writing to Mrs. Minis
as well. She had been caring for her children as well as Mordechai
occasionally since Perla's death. She had been the one who insisted
he visit Pennsylvania and remain there if need be. She promised
to raise Mordechai as her own if the inevitable happened during
the siege. Most of the Sephardim fled northward, seeking their
fortunes elsewhere. But Mrs. Minis couldn't complain much.
Since the war, her husband, the main supplier of weapons and
ammunitions, had profited well. Enough for a larger home, more
help around the house, including a nanny and nurse, and a full-
time cook. Mrs. Minis still oversaw the entire household, assisting
and aiding in every aspect of housekeeping, but had more time
for the little leisure she allowed for herself. Teaching the young
ones the Hebrew letters had been her responsibility until a proper
tutor could be found. The girls needed attention as well—to
remember their place in a threatening environment. And in all
that, Mrs. Minis found the heart to care for Benjamin's son. As
such, Benjamin quickly jotted down the following:

Dear Mrs. Minis,

Significant losses on Spanish side. Any day now should mark
the last moments of this siege. Prepare house for my return
in a week's time.

Pray for our success,
Benjamin

*

Oglethorpe, in his tent, three days from that moment in time previously mentioned, scribbled in his journal:

At last! The British crown had regained its senses! Five British
naval ships, the very best of the lot I dare say, arrived earlier
today. Fort St. Simons was taken down in less than three
hours time, with the Spaniards and de Montiano himself
heading back south. Our garrison in Frederica remained free

from intruders. Burial of deceased enemy carcasses ensued as fear of enemy reprisals decreased considerably. Received notice that de Montiano is devoid of funds and mercenaries. At last, we may all return to Savannah and begin our sojourn anew.

Benjamin returned in less than a week to an entourage of men and women, cheering his praises. The Savannah men and the Carolinians, as well as the trusty Creeks, defeated, at long last, the nasty and treacherous intruders! Benjamin, with a sack filled with rags, a tin can, phylacteries, a prayer shawl and a *siddur*, bent down to lift his son in the air. The boy squealed and hugged Benjamin's knee. Abba! Abba! Did you bring any gifts from your trip? Benjamin smiled weakly and handed his son a beautiful ring—it was a red ruby set in yellow gold and small diamonds, roughly hewed. "I brought a gift that will one day help me find you an Ima! What do you say? Isn't that a great gift?" Mordechai furrowed his brows, a bit confused. Benjamin laughed. He tousled his son's hair and gave him a treat of Turkish delight, a treasure Benjamin had stowed for such occasions. Mordechai kissed his father's cheek and ran to the house to show off his treat to Mrs. Minis's youngest child, Reuben. To his surprise, he saw Hannah Solomons smiling in the corner, her hands neatly folded in front of her. Her head slightly tilted, she beamed at him. It had been true, then. He truly had a warrior's blood running in his Ashkenazi veins! It had been marvelous seeing him decked and lauded by the townspeople—even the Christian neighbors clung to his every word. Another man stood not far from Benjamin, a tall blond man with a rough face, nodding his head to another Christian woman. "Who is that?" She asked Mrs. Minis. Benjamin overheard her question and answered, loudly, "That is Mr. Hale, Hannah. He was a lieutenant who saved James at one point, no?" and such their conversations continued until the men had to pray in the makeshift *shul*, thanking the One God of Abraham for their successes in the jungles of the American heartland.

185

"East of Eden."

OF BELLES AND BELLS

CAPTAIN MCINTOSH ENJOYED THE MYRIAD glares of admiration from the belles of Savannah. Although the town's population had diminished, the young women somehow seemed, at least to McIntosh, enough in number to satisfy a young man's growing ego. Rebecca had greeted him, with a laurel made from the trees of the Savannah wilderness. Her mother, Mrs. Shires, baked a crisp pecan pie with real cream and strawberries to honor his successes. Somehow, a soldier's welcome infused McIntosh with the energy to regale the ladies with countless tales of heathens struck by tomahawks and bloody Spaniards dying while cursing in their blasted language. *O Maria!* McIntosh imitated, wondering why the ladies did not see the humor in his mockery. Weeks after the successful mission at Frederica, McIntosh found himself signing up for Oglethorpe's militia and abandoning his solicitor's post.

Oglethorpe sat in his comfortable townhouse contemplating another visit to Parliament. It was certainly due. Funds had disappeared, and rebuilding the colony that helped eliminate a considerable foe became his priority. Mother would certainly be very unhappy about this decision—it portended an extended stay in Georgia, which, of course, she did not desire. But James could not imagine forgoing on Georgia. Indeed, he had taken vows to protect her, for better *and* for worse, had he not? Now that McIntosh was eager to share post with Hale, he could rely on two very loyal men. Causton and Williamson were hanged the previous year, so no worries from that end. Many inhabitants left the Georgian towns—he had to petition the trustees for more monies and convince them to open the doors to more debtors, Jews, Protestants and others the mother country was not too eager to retain. A great deal of more work was in the forecast. And there was Elizabeth too. He had received two letters from her while away—surprisingly dated months back. They were not very extraordinary except for two lines which seemed to insinuate extreme loneliness and her concern for James. Her writing technique was similar to her persona: subtle and somewhat mysterious. Suddenly feeling guilty for his thoughts, James recalled that she was married, and a proper English woman would not deign to shame herself in indelicacy. James felt spent all of a sudden, and Captain Hanson's tortured expression suddenly accosted James. How mad he must have been to slaughter the man! Perhaps it would have been better for Hanson to have stood trial, like Causton and Williamson. But it was the heat of battle; the scoundrel was a turncoat. Treason is punishable by certain death. James instinctively reached for his flask of whiskey and rehashed his decision making—it had been for the best. De Montiano was helpless without Hanson. There was no risk taking involved with Hanson—perhaps he would have escaped their prisons? He wouldn't have been the first, God knows. With all his jewels, he most certainly could have bribed any starving soldier to do his bidding. No. James took a quick swig. His instincts on the battlefield were right on target—which is why his name began with General and not Corporal.

James, unwashed and unchanged, collapsed onto his bed. With his boots still on, and without caring to use the closet, James fell into a sleep where Hanson's image did not seem to strain the clear image of Elizabeth, smiling with a radiant glow of joy.

*

Benjamin Sheftall contemplated the fine color of Hannah's eyes. The deep brown of pensive thought intrigued him. She seemed so different from Perla, that, in all honesty, it took getting used to. Hannah's eyes were large, but they weren't crisp and light, like Perla's had been. Each time he had stared into Perla's eyes he imagined an ocean or an endless stream of flying stars. If he had not been so impossibly constrained by his many responsibilities, Benjamin imagined he would have remained single for a little while longer— at least until Perla's ghost haunted him less. But the luxury was not his to be had. Instead, he knew precisely what he had to do— he just wished he knew for certain, as he had known with Perla, just what the outcome would be. Hannah warmed to his son. Still a child and utterly adorable, albeit mischievous and shrewd, Mordechai quickly won many hearts. Even John Hale was taken by Mordechai, a surprise by all of Savannah's Jewry. John had taught Mordechai how to throw a spear onto the target of a tin can tied to a desiccated tree. It had been John Hale who offered to teach the lad a growing number of tricks—including finding coins in other people's pockets. Mordechai's charm softened hardened hearts, it seemed to Benjamin. Hannah certainly seemed bewitched, which Benjamin was grateful for. He had been incredibly worried his son would not know the warmth of a mother, the kiss and the hug of a beloved matron. The only question remained if his heart had room for another, in a complete capacity, one that would be generous and giving. Why all these misgivings? He berated himself. As he stood behind the underbrush in Bloody Marsh, all he could think of was Mordechai and Hannah! Reliving the moment, Benjamin recalled how James had slithered into the enemy terrain, shooting and hiding, basking in McIntosh's watch. It had been obvious James needed assistance. Benjamin remembered closing in, becoming more vulnerable himself to a deadly shot. But it had to be done— and yet, in that moment of intense fear—he recalled the dinner by the Abrams and the delight of feeling alive and youthful again. How Hannah delighted in his tales! He felt invigorated! Suddenly, his prospects seemed to gather momentum. So why all these thoughts? Agitated, Benjamin left his parlor, which was cooler in the evening, and headed out doors for a cool walk.

Hannah lived nearby, he thought. She lodged near John Hale's place, two doors down to be exact. She had dined with him and the Minis family for three consecutive Friday nights since late July. She officially moved into town in early October, if he recalled— which meant the winter months would begin soon....

Benjamin considered his age; he was no longer a bachelor of thin stature. His middle was round, plump would be more accurate, he thought. His cheeks drooped a bit, but not that much, he consoled himself. At least I have most of my hair. He chuckled to himself. And then there was the intimacy. He had never been intimate with any woman save Perla. Hannah was somehow, miraculously, Benjamin believed, a virgin—for her, he would be her only one. But despite Perla's untimely departure, he somehow felt touching another woman, even in matrimony, would be a lack of constancy. But how could it? He walked across the bends of Savannah's wild gardens, strewn with overripe peaches and withered rosebush hedges. He smelled the half-rotting smell of the rosebush and considered that in due time buds would emerge, waking to splendor. The many trees of this country, and the fields as well, lay dormant, covered in a safe blanket of snow, appeared to die, only to bloom. Savannah would once again become the picturesque town, now slowly becoming a charming place. Benjamin turned the bend once again and walked across the street, right adjacent to the main road, and held his arms behind his back. Yes. The houses had a distinct colonial feel—the stucco was white, the choice color of many homes. The sun of course was responsible for that, he supposed. And the wealthier homes, including the Minis mansion, boasted a fabulous russet brick, very rare indeed. The river's inhabitants could be heard lurking at night—if passersby were open to hearing the sounds. His Prussian town fading in his memory, Benjamin began to consider his life anew.

Taken by the moment, he found himself walking briskly toward Hannah's home. It was not customary for a Jewish man to visit a single woman at night. Past eight was certainly unheard of, but there were few bystanders who would take note. He found his feet somehow light and airy, somewhat like a sprite, he supposed. He ran up the three stairs to Hannah Solomons' place and knocked with his hardened knuckles on the door. Hannah opened the heavy door, in a fine nightgown and robe, with a lace night cap covering her hair. The outline of her breasts was visible through the gown, and Benjamin detected a rush of his vigor return. She peeped out of the door, holding a lamp in her right hand.

"Yes? Who is it at this hour?" She wondered.

"It's me. Benjamin." Excited and a bit shy, she gathered her robe and looked Benjamin in the eyes.

"Is everything all right?"

Benjamin, animated by his renewed vitality, held the door and said, "Hannah! I beseech you to consider my words deeply, as I have long contemplated speaking them. Hush now, just listen. You need not answer until you are fully satisfied with your decision. I humbly ask you, and I know I am very far from a gallant man, but in feelings I am yet robust and capable. We can learn to love one another dearly—but if only you will give us the chance. What say you—will you be my wife?"

Benjamin's heart quickened pace. Hannah's certainly skipped a few precious beats too. Could it be? In the middle of the night, Benjamin Sheftall could not hold himself any longer and propose matrimony? Hannah couldn't help imagine the amount of gossip this would have spurred in her little Dutch town! She began to laugh and smile robustly. Benjamin looked into her eyes, and realized she had been laughing in earnest—out of joy that is! Overtaken himself with the prospect of beginning a new life, he began to laugh as well. The two stood there, smiling at one another, like scheming youths, behind their parents' back, forging a bond of the most intimate kind.

"Yes! Benjamin. I have thought about becoming your wife for a long time now! Why do you suppose I live in this cottage? Did you not see my intention? I had to make sure of my heart—but now I see you have come to ask for my hand, and I am truly taken—with joy! I don't know what to say! Truly, come in! Why are we standing like this?" Forbidden to touch, the two stood by the lintel for a while longer, perhaps afraid of the intimacy the house afforded them. Benjamin had been quite scrupulous in these matters, and Hannah realized his intentions in remaining outdoors. Benjamin ignored her suggestion and just smiled at her for a brief moment and thought of the temptation of the moment, how easy it would be. To break the code of moral law and lie with her. She had agreed to the matrimony—but she had yet to become ritually pure; he had yet to sign the Jewish marital contract, the *ketubah*. Such was not to be transgressed.

Benjamin looked into Hannah's eyes. Had she been just as eager as him? "We must set a date as soon as possible, Hannah. We must not tarry. When would you like to be wed, my dearest?" Hannah couldn't believe how sweet sounding were the words "my dearest"! For how long had she yearned for honey and sweetheart and lovely and dearest and my rose... but if only this moment should last! Laughing once again and smiling like a princess in a fairy tale, Hannah stepped a bit closer to Benjamin and nearly collapsed with desire, "As soon as possible."

Oh! How I wish that could be right now, thought Hannah. This is the most perfect moment for lovemaking. How I wish right now. It had been so long, yet the law required her to follow the disciplinary measures of ritual cleansing! How temptation sought her at that moment, she blushed to think too much on it. Benjamin realized the moment had reached a climax, in which if he did not return to his home, he would surely collapse into her arms.

"Then check the date of your womanly times and let me know when is the auspicious date! Until then, my love, I await the moment we can unite as husband and wife." Blood rushed through her veins with the mention of union. It had been a desire she had buried so deeply all these years. She smiled weakly, nodded, closed the door, held her heart to her hand, and felt a sharp pain deep in the recesses of her womanhood crying out from years of neglect.

Crying, she stood by the door, for a while longer, feeling the pain increase, and slowly, after the moon had long ceased to shine, had the pain slowly subsided.

*

McIntosh reached for a fine quill and decided to execute a bold plan, as he newly discovered he enjoyed risk-taking:

Dear Rebecca,

Tonight, by the Savannah River, I have placed a surprise under a rock inscribed with the words, "East of Eden." You must bring a lantern and a blanket; therein lies a secret only you can unfold.

Signed,
Lachlan McIntosh

Rebecca was astonished. Should she meet him in the evening? Would her mother approve? For goodness sake! She trembled. What could his intentions be—with the blanket and all? Did he want to make a wanton woman of her? Rebecca was attracted to McIntosh—nearly every girl she knew spoke of him as though he were a Greek god. His hair was the topic of conversation amongst the girls; he seemed to have such wonderful tricks up his British sleeve! And truth, she did witness him bathe on more than one occasion—she'll admit to the sin of voyeurism—but that was out of sheer curiosity. What could he mean by East of Eden? She had been warned of the soldier's disease by Old Mrs. Higgins; perhaps McIntosh was plagued by this debilitating illness. More than one soldier made his way to Mary Musgrove's "tavern by the cove"; rumor had it some of the orphans by the church door were testament to the debauchery of Savannah's ruffians and desperate men in arms, afraid of death, craving one more thrill of immortality.

Rebecca read the letter one more time and placed it under her pillow. She knew of too many girls who gave themselves away, only to look for an ill-suited but eager man to wed—a cuckold before his nuptials. She wouldn't be one of those—no matter what he wanted. She brushed her long hair, which tended to curl by the edges, and then cleaned her delicate skin with water and soft soap from the New England colonies. How she wanted to visit New York! She heard the colonies up North were far superior to the jungle of Georgia, and more populous as well. There were many Negroes now in Georgia; she wasn't sure if that was different in the North. She didn't dislike them or think ill of them at all; but she did fear some of the men. Her mother put the fear of God in her when it came to that. But in all honesty, most of the women she knew had to fear their own kind. The men who battered their wives and the terrible temptations most women succumbed to were, in all honesty, from their own lot. (How ugly was the truth! How she feared it!) But she did not question so much the institution itself, having accepted it as the way of life in Georgia, despite James Oglethorpe's laws and his personal agenda against rum and the Negroes. James Oglethorpe had also been a man of fascination for Rebecca, and for her close friends as well. But he kept to himself in that way, and he never truly showed an interest in the belles. Not altogether. How her mind wandered! What should she do about McIntosh?

As though plagued by a variety of McIntosh's illness, Rebecca followed the poorly lit path with a basket in her hands. She did not bring the blanket—she was wearing a shawl instead. She had lied to her mother—not the first time—and told her she had mending to take care of for the poor widow, Old Higgins. Having taken care of all the domestic duties, her mother was unable to object. Rebecca felt guilty for misleading her mother, but how else could she fulfill her curiosity? It had to be understood. It must, eventually, she supposed. The lantern in her hand helped ease her way through the vines and leaves. Her feet brushed against the long grass by the sides of the river bank. The path to the river was easier to follow during the day. She began to regret her choice. Oddly, she began to shiver, even though it was more mild than usual that particular night. She also felt a strange itch across her back. Her long dress and her bodice weighted her down all the more. Her dark hair began to unloosen from the winds. Heaving, she finally reached the edge of the river, and began scouting the terrain for the rock. She did not hear a sound—was he here too? It was so very hard to tell. She squinted in the dim light and bent down to aid her search. What does this say? It was an arrow! Excited, she ran to the next rock, a bit away from the previous one, and found yet another arrow. How frustrating! She thought. Again, she saw a small stone, and this one was covered with roses. Where did he get the flowers from? Utterly surprised and excited, she touched the flowers. The petals were silken—how she dreamed of gowns with the same texture! And the scent was the heavenly scent she pined to represent: romance, desire, vibrancy. She placed each delicate flower into her basket, first taking in a full breath from each one. Inhaling and pacing. Inhaling and closing her eyes. And then, she saw the inscription. "East of Eden." What did it mean? How did he manage to hew the letters in so nicely? Is this what soldiers learn at the front? She felt each dull curve. The *s* was so finely sculpted. And what was under the rock? Didn't he say there was some kind of surprise under it? She slowly lifted the small stone and found a wooden case. She opened it, prying it gently. Could it be? She held her breath as she touched a ring with a fine salt-water sea pearl. Where did he get it from? It was exquisite! How odd. She could have sworn she heard something. She turned around and saw bright yellow lights. Candles! One… two… three… all of a sudden candles lit up the dark, and she saw the form of a man with another two men… and violins? They began to play a fine melody, and McIntosh slowly began to pace toward her. Could this truly be happening to me? She gasped and held her small, white hands to her mouth, covering her lower jaw.

"Take your hands down," McIntosh whispered. "How can I see your beautiful lips when you cover them in that fashion?"

McIntosh stood a few feet away and then inched closer. Rebecca's hands were streamed with tears. It must have been the melody! It was so sweet and tender! And truly. How did he accomplish all this?

"Will you pleasure me with this dance?" Like a true English gentleman, he bowed and held his arm.

Rebecca stared into McIntosh's eyes and realized the blue azure turned into a dark grey at night. How he stared at her, with such intensity! She felt the fire of the candles perhaps burning within her. Had she never truly felt this way before? She wiped the last tears from her face and smiled wide—revealing a beautiful smile rare in those parts of Georgia. McIntosh knew he had seen the face of an angel and danced with her until the candles long burned and the moon long shone.

James Oglethorpe walked on the main street of his town and lifted his hat for the familiar faces. He had not been inducted as Governor proper of Georgia—but he had all the vested powers of such. He had been the founder and the defender. Indeed, in Georgia he was probably a hero of such proportions he was sure the annals of history would long remember his services to the great King George. He had to leave, as much as he detested the voyage. (The threat of sickness and the scurvy were his companions on a few occasions.) The colony was akin to the ancient sirens at sea, he mused. This continent keeps luring me back, into its alluring tide. But he had no choice; if only he hadn't felt lonely at times, it was truly all very bearable and very much to his liking. Adventurous forays were his main pursuit since his youth. The army had been suitable in that regard. He traveled across Europe in his youth, learning of the French ways, an altogether unscrupulous nation, he observed. The Parliament may not have been the most efficient governmental form, but the stories clouding the French monarchy were appalling. The Divine Rights. How long would the Divine grant these rights? In America, there was truly no "divinely" ordained class—on par with the British aristocracy, that is. And the concept of the gentry! Where a job is anathema! He laughed aloud, surprising some of the passersby. Yes. America was a new world order. And now, for my departure, he thought. I must place a visit to Sheftall and McIntosh: the former for congratulations and the latter for dissemination of duty.

*

"Like this, Mordechai. You place your right hand over *both* eyes. Yes! Very good. Now repeat after me: *Shema Yisrael Hashem Elokeynu Hashem Echad.*"

Mordechai repeated these words, as his father covered him with a prayer shawl.

"Very good! Now repeat the following and I'll let you play with Reuben: *Torah Tzivah Lanu Moshe Morasha Kehilat Yaakov.*"

Mordechai did as he was told, kissed his father, and merrily turned around to his playmate. Benjamin smiled. The child, in Benjamin's older age, transformed his life. How much joy he brought into Benjamin's life. Mordechai's eyes had the same luster as Perla's—only they had Benjamin's coloring. Dark. Very Semitic in that regard, he thought. It would be hard to mistake him for an Irish boy or a Protestant. Our faces mark our identity. We must not lose it in the wilderness of this great country, he thought. Here, unlike in the Prussian ghetto, Mordechai would be free to roam the countryside, free to interact with heathen and gentile, Jew and Catholic. This was not a monolithic society. The Germans in Ebenezer were on good terms with the Sheftalls, and Mordechai would probably learn in their schools one day. He had to sustain the child's religion. He repeated the *Shema* with his son twice a day—once during *Shacharis* prayers and once before bedtime. It had become a routine Benjamin enjoyed. Soon he would cut his child's long hair and place a skull-cap on his head. Benjamin still proudly wore his—even though his Sephardic brethren insinuated that pointing out his Jewishness was not necessarily the wisest move. Why focus on religion, here, in this new country? Don't you see how the different denominations interact? So they don't agree on ideology or theology or any -ology. But we live together—a miracle, no? Who would have heard of praying outdoors, as we sometimes do during those sweltering summer days? For years our grandparents pissed in their pants in fear of the Christian neighbors. You heard of all those horror stories of children revealing their Jewish heritage to the parish priest, so innocently of course, but with terrible consequences for their Marrano parents. Burned at the stake. Nunez had a couple of family members burned to dust, may they rot in hell those evil priests. The Jews will make their way here, Benjamin. More of your kind, hopefully. Benjamin would jest—and why may your kind not join me here in my makeshift synagogue? You are all most welcome, despite our different heritage. Certainly, if Catholic and Protestant can find a way to live in peace, we Ashkenazim and Sephardim can learn to do the same? What say you, ha?

Oglethorpe knocked on Benjamin's door and let himself in. Sheftall had been oddly encouraging members to walk into his house during the morning hours—for prayers, of course. James observed Benjamin kiss his child and place some type of shawl over the child's head. The child repeated some strange Hebrew phrase and then ran off. A beautiful boy, with delicate features. It was as though the mother lived in his breast. Benjamin waved at James, walked over, saluted, and then shook the general's hand.

"Sir!" Benjamin said, "Why the honor of your general's visit, this morning!?"

James chided, "I have come to convert!" Both laughed for a moment and shifted slightly. James cleared his throat. Remove your hat, he told himself. Don't forget your manners! "Mr. Sheftall. I am here to congratulate you on your forthcoming marriage to Ms. Solomons. I have heard she is a marvelous woman. I wish you much joy!" James smiled gallantly and took Sheftall's hand. The Jews were a resilient lot. James considered all of Sheftall's losses and hoped there were further gains for the chap. But how did he manage to woo a woman? Benjamin was by far not more attractive than *his* person! And the lady in question was attractive, no doubt. No point in envying the poor man; after all, he lost a wife and child not long ago. Indeed. No point at all.

Benjamin thought highly of Oglethorpe at that moment. How strange that this gentleman should behave in such a violent manner one moment and in such a gallant fashion the next. These British never cease to amaze.

"But why now, Sir? The wedding is scheduled for November the twentieth?"

James sighed and smiled. "I'm off to London. Part of the bargain, I suppose. Well, I'll be off now. I am to board in a few hours. And please inform Ms. Solomons of my very best wishes upon her betrothal." Ever the suave speaker, James slightly bowed, placed his finely woven hat on his aristocratic head, and headed out the door, noting the strange *mezuzah* by the doorpost.

As James continued toward McIntosh, he saw Nunez walk in. "Old chap! It is very good to see you this morning. How fares Ms. Shires? There is rumor she has caught a dreadful cold dancing the night to McIntosh's romantic melodies. Is the rumor substantiated?" Nunez held onto Oglethorpe's hand for a while, warmed by the gentleman's cordiality.

"No, sir. She is simply tearing from an allergen in the grass by the wayside of the road leading to the river. It was caught in her dress, and it rubbed off of her as she undressed in the evening. She shall recover just fine for her suitor to seek some more dances—perhaps in the town hall, if that should suffice this wonderfully tender couple." So it was true. What a rascal that McIntosh was after all! Wooing a girl underneath the stars, with fiddlers. Half the town was abuzz with the affectionate tale. Perhaps that was the new way to win a woman's heart. Sitting in parlor rooms with chaperones never did permit for moments of much intimacy. Lucky chap! That Ms. Shires was a true southern belle, she was. With a mound of dark hair and fair skin, a figure elongated and fine, a waist as small as a doll's, she had been the object of admiration of many a gentleman. Well, enough of that. Perhaps if he had used the same creativity in battle to court Elizabeth he would be in far different circumstances today. A bachelor. A wretched one, if he truly were to admit the truth. Ever since the tragedy of his secret lover, the exotic Florence, he had been very watchful. Indeed, come to think closely on the matter, his energy had been focused on the safety of his colony! Love had eluded him. Well, at least McIntosh had this wonderful woman to warm his heart.

Nunez waited for a response from James; James was oddly unfocused. His eyes watered a bit and turned off to the side. Perhaps he too was touched by the youth of this country.

"Thank you, Nunez. It was good to see you!" Once again, James shook the doctor's hand and continued his way toward the Romeo of Savannah—no other than the solicitor from Manchester.

McIntosh contemplated the method by which he would propose to Rebecca. He could not rest his head the entire night! After dancing he had felt such elation he could not sleep. He had been drunk, it seemed, with an elixir of such freshness! Her hair grazed his cheek on too many an occasion, and the scent of the roses in her basket wafted in the moonlight. The crickets added a bit to the harmony of the fiddler's tune. That was a nice touch, he mused. He tried to whisper into her ears, but she kept giggling. At one point he did manage to say he thought her the most precious pearl he had ever seen. She wore the ring the entire evening— indeed, it fit perfectly well on her middle finger. (No sense in thinking where it originated from. War booty was a prerogative of sorts, he supposed.) She was silent for most of the dances, as though somehow speaking would erase the magic of the moment. How would it be to become lovers? How much longer should he wait? In those terrible battles not long ago he had held onto her smile as though the world depended on its radiance for sustenance. He would close his eyes and think of all the wonderful ways they would bask in their lovemaking. And then he would somehow face the enemy with renewed spirits. And he had been right all along; she was a dream. How kind she was to that old wretch, Old Mrs. Higgins! Not a single soul cared for the old widow! But she had been so kind, feeding her and supplying the old wretch with victuals. McIntosh imagined the way Rebecca would attend to *him*, and he considered himself a king. Yes. A *king*.

James found McIntosh pacing the front enclosure of Rebecca's house. He seemed preoccupied. James continued his vigorous pace until he stood face to face with McIntosh, who was eager for a distraction.

"General Oglethorpe! Good morn!"

"I have heard you woo better than Don Juan himself, young man. Is this true?"

McIntosh smiled, a bit sheepishly, and allowed James the jest.

"Yes, sir! Do you approve, sir?"

"Yes! A man must do his very best, in every inventive manner, to win the heart of his beloved."

McIntosh felt a strong impulse to hug Oglethorpe, out of sheer bliss. Truly, how *does* one contain all that ecstasy? How this lad does seem to be beside himself, James realized. He stepped aside, and explained the nature of his departure. McIntosh's brows, every so delicate and fine, wondered what this meant for his future with Rebecca.

"Should this interfere with my wedding, sir? What then?"

James knew McIntosh should ask the question. It was only fair, after all.

"Hale can always be called upon, most certainly. And, if exigencies shall occur, you may rely on Bull. I hear his wife is expecting again, but he may avail himself as her mother has immigrated to the Carolinas."

McIntosh did not hesitate this time. Completely out of his character, he grabbed James's hand and nearly, truly, *almost nearly*, hugged the general.

*

On a brisk but bright morning, Benjamin took Hannah Solomons for his wife. The *chuppah* was simply festooned with vines and lilacs from the gardens of the town. Minis placed a shawl over their heads, and Nunez blessed them both. The witnesses were eager to sign Benjamin's contract to his dear wife, the *ketubah*. Mrs. Minis brought her brood to celebrate, and Reuben chased Mordechai round the *chuppah* just as Hannah circled her husband. The fiddlers played a fine tune, one that was as somber as it was tender. More than one woman had tears streaming down her cheek. The bride wore an embroidered white dress with fine lace all across the sleeves and collar. Her hair was braided and pinned, with flowers and some beautiful ornaments: a crystal butterfly from Mrs. Minis and a pearl from the Abrams, who travelled from Pennsylvania to attend.

That very morning, Hannah awoke to the knowledge that *today* shall mark the anniversary of a new life. Perhaps God will grant her a child, just as He granted her a husband. The thrill of newfound love, and the potential for even more warmth, filled her heart with a sense of purpose. Somehow, she felt as though she was twenty again, and all those years of decay disappeared in a strange moment of reversal. The earth's axis shifted, perhaps—her world had so changed. All its prospects have altered to the degree to which she would finally be *known* to man, in the way a woman is truly, and properly, *known* to a man. She could hardly breathe thinking on it. Just the night before, she had cleansed herself properly and dipped in the waters of the great river of Savannah. The body of water was warmer than the ocean, and Mrs. Minis kept close watch so that no man should see her pristine body dipping in the waters. She had counted the days, five in total, of her menses. She then counted another seven, just as she had been schooled, of clean days. No blood. No stains. Pure and clean. Under a fading ceiling of ever-appearing starlight, she then submerged with words of holy blessings to her God, the One God of Abraham, Isaac, and Jacob, her forefathers who had agreed to the law of purification, and whose progeny signed a binding contract on the famed Mount Sinai in the year 2448 from the year of Creation. Part of the progeny of Jews, long since the time of the lost Temple in Jerusalem, her women have adhered to this secret code of law. She was a single link in the long line of Jews, and she shall transmit this secret to another chain, to another generation of Jewesses, who purify their bodies before allowing their husbands to submerge themselves in their bodies. It was the very core of the Jewish home, she was told. The secret that held the Jewish people bonded throughout the ages. It is the very secret that will allow for endless promise and endless desire. The anticipation for reunion after long separation ensured the rejuvenation of a man's union with his wife. Hush. This is the reason for their caution and prudence; it is not to suppress entirely, but to patiently and precisely liberate the intensity of their desire in bursts of disciplined passion. Thinking of all this, as she paced slowly around her husband, seven times, the number of submersions in the purifying waters of the river, Hannah quietly breathed, imagining her body finally giving way to its full promise, with a man who emerged so promisingly in the backwoods of the New World.

*

James gasped as he read Lady Elizabeth's letter. Could it be? He read it a second time:

Dearest James,

I hope, with dear God's blessings, that you are safe and secure in Georgia. There are murmurings abroad regarding the Spanish invasion of the colony, and I am most concerned for your safety. I have longed to write to you in previous months, but, alas, personal matters have prevented my doing so. James, I am a widow now. My late husband fell ill, quite suddenly, with a terrible illness. The physician informed the family that he had not but a year to live with this most dreadful ailment. Although I cannot say with assurance that he had been a warm and congenial partner in every regard, he had been devoted and generous until his last breath. I currently reside in Cranham, which, I am sure you know, is located in Essex. I am lady to an empty manor. My daughter Anna warms my spirits, but the doors are mostly locked; the drapes collect dust. This empty place lends to contemplation, and I have come to see the folly in my keeping silent all these years.

James, I have longed for you. In my more mature years, for I am a woman in every regard, James, I have come to realize the error and folly of my youth. To replace warmth in one's heart with the cold guarantee of financial security is a terrible, terrible misfortune. The days of loneliness have been seemingly endless—and all due to a brief, unwise choice. I have been untrue to myself, and I fear I may have harmed your precious soul. I cannot continue to sit in this grand library without finally confessing my long-buried secrets. My regard for you is immense. Your work in the States is truly exemplary; the sacrifice you endure—and all without recognition! How often can one meet such a grand gentleman? All the men in this town, those that I know, yearn for recognition, yet duly undermine their fellow men to achieve honor and prestige. But you have always remained steadfast, and most truly, a pioneer of grand vistas. How I admire your resolute nature! Yet, I do fear for you! The scourge of this terrible invasion weighs heavily with me, sweet James. Please! Take care!

And know, in a barren manor in Essex, sits a woman praying for your safe return.

Yours affectionately,
Elizabeth Wright
Cranham Hall, Essex, 1743

James sucked in air and sat by the side of his bed. So she had been a lonely widow and he a lonesome bachelor. Had she truly lived an empty life all this time? Ten years in Georgia had transformed James, but it had not dispelled the yearning for Elizabeth, not entirely. He had seen her during his last trip, but she remained aloof. He had all but given up hope; surely their attachment was a thing of the past. Suddenly, the weariness he had felt for so long now, yet had never truly acknowledged, began to dissipate. Perhaps this was an invitation? Could it be? A demure insinuation? He read the words again, "James, I have longed for you." All of a sudden, James was transported to the Wright's London home years prior. The splendor of the room, the lushness of Elizabeth's figure; the rash kiss, furtive and ardent. He felt a rush of vertigo and fell on the bed. Elizabeth! Her elongated neck, her soft skin. The perfume of Eden. Elizabeth! Her pink gown, shadows of his nocturnal imaginings.... With speed commensurate to Fleance, James searched his desk for a clean sheet of paper. Rummaging for a sharp quail, James composed the following letter:

Dear, Dear Elizabeth,

How sorry I am to learn of your grief! To think that you wallow in wretched solitude! But know this—I had nearly given up all hope of winning your affection. And, in that regard, I am most pleased—for you have opened up a sore hole in my desolate heart. I had imagined it was sealed for good on that fateful day, in which you shared your vows with Sir Wright. I have been a wretched soul, my love. Yes, I have. But now I feel as though I am ever so youthful again! I have never ceased adoring you, my immortal beloved. I have learned to live in denial of your love, but if you should just let me into your own, the gaping hole in my heart of hearts shall be crowned with the glory of your love.

I shall set sail for England and leave Georgia for good if you but pledge an oath to reunite and somehow begin anew.

Ever so furiously awaiting your response,
Your James

And so, it had come to pass that James returned to his homeland in the year 1743 to Elizabeth Wright's manor, subdued by the adventures in America and ready to settle for the adventures of married life. A bachelor until the ripe age of forty-eight, James joined Elizabeth in holy matrimony. Not entirely convinced his marriage with Georgia had been fruitless or barren, James decided it was time to replace one vow with another. And so he had wed Elizabeth and finally shared the canopy of marital bliss with his beloved, satiating his desire and love in one momentous sweep of luck and good timing.

"I have always been fond of you."

Promising Delights

APRIL SEVENTEEN HUNDRED AND SIXTY-ONE marked a day of joy
for Benjamin. Sixty-nine years had not diminished the charming
shimmer in his eyes. Hannah Solomons proved a hardy woman
who bore two children—only one of whom survived infancy. *Ach.*
How the years have gone! He mused. Both Mordechai and Levi
were young men now. And on that Passover eve of that particular
year, Benjamin reclined on the embroidered chair and sighed for
Mrs. Abigail Minis. Her husband had succumbed four years ago
to illness, leaving poor Abigail to care for her brood. Now it was
Benjamin's turn to repay Abigail's kindness during *her* time of
need. How fate has a way of surprising us, he thought! To think
that now *she* is the widow and I the married man! Benjamin
insisted Abigail spend Shabbat meals and the Passover Seder, the
commemorative feast celebrating the Hebrews' redemption from
the onslaughts of Egypt, with his dear family.

For most of the 1740's the Minises and the Sheftalls were
the cornerstones of the Jewish presence in the thirteenth colony.
Indeed, Benjamin helped found the St. George Society, which
assisted orphaned children. Due to his concern for the Georgian
colonists, he was accepted by his gentile neighbors (and that
included John Hale!) into Solomon's Lodge, a prestigious Masonic
order. In all, Benjamin felt very much pleased with Georgia. For
a while after Perla's death, he believed his life would be burdened
by caring for Mordechai. But it had been Hannah, after all, who
relieved him of that duty and enabled him to prosper. Out of the
seeds of need, he came to realize, a blossoming love emerged. Their

union had been blessed, and her generosity was equally bestowed on Perla's child as well as Hannah's own. Levi and Mordechai were only a few years apart; somehow, God had granted him another son despite Hannah's age, and the two were equally raised as brothers.

"Raise the glass of wine, ladies and gentleman! Let us sing the *Hallel* together, in unison!"

Levi glanced at Mordechai. Mordechai stifled a belch. They had eaten a bit too much. Abigail poured the wine for the older children and insisted the younger ones drink grape juice. Levi began the prayer, wishing to continue his conversation with Abigail's beautiful daughter, Hannah, as soon as possible. But Hannah remained in the kitchen, cleaning the dishes. (Benjamin relieved his slaves of all duties on Passover, a benevolent gesture Hannah Sheftall wasn't entirely pleased with.)

Once the *seder* was fully conducted, Hannah Minis asked Benjamin if she could borrow his treasured *Dictionary of the English Language*. The book was a gift from General James Oglethorpe, who had befriended the author, Samuel Johnson. The author had inscribed the front pages with a witty remark, "to mark with great care the book's remarks on language." Benjamin often corresponded with James Oglethorpe, the general her father had helped during the War of Jenkins' Ear. Her father had sent a key shipment during the siege in which a fleet of thirty-six boats appeared at the mouth of the Altamaha River. When her father died, James had felt obligated to keep correspondence with her mother as well. Oglethorpe no longer lived in Georgia, but he kept close touch with Benjamin, who had fought alongside James. Many stories were told about the general, who had never assumed a title nor had been appointed one. Some say he had an illegitimate child, others that the King was displeased with his anti-slavery policy. She was sure the rumors were a mixture of sense and pure nonsense. His policies were too unpopular to sustain themselves: Negroes abounded in Georgia, and people's throats were well-watered with rum and ale. To think of her father's estate without Negroes? To think of all those farm lands without their hands?

THE REBEL OF SAVANNAH

Hannah turned to Levi, and asked if he had read the book. "No need! I should read a dictionary of the Indian language!" Hannah knew why he was keen to do so—Levi regularly traded with the Indians. Deerskins. Since Levi was thirteen (was that 1752? Hannah wondered), he had spent many laborious hours dressing the skins. His hands became filthy, and he smelled of musk and of some hideous odor no human could properly identify. They had been such good childhood friends! But, almost overnight, Levi became determined to profit from his "deerskins investments" and neglected himself and their friendship. His half-brother Mordechai was more attentive to Hannah during those years, and Hannah felt a strong attachment to Mordechai since their very early years, the years her mother nearly adopted Mordechai. And then, just when Levi's clothing no longer stunk of rawhide and pigskin, he began to reek of blood and animal guts! He spent an entire year as a butcher, working double-time and never spending pretty pence on anything but a new shirt for Rosh Hashanah or a waistcoat for Passover. Venture after venture, Levi managed to do well in business. Even the governor was keen on aiding the ambitious youth! Levi was now a landowner—of more than 100 acres—and he also owned seven good slaves. Since then, Hannah admitted, Levi no longer stunk of buckskin. But he had paid the price of neglecting her; she had grown too fond of Mordechai while Levi accrued his fortune.

Mordechai, on the other hand, worked assiduously in his family retail shop on Broughton Street. Benjamin had managed the store after his marriage to Hannah Solomons, but since Benjamin had lost ground to old age, Mordechai gradually assumed the responsibilities of clerk, manager, and salesman. Then, during the same time Levi had amassed his lands, the two became business partners. It was odd; indeed, up until then, when was it? Oh yes. Not too long ago, Hannah realized, Levi grew interested in becoming his brother's commercial counterpart.

Levi accompanied Hannah and her family on that Passover eve. The air was typically humid; the spring had settled earlier than expected that year. Levi had prepared his entire maneuver: the quiet walk home, standing outdoors, catching a glimpse of a smile from the melancholy girl. Ever since his youth, he had eyes only for Hannah. But how could he dare ask for her hand in marriage with nothing to his name? It came to him rather suddenly: he must first accumulate wealth and only *then* would he deign request her hand. Capital investment became an obsession from thirteen years of age. And each time he slaved away and pocketed sixpence, he imagined Hannah's wholesome face smiling with fondness. Images of bliss kept him from becoming sick in the butcher house and from near collapse on the sultry days of Savannah's summers. Few knew just how squeamish he truly was. Levi revealed his truest intentions to no one. And least of all, Hannah Minis.

Levi gazed at Hannah's long curls, falling from their up-do after a long evening. She had the posture of a British Duchess, and a slightly elongated nose of the upper echelons of Britain's great aristocrats. Her eyes were oval-shaped, and her left eye was a bit more almond-shaped than the right. Her lashes were darker than her hair and quite long. When she rolled her eyes at her siblings, the irises seemed like two globes set in iridescence. Hannah was soft-spoken but capable of putting her foot down when displeased. Unlike Mordechai, though, Levi didn't distinguish a single fault in the young girl in question. Hannah captivated him, and he had felt that way since he had become a man.

"Hannah—Did you enjoy the *seder*?"

Hannah turned to Levi and shrugged, "I guess I did. But I miss my father. I'm sorry. I should be more grateful. After all, your family—"

Levi stood and held her arm. "You don't need to apologize, Hannah. Your father *is* missed, by all."

Hannah searched Levi's eyes for comfort. "You can only guess how many tears Mama has wept since he perished. She refuses to seek another husband, and we are certainly grateful for that. But she is miserable! I tell you, if I were careless and neglected to bring her tea or sit with her one afternoon, conversing the next day becomes a nearly insurmountable feat!"

Levi felt a pang of regret; he had never guessed such! All those years of competitive gain had left little room for sympathies and dialogue. Did he detect a tear in Hannah's eyes? Had she truly been tormented all this time? Of course she had been. He knew that Hannah Minis was a compassionate girl. The entire town was abuzz when she cried so loudly upon her father's death. *He* witnessed it, but surely she had overcome the trials of her father's death. Mysterious one that she was, at least to Levi, he hadn't detected as much as she seemed to reveal at that moment. Levi couldn't quite find the words to cheer up the girl. He was content with her attention. Hannah looked at her shoes, which were ivory and slightly pointed, and then back again at Levi. "Well, I guess I better go in now, Levi. Happy Holidays."

Hannah turned around slowly, slightly uncomfortable in her bodice. The humidity caused her gown to cling and the feeling of dried sweat unnerved Hannah. Levi, of course, was ignorant of her discomfort. He grabbed her arm, "Wait!" She lifted her left brow, slightly, and delicately removed her arm from his grasp— "Yes? What is it?"

Levi's palate dried up and he felt queasy. Her eyes stared directly into his own; he didn't know what to say. He nodded his head and mumbled, "Sorry." She shrugged and whispered good night, as she gathered the folds of her dress and stepped into her house, relieved and spent from the *seder* night.

Levi suppressed his disappointment. How could he? He had it all set in his mind. Word for word. But when she looked at him so, with that quizzical expression, he felt as though a vast chasm separated them. He must have carried on in his third ear, for years, conversations and wonderful chats with Hannah Minis. But then. When the moment arose. He was silent.

Levi returned to find Mordechai reading by a dim candle.

"Why on earth are you still awake?" asked Levi.

"I could ask you the same," Mordechai retorted, with a click of the tongue. "So? What did she say?"

Levi shrugged once again, this time with shoulders slumped.

"I see," Mordechai sighed.

Mordechai closed the prayer book, kissed it, and walked up to Levi. "Attempt to court the young woman, Levi. For goodness sake! Flowers. Roses are a charm. Just look around you! Savannah is *teeming* with gardens—enjoy long walks! You must *seduce* the woman—not kvetch to her about your love."

Offended, Levi retorted, "That's easy for you to say! You know how busy I've been all this time."

Mordechai picked up the candle and stood face to face with Levi, "Maybe that's the problem, fellow." Mordechai patted Levi twice on the shoulder, and, without a word, marched to his bed chamber.

*

Mordechai left Levi standing in the parlor. The chap was mad for Hannah, but Hannah was a reserved, quiet girl. True, she was beautiful. But not as beautiful as Frances. Hannah, to Mordechai, was more of a sister. Frances was the exotic fruit of his *every* fantasy. (Not that there were many choices in his part of the woods.) In fact, if it hadn't been for his loyal friend, Joshua Hart, he never would have known of Frances's existence. (Good chap!) Marvelous young woman! And if he hadn't ventured into the shipping trade and traveled to Charleston every so often, he never would have met Joshua Hart. What a fancy!

It was only three years ago he had decided to expand his small mercantile business by constructing a wharf and warehouse on the Savannah River. Georgia, as a royal colony, traded regularly with the Caribbean islands, the West Indies, and England. Abraham Minis had made his fortune in the trading business; it only made sense to join the merchants of the burgeoning Georgian towns. His mother (he referred to Hannah as Ima) had always warned him that small steps are safer than large ones. So, he had decided to gain experience by acting as merchant trader. He began with warehousing, importing, and exporting his own products and those of others. The Royal Governor James Wright deeded the necessary land—one hundred feet under the Savannah bluff—and traveling to Philadelphia and Charleston began in earnest. He had successfully traded with Thomas Bruce and even managed a sometime-partnership with the hotheaded Joseph Wood.

Joshua Hart, unlike Mordechai, wasn't born in the colonies. Joshua, very much like Hannah Sheftall, was born in the Netherlands. He didn't have much of an accent, since he settled in Charleston as a youngster. Mordechai had known Joshua for quite some time, and in all that time, Joshua had not revealed that he had an eligible sister! Naturally, Mordechai was taken aback when he saw a young woman with a small upturned nose gazing at him from a chaise longue. Her dress was markedly European in style with frills and lace and a heavy bodice. Her petite frame gave the impression of a Russian Doll, and her plump arms and bosom seemed to yearn for a looser corset. Mordechai had never seen a young woman with such a small mouth; it seemed to belong to a child. Her eyes, round and honey-dewed, were encircled with high arching eyebrows. She seemed, without saying a word, to be immensely interested in her surroundings. The brows lent her a sophisticated air, while her mouth seemed to contradict the air of natural maturity. Mordechai recognized her as Joshua's sister. Indeed, they shared the roundness. But she seemed more like a sprite! From whence did *she* come?

Mordechai had seen many young women before, but never had he felt the odd sensation of being at a loss for words or gazing (for more than the appropriate time) at a woman's bosom. The love sonnets of Shakespeare sprung to mind: he felt as though "he had eyes to wonder, but lack[ed] tongues to praise." Taken by the arched brow and her expression, he thought, "there lives more life in one of your fair eyes / Than both your poets can in praise devise." Since then, Mordechai had traveled to Charleston on more than one occasion. He had yet to reveal to his family the source of his every promising delight; indeed, he had yet to reveal to Frances just how greatly his love was like a fever, "longing still / For that which longer nurseth the disease." Feeling as though he could not fully express his experiences, he turned to the poets for consolation. The Songs of Songs provided ample imagery, and his imagination waxed with each verse: "the great waters cannot submerge my love…." With King Solomon's words echoing in his mind, Mordechai fell fast asleep on that Passover of 1761.

*

The next few weeks passed by in a haze. Mordechai traveled to Charleston with one mission in mind. And with the same focus and determination Mordechai previously utilized to seal commercial deals, he set off, together with a dash of charm, no doubt, to gather Frances' heart and seal it off from foreign influence. Joshua had arranged a room for Mordechai, and so, the time arose when Mordechai found his sweetheart stitching ever-so-delicately a handkerchief with a fine, floral design. The Hart's abode was decorated in the Dutch style, which was more common in New York estates, those of the New Amsterdam influence, and far less of the Charleston style. The drawing room was farther apace from the kitchen quarters, and the shades were all Venetian lace—a mark of distinction. The housemaid wore a bonnet, and Frances preferred fancy Dutch chocolate to the English breakfast teas. America was a bit behind in the fashion sense, Frances realized, as she perused the shops of her brother's hometown. But there were markets here, and a chance to enrich one's coffers. Her kind had learned mercantile trade along the Atlantic and Mediterranean coasts for centuries. Frances was proud of her Dutch heritage. Besides, the Dutch were tolerant of other religions, unlike the English with their fair distinctions between religious denominations. Indeed! Didn't Mordechai's parents prefer living in the colonies to the Old Country? The shoes these English women wore! Frances lifted her dress just a bit to admire her shoes—they were in the Parisian style, with satin bows and a slight heel and triangular toe. Hers were blush, a pink hue she adored. Most of the women wore shoes made from the same material as the men of this town, she lamented. How dreadful!

Mordechai stood in the corner, removing his merchant's hat. "May I come in?"

Frances's heart skipped a beat. She hadn't been expecting him! Passover would continue for the next two days; when did he manage the travel? Frances stood, smoothed her gown, and looked Mordechai in the eyes.

212

"Of *course.*" She bowed slightly, keeping a steady glance at his torso. Mordechai was built like one of the sculptors in the museums she had visited the year prior: he was broad by the shoulders and narrow by the hips. She wondered if he had chest hairs like her Sephardic relations, who were more "endowed" with masculine features. She didn't know what she preferred, but she was curious just the same. She blushed slightly when she glanced at him a second time.

They spoke of trifles; the *seder*; and oh, didn't you just sleep like a drunken sailor after all that wine? Laugh. Pause. And Joshua? Did you not hear? He could not rouse himself the next morning for prayers? Giggle. Matzah, the ritual, unleavened bread? It's a treat for the children back home! Who bakes the matzah by the Sheftalls? Oh. Yes. Hannah Solomons was her maiden name? Yes. We knew Solomons once, I suppose. Pause. Awkward moment. Beautiful shoes. I noticed them earlier. Blush. Yes. We can purchase those shoes here too, but the travel time may damage delicate goods such as those. Yes. The fashions here differ from the Continent. So I've heard. But those who travel see the world and purchase goods from all over the Indies and England as well. The English require our cotton—it is by far cheaper. Shall we take a walk in the garden paths?

Frances bowed her head. She enjoyed walking with Mordechai. His eyes, which were deep, twinkled with a few merry tales of his family and his youth. How he hunted a few Indians out of his lands, avoided his schoolmaster's blows, and even fooled his poor mother into believing he had showered when he had only soaked his head in some dishwater. Most anecdotes involved his brother, Levi, who was truly his half-brother. And what of his true mother? Did he remember her, at all? Mordechai's eyes would turn away, cheerless in expression: there was a cloud in his memory he could not dispel, and his mother's face was lost to him forever. But why speak of such things? But did he not have a sibling from his mother? Why speak of such things? He had perished. Pause. Poor Mordechai! How she yearned to hug him! Better yet, promise him sons to compensate him for his loss, his family's terrible loss! Let us walk to the rose gardens; and let us sit? Frances nodded and walked beside Mordechai. His dark suit was sewn from fine yarn; it was lightweight. Keeping slightly ahead, Mordechai found a rose, of dark burgundy, and nicked it. He turned to face Frances and placed the flower in her hair. This is what you look like in my dreams, he said.

*

Levi strained to loosen his collar. The Savannah heat advanced on the inhabitants of the coastal city, to the dismay of all. Levi wondered why Mordechai decided to take off during the Passover week, of all times! The store was left to Levi to manage, and the influx of costumers only increased his nerves. Levi glanced at his pocket watch; soon it would be time for midday prayers. As he turned to count the change in the cashier, he caught sight of Hannah Minis in the mirror adjacent to his left, strategically placed to spot any pickpockets. Levi felt his palate dry up. He glanced quickly at his reflection and removed a bit of snuff from his nostrils.

Hannah's hands, white and neatly manicured, lay folded by her bodice. She smiled but did not look Levi in the eye. Instead, she peered around the store, and said, "Levi. Hello. Mother is looking for black tea." Her delicate voice trailed, and she patted her hair down.

Levi nodded and walked over to Hannah. "Of course, Hannah. How have you been?"

"Well, I thank you, but this oppressive heat! I have half a mind to dip in the ocean waters! It is simply *unbearable!*"

Levi took note of the sweat accumulating on her brow, and marveled just how *warm* she was in her gown. He began to undress her, slowly, and realized he should desist. After all, the rabbis warned of improper thoughts.

Hannah removed a fan from her pouch, which was embroidered with fine English needlework, and began to cool herself. "I cannot stop for a single moment; if I do, I will most certainly *faint!*"

Levi laughed as she stopped fanning herself to pay Levi the fee. "May I?" he asked. Hannah blushed as Levi fanned her, only so glad to assist. "Will you dine with us tomorrow evening, pray?"

Hannah smiled. "Yes. Of course. Will Mordechai return from Charleston by then, do you suppose?"

Levi frowned. "No. I am afraid business matters detain him. Do apologize." Hannah nodded, appeared disappointed, and left the shop. Levi stood in the shop wondering if there was more to her disappointment than she let on.

Levi turned to glance at his reflection once again. He was by far, if one could be objective about these inherently subjective matters, comely. His hair had a tinge of light brown streaks, and he did not cut his hair very short. Instead, he brushed the strands off to the side with a bristle from coarse boar hair. His eyes were grey in hue, a compromise between his mother's Sephardic genes and the Sheftall Ashkenazi ones. He was of commanding stature, and he was trim. He inherited his mother's large eyes; Mordechai's were deep, like Benjamin's. Their father. Benjamin Sheftall had been slowly aging all these years, and the boys learned to become self-sufficient. His father's hard work carried over to the boys—both Mordechai and Levi. But Mordechai had more luck, Levi believed. The man had some secret up his sleeve in Charleston, he was sure of it. And now Hannah. What did she mean by that expression?

*

Mordechai enjoyed his Passover meal, even if it meant more potatoes boiled in dillweed sauce. Joshua kept pouring more wine into Mordechai's glass; Mordechai's jolly nature increased with each swig.

"So long as I do not try to stand, Joshua, I presume I shall remain sober!" The beef was tender; the cook quite experienced. The Harts had a few good Negroes and hired workers to maintain their estate. Frances enjoyed a glass as well.

"A toast!" She insisted. Mordechai's eyes twinkled, and he stood, nearly keeled, but held steady by his comrade, and then declared, "May this be the first of many Passover meals together!" Frances blushed and enjoyed the rich aroma, wondering if Mordechai had intended every word or if he was, simply put, intoxicated. Joshua glanced at his sister and thought, "The two would make a marvelous pair."

Hannah wondered what Mordechai was doing for the Passover meals in Charleston. Goodness knows there weren't many Jews in Georgia. Ever since she could long remember, Mordechai had been her companion. Ever since her father died, it had been Mordechai who would listen to her, especially on those long Friday nights. She had relied on him during the darkest moments of her mother's sorrow. In her imagination, he had been the tireless supporter of her youth. She perhaps never truly realized how integral he had become until he had begun to disappear. Business and trade—her father had been active similarly. It was due to those war years that her father made a fortune, a supply of monetary funds they *still* subsisted on. And now Mordechai. She no longer had much of an appetite. Passover meals were inventive, but tiresome after a while. Hannah's family ate rice and lentils, since she was of Sephardic heritage. But since she married an Ashkenazi, the rice stuffing on Passover was a thing of the past. Hannah wondered if she would have to change her customs and traditions when she married. The wife usually follows the customs of the husband. Pity that, Hannah Solomons liked to say— we could all enjoy delicious rice balls if Benjamin followed *my* heritage! Each year, Mrs. Sheftall would repeat that refrain, and Hannah Minis wondered if life were always full of such circles.

Coming of age in Georgia was a great joy for many of the Savannah youths—particularly girls Hannah's age. But Hannah was Jewish, and her family was quite observant. She did not mix with the townspeople. How she wondered what those town-hall balls were like! Granted she could never associate with the *goyim*— intermarriage was forbidden—but she was curious—oh so curious! Her mother would soon send for a *shadchan*, the matchmaker. Perhaps a gentleman caller would travel from Pennsylvania or New York. Larger Jewish communities resided mostly *out* of Savannah! But she couldn't leave her mother and travel. It wouldn't be just: her mother *needed* her assistance at home, particularly with the education of the young ones. The Hebrew letters and such—

who would teach that? No. It was her duty. But her joy had been listening to Mordechai's tales, his antics, and his occasional sober moments in which they discussed interesting philosophical ideas, particularly of the English writers, such as John Locke. Locke was immensely popular in America, and both Mordechai and Hannah read his famous works. Granted Hannah needed assistance with some of the difficult terminology, but Mordechai seemed to grasp the ideas of the English Enlightenment with great ease. "The whole concept of the social contract is not foreign to Judaism. Think of all the Jews before receiving the Torah on Mount Sinai. Didn't God first ask for their consent? Didn't they agree? And what about Locke's call for religious tolerance!? You know, when I sign contracts with Christians, we put our differences aside so as to come to an agreement—and in this country, the capital investment supersedes personal religious inclinations." Mordechai, his mother liked to say, "was a revolutionary." She did not necessarily seem to agree with his fervor, but kept silent. During those long conversations, come to think of it, Levi had always remained in the room, quiet but *present* nonetheless. How odd that she did not realize that Levi had shadowed their conversations, with the vacuum that Mordechai had left… it had become clear. Hannah Minis looked up; it was an instinctual response. She had felt Levi's intent glances. He smiled and slightly winked.

"Don't eat all those potatoes at once, Hannah. You may never fit into that bodice again if you do!" Benjamin smiled. "Hannah. Would you like some poached chicken, young lady?" Hannah blushed, unsure if she should refuse. She hated to disappoint Benjamin. He was her uncle in every sense, save for the blood. Benjamin shivered for a moment—Hannah's youthful face hearkened that of his late wife, Perla, with its melancholic expression. "I wonder why she is despondent tonight," Benjamin wondered. And to ease her woe, Benjamin decided to regale his guests with tales of Tomochichi and the dancing Indian boys of 1733, much to the delight of the young ones.

*

Mordechai patted his friend on the shoulder. "Are you certain, Joshua?"

Joshua nodded. "Yes. Now excuse me, for I am tired from last night."

Joshua let out an enormous yawn, exaggerating his exhaustion. Frances raised her brows. "So soon, good brother?" Joshua bowed gallantly, and smiled on his way out of the parlor. They had just completed their day festivities—prayers, mealtime, and a bit of chess. The nights were long, since the festivities at night had only begun past sundown. Frances nearly suppressed a yawn as well, but held off. She didn't want to give offense to Mordechai, who had refused to take a mid-day nap. The fervor of youth had caught his sails, and he seemed tireless.

The room had begun to warm due to the mid-day sun. The shades were drawn, and the windows let in a delicate wind. Every so often, Frances felt wisps of hair falling from her intricate up-do. Her handmaid, a Creole woman who went by the name Rochelle, braided her hair every night, unraveled the locks in the morning, and set her hair in elaborate styles. But today, for some reason, her pins weren't holding her locks in place. Frances was about to leave the parlor and call for Rochelle when Mordechai suddenly moved closely to her and whispered, "If I wait another moment I am sure my heart will burst! You must hear me out, dear Frances."

A bit surprised, Frances remained seated and glanced at the porcelain set of tea cups left untouched by the corner of the table. It's too hot for tea, she thought.

Mordechai stood by the opposite side of the table, moved to the left and then to the right. He sat, and then he stood once again. Frances wondered what was agitating the poor man. She stood to ring the bell, but Mordechai blocked her from reaching the entrance.

"Frances. I don't know how to say this. But you must be patient. [How does one go about such things?] When I first met you, I felt as though I had always known you, as though my entire life was waiting for this moment. Up until then, I had gone about my life as a half-soul, never realizing it until I glanced into your special

218

eyes. You're more beautiful than all the verses of Shakespeare—and I am most certain not even *he* could sing your praises! Not properly. Please. Let me finish. Every moment in your presence is a delight; your laugh, smile, even those tiny lips of yours! I am spellbound, Frances! Completely bewitched. Now before your cheeks turn another shade more crimson—oh! How beautiful you are—[Let me do this properly]," He desisted his speech, and with one hand on his heart, Mordechai fell to the floor on one knee and asked Frances, "Will you do me the great honor of becoming my wife?" Taken aback, Frances placed her gloved hand over her mouth, and stared at Mordechai before she gathered her words.

*

Levi rummaged through the cashier for some change. Rebecca Shires was the wife of his father's friend, Mr. McIntosh. The two had fought alongside James Oglethorpe, but that was before Levi was born. She was still a pretty woman, but worn from many pregnancies. She had lost two infants in their youth, a common occurrence. Levi knew his mother gave birth to a child not too long after he was born—but that child died in infancy. In fact, his father's first wife suffered a similar fate. Levi wondered if there would come a time when infants would make it through their early years unscathed. Rebecca smiled at Levi and left the store. "I am glad I am not a woman," he thought. They have to pay a hefty price for the joys of the flesh, he sadly realized. He immediately thought of Hannah. It was strange; ever since Mordechai left for Savannah she had been even more reticent than usual. Could it be? Could it be all this time she had grown fond, *very* fond of him indeed? Levi's thoughts were slightly interrupted by the sound of the front door jangling open. Levi saw the post carriage outside, and the horse kicked its hind legs. The postman entered the store and handed Levi a letter. Levi didn't expect any correspondence. How odd, he thought. He opened it and read,

Dear Levi,

I have wonderful news for you, but I wish you to wait for my return before you tell *Aba*. I am to be married! The most glorious woman

219

will soon become my wife! I am uproariously blissful; if I could just describe to you this feeling, but I lack the words dear brother! We do not wish to tarry; the date is set for October of this year. Frances insists the wedding shall be celebrated in Charleston, and so it shall. I plan to sign a Deed of Trust to ensure legal protection against property loss—I want Frances to be taken care of. Isaac de Costa agreed to the arrangement. Of course, almost certainly upon our marriage, I shall take my bride to our home on Broughton Street where we hope, with God's will, to hear many wonderful joyous sounds of laughing and singing children! I am immensely joyous and only wish the same for you dear, dear brother!

With much gratitude to the One Above,
Mordechai Sheftall

So this was the cause of those hasty trips to Charleston. Of course. Levi's heart colored with tinges of joy and envy. Ashamed of the latter, Levi immediately resolved to share in his brother's joy and maybe to push his own luck with Hannah. Surely it was time! Remaining a bachelor was slowly eroding at his self-restraint: too many temptations lay in Savannah. Females of ill-repute loitered about, particularly by the shoreline, where Levi enjoyed long strolls at night. He never imagined taking off with any one of them; but even *he* hearkened the caveat to "never trust in yourself until the day of your death" from *Ethics of the Fathers*. (Soon he would study the tractate with his father.) Several of the Indian tradesmen hinted their daughters were suitable for "leisure," but Levi scoffed at the insinuation. His mother had been keen on protecting him from the "ills of *goyish* life," and she warned him since his bar mitzvah of the sins of the flesh. Levi and his mother had been very much attached—he was her only child after all. (A gift in her old age, she quipped.) And any disregard for her moral lessons was anathema to Levi. So! He reasoned, he must wed; Wasn't Mordechai, as always, the best role model?

*

Abigail Minis smiled at her daughter, "Don't be silly! Mordechai always treated you like a sister. It is Levi who you should concern yourself with. Of course he is to marry! You met her; she's lovely. Very refined, with European manners."

"I'm foolish for crying, aren't I, *Ima?* He never loved me. Not like I hoped." Hannah began whimpering again, as she was wont for several nights now without revealing her soul's misery. Abigail had figured her daughter was bent on Mordechai, but she hadn't expected her daughter's tears of unrequited love to flow so, what's the right expression? Voluminously?

"I was always hoping he would take me for strolls in the park, in the evening, without the family or the children tagging along. But I waited in vain. It's over. My life is over."

"Don't be silly, Hannah. You are very young; there is no reason why a girl your age should condemn herself to such misery. If you open your heart, you may just see love sprouting from a different source."

Hannah looked quizzically at her mother. Whatever did she mean? Hannah wiped her nose with a handkerchief, kissed her mother and turned her back to wallow all the more in her misery. Abigail sighed as she closed the door, holding a dim candle in her right hand. Perhaps it had been her error as a mother to keep her too close to the Sheftalls and prevent her daughter from seeing more of the world.

*

Levi turned the silk ascot round his collar; he wondered if he appeared too European for this part of the globe. Despite the heat, he wore long silk socks and breeches. His gray eyes shone with excitement, but the delicate skin around his eyes matched his irises—he had slept intermittently at best the night prior. The past month had provided ample occasion to speak with Hannah. Attempts at wooing the woman weren't an easy task; Hannah deliberately quarantined herself in the kitchen. She avoided small talk with Frances and her family. She wore the same dress to each occasion—the meeting of the family, the engagement, and the Shabbos dinner parties. She didn't sing the *zemiros*, hymns, on the Shabbos table. If Mordechai noticed Hannah's melancholic air, he did not let on. Levi often sat across from Hannah, but she barely met his gaze. Mrs. Sheftall whispered into Abigail's ears, "She's turning into a waif. You must force her to eat, even if she doesn't want to. This is an absolute absurdity! If *I* had a daughter, I would scold her." Abigail nodded in agreement, to be polite to her hostess; however, Abigail knew her daughter was a stubborn girl who had her mind set and barred from influence. Mrs. Sheftall turned to Levi and suggested he take her for a walk after dinner. Levi acquiesced, and Hannah simply followed orders.

On those late night walks across Savannah, Levi imagined his life unfolding with each step. They had ventured towards the shore as a ritual, both preferring the cooler air. She held her hands behind her, sometimes folded against her dress. He tried to keep steady, falling into her step every now and then. He took pride in his daily walks with Hannah. He felt as though Hannah's presence were an honor of the greatest kind, as though an aristocrat deigned honor him. Of course it was odd she shared the same name as his mother, but Levi didn't dwell on that.

Instead, he focused on her charming figure and beautifully sculpted features. And the glow of her skin was astounding: a shimmering white. But there were all these awkward silent moments, which she seemed to value, but which he had preferred to avoid.

"The air is beginning to become less and less humid," he whispered.

Hannah stared into the distance, the black sea splashing with familiar sounds. Levi edged closer to Hannah, trying as much as possible to breathe her presence.

"Let's turn back, Levi. I'm tired."

Levi nodded his head, and was about to enquire how she was feeling, when she began to cry.

Levi wondered if he had in any way provoked her outburst.

"Whatever is the matter?"

She covered her face with her hand, wiped the tears that kept streaming down her fine chin, snuffed repeatedly, and whispered, "Levi—I'm sorry. I don't know."

"Do you miss your father? Are you ill?"

Hannah began to cry once more, wrenching Levi's heart in two. How much he wanted to hug her and console her! But he was taught that all *negiah*, touching, was forbidden. He was forced to communicate with Hannah verbally.

"Will you tell me, Hannah? Unburden yourself, to me."

"You wouldn't understand. And besides, you would think less of me. You would think I'm silly!"

"Why don't you test me before you judge my character?"

Hannah stood there and for a moment contemplated unburdening her heart to Levi, but, right at the last second, she decided to keep silent. The matters of a maiden's heart, she believed, had best be kept sealed and bolted.

The wedding was set for after the High Holidays. Benjamin Sheftall approved his son's choice of wife. He would have preferred some form of consultation *prior* to the announcement, but Mordechai had become too independent at an early age, and although Benjamin took pride in his son's self-sufficiency, he was uncomfortable with Mordechai's *modern* approach to matrimony. In the old country, the parents found the suitable partner through an established *shadchan*, matchmaker. Here in America, a friend "introduces an acquaintance." His son refused to wear the skull-cap to meetings at times, preferring the colonial-style hats very much the fashion. But Benjamin trained Mordechai well; he carried the *koshering* knife with him, and he knew the Jewish laws. Benjamin had ensured his son was able to read and learn from the Hebrew books. Reading, writing, figuring—his sons learned the rudimentary subjects under the tutelage of Master John. The Hebrew tutor cost him, but Benjamin never complained. Hannah assisted as well in Mordechai's (and Levi's) education. And now Mordechai finally chose a girl who would hopefully continue in a righteous path. She agreed to cover her hair, in the fashion of the married women of his ancient religion. She said it would probably prove difficult at first, but the bonnets in fashion are very suitable for married life *and* very pretty.

Benjamin was satisfied with his lot. Although he, personally, had not gained a fortune in America, he had ensured his son would be able to maneuver his way in the New World. From an early age, Benjamin inculcated in his son important business sense and even invested in Mordechai's ventures. Mordechai seemed to have luck on his side. Soon enough, he'll be a home-owner with a bride to warm his bed. It was more than Benjamin dreamed of and hoped Levi, his gift from God in old age, would enjoy his brother's success.

It had been a long time since Benjamin thought of his early married life with Perla, but Frances forced the repressed memories to jut out of his consciousness. He missed Perla. Those long, winter nights in Prussia, during their early years, served as excuses for warming the sheets. Generally shivering from cold and complaining that she should "turn to icicles on the great Vistula," he had promised to keep her properly warmed. Although their union was not fruitful for many years, they had enjoyed each other's presence. How soon she had been plucked! Benjamin prayed his son would not suffer a similar fate; he hoped Frances was built of greater stock; hopefully, Frances will be more like Hannah: strong, fierce, and capable of successful pregnancies, even in the advanced fertile years. There was no way to truly know, which only added a bit of anxiety to Benjamin's already anxious heart.

Benjamin recalled those early years in Savannah; his son won't have to endure the poverty he had known. Benjamin thought of all the men Mordechai had never known, the men who had contributed to this very town. James!

"I must inform James Oglethorpe of my son's wedding. After all, if it weren't for James, I would never have settled in Georgia!"

Benjamin was of the old school: they never forget an important figure. Since his departure after the war with the Floridians, James Oglethorpe had on occasion requested news from Georgia. James had promised to keep an eye on the colony, despite the distance. Settled in Essex to a fine Englishwoman, James continued to demonstrate a vested interest in the success of the thirteenth colony. Benjamin obliged, and was quite glad James had not forgotten Savannah. The new governor was quite successful—James Wright—but he lacked the heart James Oglethorpe surely had. James Wright did not object to the whipping of slaves nor did he prevent men from drinking themselves to oblivion. Perhaps for this reason Wright was more well-liked by the townsfolk; James had garnered admirers—but too many enemies along the way. He had too many run-ins with Parliament, but regarding what, exactly, Benjamin could not entirely understand.

"Benjamin, Mordechai insists you speak with Levi. But he hasn't seen him in a few days. Where in Heaven's name is he; do you know?" Hannah said.

Oh—why did women interrupt pleasant reminisce—with troubling *present* woes?

*

Levi replayed the scene in his head over and over. Between drinks. And more drinks. And vomit. It had gone so well. It had started so fine. And then a sour turn. What had gone wrong?

Levi replayed the morning breakfast. Tea. Biscuits and a bit of boiled eggs. Too eager to find Hannah, he had neglected to say goodbye to his mother. The one woman who would always love him. Frailty. Thy name is. Woman. Drink. What had gone wrong?

Having knocked on the Minis home, and finding the Negro housemaid at a loss as to Hannah's whereabouts, Levi began to stroll toward the wharf. The weather had been pleasant that morning. The humidity of the summer dissipated. The homes and gardens flushed like a maiden's plump cheek after much exertion. The verdant fields bustled with Negroes gleaning their day's quota. Children squealed in their long dresses, and the old men sat beside the bay drinking cider. Levi searched the streets of Savannah for Hannah, appraising women, from the posterior, wondering where Hannah had disappeared to first thing in the morning. At length, he found her standing among a group of squalid townspeople, a motley crowd, at the edge of the dockyard. The ocean breeze lifted her dress just a bit, revealing her thin ankles. Her long gown shone in the sunlight. Its hue was a beautiful azure, and her head was bare. Levi stared at her for a while; she seemed so content. A steamboat laden with all kinds of cargo usually generated commotion. Merchants, awake long before the sun splashed its rays on the settlers of King George's colony, bustled about, babbling and scheming.

Hannah turned her head slightly; she felt someone. *Strange*, she thought. She shrugged her shoulders and continued watching the steamboat slowly close in. Her hair, in a loose up-do, undulated and quietly grazed Levi's neck as he discreetly stood next to her.

"Hello, Hannah," he whispered.

"Levi! My, you startled me!"

"You seem to be enjoying yourself. May I join you?"

"Certainly."

Levi turned the glass round and round his head. He could still smell the perfume wafting from her freshly cleansed skin. Lemon zest. Levi closed his eyes. Vertigo settled in, and he fell to the floor, sick, and saliva pouring out of him. Gushing forth. Was it what he had said?

"What brings you here?"

She shrugged her shoulders. "I really can't say. I just was tired of my room, the walls, the house. Why don't we go to the market? I'd like to see the new goods from the Continent. What do you say?"

"I was hoping we could stroll about a bit."

"Why not let's do both?"

Levi acquiesced. Hannah's gait was uncharacteristically light; she seemed cheerful, somewhat. She pointed to some rose bushes, and they marched toward the marvelous flowers. She breathed them inwards, breathing a sigh of pleasure. A few dogs barked in the distance, frightening Hannah along the path. "I've always been frightened by loud noises! I am *silly*, aren't I?"

Levi didn't want to offend Hannah, and his hands had begun to perspire. How did Mordechai propose? Did he kneel? How does one make love without touching the woman you so desire?

"Why are you so quiet today, Levi?" Hannah seemed concerned, and so Levi stopped just as they reached Broughton Street.

"Hannah," he began, "I have deprived myself of every indulgence, spending my earnings on the barest of necessities."

"Yes. Mordechai has told me so once." She seemed gloomy all so suddenly.

"Well. He did not tell you the reason, did he?"

"No. That he did not."

"It was for you, Hannah. For you." Levi stared at Hannah, hoping she understood the implications. She only returned a quizzical expression, somewhat frozen in confusion.

"What do you mean? My father bequeathed a generous—"

"My hard work, Hannah, and all my determination was for the hope of one day meriting a life companion, which no sum in shillings or pence can provide."

Hannah began to comprehend Levi's intentions. Levi deliberately made room for some silence.

"We've known one another since our childhood. You and I are companions—I wish for us to become more. My new house will be completed by the end of the year, Hannah."

Hannah's lips began to tremble. Her eyes began to dart. This way. That way.

"I have not built this house so that I should remain there alone, a bachelor all my days. I wish to start a family of my own, Hannah. And I beseech you to do me the great honor of becoming my wife."

With the mention of wife, Hannah's eyes began to tear ever so slightly, and an audible gasp escaped her delicate mouth.

And again and again, Levi replayed her words, as though to torment himself in a crucible of agony and misery:

"Levi," she shook her head. Swayed back and forth. "I never suspected your feelings. This, this. This declaration—"

"I hope my protestation has not offended you!"

"Levi! No! I have always been fond of you. I am simply shocked."

"But what could have been clearer? Was it not obvious from all our time spent together—"

"Yes. It now *does* appear so." Her eyes shifted to the left, as though she were reminiscing all past encounters. Hannah looked at the silky white skin of her hands. She wore a gold ring her father had bought from a West Indies merchant. She twirled it round her finger.

And then she spoke the words, "I cannot, Levi. I cannot marry you." She began to cry. She covered her mouth, ran home and left him standing in the middle of Savannah, mystified. And utterly defeated.

Levi heard the echo of her voice in his head. I cannot, Levi. I cannot. I cannot…. Levi lifted himself from the pub and walked towards his half-built house. The home where he imagined his body entwining with Hannah's. The house of his daydreams: of warm morning biscuits, blooming yards, cattle grazing the lush fields, and children playing with the farm animals, with milk stains on their lips. The house of his labor: endless hours sweating over deer skins, bloody animals after the slaughter, and foul-smelling merchants from the Indies who had not bathed in epochs. But he had the stamina to endure it all with the brief picture of Hannah in his mind's expanse. It was Hannah's sweet countenance that energized him during those long treks to the wigwams and her beautiful voice that carried him through the severe heat of Savannah's seemingly endless summer days. All for naught. I cannot. I cannot, Levi.

"I cannot marry you."

*

Mordechai glanced behind him. Who was that walking like a midnight drunkard? Mordechai turned a corner. Maybe Levi had gone to Abigail's home to call on Hannah. He had set eyes on her for some time now. In all the excitement relating to his own joy, Mordechai had neglected Levi. For a couple of days now Levi had not prayed in the morning nor had he taken up supper. Their mother sensed there was something amiss. Perhaps she was overly-worried. Mordechai knocked. No. Sir. Levi Sheftall is not here. Yes, Sir. Two morns ago, that he did. No, sir. I do not know where he had gone, only I do know he was wondering where the Miss had gone off to. Abigail came to the door.

"I'm so sorry, Mordechai. She refused him." Mordechai immediately realized what had occurred, and a gaping hole began to etch away at his heart. Mordechai lifted his hat, whispered good night, and began to walk briskly toward the pub. Few knew Levi's tendencies like Mordechai. Not even their father knew Levi would take to drink when business deals struck debt. But Mordechai had usually been there to support him. Mordechai entered the noisy pub. The usual. Loose women. Dirty sailors. Dissolute businessmen on holiday from loyalty and featly. But no Levi. He left, sir. Hour or so. All sick. Sick. That way, sir. Take this, Sir. You'll need it. Mordechai grabbed the lantern. No time for gratitude.

Mordechai ran through the town of his youth; the streets whizzed by. And then he saw Levi, draped over a pile of wooden beams, coughing, cursing, crying. His partially completed home stood in an eerie gloom in the darkness. Levi's wails filled the air, and Mordechai began to cry as well. Mordechai's heart sank.

"God in heaven!" He uttered.

"You must despise me too. Look at me!"

"Levi! You presume wrong. We imagined the worst. I am relieved!"

"The worst perhaps would have been better." Levi groveled on the ground, moaned, and expunged the final contents of his poisoned stomach.

Ugh. He sighed. Ugh. "Look at me. I know how I must appear. Sunk so low. Perhaps you wonder why I have reached such lows, brother? Do you wonder?"

The stench of alcohol and acid tormented Mordechai. Mordechai kneeled towards his brother.

Although by now Mordechai knew the answer, he asked his brother, "No. Why Levi?"

"Ah. The inescapable question. What could possibly happen to you, Levi? What? If not that Hannah Minis cannot marry me. She daren't. Tell me, brother—am I nearly so bad as I imagine? Am I truly such a terrible wretch, a dreadful bore, an ogre? Tell me? If you pluck at my heartstrings, do I not bleed? Is it true? Is no woman to love me?" Levi began to cry in drunken stupor and with excessive self-loathing.

"To be thus rejected is but the pains of the most acute kind, dear Mordechai. How can I look into her eyes again? How? Tell me—what should I do? Where should I go?"

Mordechai clasped Levi's shoulders, grabbed him by the waist, and hoisted Levi home, listening to Levi swear to never open his heart to the wounds of love. Now the hopes of every man belong to all save for Levi.

*

It was entirely his fault. Trees spread foliage on Mordechai's path while the indigenous creatures remained underground. Mordechai galloped on his trusted horse since six in the morning. The previous night forced him to reconcile his own happiness with his brother's misery. Nothing cleared his mind like the cold air. It was his fault. Hannah had been smitten with him for a long time, only he had never admitted the intensity of that infatuation. *Because I enjoyed it. Just be honest.* As the horse galloped, hard and then harder, Mordechai berated himself more and more: you knew Hannah was attracted to you; you knew she deliberately sought your counsel—and for what? Your every gesture was cause for her rhapsody. And now, when you've long outgrown Hannah's admiration, you forge ahead and find a woman to woo and wed. Leaving Hannah behind. You knew the poor girl thought of you in a romantic light; it had become more evident than the bump on your long nose! You never truly intended to mislead her, but you've managed to entangle her heartstings in a ridiculous web— now try to undo the mangled threads, you wretch! Buying her trinkets from the Indies—of *course* she imagined you loved her. But what were you feeling all that time? Responsibility? Can you really hide behind that cloak of "adopted brother"?

Mordechai began panting as the horse's hooves hit the ground. Mordechai lifted his legs and buttocks from the pounding horse's flesh; his knees began to ache. The image of Levi's half-built house covered in vomit and saliva flooded his memory. Levi. How he pitied himself—like a neglected child upon the birth of a beautiful and fresh newborn. Levi had become a pathetic figure, giggling every now and then as though an idiot were telling him some absurd tale. What did Shakespeare say? "A tale told by an idiot." Yes. *That's* what Levi repeated! "I'll tell you a tale told by an idiot, Mordechai. I'll tell you!"

There was only one thing left to do. And with that, Mordechai turned the massive creature back toward the Sheftall home and out of the dense Savannah forest.

"Yes, Suh. Yes. She's a-comin' from her room. Can I offer you tea, Suh?"

Mordechai had no patience for delays. The matter had to be settled. He waved his hand, dismissing the Negro woman. Mordechai heard the unmistaken rustle of Hannah's long gown and removed his cap. Hannah smiled and slightly curtsied.

"Mordechai! What a pleasant, pleasant surprise!"

"Hannah. I believe you know why I am here."

"Indeed? I know not! Would you care to join us for breakfast?"

Mordechai frowned. He was most familiar with her obstinacy. She gestured to the dining hall, but Mordechai took one step closer to Hannah and realized the fix he had placed himself in by barging in. Perhaps a letter would have been a wiser tactic?

"Is anything the matter, Mordechai? You seem wan and flushed. Let me get you some water."

"No! Please don't go anywhere, Hannah. I have to ask you an important question. Indeed, I came all this way. It's of a personal matter."

"If you mean to ask me if Levi proposed, and if I rejected him, then on both accounts I answer positively."

"I am *fully* aware, Hannah. And may I ask, I believe I *must* ask, the reason why you had rejected his hand! Is he not most suitable? Does he not admire you?"

A bit surprised and feeling altogether on the spot, Hannah responded by nodding her head, swallowing, and answering, "Yes, yes, of course."

"But do you admire him, Hannah? Do you not feel warmth and affection for Levi?"

"Please, don't oblige me to answer your question, Mordechai. I—"

"Nonsense! You must!"

Hannah breathed in deeply and then deliberately let out all the air.

"If I must, then. No, Mordechai. My feelings for Levi are not deep. Not like the feelings—"

"Allow me to finish your thoughts. Please. [Look at me Hannah—is it true?] 'Not like the feelings I have for *you*'?"

She looked down. Mordechai stared at her chin, and from its point he saw drops of fresh tears slowly drenching the fine European carpet.

"Then I must apologize, Hannah! And I only blame myself, the wretch that I am, to have caused my brother this great harm!"

"Do you not love me, then Mordechai? Not at all?" she groaned in a tight whisper.

"Not as you would imagine, Hannah. I *do* love you, but as a sister. A friend. Not more. You mustn't allow your maiden fancies to rob you of joy! Levi loves you and he is generous! Far more than you are even aware. His entire life, save for his early youth and childhood, has been in pursuit of one aim; I can guarantee that aim was none other than your hand, Hannah. But he has no eloquence of manner, only feelings of heart. Can you not see that? Is it not clear? Please, Hannah. You must reconsider and *believe* what I say—that he longs for you in ways I do not."

"But you *do* love me—you did say so yourself. Just now, if I recollect."

"Please, Hannah. Don't force me to say words you may bitterly recollect—"

"Then it's enough for me. I thank you, Mordechai. You have said all I need to hear."

"But will you reconsider?"

Hannah's eyes dried and a cold stare overwhelmed her, "No. I'm sorry."

*

Frances admired her lovely figure in the looking glass. She took another sip of tea, with a hint of lemon and honey. Abigail Minis taught her the ritual laws of purification. So even when married, Frances learned, she must sleep in a separate bed from her married flesh, her husband. Even while married, she must learn the art of self-denial. The courtship phase will continue, with its flavor of restraint and abstinence. Abigail swore Frances would benefit—for Mordechai will always desire her with the same intensity he feels *now*, days before the wedding. The duration of platonic love shall only last twelve days, two weeks at most. Abigail had said brides are too romantic to realize the inherent wisdom of separation on a rhythmic beat. "It will ensure the rejuvenation! I assure you! Remember this: Separation ensures rejuvenation!" Frances knew Abigail must be right—she was a wise woman after all—but she could not help but wonder how desire abates altogether. Mordechai insisted on hastening the nuptials—for she had been a *niddah*, ritually impure—and that meant they were forbidden to embrace, kiss, or even touch one another! Up until last night, she had been ritually impure. And, with just one proper dip in the ritual bath, she was now cleansed. "Gone! All the world is ours to explore! Gone is the impurity! How wonderful it is," she thought. Abigail explained that these laws are passed down from mother to daughter, woman to woman, since the time of Moses. Frances wondered—what about Mordechai? Don't fret, Abigail reassured her. Mordechai learned of these laws too, from his father. And the imposed separation prior to the wedding—is that a law as well, Frances asked. (Mordechai and Frances refused to see one another for a week before the wedding.) No, this was a tradition Mordechai's Ashkenazi family adhered to. At first, Frances was a bit upset about it all—she wanted at least to *see* him. But, truth be told, she was terribly stressed and overwhelmed, and in the very end, she decided she rather liked the tension. She began to enjoy the week of anticipation all the more: Mordechai wrote each evening a note with romantic flairs. Frances re-read each letter during the morning hours and right before bed. Her favorite was posted two days prior:

Dearest Frances,

Two days. And then one more. Frances, it seems like an eternity! I can't sleep at night, for I think of your sweet self sleeping beside me and my overwhelming desire holds me

233

bound! How have you bewitched me! And when I finally
drift into sleep, your voice trails in my head. You are my
siren; you call me to your lair. You entice me with those
marvelous curls, those large, expressive eyes with lashes as
long as blades of grass in the Savannah pastures. Tell me it
isn't so! Tell me you haven't robbed me of my sanity; indeed,
I am on the verge of breaking down the walls of your home—
but for the reminder that soon you will be mine, a few days
more, and you will become *my* wife, and never shall I have to
tear down any wall, nor will I have to refrain from expressing
my pent-up love and desire for you.

Always yours, most affectionately,
Mordechai

It was too bad Mordechai's brother left town abruptly about
two weeks ago. Frances wanted to introduce him to her cousins
who traveled from Pennsylvania for her wedding in Charleston. He
left a hefty sum as a wedding gift and summarily boarded a vessel
to the West Indies. Mordechai said Levi had grown a beard and
lost the gleam in his left eye—the one that smiled, while the other,
the right, remained unmoved. It was really very uncharacteristic
of Mordechai to sulk, but he *had* been quite upset for a while. Mrs.
Sheftall explained to Frances that when men become entrenched
in "moods," the ladies had better retreat. "Take up your needle
and begin stitching away. When the time is right, my dear, he
will surely seek you. You must learn from the wiser women, dear,
so as you can benefit without the harm of learning by virtue of
error." Frances believed her future mother-in-law was an astute
housewife, albeit with the attitude of a previous generation. Living
in Savannah means I must get along, Frances repeated to herself in
self-persuasion. No point in finding fault.

The Charleston Hart home bustled with guests from varied
countries and colonies. The Harts arrived with a flurry of gifts
for the newlyweds and an insatiable appetite—they had nearly
"starved" at sea. The Sheftalls gladly paid the expenditure for
victuals, and the Savannah crowd lodged in the Charleston estate, a

measure of gratuity and appreciation. Mordechai was disappointed Levi absented himself from the merriment, but Joshua posed as a replacement. The two joshed and amused one another with the characteristic jokes of youths soon verging on manhood. Lace, French tulle, and satin bedecked the fine ladies, and the men paraded the latest fashions in silken socks and buckled shoes. Hannah Minis thankfully donned a pearly white gown, oddly resembling the hue of Frances's dress. The few remaining Jewish families were in attendance, as well as the governor, James Wright. Mordechai had invited Governor Wright as a matter of propriety, truly anticipating his absence. However, Wright had rather believed it wise to be on good terms with all his constituents, especially the budding prosperous ones. Mordechai Sheftall had garnered quite the reputation with his untried yet surprisingly lucrative business arrangements. Business was booming—and Mordechai was a burgeoning bolt fastening the successes of the Georgian colony. Wright rather enjoyed the bustle of weddings. The maidens frolicked and the young men gathered in small crowds to comment on the prettiest pair of eyes. James imbibed a glass of fine wine and imagined the bride and groom should soon wed. It was nearly time.

*

The nuptials soon arrived, and Mordechai took his new bride in the manner of bridegrooms—with sheer elation. How could it be? That such a beautiful woman should choose to marry me? He wondered. Benjamin and Hannah gave their son away to the petite bride whose eyes shone with gaiety. How could it be? I have barely known the man! And yet here I stand, with bouquet in hand, veil across my face, and a white gown of lace and silk. Willing to say goodbye forever to my hometown in Holland and embrace the wilderness of America? Is this the power of newfound love? The ministering rabbi recited the blessings, and Frances's parents, who traveled for the occasion, held each other's hands—they had trusted Joshua with their daughter's future, and they have been most wonderfully surprised with a generous son-in-law. The *ketubah*, the marriage contract, provided for Frances lest her husband fell ill or worse, and Mordechai even provided their daughter with a deed of trust; a revolutionary endeavor from their standpoint. (Dutch Jews did not necessarily sign marriage contracts to that extent.) Frances would settle in a home, and Mordechai was clearly smitten with her. The Harts were indeed grateful for what they deemed superb *mazal*, good favor and luck! Mordechai listened intently to the rav's words thinking of the momentous night yet to follow. Mordechai tried to focus on the seven blessings, but found himself slightly distracted by Frances— how radiant she appeared in her bridal gown! Their eyes met, and both smiled at one another with the knowledge that their flesh shall soon cleave and become one.

*

Hannah Minis witnessed the *chuppah* with a mixture of envy and gladness. She believed Frances looked rather ridiculous in all that lace, and that Mordechai's smiles could only be reflected in her own, if she truly had a heart capable of compassion. Since she most certainly *did* possess that trait, Hannah smiled as tears streamed down her eyes on the late October eve of the year seventeen hundred and sixty-one.

PART II: 1765-1791

"This is absurd!"

WRIGHT IS WRONG

How did Oglethorpe *ever* entertain a colony without the basic distractions of rum? The Georgian towns were abuzz with newcomers and commerce—thanks to vacant lands, slaves, and all that precious rum. James Wright knew he stood head and shoulders above the two royal governors who had preceded him. (If he could allow himself the compliment, he was indeed superior in almost every respect to the Royal Governors of the *twelve colonies*.) The free-flowing alcohol assisted the colonists; they could feel optimistic about the future. Although only James Oglethorpe could perhaps match his interest in the welfare of the colony, Wright *clearly* was unmatched in his experience, training, and executive ability. His father served as Chief Justice of South Carolina, and Wright spent most of his youth there. From a young age he had succeeded at law. He served as Attorney General of South Carolina. Which other governor could say the same? But his days of reaping the benefits of optimism and basking in his own achievements would be tested by his mother country—Great Britain Herself.

The Crown had to raise funds. That dreadful war incurred dreadful expense. The colonists across the Atlantic were expected to help defray the astronomical cost of warfare. And the people of Savannah and all the colonies had to pay a little extra for their indigo and coffee. It was a matter of course; Wright understood that. A small price to pay, come to think of it, for being under the aegis of the English Crown, May God Bless the King. Why did the New Englanders have to protest the Sugar Act of April

1764? Georgians at first took very little notice of the protests—after all, the New Englanders feared virtual destruction of their valuable rum industry, not the Georgians. But lately there's been great consternation regarding Section XXVIII: a bond on all wood or lumber aboard naval stores. Savannah's merchants began to complain. The levy was burdensome to many, straining pockets of much needed liquidity. Yet again, Wright believed the taxes were due and a necessary evil. "The English system is benevolent, and I'm sure most colonists would agree," he thought.

Wright sighed. The year 1763 marked the end of the Seven Years' War in Europe. The Treaty of Paris solved Georgia's most pressing problem—the Spanish down south. Florida established two British provinces, and for the first time, Georgia's boundaries were secure. Finally, the poorest and weakest colony could begin to expand and nourish itself. Many colonists indeed poured in from the existing colonies. But that dreadful European War with France and Spain left the British near penniless. And now the colonists are beginning to grumble. Truth be told, the new acts were burdensome on Georgians—they required imposed forfeitures be paid in *gold* or *silver*. Georgia has a limited supply of both. Wright sighed again. The constituents had reason to grumble. No doubt the tax on sugar, which will affect the price of rum, will not inhibit its purchase. For now, rum served as a warranted diversion.

Wright felt a bit drowsy, even after tea.

"Let me rest a bit," he thought. He removed his trousers and lay on his bed; just as he began to drift into midday slumber, Percy, his Negro butler, awakened him with a hurried knock on the door. Percy continued to harass the door; "Desist!" Wright bellowed. "For goodness sake! Just a moment. A moment."

He nearly lit a candle out of habit, but recalled it was no later than four in the afternoon. Frustrated his sleep had never truly begun, he nearly yelled at poor Percy.

"What is the meaning of this?"

"Mastuh Eddings is here to see you, Sir. He says it's urgent, Sir."

"And did Eddings share with you the nature of this *emergency*?"

"Nossuh."

"Ahm. Very well."

Wright closed his door and quickly dressed once again. Victor Eddings was a serious fellow; he was after all Minister of Trade. He knew better than to barge into Wright's home unannounced or uninvited. Eddings was by far the dandy, and a pedantic one. Even Wright, who had been trained as an Englishman from youth, found Eddings' mannerisms tiresome. Eddings suffers from a sycophantic obsession with mores, Wright believed. Yet here he was interrupting the Governor. Something was amiss.

Percy prepared another set of tea and biscuits. Victor was too anxious to pay the black servant much attention.

"My apologies, Mr. Governor," Victor bowed slightly and even tilted his left leg in deference.

"Not at all. Not at all. I presume this is a matter of import."

"Indeed, Sir. It is quite serious. I would not have intruded upon the governor if it were not, Sir."

"On with it, then."

"If I may, Sir."

"Yes, you may," Wright subconsciously flexed his wrist in irritation; my, how he grates on my delicate nerves, Wright thought.

"A group of merchants refused to comply with the Writs of Assistance. As you know, this law stipulates that search and seizure of premises are permissible without adjudication. The inspectors, following British law, demanded entry. Mr. Axelrod (yes, he with the cocked hat) struck one of the officials square in the jaw; a few followed suit. Mr. Axelrod claims the Writs are illegal. I thought we should, with your permission, discuss this matter at once before the merchants, in their fury, storm your estate and demand you beseech Parliament to rescind the Writs. I need not tell you, Sir, what has transpired in the Northern colonies of late. We must be prudent, sir."

Wright held in his breath. So the masses are discontent. He thought for a minute longer. Custom officials do not justify their suspicion. They simply obtain the warrants. Surely this is not matter of grave concern!

"This appears to be a troubling development, but I see no cause for alarm, Eddings. Renegades and ruffians who defy the sovereignty of the law exist, and we must accept that they will act out every so often. Mr. Axelrod shall find no clemency; he shall be jailed and fined for his misdemeanor and released in two days time. Is that all, Victor?"

"Perhaps, Governor, Mr. Axelrod shall find a compassionate ear amongst the citizenry?"

"Come, Mr. Eddings. You are surely overly anxious. Now be on your way, and let this matter trouble you no more."

Victor, somewhat dismayed Wright did not perceive the extent of resentment and antagonism of the general public, bowed his head. "I suppose so. Yes, Sir."

Wright escorted Eddings past the magnificent library and grand staircase toward the door, where Percy naturally assisted Eddings with his waistcoat, and closed the door to the carriage.

Wright noted Eddings did not wave nor did he lift his hat before taking leave.

"He must be preoccupied to forget his manners," Wright mused. "Perhaps it is better this way. I simply hope there is truly no backlash from this mess," he reflected.

*

Mordechai leaned back on his horse for a brief second, to stretch his lumbar. The ride to Augusta was strenuous. Mordechai traveled through the dense forests of Savannah, preferring short-cuts, even if they came with a bit of a price. During his long journey, his mind wandered to his beloved, now busy with motherhood. Frances sent for the physician; she had been ill of late. He was loath to travel and miss supper, but he *had* to meet John Wereat, a gentile Mordechai befriended of late. John planned on a clandestine meeting after Axelrod was imprisoned for protecting his privacy. Mordechai desired to be part of the "tete-a-tete," as John liked to say. Mordechai felt a bit uneasy leaving his children behind with Frances, but the economic situation was beginning to appear bleak. He truly did not wish to burden Frances, so Mordechai did not see the point in stating too much to his wife. This time, Mordechai didn't forget to carry his koshering knife with him; he had returned to Broughton Street hungry too many times as a youth to neglect the knife as well as "Necessaire"—a carrying case with eating utensils for on-the-go meals.

Poor Frances! Not even two months married, and she had become pregnant. The first pregnancy weighed heavily on her petite frame. She gained many pounds, which she quickly shed when their first-born sucked her near dry. Mordechai thanked God his wife delivered the first one and survived at all. She had labored for well over twenty-four hours before she even felt the baby's head sneak out from her sore crevice. Susan Hale was called in, a noteworthy midwife well known in town. But she didn't help Frances much; Mordechai believed it was his dear mother Hannah who truly helped Frances maintain the stamina to deliver the child. She must have screamed for half a day, and then fell silent like a dying chick. And then, just as Mordechai began promising all kinds of sums for charitable donations in lieu of a healthy newborn, a beautiful cry filled the room. Mordechai remembered rushing into his wife's bedroom, nearly collapsing from all the blood on the sheets, and held steady by Hannah, beheld his newborn son—healthy, hearty, and hungry. Benjamin waited patiently in the parlor, reciting psalms and crying like a baby himself. He relived Perla's deliveries, and the memory of Sheftall, his infant son who never learned to pray, bombarded his reveries. The baby's cries! How it resembled his lost son, Sheftall—the beautiful boy with blonde ringlets and precious, expressive eyes; the baby who finally turned a barren woman into a mother; Benjamin shed tears, as though he had been holding them back since Perla's untimely death. Hannah came down the stairs after a while and cradled the baby. She saw her husband wiping tears, smiling.

"Let me see him, Hannah."

Hannah whispered, "He is precious, Benjamin. You have never seen such an angel." Benjamin glanced at his newborn grandson and nearly collapsed—he was a replica of his dead son, Sheftall. Benjamin kissed the boy and cried once again.

"God has repaid me after all these years, Hannah. This baby," he choked, "this baby reminds me of Sheftall. My God! How wondrous are His ways!"

Mordechai overheard the conversation as he walked into the room and knew precisely what to call his son on the day of his *bris*, or circumcision. Sheftall Sheftall—a name to honor the dead as well as the living.

Frances soon became pregnant again. This time, her body had grown accustomed to pregnancy; she had gained weight, but not as much as with Sheftall. Soon enough, another child was born. The child was not as large as the first; its head eased its way out of the canal with surprising ease. The recovery time was longer, however. The reverse contractions triggered nausea and severe headaches in Frances, which worried Mordechai tremendously. Thankfully, she recovered, only to become pregnant once again soon after. Now Frances was expecting as he galloped toward a meeting, and Mordechai believed he had left her all alone—even if they owned a few good slaves. Frances was young and soon becoming more and more womanly; having known the pains of childbearing, Frances was now less of a girl. Mordechai noticed she did not smile as often as he remembered; this was perhaps due to the emotions of a woman whose body is constantly in flux. She slept, but not enough. Dark rings began to form underneath her eyes, and Mordechai's mother insisted on helping Frances care for the little ones so she could rest her eyes. Frances took to knitting the babies all kinds of clothes, and spent her time with little else. One of the Negro housemaids assisted in the day-to-day cares of the infant and toddler. Mordechai was well off, and his fortune was diversified; income was influx, and Mordechai spoiled Frances as well he could. But he wondered, how would Frances manage with a third child? He prayed to God for strength and courage—much was needed of both, he imagined.

John Wereat wondered what was detaining the Jew. God he was *wealthy*! He owned acres and acres of land and a grand estate—and all this prior to the age of twenty-five! But it didn't show. Mordechai rarely displayed his fortune; his attire was respectable but not ostentatious. Indeed, those with less equity tended towards grand displays: French lace, Italian-spun yarn, fine silk sashes. John admired Mordechai, and he was a bit surprised Mordechai agreed to meet him. Not because he didn't expect a Jew to associate with Christians—or "Gentiles"—but rather because he had no inkling Mordechai was *political*. Mordechai was an interesting fellow, John believed; he didn't have the horns his parish priest insisted upon. No. All kidding aside. Mordechai possessed that air of confidence that comes with wealth and influence. Even Governor Wright attended his wedding in Charleston, and Wright was well-known for courting the "better sort of people." (Very British, Wereat begrudgingly acknowledged.)

Augusta was a small town by colony standards, but there was land to settle. Wereat owned an estate too, and he was satisfied with his lot; that is, up until the ordinances from Parliament, thousands of miles off shore. When it comes to American pockets, the British had better desist, Wereat believed. Too bad that aristocratic Brit Governor Wright is wrong about the appropriate stance—Americans should resist the ordinances, particularly the Writs! By God! The "Writs of Resistance" not "Assistance"! Who the hell can pay in *silver?* Wait, wait. Or better yet in *gold?* And the people of this town are slow to place pressure on government—the Northerners were far more vociferous on account of the injustices. A tax on *sugar*? What are the poor devils to eat? It was enough settlers abandoned London and debtors' prison—should they now be incarcerated for a crime inflicted by the self-same "mother" country? Madness, I say! Wereat muttered; he couldn't *wait* to vent all his frustration and pent up bitterness to Mordechai—a fresh and patient ear.

Mordechai, out of breath, knocked on John Wereat's front gate, a wooden structure covered in vines. Augusta was slowly becoming more and more populated. A good place to do business, Mordechai figured. The moon hung low; its dim yellow light becoming brighter with sunset's passing and twilight's slow, creeping entry. Mordechai held his riding hat and looked up—the starry sky provoked awe in the young man; he thought of God's promise to Abraham—"your offspring shall be like the stars." John identified Mordechai in an instant. The Jewish merchant had an intense look in his eyes, which were smallish. Mordechai's ears were large, which balanced well with his nose. Of course, the nose was the most prominent feature. The ridge of the nose was narrow, but quickly tapered off into a swooping equine tip. The nostrils were a bit round, with a nub of fat. His lips were pursed and thin. To offset the sharp look in his eyes, Mordechai boasted a wide, M-shaped forehead that, despite the youth of its owner, displayed fine horizontal lines, altogether adding an air of sophistication to the young man. His hair was dark, black almost. His eyebrows were thick and well-groomed. It appeared, from the angle of Mordechai's tilted head, that one eyebrow, the left one, was slightly longer than the right. When Mordechai turned his head, and his profile disappeared, Mordechai's physiognomy appeared quite handsome. His was a searing look; his eyes were all intensity, with a striking glow.

John held his hand in deference and respect. Mordechai gripped John's with vigor and poise. *My his hands are calloused*, John thought. It was true, of course. Mordechai had trained from childhood in various "hands-on" labors, including ranching and tanning. But he did not feel as though he ought to shy away from any form of arduous activity; in fact, Mordechai prized toil; he believed industry liberated a man. John realized Mordechai may have been a well-to-do merchant, but here was a man who knew how to get his hands dirty if need be.

"Our countrymen are discontent, Mr. Sheftall. I am sure you are well aware. Needless to say, gathered in my home tonight are well over twenty men from various parts of the colony. We are here tonight to share our grievances and to perhaps proffer solutions to our quandaries. You are welcome to suggest your own."

"Naturally. I am here to ascertain the winds of discontent as well as to learn the ramifications of England's laws and ordinances. I thank you very much."

The two seemed to share the same regard for small talk—concise and brief, please. Mordechai spent the evening mostly listening to the Georgians' gripe. Truth be told, most merchants such as he were not present. Perhaps they are afraid to be seen, lest buyers should suspect they do not have professed equity, Mordechai conjectured. Wereat busied himself with making his guests feel comfortable. His Negro slaves fanned some men who were perspiring profusely; other Negro boys offered refreshments. Smoke filled the room. Mordechai's eyes began to tear. He refused to drink an alcoholic drink; it was forbidden by Jewish law. However, he certainly drank as much cider as he could.

Mordechai was part of a generation of Americans who believed they could only be taxed through their legislative body; the assemblies in America should decide matters of revenue. The Parliamentary Acts tried their patience. Mordechai thought of his father, Benjamin. Benjamin felt an underlying loyalty to King George. Benjamin would probably not have agreed with Mordechai's attendance at this meeting of "ingrates," as his father would most likely say.

"Where's your *hakarat ha-tov*? Your appreciation? Hmm? So the British Crown requires taxes—that is the way of *all* governments. America belongs to the great British Empire—and who are we to tell the British what to do? We should be grateful we do not have to live in squalid ghettoes, Mordechai. Have you any notion where your father lived in Prussia? The type of slum I was born in? This America is benevolent—why stir trouble? Why kvetch? Eh?" But Mordechai couldn't feel the same loyalty his father keenly expressed; after all, Mordechai was an American, born and bred.

"We sons of immigrants have matured! We must grasp the reins of colonial control—and by that, we mean the government," Mordechai said aloud. The crowd grew quiet. John Wereat nodded his head.

"Hear, Hear! Did you hear that, men? We must rein in London! They cannot dictate laws without our governance, here in Georgia, stipulating *first*! This is our land, and *we* appoint magistrates and assemblymen!" Mordechai lifted his empty glass, "Amen!"

*

William Knox regretted, quite bitterly in fact, becoming a colonial agent of the Georgia Assembly. The Georgians had been pressuring him for months now to oppose the Sugar Act in Parliament. *Damn*! Knox owned a plantation in Georgia, and by virtue of his grand assets, incurred the loyalty of the colonists. Thus he served as Provost Marshal of Georgia for several years. Once elected colonial agent, Knox had the privilege of settling in England. Living in London most of the year was a benefit he could hardly resist: theatre, fashion, arts, society, excellent food, and the libraries. London was a dream compared to the plantation in that regard. But the pressures of late! Governor Wright, Knox's great friend, *insisted* Knox "resist all temptation to oppose in any which manner the Sugar Act. Such opposition would be an act of sedition." *Sedition*! With the use of such rhetoric, Knox knew he had recourse at his disposal—one that would not be met with much glee. Knox then wrote a pamphlet defending the Parliament: "The Crown has every legal authority to tax its colonies in America. Such is the manner of governments." In the eyes of his constituents, Knox committed perfidy as well, thus forfeiting their loyalty and gaining their animosity instead. At the end of the day, Knox bitterly realized, he had gained contempt from many to appease the few.

James Oglethorpe wrote letters to Knox too, as though pressure from Wright weren't enough. Oglethorpe, surprisingly, seemed in favor of the colonies:

> The men and women of Georgia are slowly building their livelihood. To burden them with levies is simply inequitable. Since my years in Georgia, I have come to realize that one too many burdens on a youthful colony, one in which members from all of its various parts seem to be justly distressed, must not be disregarded with contempt. The disgruntles of the masses will seek recompense; it is our duty to hearken the voices of the masses to duly reconcile their grievances— the more efficiently you succeed at this task, the less likely

you will have to grasp for a dire remedy, which will be very difficult to conceive and execute by and by. Although I have not stepped a single footstep in the colony since my departure, I have never forgotten the kindly countenances of the people there—and I would most despair of learning of their suffering, or their children's suffering, at the hand of Parliament. It is your duty to lend, vociferously, a fervent stance in London in favor of the colonists.

In this and all,

James Oglethorpe
Essex, London

Knox knew Oglethorpe's letter was well-argued. After all, the man had dealt with Georgia long before James Wright governed. But Knox's relationship with Oglethorpe could not be compared to Wright's: Knox felt too much duty to his friend; thus, Oglethorpe's letter eventually landed in the ash heap, together with all other correspondence from relatively "influential" Savannah and Augusta figures. Men of little influence, Knox believed. This was the way the world turned on its axis, he theorized—through webs of power of those with grand-purse strings and attachments to Crown and Scepter.

*

"Would Frances support my political leanings?" Mordechai wondered. Since their first months together, Frances and Mordechai rarely had cause for friction. He had met all her needs, and quite happily too. They had all but devoured one another, especially in the first year. The pregnancy did not seem to deter them. Frances had not become a *niddah* throughout the pregnancy, and the two enjoyed a near year-long honeymoon. Levi had been absent all those months, strategically so. Perhaps it was better off that way—it would have only sharpened Levi's pain. Joy in others is a bitter reminder of one's woes, Mordechai well knew. But the question remained, despite Mordechai's wandering mind—what would Frances say about the clandestine meeting, the emerging political landscape? Should he burden his ailing father with his growing ideology too?

John Wereat's cabal met in Savannah on occasion, where Mordechai met other revolutionaries: the Sons of Liberty. Now those were a group of rowdy men, but they had a purpose and passion. Mordechai sensed a paradigm shift in the American dreamscape. But how could he even begin to express these beliefs to Frances? The Sons of Liberty boasted a few women, even Negro slaves. But they were on the sidelines. The real issue at hand was political freedom, not an entirely new social order. Men throughout the country were speaking up. The firebrand Thomas Paine published works; even the town papers roused unrest. The wretch Knox in England rapidly lost popularity. Merchants tried to work against the system, cooking the books and hiring shady characters to buy and sell below decks. And the governor was *completely* out of touch! Mordechai was surprised Wright supported the Writs and the Sugar Act. Wright had been very accommodating on the economic front, granting him wharfs and land. Wright seemed to have understood the dire necessity for trade and mercantilism. But now it seems for the sake of the throne Wright is willing to follow orders blindly! How maddening.

Mordechai paced across the hall to the bedchamber. Peering inside, he saw Frances soundly asleep, clutching her pillow lightly. She wore a lace bonnet to sleep, a trademark Mordechai found quite sweet. Her nightgown covered her well, but crumpled, revealing her lean, petite legs. She snorted lightly, breathing deeply from her nostrils. The sound of a woman with child, Mordechai thought. He began to remove the bonnet slightly, trying to find a long strand of hair to twirl. He loved Frances' hair; it was long, light, lustrous. Frances, a light sleeper, roused and turned, slightly surprised to make out her husband's contours. Barely visible, he whispered, "I'm sorry love. I missed you." Frances' lips parted slightly; "The children missed you too." Mordechai nudged her slightly—"And you? Did *you* miss me too?" Frances' lips widened.

"Of course. But I am worried for you, Mordechai. I don't know if I want you to associate with those types of people." Mordechai sighed deeply. So she knew. "Your mother told me, Morde-chai. Don't be upset. I just don't want—"

Mordechai stood and straightened his waistcoat, despite the late hour. "Don't worry on my account, dearest. For now, all we do is kvetch. Influential men attend the meetings—the same men we see during the day. Johnston's there—"

"The newspaper man? The one who works nearby, on Broughton Street?"

"The one."

"Who else?"

"Joshua. Da Costa. And a new friend, John Wereat."

"The *goy*?"

"Yes! The *goy*. What difference does it make? The Parliament doesn't distinguish between our monies and theirs!"

"Indeed. They most certainly do not." Frances felt over-whelmed. Her husband was very headstrong—she didn't need a fortune-teller or a wizard to impart her with that knowledge. All her little ones seemed to have inherited the same attribute—that tenacity to do precisely as they pleased. Suddenly, she felt quite laden and overtired. Her arms went limp as Mordechai began to remove her bonnet and rest his head next to hers. "My love, you needn't worry. Such domestic tribulations are resolved in due course. But certain pressing needs must be attended to, or else much will be amiss." He began to remove his garments, as though its weight, once removed, would free him of all burdens.

Frances wanted to laugh off her worries; she had grown rather lonely, craving companionship. Her evening repast had been quiet and laden with anticipation. She welcomed her husband's attention and easily reciprocated his gestures. The fear of his passing or being harmed had a strange effect of increasing her desire and longing. Theirs was a passionate session, full of fear and longing and urgency. And tenderness. Always tenderness.

*

Benjamin Sheftall re-read the letter. He was surprised. Truly. Oglethorpe supported the Americans. Benjamin read the letter again. His son would feel justified after all. But how could a British officer of high repute disagree with his own Parliament on this issue? "Perhaps I am growing too old for this world?" Benjamin despondently thought. Since Mordechai had become increasingly successful at work and occupied at home with wife and children, Benjamin had come to feel increasingly alienated. The political situation was the topic of most dinner conversations. Benjamin dined with his son. So he was privy. Philip Minis and his brother Abraham shared most meals at the Sheftall household too. Hannah, their sister, would join the crowd only to sequester herself with the nanny. The dialogue quickly advanced on the issues: Governor Wright. Knox. The hot-head Axelrod. Writs. Boats and illegal trade. Decreased profits. And Da Costa on occasion would attend too. Joshua, with news from Charleston's ports: no money. No business. No markets. More guests arrive daily. And the newest addition by far to arouse alarm: a *goy*. This man John. Eating with his son. Discussion of publications in the *Gazette*. Underwriters. Ghost writers. Secret societies. Even some Indian tribes. Negroes too. It's ubiquitous. John had *influence* beyond the Jewish borders of merchants. Benjamin remained quiet on the subjects. He felt terribly anxious regarding the entire matter.

"Jews should keep a low profile! How many times have I demonstrated this to my son? Have I not fought alongside James Oglethorpe as a loyal soldier to the British cause? Have I not nearly lost my life to a dreadful Spaniard? And now my son plots against the same British lords? What has become of this generation? Speaking with such arrogance against a country of bounty and benevolence! And should he but *value* my opinion? But fancy that—I am the *father*!" How he listens to this John Wereat! All the Jewish boys do: Hart, da Costa, Minis, and his son. What do these young men know of suffering?! What do they know of near starvation? Who spit into their long beards? Who forced them to eat potatoes, potatoes, and potatoes? Who forbade them entry into committees and organizations and universities and God knows what else is barred from our kind. And yet here they are, fighting as *Americans*. Maybe this will be our end, he fearfully believed. And if there is to be a war, and the Americans are to lose? Who will they blame then? The Jews! For this reason it is best to keep a low profile! This is what my father taught me. But I have failed to teach *my* son this important lesson. Ach. And what of Sheftall Sheftall? The boy is young—but is he deaf or blind? All this talk of liberty—what will it serve? Ach. The beautiful children. The only bit of joy in old age is the young. Benjamin placed Oglethorpe's letter in a silver platter, for Mordechai to read when he returned home. Despite his own leanings, Benjamin wanted to grant his son some joy. "What we parents do for our children!"

Mordechai lifted the letter from the silver platter during his late-afternoon tea. He recognized the hand—it was James Oglethorpe's. Mordechai's ears grew longer as his father repeated the stories of famine and fierce battle fights during his youth. Benjamin now regaled the little ones and whoever was (fortunate enough?) present. The Negroes smiled politely; even the housemaids listened intently. And all the stories culminated with some mention of correspondence. So here it was:

Dear Benjamin Sheftall,

How glad I am to learn of the birth of healthy grandchildren. The descriptions of your son's plantations are quite beauteous. It is quite clear he is successful, and I wish him continued success. On the state of affairs of late in Parliament: it is quite dire, and perhaps will swell with time. Legislators are quite dissatisfied with the American response to taxation, as they view the matter from an increasingly practical lens. The coffers are spent; there is likely to be very little compassion from King George the Third—he is *bent* on making good use of his colonies. Knox enjoys support from loyalists and Governor James Wright. I have written to Knox, to no avail. It saddens me to learn of the circumstances, pecuniary and such, that have led to much economic debilitation. Please inform me of the situation, as I am deeply concerned.

Thank you very much,

James Oglethorpe
Essex, London

Mordechai knew this was a concession on his father's part. Benjamin respected and adored James Oglethorpe almost as much as the late King George. To learn that Oglethorpe does *not* support the Tories! And all this time Mordechai had assumed Oglethorpe was just another English loyalist, a member of the British ruling class, determined to pass along his suffocating taxes and fiats. So there *were* those back in London who supported their brethren in the colonies. Mordechai appreciated his father's maneuver and believed, in part, despite his father's most obvious discontent, that perhaps Benjamin Sheftall, stalwart soldier of the War of Jenkins' Ear, trusted Mordechai the ingrate after all.

*

The forestland surrounding Savannah had remained uncultivated. Few ventured into its mysterious paths. A trodden dirt road sufficed for many—but not for Mordechai. Since his days courting Frances, Mordechai had been seeking shortcuts through the forest. Of late, he had other cause for galloping through the woods, in a manner his wife would most certainly disapprove: the liberty movements. Struck with intrigue since the clandestine parlor meetings by Wereat's, Mordechai had since traveled to Charleston on more than one occasion. Of course he had also benefited from business ventures, transactions, and multiple investments, but the real cause for his excitement was the prospect of learning about the political underpinnings of Georgia's emergent rebel class. Mordechai recruited a few of his own comrades—including Hannah Minis's brother, Philip. Philip was a strapping lad, and at thirty-one carried himself with the airs of an aristocrat. He had cause for discontent as well and was rather intrigued by "secret societies" and such. The two galloped, Mordechai leading through the forest, sharing bits of conversation.

"I've been meaning to inquire about Hannah," Mordechai said, breathing spurts of deep breaths. "Have any of the new Jewish residents caught her fancy? How about the blonde one? What's his name?"

"I forget," Philip answered. "I have no news on that front. My sister's situation begins to worry me."

Mordechai didn't respond. It was an unfair disadvantage women shared, especially in his social circles: once past a certain age, a woman was more likely to plunge into spinsterhood. Hannah was twenty-one. Most girls, gentile or Jew, married in their teen years.

"With God's help, she will find her intended one, her *bashert*."

"Amen," Mordechai whispered. Mordechai ruminated on his last meaningful conversation with Hannah. How she purposefully played the part! Refused to see reason, refused to let go of fantasy. And then his mind turned to those terrible displays of frustration and agony on his brother's poor face! Philip broke the awkward silence for a moment, "It would have been nice for things to work out between them. I am rather fond of Levi." Mordechai's heart for a moment filled with the possibility of optimism, "Do you know, Philip, if she regrets her decision?"

"To wed Levi? Not to my knowledge."

Mordechai slowed his pace a bit. He tried to look into Philip's gray eyes—how much like Hannah's they were! Of all the Minis siblings, Philip and Hannah were the most similar in appearance. "Levi is still fond of her," Mordechai's voice trailed. Still peering into Philip's concerned glance, Mordechai didn't catch sight of the strangely clad natives surrounding the vicinity. Philip suddenly yanked the reins of his horse. Mordechai instinctively lowered his head by a few good inches.

"Take cover!" Philip cried. An arrow sliced the air between Philip and Mordechai. "Blasted natives! Follow me, Philip!" In moments such as these, Mordechai's mind focused on strategy—how was he to evade the painted men? Mordechai had enough dealings with the Indians to distinguish between those that had an interest in communication and those bent on destruction. The damned arrows were dipped in a poisonous potion, which upon the disastrous occurrence of a hit, spelled an irreversible death sentence: a victim writhed in agonizing pain and died shortly thereafter. Arrows launched to Mordechai's right and left. By God! Tomahawks! Mordechai began to bellow for

Philip to remain close behind—but he could barely hear his own voice. The Indians shrieked chants. Mordechai turned his head slightly and couldn't make sight of Philip.

"Philip!" Mordechai wrenched his horse to a halt. He clenched the reins. His body snapped back. And then he saw Philip's poor horse—legs spread widely apart, a tomahawk lodged in its gut. The natives with their hysteric beats began to scramble, closing in. Mordechai's left eye caught a glint of silver light. Without a moment's hesitation, he fired his musket. A scream. Dashes to the left and right. Trees rustled. Sweat gathered between his brows, a cold sweat. Where was Philip? Mordechai caught sight of a pistol. He slowly galloped toward it. Where *was* he? Had they carried him away? A tomahawk landed beside the dead horse. Mordechai didn't shoot indiscriminately. Pumped, he slowly descended and began belly crawling across the dirt floor. Catching sight of red and orange beads and moccasins, he quickly jumped, shot, and resumed his belly posture. The Indian fell to the floor. Just then, Mordechai caught sight of Philip. Philip's cheeks were blackened by the mud, and blood stained his trousers. He seemed to be breathing. Suddenly, another Indian hurled a flaming coal. He was completely naked, save for a loincloth. His sinuous body was bedecked with burnished paints and wild stripes. Another native followed suit, with a curved knife in one hand and another between his teeth. Terror gripped Mordechai. *Is this truly the way I am to meet my end?* A flaming object struck the ground, erupting into plumes of bluish smoke. Dense fog filled the air. *I must take advantage of this!* Mordechai yanked Philip off the ground, hurled him with a strong, controlled movement unto the horse, managed to swing one leg over the horse, and began galloping toward a winding path. The horse began to gallop. Mordechai forced Philip upwards.

"Hold onto me!" Philip, regaining consciousness, held onto Mordechai with the last bit of strength. Mordechai managed to fire Philip's pistol one last time. *Shema Israel,* Philip chanted. *Ribono shel Olam,* don't let me die. Philip cried.

"Mordechai, my leg. My leg." But Mordechai could not cry nor could he pity his friend. A knife hurled by, stabbing the saddle, and then fell, almost like a raindrop. The thump thump thump of the horse's hooves silenced Philip's agonizing cries. Mordechai removed a carving knife he carried with him, hurled it with all his strength before escaping with his life and the life of poor Philip. Only later did they discover the horse had suffered burn injuries and a stab wound. Mordechai never related this tale to Frances and avoided the forests for a long while. Philip eventually regained the use of his left leg, but refused to attend meetings of rebels, believing he had been warned by Heaven. Mordechai sold the poor horse; he didn't want to arouse the suspicion of his Negro slaves who were very diligent in relating all matters to Frances Sheftall, wife of the man who had the gall to seek short routes through the Savannah forests.

Philip eventually attended meetings. Mordechai had persuaded him long enough.

*

Levi Sheftall moaned as he read the letter from his mother. His father was falling ill. Perhaps gravely ill. But she kept the news from Mordechai. No wonder. Levi's brother had enough on his plate. Supposedly, he was becoming political; few hours were spent at home in the evenings. Their father felt he ought to protect his son from worrying too much about him. What nonsense! Shouldn't his mother know better? And shouldn't Mordechai acknowledge the implications of his father's illness? Benjamin had lost most of his rigor; he spent many hours sleeping, especially after meals. He often complained of indigestion, and rarely went off on excursions. Hannah ignored the signs for a long while, burying her fear; instead, she attributed Benjamin's listlessness to old age. Surely, years of labor took a toll on any individual, she reasoned. Hannah fed him dutifully, mended his torn socks, helped soak his feet in salt water and tonic, and massaged his aching limbs with olive oil from Andalusia. Benjamin spent most mornings reading Psalms, and then paced, slowly, to his son's estate. Spending his afternoon hours with the little ones was all he truly looked forward to. Frances never objected, and the slaves tended to his needs as

Hannah went off to the market or strolled along the river bank. She knew her husband's condition would only worsen. His stools had become bloody for a while now. Benjamin had lost considerable weight. His bearings worsened. But Mordechai had surely noticed, had he not? She wondered if Levi would travel to Charleston less now; maybe he would settle at long last. Perhaps it was time she revealed to Levi just how poorly his father fared. All this must have occurred, Levi realized. The letter stipulated as much.

Levi truly had not thought very long and hard about his father's well-being, not since Hannah had rejected his offer of matrimony. Indeed, he had remained outside the colony for quite some time. He had *preferred* to consider little else besides for business. Of late, however, he had met Rebecca, and he had fallen for her. She, too, was soft-spoken. Perhaps to a fault. All this time courting her, granted it wasn't for very long, and she had not given him true reason to assume she reciprocated his feelings. How difficult it is to decipher the mysterious sex! he mused. Why were women so complex? Take Rebecca: the young woman lived with her Puritanical aunt who refused to allow any male visitors to remain in the parlor, let alone court her niece. Rebecca had to concoct strange fabrications, lies truly, in order to *speak* to men. (I'm shopping for lace, again.) And how was this young woman to wed? Her strange aunt had objected to previous arrangements: Moses the peddler was too poor; the butcher's son was too boorish, and the merchant from Versailles probably too loose. It was a miracle of no small proportions, come to think of it, that the two even *met*. If it weren't for the bakery by the ocean front the two would forever remain untouched—as two heavenly spheres removed by vast distances. Levi had been neglecting himself during those first weeks; eating only when ravenous, smoking more than recommended, and later binging on stale rum. If it weren't for *Shabbos*, he would never have bothered buying two loaves of bread and some fish by the wayside. The corner store sold all different types of loaves; he bought the ones that most appealed to his senses—the ones that looked *somewhat* like *challah*. Levi missed his mother's pots—the delectable dishes and the warmth that usually came alongside the beef or the broth. *Shabbos* was not meant to be celebrated all alone. If he was lucky, a friendly Jew invited him for the Friday night meal. When in Rhode Island or New York, that was rarely a problem. Plenty of Jews lived in that part of the New World. Levi wondered why his father bothered to remain in Georgia when so many of the Jews, particularly the Portuguese, left for higher ground—the New England colonies—years prior. Granted the poor Portuguese were petrified of the Spaniards reissuing the Inquisition in all its measures, but what was there for his father? Benjamin Sheftall refused to move up North; he believed Providence had set forth his destiny in Georgia; his loyalty to Oglethorpe, even years after his departure, had remained embedded in Benjamin's blood. But Levi was not afraid to venture forth—even farther than his brother at times. Of course he wasn't tied down by a wife and several children. That was definitely the upside of all his misery. Unfettered perhaps. But that might change now with the budding interest in Rebecca reaching its boiling point. There was only one deterrent: Aunt Beatrice. How her beady eyes narrowed in when she first appraised Levi! He felt a deep shivering sensation, one he could barely vocalize. Her stare most resembled that of a priest staring at a Jewish enemy. It was truly odious to think that Rebecca respected the hag; but Levi refused to focus too heartily on the aunt—for the time being he was smitten with the young woman whose eyelashes curled into half-moons.

*

Levi called upon Rebecca that same evening. Usually, during this time of year, Levi would spend the weeks prior to the High Holidays engrossed in economic affairs. Still building an empire of tanneries, Levi found that time of year propitious for business. The Christians were eager to find a buyer after a sluggish summer, and he was keen for profit. But this week he would have to forgo the formalities of trade and the benefits therein; his father needed him. It was a matter of course to say farewell then to sweet Rebecca.

Rebecca had been busy at her needle-point. Slender and agile, her form was nicely adorned in modest silk chiffon. As most girls her age, Rebecca wore a pinafore while at home. Tonight, however, she sat in her egg-shelled colored gown, softly praying for a breeze to cool her off. Charleston was not as humid as Savannah, thankfully, but the homes nevertheless remained warm, even late into the evening during the summer months. The church bells rang in the distance, a reminder of their Christian surroundings. The *mezuzah* by the doorpost hung innocuously, barely noticeable. Levi kissed the *mezuzah*, wondering if the American populace will one day decide to ghettoize the Jews or, if perchance, the Jews just may volunteer and ghettoize themselves, sequestering their homes into community bases, as in Rhode Island and New York. Levi shifted impatiently, anxious the fussy aunt won't meddle or make a scene. He glanced at the rose bushes; how incredible! They bloomed more than once this season. Levi wondered if his heart could bloom with newfound love, even after the buds of so promising a love had withered away. Could the soul bury itself and then rise reborn? The rose-bush reminded Levi of Hannah; she too loved flowers. On many occasions she tugged at a few of the yellow hedge roses and placed one, ever so daintily, behind her ear. Rebecca's Creole maidservant thankfully answered, bowing her head. Levi respected their mannerisms; many of the women were portly, thanks to sausage and buttermilk. But she was a breathless sight after the dread of anticipation. Rebecca heard the door open and placed her needle point by the ottoman. She glanced at her complexion in the mirror, fastened her necklace, and prepared to smile broadly. She noticed her bodice felt a bit tighter with each successive breath. How easy it was for her to appear gay when she considered Levi's visitation! How wonderfully unexpected! The curtains were drawn at this hour, and Aunt Beatrice was out visiting an old friend. Rebecca shooed a pesky fly, and bowed. Levi had finally arrived and her dreadful aunt deliciously absent! But she did not detect any cheer in Levi's expression. Quite the opposite in fact. How demoralizing! Why can't he smile? Is it my dress? Have I caused him undue harm? Whatever shall I do? Such and such were the thoughts of the young woman. Levi wished he could grab her arm. I didn't realize I felt this way.... How truly sad my mien must appear to Rebecca. How shall I phrase my fear upon learning of my father's illness? Surely my eyes betray any feigned attempt at gladness!

"Whatever is the matter, Levi? Please do tell!"

Rebecca's voice trailed softly, in the same manner Hannah's had, with a tilt of compassion. But Rebecca's brows were not curled at Mordechai, Levi bitterly ruminated.

"It is my father. I must take leave of you, Rebecca. He is ill, and I fear his illness will worsen in the days and weeks to follow. Pray for him, dear Rebecca. I regret to impart such knowledge onto your sweet self."

Rebecca felt instantly regretful; it shall be a long separation. *I feel it.*

"I shall recite psalms every morning."

Levi nodded his head. His chin crinkled. He looked away.

In a moment of absolute impulse, he seized Rebecca's arm. He held her close and kissed her forehead. Rebecca, for a moment winded, embraced him, forgetting the laws prohibiting physical expression. After a brief moment, Levi let go of her thin and graceful arms, stood a foot apart, as though he did not trust himself any longer, bowed his head, turned around and stared at the cobble road until he mounted his horse, heading for Savannah and to Benjamin, his father.

He did not take note of Aunt Beatrice holding her parasol, *tsk-tsk*ing in the shade of the rose bush.

*

Mordechai received a note earlier that morning, anticipating his brother's arrival. Levi had absented himself from Savannah, was sincerely interested in a young woman, and had begun creating his own career. And now the two must gather strength to face their father's debilitating illness. Suddenly shaken, Mordechai had felt a tremendous weight burdening his shoulders; his father had been the mainstay of the Sheftall household. It was his father who taught him self-preservation, social duty, and independence. Mordechai suddenly felt as though he were two years of age, and his father had to temporarily abandon him once again. Terror gripped him, and then he shook it off. *I'm no longer a child.* But then again, he suddenly recalled his own screams and shrieks as Mrs. Minis held him to her bosom, little Hannah looking along—and Benjamin off in the distance, striding his horse toward Oglethorpe's garrison. Reduced to an infantile panic, Mordechai's head swirled with the colors and the scents of his early childhood. His father had sworn to return, but he had tears in his eyes. *Mommy. She never returned,* Mordechai had thought. *Will daddy disappear too? Where's the baby? I can't hear him crying from his cradle under the ground.* Mordechai had never been able to leave his father's side since Benjamin returned from the battlefield early in Savannah's colonial history. As independent as he had become financially, Mordechai was *still* dependent on his father for moral guidance— and much more. Much more.

Hannah was not his biological mother, but she was all he knew. Suddenly, as Frances walked through the door, he had recalled his own mother, Perla. She too had light eyes and light hair. *Like my Fannie.* It suddenly dawned on him, that after all these years, perhaps it was his mother he was truly longing for.

"Whatever is the matter, dear?"

Mordechai walked over to her side. "How's the child?" He rubbed Fannie's swelling belly for a while, and she simply nodded her head slightly. "Thank God. I feel the child. But I fear for our children, Mordechai. Mrs. McIntosh frightened me with terrible stories—she lost her babies. I so fear it!"

"Shhh. You must never fear." Feeling isolated suddenly, he embraced her. "Never fear."

*

"This is absurd!" Wright nearly flung a vase of antique handiwork from Paris. "What is the intention of the countrymen? Do they indeed presume to impose governance *above* Parliament?"

Mr. Eddings resented James Wright's display of righteous indignation. "It is not for me to say, sir, what the masses presume."

"Indeed it is not! How say you the men of this town should threaten Knox, a serviceman of the King, with nary a word of such to *me*? It is from Knox whom I discovered the breach of loyalty and deference—not a word on the matter of *propriety*. What is to become of these Georgian men, who have misguided notions regarding their *liberty*? They most certainly took liberty with Knox, I dare say!"

Mr. Eddings nodded his head. He believed that was the *proper* response. James Wright, however, was irritated by Eddings' seeming indifference.

"Man! Do you not see the absurdity of their actions? Some of the men who had written to Knox do not even *own land* sanctioned by the colony. What is to become of the order in this country? Shall the Negro now order his master as well?"

Percy overheard Wright's tirade, and contemplated the cause of his ire. Percy gleaned from his fellow Negro men (mostly field workers) that Wright's popularity was slowly waning amongst the merchant class. They resented his undying loyalty to an overblown king in faraway white man's land—England. Some Negroes hoped the merchants would perhaps take to their bondage as well—after all, the merchants were free in many respects, unlike the Negroes. The Negro had no voice, after all. Percy helped himself to a cup of tea—a rare treat he secretly enjoyed when his master had more important matters to attend to. Percy noticed a pattern: when Master Eddings arrived, Wright would sequester himself with Eddings in the grand parlor, ignoring his little ones, his graciously adorned wife, and all the indolent servants. Eddings would venture forth on Sabbaths, and overstay his welcome. On those occasions, Percy would remain awake, with a soft candle by his bedside, and read the Holy Bible—the King James Bible. His mistress, Mrs. Johnson of good memory, taught him to read as a young one. Doing so opened his mind to God's voice, and he knew he was of Canaan, cursed to serve his white brothers. And he knew Moses was God's messenger, and just wondered if there was a messenger for his kind of people too. Ruth the scullery maid, a mongrel woman truly, (with chocolate skin, the color of ground nutmeg) sang church hymns all week long—but read she couldn't. Indeed, just this morning, Percy surveyed the headlines of the morning paper, issued in the local Savannah streets near the rich Jew Sheftall (his friend, Jeremiah White worked there) and noticed a distressing bit of news—up in the Pennsylvania colonies, men and women were boycotting British goods, and some children were real hungry. The story blamed Parliament back in London for their empty stomach, the poor children! *Don't care for their own kind, they don't.*

While Master Wright was not mean-spirited to the helping hands—including Percy—he was not benevolent either. Whippings occurred when "deemed most necessary," and Percy himself had to witness poor Ruth's son learning the way of the white man's hand. Barely baptized six years and already consigned to drudgery—feeding hens, milking the fat pigs, and chasing the barnyard dogs—the child had learned the underhand method by which his lot survived. But he had stolen biscuits from the Missus' crystal jar, a most delectable biscuit, and received six lashes—one for each year he had not digested the strict commandment of the almighty Lord Himself, down from Sinai He did utter—Thou shalt not *steal*. Ruth had cried alongside her son, feeling too much pain to scold her son. Ruth's little boy didn't bother with the biscuits after that. He just learned to hate the white man, alongside many of the Negro hands.

*

Wright opened the door to the parlor and gestured with his hand. Eddings was enjoying the sumptuous carpets and the portraits hanging on the walls of Wright's estate. The paint was finely layered in a soft translucent blue the aristocrats of London's burgeoning upper class preferred. The frames of all the portraits—one of King George the Third by far the most outstanding piece, worth many thousands of pounds, no doubt—were placed in golden frames. The gold reflected the threads in the tapestry, which were of a similar hue. The ottoman, chaise, and the large chairs were all hand-painted with fine ivory Venetian color, with a stain of gold all along the edges. Even the molding boasted slivers of golden laced paint, all perfectly lit by soft candle chandeliers, to ease their passing towards the grand foyer. The room was extraordinarily clear from dust. Wright was known to keep a strict household, similar to the grand estates of Wright's ancestry back in Old England. Wright was bred in breeches of gold, Eddings thought. Wright seemed immune to his august inheritance; indeed, the stately manner in which Wright lived was bequeathed to him, together with all the rights and privileges of his grand class, Eddings unconsciously realized. *Is it possible I take greater pleasure in his surroundings than does he?* Wright dismissed the footman, and Percy, the tall dark Negro whose eyes shone in the night with frightening intensity, assisted Eddings, rather gently, and bowed, ever so slightly, in a dignified manner that rather pleased Eddings.

*

That evening in Broughton Street, Benjamin felt exceedingly weak. Levi had finally arrived, and Mordechai trailed behind his younger son. More and more, Mordechai had begun to resemble his father. Hannah had removed all the holy books from Benjamin's bedside. Hannah's eyes belied her calm; soft, moist water lines testified to her worried tears. The room in which Benjamin lay was the same room in which Mordechai and Levi had been conceived; the room of marital bliss and agony; the tapestry had changed since Perla's days, but the aura of serenity had remained. The wooden panels had slightly disintegrated, and a slightly acrid smell permeated the room. The scent of camphor and lavender mist slightly nauseated Mordechai. The area rug had been worn. His father did not believe in throwing out what had not completely lost its value or purpose. Thus, the bed tables had a moldy residue and the mattress was folded slightly in half; but Benjamin refused to purchase new furniture. "For what the expense?" He would insist on enjoying what he had purchased; and so Mordechai had imagined the room had not changed much since he had been a child living with his father. A silhouette of Perla was removed from its hiding place;

Benjamin held the portrait in his hands. A book of psalms, for years, served as its secret home. Now Mordechai had the chance to recall, if just a bit, his mother's lost face. Levi realized Mordechai's intent, and left the room. Mordechai barely noticed. With his father asleep, he gently removed the portrait and stared into the darkness of Perla's soft profile. Her nose was so delicate! Unlike mine, he thought. Of course, I do take after father. But should my daughter one day… But of mother! Perhaps I truly *do* recall her. Mordechai felt emptiness inside, the emptiness he had submerged all his life with a façade of cheer. Hannah was his mother, but it was Perla who had captured his imagination and his loneliness. Since marrying Frances, Mordechai had forgotten, long forgotten, his desperate longing for warmth. Hannah had done so for him, he knew that. Hannah was his mother, but even his father could no longer bury his longing. Lost love is never truly gone, and Hannah must lose a double loss….

Mordechai glanced at his father's face; it was etched in fine lines, lines that had accumulated over years of agony and joy, labor and serenity, toil and ecstasy. These were the same lines that drew the story of his life, from the early summers of his Prussian youth to the winters of Georgia's darkest hours. The wrinkles on his skin reminded Mordechai of fallen leaves; his tears flowed. It was a response he had held back since Levi had sat across from him and informed him of what he had probably already known, but had not the courage to admit.

Benjamin began to rouse, and Mordechai was about to leave the room when his father called his name. "Under the bed is a pan. Call Hannah. She knows what I need."

Mordechai did precisely as he was told. He had left the room and stood outside. The terrible stench reached the other room.

"The doctor says it's a terrible disease," Mordechai whispered to his brother, uncomfortable with silence.

Levi nearly began to laugh in hysterics. Was this not an egregious understatement? He barely recognized his father! His cheeks sunken in; shriveled like a dried tomato. Barely recognizable.

His mouth was dry; he was bled daily. Few contents remained in his rebellious gut and few more in his miserable stomach. Why had his mother waited this long? What was left of him; it was too terrible.

Hannah motioned for the two to step into the parlor. Benjamin needed to bathe. The Negro hands began to boil water, carry buckets, and fill the tub in the wash closet with cleansing agents and very warm water. Benjamin would become ill if he shivered too much. The vapors of the warm water massaged his intestines. The doctor recommended warm baths to calm his sulfurous belly.

It wasn't working much. Benjamin's moans filled the room, and Mordechai could barely withstand the sounds of his father's agony.

Levi paced around the room, counting the planks. Beneath the rugs are planks, he thought. *We cover it up, don't we. The body with decorated frills, the face with powder, the hair with bonnets, and the legs with fancy boots. We chase after beauty, living as though life were not a butterfly, but a long butterfly's day. He paced faster, counting the planks. Life. And I have not made any of my own. Who will I bequeath to when my day comes? What have I done? Gathered a fortune without a soul to confer my blessings upon. My years may just become days.*

Mordechai stared at his brother and wondered what he was thinking. Levi had not seen the deterioration progress slowly. It had come as a shock; it was much to bear. His father had prayed for Levi to find happiness. Would he witness that now?

Eventually, Hannah returned, her back bent even more, and sighed.

Levi hugged his mother, glad she was still strong. "Ima," he whispered.

Hannah hugged him dearly. He was her only surviving son.

Mordechai had felt a strange pang of self-pity; *why am I conscious of all this now? He wondered. I thought I had long-buried my jealous heart.*

"Come, Mordechai. He wants to see you now."

Benjamin felt as though he could finally look into his sons' eyes again. How his body betrayed him! For years it had served him well. It had provided him with countless hours of energy; even when deprived of countless hours of sleep, Benjamin had rocked his sons to sleep with his arms, cooked for his wives when they fell ill, read the Torah on the Sabbath, and bore sons—two of which stood before him. He began to tear so suddenly when he considered the light that had been spent—little Sheftall; he could have been a father now. Such a beautiful boy! He didn't need to die! He did not have a disease, as Hannah's second son had! He could have lived to a fine, ripe old age. Imagine! Three sons! Benjamin held their hands.

"*Yevarachecha Hashem, Ve-ishmarecha.* May God bless you and protect you." Addressing Mordechai, he smiled. "I know you, Mordechai—you won't rest until you change the universe! Let me kiss you, son. Let me kiss your cheek."

Mordechai began to bawl. *I'm losing him.* Levi cried too. He kissed his father's hand and begged his father to bless him too.

"*Yesimecha Elokim K'Efraim u'Menashe.* May God bless you as he had blessed Ephraim and Menashe." The two beloved sons of Joseph the patriarch. "I know you too shall spread far and wide, Levi."

Incapable of speaking too much, Hannah removed her sons from Benjamin's bedroom and closed the door. It was a dreadful thought, to lose her husband when she had felt as though she had gained him late in life. To lose ere half your days….

Seventy-three years since his birth, Benjamin closed his eyes for the last time the following evening, having recited the *Shema* in the presence of his family. It was October. And the "yellow leaves" were "few" that "did hang" by the door of his home, the same home that held so much promise, the home where lovely Perla had kissed little Sheftall before her soul kissed itself away.

That same year, Parliament buried itself as well, with the Stamp Act, and Wright's opposition increased. The years of Georgia's tranquility had died.

*

The year was 1765 and the worst was yet to come.

GAGE MUST GAUGE

FRANCES HELD HER SON'S HAND. Sheftall Sheftall had grown into a fine child; he was by far more charming by the day. His little fingers, snugly placed in Frances' hand, touched Frances in a way she had never envisioned. Little Shefy loved to imitate his father and insisted on following Mordechai's every step.

"But why not, Mother? Why must I join the *babies*? I am not a baby anymore!"

Frances laughed. "Of course you are! These men will be speaking about *secret* matters, son. And Father doesn't permit it."

"But when then? When will Father allow me to sit in on these secret meetings? Next year, when I am forty-four?"

Frances raised her son and kissed his soft cheek. She giggled all the way to the nursery. "You are not even FOUR! And you will be *forty*-four in a long, long time, silly boy!"

Indignant, Shefy removed his little fingers from his mother's grasp. "I want to go now. I am almost forty-four!"

He darted for the stairs, and Frances had a difficult time catching up with her son. Amused, she nearly collided into Mordechai, who had just bathed for the evening's meeting. He chased after his son and caught Shefy.

"Aba! Aba! I can come tonight! I know I can!"

Mordechai glanced at Frances. He had a strange expression, Frances believed.

"I am afraid Mother does not permit little boys—"

"But I am *not* little!" Mordechai held his eldest tightly and ruffled his hair. "You are right! You are not little. Let's make a pact, son. When you turn ten, you shall attend all meetings. What say you?"

Delighted, Sheftall Sheftall believed he would be able to partake of the "special" gatherings quite soon. In fact, he believed he would turn ten quite soon. He kissed his father's cheek and ran to the nursery without another protestation.

"You know he will ask you tomorrow if he's ten," Frances said, with a bit of a teasing intonation in her delicate voice.

Mordechai's head instinctively cocked backwards. He laughed and held Frances. "Of course he will! And I plan on keeping my word, wife." Frances was duly disappointed, but Mordechai left little room for protest. With his charming maneuvers, which truly did not fail *most of the time*, he lifted Frances just a bit off the floor and kissed her forehead and then her mouth. Frances knew his tactics were effective, which confounded her ever so slightly.

Frances knew she was meant to support her husband. She had been taught that much from her early years. A valorous woman. Cares for his needs, respects his desires. But what good can come from political dealings? It didn't help that all these important men knocked on her door, incessantly begging for her husband's attention.

At first it was John Wereat. Frances didn't like the idea of his being a *goy*. She was taught that *goyim* do not enter a home. But her husband had no such beliefs! He *dines with them*, spends *countless hours guiding* them…. The Sons of Liberty have taken a liking to him now as well, and Frances was beside herself. *Ruffians. Loose men.* She did not approve of many of the characters looming in the landscape of her peaceful home. But Mordechai was exceedingly *charming*; embracing this one, aiding that one, funding this venue, feeding this stomach and that belly.

And then he involved the Minis brothers. Even after that mishap in the forest, which she eventually *discovered thanks to her loyal slaves*, Philip had been persuaded to join. Meetings in taverns. Gatherings in town squares. Mordecai Sheftall was *too* well-known for her liking. Goodness! When she agreed to marry him she had never dreamt of this *notoriety. I don't like all this attention, all this organizing.* Frances feared the English government. The English were well-known throughout the Western world as a formidable empire. They crushed the Spanish; they nearly owned the seas. They surpassed the Dutch years ago. They funded the colonies, and engaged in world-trade. How could her husband stand up to Parliament, the symbolic gate round the Crown itself? It was absurd. Surely taxes, even the Stamp Act which ostensibly raised every single commodity by a degree which irked *each* colonist, were not just cause for all this *rage*. But Frances had to keep her mouth tightly stitched. It was a matter of course that women, regardless of rank, did not overstep their positions as housewives. It was a world of men; men decide. The women can only stand *beside*.

*

Quoting John Locke in taverns, surrounded by all sorts of riffraff, Mordechai tantalized Georgians with thoughts of *revolution*. Unafraid to speak against the Crown, Mordechai felt responsible for articulating the discontent of his fellow men. Plenty of reading material was readily available, including translations of Rousseau and Voltaire. A grand fellow by the name of Thomas Paine regularly published short essays well worth reading in public. Granted Mordechai was not always responsible for every scoundrel in attendance; but whether the attendee was a pauper, plebian, or patrician, Mordechai riled the masses with his formidable presence. Those who were incapable of reading relied on Mordechai's opinions. Even the few Catholics who lived nearby overlooked Mordechai's religious background, briefly in the least, while he paraphrased the Bible's injunction against thievery and injustice. Integrating the Bible, the most credible source of Divine origin, with luminaries of the Enlightenment, Mordechai was able to weave an American quilt. Mordechai, though, could not always determine who was an innocuous member or who perhaps considered him a foe. Besides for Wright, who debased the group with the appellation "Sons of Licentiousness," Mordechai garnered much honor. That's not to say that Wright did not admire any man so capable of rhetoric. But the governor found the subject matter, needless to say, scurrilous and outright treasonous. Having known Mordechai as a burgeoning nobleman, the Englishman was rather crestfallen and demoralized that such as he should not take up the Tory cause. Among the Tories were the great landowners, not to mention statesmen, such as James Habersham. Assuming Mordechai's influence was waxing (while his waned), Wright found and directed his own kind to observe the "anarchists."

Truth be told, the worst began shortly after Benjamin passed on. *The Georgia Gazette* published the Stamp Act Congress documents only three weeks after his passing. James Johnston was appointed public printer by the Georgia Assembly, so he was only acting out of duty. Ironically, the Stamp Act prevented Johnston from profiting from the publication. Every page was to be levied! Every damn piece of paper! Well, Johnston's paper caused enough rage and bedlam, so perhaps it was for the best. That night, on the thirty-first of October, 1765, a mob sprouted from every Savannah corner. McIntosh's son, a couple of half-breeds, and plenty of irate women carried an effigy of a stamp officer through the streets, up and down Broughton in fact. They later hanged and burned the effigy. A few mutineers shot their rifles for effect. James Wright heard it all, from Habersham and from a couple of trusty moles. The Stamp Act was meant to go into effect on November 1. No officer was in sight. Any British man or loyalist who dared to enlist as a stamp officer was a damned fellow.

The Savannah ports were ominously still that evening. The clouds darkened the horizon, and the terns circled round the ships. Rows of wooden boats were docked, buoyed by the placid waters. The anchors had begun to attract barnacles. Perishable goods served to placate the hungry seashore rats, those that fed off of bloody carcasses and half-rotten sturgeon. The vessels carried goods from Britain and from the northern colonies. But they were unable to clear their merchandise. No one issued the stamped paper. So no one could unload the goods. At first, the odor was reminiscent of stale biscuits accidentally toasted by a nearby fire. Then, the rancid tomatoes, squash, and pumpkin, cooked by the midday heat of Savannah's raging sun, intensified the stench. By the time Mordechai tied his stallion to the pole by MacHenry's tavern, which was inconveniently situated by the shore, the breeze wafting from the port was a great deal worse than the waste of humans and creatures alike. Those that had been to battle swore human bellies, after days of swelling post mortem, gurgled and exuded vile juices which were somewhat reminiscent of the Savannah shore. Few ladies saw cause to venture out.

Mordechai had debated leaving his wife and still-bereaving mother. After all, his father's corpse was freshly interred. He had just completed the mourning period of seven long days. For seven days he wept, shook hands, and listened to words of consolation. Clean water to bathe his flesh—no longer permissible. The agony of his body was to mimic his father's. That week Benjamin stood in a Heavenly Tribunal. And should his son partake of the flesh? For seven days he recited psalms, praying Benjamin's soul should sojourn in the Land of the Living. Before the Sabbath, Mordechai rinsed his body in cold water. He refused to pleasure himself. *In remembrance.* He slept in a separate bed; his wife was forbidden now. All sorts of men tried to comfort him. John Wereat sat and held his hand. Few words passed between them. Jews from Pennsylvania who had known his father, those Sephardic men who remembered Mr. Sheftall from Georgia's early days, visited Mordechai's estate. In that week, Mordechai learned of his father's great valor in battle and his uncompromising determination to assist the orphans of the town. Heaps of old women recalled Mr. Sheftall—he had aided their daughters' poor orphans. Susan Hale came too; she spoke kindly of her long-ago employer, who had been wed to a fine European woman with the name of a precious gem. Captain McIntosh too, once a fine man of Manchester, gallantly regaled the company that week. Mordechai had never envisioned his father in that particular way. Could it be his father was speaking from *she'ol*, the deep grave? Should Mordechai battle as his father had? Should he become a spokesperson for his brethren in America? Is he meant to remain a silent citizen?

Should he involve his brother? What should the onus be—the one that he were to bear? Oh! Why had his father remained silent on this subject? If not for the gesture of that letter from Oglethorpe, or Benjamin's seemingly prophetic mumblings before he perished, Mordechai would have truly felt at a loss. But it was Levi in the end who pushed him. It was Levi's noncommittal stance to join the Sons of Liberty that propelled Mordechai. *If not now, when? If I am not for myself, who will be for me?*

*

Mordechai held a handkerchief to his nose. The impulse had caught him by surprise, and he retched in a bucket by the tavern. This was the first *public* meeting. Up until tonight, Mordechai had attended closeted meetings, a few good times in fact. Tonight. All was changed.

A motley crowd of Georgians gathered round the main tender MacHenry, a stout man with ruddy cheeks. MacHenry's partner, a woman of thirty years of age, gladly poured the ale into flasks. The men preferred to drink from their "pockets" as they roamed the tavern. The usual sailors weren't leaving town until the stamp officers levied the proper taxes. MacHenry's was profiting in all this political stalemate. A few farmers complained of the overbearing heat on the crops. Some peasants, rather boorish and all missing teeth, begged for another draft of ale, just this one more time if you please. They were the usual. A few aristocrats who had their dealings in imported goods attended as well. Renegade scholars and solicitors quietly made their way through the doors of MacHenry's, embarrassed somewhat but then easily contented to join in the fracas. All were to be unjustly affected by the Stamp Act.

"Dice! Why! It's as if Parliament *knows* we play with those damn dice while we wait for the crops to sprout!"

Johnston bobbed his head and overheard the downtrodden farmer, O'Brien. "Fellow—what am I to say? Advertisements, pamphlets, newspapers, almanacs—these are the elements of my trade. I am now a beggar—at the expense of Parliament's cupidity! What say you, Sheftall?"

The Jew. All eyes turned on Mordechai's countenance. His eyes had sunken in deeper and he had cultivated a beard. His dark piercing eyes shown, as though he had recently cried a bitter hour. His long, prominent nose seemed to protrude even more, lending Mordechai an air of authority.

"Governments do not have the right to mock its people. Nor should government impose such weighty levies on a fragile colony without the consent of the governed. Do we not have the right to oppose an act of direct wrongness? Johnston, I hear you shall soon be unable to print the *Gazette*. And who are we to blame? And you, Mr. McIntosh, I hear your son cannot claim his academic degree without the levied tax on *each paper*. Is this just? All goods wrapped in paper are to be levied as well. And which merchant or farmer is not reliant on paper? You—MacHenry—where should you pay for your liquor license? It is to be reissued, but this time at greater expense. Does that entail a greater price for a draft of ale? And what of cotton, lace, soaps, sugars, teas? Are not these goods wrapped in paper! The Stamp Act is no more than a rat chewing at our very legal notes! Every legal tender you now hold will increase tenfold in the hands of Parliament—and shall decrease in ours. Look you—O'Brien. I hear your crops are suffering. Add to that the added expense of this tax, and soon your pretty wife will have you cooking too!"

"Hear hear!" One of Wright's men, Habersham's boy, confronted Mordechai. His tender skin radiated a well-bred youth, one of equestrian escapades, fencing, and delicate mannerisms. His tongue was pink and his teeth exceedingly white. His fine-tailored waistcoat boasted brass buttons and nicely displayed his physique—broadly shouldered with wide hips. A few of the women were pleasantly distracted by his fine features. A delicate mole, almost placed by a painter's hand it seemed, by his upper lip captivated his audience. His eyes, green and dusted with mauve, darted at Mordechai. Everyone knew James Wright dined with James Habersham and that his son was a well-bred boy. "What do you make of the letter in *The Gazette*—the one signed by the notorious and nameless 'Townsman?'" he demanded.

Habersham's boy was referring to the threatening letter published in the paper. Five leading citizens received the letter, which was published for all Savannah to read. These leading men, the "elite," were suspected of harboring imported stamped papers. Some were even believed to have accepted the appointment of stamp official. Habersham knew of all this, of course, because of his father's close connection to Wright. Wright thought he could reason with the nameless Townsman. But yet again, Wright was wrong. On the issue of the anonymous "Townsman," all Savannah folk seemed united in their reticence.

"James Wright may issue a public notice offering a fifty-pound reward for the identity of the Townsman all he likes. He is missing the *point*. We act as a committee of *men*. We do not conspire *against one another*. The Townsman, be he who he may, was simply warning the government of the *foolishness* of this Act."

"And what if Wright fines the town, or discovers the identity of the Townsman, what do you propose?"

"My boy—the issues here are far grander than any one man, Townsman or not. We here, and tell me if I am mistaken Sirs, do not abide by the lunacy of mandating taxes!"

"Hear! Hear!"

"And yet, Sirs," Habersham interrupted, "You rather bewilder me! That you should hearken the words of a *Jew*. Tell me, why shouldn't you speak of such matters? After all, when it comes to your coffers—"

A few men giggled at the insinuation. It was *true*. Mordechai was an affluent Jew who was probably concerned with his pockets. But they all were, weren't they? But laugh they did all the same. Unmoved by the boy's innuendoes, Mordechai averred:

"So is *this the extent* of your fine education? This *rubbish!* Place yourself in the soles of these wretched men, young man. Have you ever labored for any stitch of fine clothing you now don? Have you ever toiled for a trade, as these men have, only to be robbed of every pound and pence, by a government, no less, who adjudicates beyond the great sea?"

"And should you speak! What do you know of labor? Your fine estates belie your so-called entreaty for equity!" Habersham retaliated.

A silence filled the room and Mordechai nearly lost his sense of reason. The gall of the entitled youth!

"And what do you know of the sweat of my brow? From the early days of my youth I have labored in tanneries and farmyards; I have been raised among the herds and hogs of Georgia—not unlike these men standing here. With God's grace, and with the toil of mine own hands, have I been blessed to stand and state, with all the confidence of a hard-calloused hand, pounding on this, my heart, the solemn oath that this great country shall not become picking ground for avaricious men! Now go scurry over and repeat *that* to Mr. James Wright. We are all but men here."

Silenced by the uproar, Habersham's boy disappeared into the crowd. A few men left the dank tavern and made way to Wright's estate. Inside, the men were boisterous and giddy. They had found a leading voice in the Jew Mordechai Sheftall.

"It is time to decide our course of action!" The leading man, Archibald Bulloch, took over at this point. Mordechai sat near Bulloch, refusing a glass of beer, and trying to ignore the portly woman beseeching him with her alluring eyes. After a few good rounds of discussion, they finally agreed that if any Stamp Master should so much as deign to step foot in Savannah, he should expect "trouble" from the people who were justifiably opposed to the vile Act. Ill-advised. The people urge this Stamp Master, whoever he shall be, to resign his position immediately, as the Stamp Masters in other colonies had wisely done.

*

James Wright frowned and bitterly recollected Knox's warning, "Expect to be the next one to receive a wretched lashing." Poor Knox! Ousted by his own constituents! The barbarism of those who uphold their "liberty," denying others their rightful duties! It was mad; the *people* were mad. Burning effigies of Stamp Masters—what would they think of next? By golly he was glad he did not live too close to the stinking shore. Those damned boats were breeding ground for treacherous disease, least of all the malodorous fumes. Even the Indians refused to trade, now that the ports were idle. But in all the "hurly-burly," Wright had yet to lose face. Ignorant men of questionable breeding entertained the most ridiculous notions—Independence! From Great Britain? The seat of Western Civilization, Shakespeare, Milton, Newton! All of the Iberian Peninsula now bows to George the Third's imperious satin laces. The governed, with a seat in Parliament, arbitrate while the Arabians and the yellow men of heathen origin conspire against their chieftains. Are the Americans to retrogress and revert to the stage of the aping figures of mankind of the previous generations? Had not Seneca proven the superior mode of a republic? Why should a people desire to separate from the great legions of Western Civilization? Could they not see the honor and *damned privilege* of being a British colony? And who would govern these anarchists? Could they even *agree* in a *civilized manner* on a code of law, on jurisprudence? Most of these men just want an honest beer alongside their loose women! MacHenry's tavern was no more than a brothel, even his wife knew that, and she was a *decent* covenanted woman. Under the pretext of "paying too much" for "paper goods," the Sons of Liberty had ample pounds to splurge on buxom women willing to reveal their not-so treasured chests, and to uncover their shame! *Prostitutes in petticoats;* these women have their liberty, all right!

Do they not enjoy their freedoms in America? No man forces those in Ebenezer to forsake their religion. So why all the fuss? Do the Jews live in ghettoes here? So why should the likes of da Costa, Minis, and Sheftall take cause against the British? Where was the justice in this universe!

Utterly spent and disgusted with humanity, James Wright walked into his parlor and made way for his grand library. The bibliophile that he had become was only due to his fine breeding; his study of law was most prolific. How many men in this town could boast of reading Plato? How many had indeed heard of Aristophanes or Euripides? Even the grand work of Milton—

why, how many could quote, verbatim, verse upon blank verse of *Paradise Lost?* But man was cast in the light of Satan after the Great Sin of Disobedience, and Wright was damned if he could not set the tone in his own town. The Stamp Act was legal, proper, and no matter what licentious boys should consider, fit for compliance by every dutiful citizen of the British crown.

Energized by a sense of filial duty and honored by a code of chivalrous submission to the Regent, Wright wrote a letter to the King promising him that all should be quickly resolved and the monies levied should soon help defray the cost of hefty wars. The ports shall be cooking its fetid odors until George Angus, the English Stamp Master, would arrive on the *Speedwell.* Godspeed, Wright thought. Godspeed.

*

"But if you are already active in the Sons of Liberty what need you of joining the Parochial Committee?"

"I cannot say. The Committee beseeched I join their ranks. There is no *inherent* difference, Frances. Not one in beliefs. Our objectives are similar."

"Do you not believe influence in one is sufficient?"

"I must follow the duties the men of this town properly deem for me."

"But surely your wife's opinion should not be disregarded in this matter?"

Mordechai turned his head to the side. Ruminating, he considered his wife's protestation. These meetings were tedious, to be sure. Many Christian men sought his counsel, and his house had become a haven for discussion and debate. While his father had run a synagogue from his home, Mordechai, at least during this turbulent time, had furnished his house with chairs to seat the many men who voiced complaints over the long days of discontent. Doubtless, she was overburdened with children and household; every woman desired her husband's attentions. But these were not ordinary times, and Mordechai had every intention of aiding those who were less fortunate than he, even if he would incur discomfort or tedium.

He did not answer his wife; he only nodded his head, hoping the Sabbath meals would suffice for quality time for now.

*

Dear Rebecca,

A long winter has hampered us all, and it is not even remotely near its close. My delicate mother Hannah mourns the loss of my dear father, and I have assumed the role of comforter. How I yearn to find comfort myself! Alas, I have been occupied with my mother's pain that I often neglect my own. Please forgive me, dearest; I did not intend to neglect you in any which way. I have longed to see your beautiful face, but I have neither the time nor the luxury to do so. My mother is in dire need of companionship; I fear that if I should leave her, she shall succumb to melancholy.

I hear your father's plantation thrives. I am glad of it. But how do *you* fare? It is of no small consequence that you have remained patient all this winter. Brewing of all sorts is fomenting in Savannah, and I am sure the same is true of Charleston. Although it is not for me to speak of such matters to a genteel soul such as yourself, the Stamp Act indeed affects us all, one way or another. I have been disabled by the Governor's stance and Parliament's edicts. Unlike my brother, however, I am unwilling to sacrifice or risk my inheritance on a mere formality that shall soon become a way of life. On this matter I feel most passionately, whereas my brother could not disagree more. Oh Rebecca! How I desire to get lost in love, but talk of revolution and rebellion is stirring my household—I fear at this time, I am my mother's bulwark and only rampart. She longs for my company. She insists I sleep next door to her bedroom chamber. The loneliness of old age drags her days, and I am loath to deny her comfort. Yet how can I forget my own?

Forgive me for this delay. I do promise, Rebecca, to greet you in Charleston as soon as the scuffle in Savannah subsides and the spring buries all weeds of sorrow.

With all my affection and highest esteem,
Levi

Levi folded the letter and hoped its recipient would find the contents reassuring. The entire town was on edge. A stamp master was due any day, and up until he graced American soil with his British airs, Savannah maritime was ostensibly at an impasse. But Levi secretly feared Habersham's lot would undermine the appeals of the merchant class and deal dirty, below-deck that is. Governor Wright was more astute than most men gave him credit for, Levi knew. First of all, Levi hated to let Mordechai realize this, but Governor Wright has access to the *militia*. For all they knew, the loathed Stamp Master "George Anus," as he was dubbed by the Charleston Sons of Liberty (Savannah and Charleston both hosted miscreants known as Sons of Liberty), was in the company of British militiamen. These men were doubtless conscripted for the sole purpose of *implementing* the Stamp Act. Trouble or no, Wright was no idiot either. He kept close watch on the Sons of Liberty. Even Mordechai knew that. But it was useless; his brother was headstrong.

Levi and Frances often whispered that should the time come, Wright would be quick to blame the dirty Jew Sheftall for his diminished authority over Georgia's increasing rebel class. Levi was all too fearful that the governor would release torrents of hell should the Sons of Liberty prove a pain in his royal seat.

*

James Habersham enjoyed breakfast by Wright's estate for some time now. Wright was unusually late this morning. *The Gazette* lay on a silver platter by the mutton. The dining hall, which was situated beyond the grand library, was relatively empty at this hour. Mrs. Wright and the children did not come down yet as well. Usually, Mrs. Wright tended to her toilette, and only the older children dined. The housemaids, including the Negro hands, served fresh fruit, biscuits, black teas, and strawberry jams alongside the cold mutton. The tall glasses of fresh cider were filled by Percy. The butler stood in his black and white attire as though he were an exhibition or a statue in one of London's majestic museums. The table was polished, and the oak revealed varied hues in the morning hours.

James Habersham noticed the chair by the window, the one facing east particularly, was of a lighter shade—the result of the sun's rays whitening its rich cognac color. Percy's blackness accentuated the crisp ivory walls, inlaid with fine Venetian molding. The drapes were exceedingly long; the manor enclosed elongated walls, buttressed by high ceilings and Doric beams. The planks of wood running the length of the house slightly creaked as James Wright strutted into the dining hall stirring Habersham from his thoughts.

"Did you read *The Gazette* this morning, Habersham?"

Habersham noticed snuff stains on Wright's fingertips and his cravat. Some remained on his nose.

"No, but I imagine Johnston gleefully relays all the clandestine activities of those blasted Sons of Liberty."

Wright nodded his head, and moved his arm so Percy could place two pieces of fresh biscuits into the porcelain plate that gleamed with a pristine shine. Wright motioned for the paper, and Percy, with his gloved hand, offered the sterling silver platter to his master. Wright groaned ever so slightly in recognition and opened to the front page. He placed his fork down, pushed the butter aside, and yelled, "Preposterous. Simply outrageous!"

Habersham, aroused with curiosity, turned to Wright, "Well, what is it?"

Wright cleared his throat, "Let me read this rubbish and you'll understand: 'The Sons of Liberty have called a unanimous vote to commit violence against the unfortunate fellow who shall become the Stamp Master.' Can you believe this, James?"

Habersham sympathized with Wright. But he had a slightly different take on the matter:

"They most certainly are foolish in resorting to hostility. But think on it James: compared to the other colonies, our citizens have been, well, what can I say? Rather *civil*."

"*Civil*? Mutiny is far more fitting, Habersham. Really now!"

"I cannot repudiate the notion. However, James, let us be honest now. Parliament has clearly erred."

Wright emitted a long and heavy exhalation, "It is somewhat conceivable that they did, indeed, misjudge the delicate nature of this tax. But these miscreants! These violent demonstrations! They will only make matters worse, far worse I am afraid." Wright nibbled on a small piece of overly dried mutton and a bit of hard cheese. He jabbed a finger at his crony and swallowed the bolus. With the aid of a bit of cider, he muttered, "Have you so quickly forgotten that insolent letter? Hmm? The infamous 'Townsman' has yet to surface his craven visage."

Habersham nodded. Yes. James was right. I guess that's what happens when you reside as President of the Georgia Council. Certainly the Governor's second-in-command receives threats. The Townsman had the deleterious effect of tearing his family apart. One son stood by him, but the others have been swept by the liberty bug.

"We are essentially in agreement," said Habersham, "but where I see recklessness you see mutiny."

"Indeed. Mutiny is the flavor in this," Wright retorted, slapping *The Gazette* back onto the silver platter and pushing it away.

*

Levi made his way to Charleston. An unexpected visit is always a welcome surprise, he believed. Hannah had insisted he take leave; she would remain with Frances and the children now. She prayed by Benjamin's grave and recited psalms between stitching pretty bonnets for the little ones. Frances believed keeping busy was therapeutic and insisted Hannah take house in their Broughton home. Hannah felt obliged to cooperate. The children truly implored her, especially Sheftall Sheftall who was a delight, an absolute charm. Reading to him was one of her few pleasures, and she somehow felt young again. She remembered the days of Levi's youth, when he sat firmly in her lap for precious hours, asking many questions and enjoying her storytelling. Mordechai would relax beside her, reading from the Bible, and every now and then listening to her tales. Frances' children were just as sweet, and she could forget her misery every so often. The baby was a delectable button. Hannah's home remained in her possession, but for this brief fortnight she had decided perhaps it was best to remain with her grandchildren.

Mordechai's plantation fed and housed many fortunate souls. The barns were well-operated. The family enjoyed poultry dishes at least once a week. Eggs were certainly a staple. The gardens were also well-cultivated, and the domesticated animals were well-cared for. They grazed the land, and the hands cultivated the vast orchards. The Savannah forests lay in the distance, and the River to one side blended with the slender, tall trees across the landscape. On the other side, the great Atlantic Ocean and the harbor offered solace from the verdant fields. Azure skies festooned the city, and the inhabitants enjoyed citrus fruits in abundance. Clean water was habitually drawn from the wells, which the River continually bathed. The city was no longer the primitive hut-based land James Oglethorpe had originally built. Mordechai's home was by far one of the more marvelous estates in the countryside, and Hannah enjoyed long walks across its width. Benjamin had raised his child to become the affluent man he had never truly been himself. She hoped Benjamin was glad of his choice to settle in America. Certainly his son was testament to the goodness of the land. The abundance and freedom, but that may be in question now. Benjamin had always praised James Oglethorpe, even though, from what she understood, Benjamin had initially formed a rather prejudicial stance on the general. But the governor, James Wright, only shared Oglethorpe's Christian name. Their politics could not differ any more, in her estimation. First of all, Oglethorpe had never been afraid of contesting Parliament. He had butted heads with a few influential members as far as she knew. But Wright was as fierce as a falcon; his loyalty was truly astounding. In that regard Wright was a man of honor, truly. But this was not the wind swaying people's principles. The creed emerging of late was one of departure *from* Parliamentary influence. Mordechai had surely educated them all in this matter. He was of the firm conviction that Great Britain, with all due respect, must allow the Georgia Assembly, both houses of course, to arbitrate on matters of civil law. But Hannah knew it was more than just that for most people. Mordechai was an idealist, but many in Savannah were truly opportunists. And they resented *any* form of true sovereign power, in her belief. It was the wallet that spoke to most. And the very belief that they received nothing in return augmented their grievances. They did not elect those in Parliament who had settled the laws. This was their main concern. They feared this was only the beginning, and in that case, perhaps they had due rights to resist. What did she know? Politics is for men who have purse-strings that can pull and maneuver about. What did she know of politics? Every country had its own, and every era had to deal with the dirty plates left over from the previous generation. It was a mess, and Hannah had become weary of the subject. Why! Even during moments of reverie, while stitching that is, she had been contemplating her son's activities! Well, either way, she hoped Levi would enjoy his time in Charleston. From what she understood, there was a woman in question, and that was promising.

*

Levi walked past the bakery where he first caught sight of Rebecca and a warmth filled his heart. Optimistic suddenly, he increased his pace. Charleston's Sons of Liberty littered the streets with pamphlets. Trees were nicked from previous papers, and Levi read one particular phrase as he prodded along: "Beware those who dare to charge a fare. Our pockets are not for sale." Corny, he thought. He brushed aside a few bottles of beer, and he peered into the pubs by the wayside of main street. Yep. Just as in Savannah. Drunken men raving about Governor Wright. His tactic of bribing men to come forward and reveal the notorious Townsman was stirring heated debate. Could money buy loyalty? When do the needs of the people come before fealty to the crown? And such. Levi was concerned; even a blade of grass can get caught up in a storm, he knew.

He finally reached Rebecca's quaint cottage and noticed the rose bush was no longer in bloom. His heart speeding a bit, and he hoped Rebecca would be the first to answer the door, but that rarely was the case. But there is always a chance.

Just as he was hoping to lift his eyes onto the beautiful face of his new sweetheart, the pock-marked expression of her aunt scorched his hopes.

"Well, well! What a surprise. We weren't *expecting* you!" she said, in a rather mealy-mouthed way Levi detested.

She let him in, and he felt as though he were intruding. The last time he had stood in the foyer, he had hastily kissed Rebecca. He truly should settle down, he knew.

Rebecca's aunt despised men who win a woman's heart by gestures. Any man who so much as touched another woman prior to marriage had a black scar across his family name in her opinion. Even if it is in earnest; such was not to be tolerated! And here he comes, this suitor, as though he practically *possessed* her niece! She knew *exactly* what men like him were up to. It has a name, and it's as old as Methuselah. It was a wise choice to check the post, otherwise her niece would have received countless letters from these men, particularly Levi Sheftall. Rebecca *needed* guidance. And thankfully she respected her aunt. Levi's averted gaze and folded forearms betrayed his anxiety. *Of course!* She *knew his intentions,* she did!

Rebecca sat quietly in the parlor, tired of stitching and bored of her surroundings. Aunt Beatrice meant well, but what could she possibly discuss with her, and for hours at end? The tea was cold; it had been sitting in its pot since the morning. Rebecca hadn't been feeling too well; the winter days lent little by way of entertainment and gaiety. She had remained utterly unaltered in her melancholia, until Levi's full figure graced the entrance. *My goodness! So he hasn't forgotten me! But why had he not written all this time? How neglected I feel! Does he know? He seems so confident!*

"Rebecca," he whispered. Her eyes were wan; her complexion whiter and slightly more ashen than he recollected. The room's interior did not highlight her features. But when she smiled, the irises appeared brighter, and her smile illuminated the darkness that remained between them.

Aunt Beatrice rummaged for her spectacles amid the morning papers and the myriad yarns. She kept muttering to herself, as though preoccupied. *For once let the old hag be gone!* He thought.

"Let us stroll, Levi? Hmm?" Rebecca intimated. "Surely. Let's."

Just then, her aunt said, "Aha! Here it is!" and commenced to speak in a tone Levi detested. "Rebecca, dear, you have not begun your chores for today. Perhaps Mr. Sheftall can return at a more decent hour. Perhaps he can announce his arrival."

Rebecca turned to her aunt, her front still turned to Levi. "Aunt, there is little for me to do!" She turned to Levi and whispered, "Let us spend some time together."

Rebecca's aunt glared at her niece. She had never contradicted her before she met this man. What other alterations in her dear niece is she to expect if he is to wed her? But Rebecca must realize this on her own. The sooner, the better she believed.

"Very well. Please return by supper. I do not intend for you to remain idle all afternoon." Aunt Beatrice carried some books and the tea to the kitchen and left the room with a rustle and a slight curtsy.

Levi knew Rebecca's aunt disapproved of him. But why? He had a decent reputation, did he not?

"Thank goodness," he sighed. "She began to weigh heavily on my nerves!"

Rebecca's chagrin was clear. "Whatever do you mean?"

"Why, your aunt, Rebecca! She is a tyrant in this house, do you not see this?"

Rebecca continued to stare at Levi. The room suddenly felt smaller. "She is suffocating us, Rebecca. I thought you believed the same—"

"I most certainly *do not!* How cruel of you! Had you truly known what this woman has done for me, you never would speak in such a tone! She is the only companion I have known since my mother's untimely death. And my father... he's never in town. And yet she is all I know."

Rebecca sat on the divan, most perturbed. First he insults her by walking in unannounced, and then he offends her aunt!

Levi thought she was surely sporting with him. He waited for a burst of laughter, some indication of cheer. But none was forthcoming. Rebecca's back was turned to Levi, and he felt at a loss for words. He walked to her and stood face to face, "I meant no harm. I intend no insult, Rebecca, but she gives us little chance to be together, surely you see that."

Irritated, she suddenly unfolded her arms and pointed at Levi, "You blame *my aunt* for *your* neglect? Which betrothed woman waits for months to hear from her beloved? For months! And you *dare blame Aunt Beatrice!*"

So this is what she thinks of me, he sadly noted. If he were a child again, perhaps his eyes would tear. But he was dried of tears since Hannah Minis had torn his heart.

"You misjudge me, Rebecca. And I won't have it."

Hearing his voice so down-trodden and distanced, she suddenly glanced at him longingly, "Levi. If you can barely stand her, then tell me, what will you do when she purchases a lodge in Savannah, as she plans, just so she can be near us at all times? What then?" Rebecca looked intently into Levi's eyes and had yet to decipher its expression.

*

George Angus arrived in the British vessel *Speedwell* in early January. He held a letter in his hand:

> To George Angus:
>
> Please be advised that I issued tax stamps to sixty vessels. There are certain merchants in Savannah who are eager for their boats to set sail. Do not fear the ire of the masses. There are yet those who are loyal to the crown and willing to respect Parliament's Stamp Act.
>
> Signed,
> Governor James Wright

George Angus was a stout man; a servile one. He had been charged with the menacing duty of Stamp Master. Odious to many, yet his livelihood. The governor of Georgia proper had no intention of negotiating with licentious youths or unscrupulous men. So, as duty-bound as he truly was, George Angus followed orders. But truly. Word did get out regarding that effigy that burned so terribly on Guy Fawkes Day. And of all days! Every school child learns of the Gunpowder Plot, the very one, indeed, that nearly ended the monarchy of King James and his sons, those blasted Catholics. That was a day meant for merriment, yet now bodes of rebellion, thanks to riotous youths. Would these unfettered Georgians dare to burn him at the stake? At first the Council ruled four to five *against* a stamp master, only to rescind their initial stance. Yet up until George Angus arrived (nearly vermin-ridden and starved), not a single human being dared apply for the most reviled position— Stamp Master. *Why should I feel like a devil? Blast it all!*

George dutifully cleared all the vessels and documented their leave. He was not *entirely* astonished to learn that the citizens of the Crown had refused to accept his authority. But he was appalled by the Americans' lack of *civility*: MacHenry's refused to offer him a drink; women spat in his direction. Wright told him not to worry. George just held his sorry head and wondered where he could find a tavern that didn't shut its doors in his face. His appearance didn't credit him either; a red-haired man, many mistook him for an Irishman. Sitting in the *Speedwell* didn't do much for his complexion either. The Irish were disliked for their Catholicism, another cause of contention, and certain women were wary of sailors, for good cause. The Savannah ports were finally empty, but the stench of some indescribable nature remained. Where was he to lodge in this stinking, god-forsaken town? Thankfully, George found a welcoming gesture by the wealthy merchants, Whigs all, and James Wright housed George for the duration of his stay in America.

George couldn't fathom the ire he had caused. But George Angus served as a catalyst for what occurred that eve. And what occurred was only a fraction of what was to come.

*

Mordechai closed the doors to his parlor. The children were "safely stowed," as Shakespeare perhaps would have stated had Hamlet concealed a doll instead of a corpse, and Frances was off to bed at an early hour. He cleared his throat. It was parched. The parlor was well-lit with many and varied oil lamps. His Negro butler, Uriah, placed another platter of apples and peaches, cobbler and pie. No one was eating a morsel. Mordechai gestured for silence.

"Our plans have been well-concealed, despite our numbers. With luck, we shall not meet opposition. But let us not presume fortune is necessarily on our side. The faint at heart should take leave, and no one shall judge him." Mordechai paused and looked around the room. Philip Minis stood by the doors, securing the entrance. John Wereat sat, by the edge of his chair smoking a reed pipe. A few regulars from the Sons of Liberty, undoubtedly recognizable by now stood in the corner. Many new faces without names crowded the room. A haze obscured their features.

No one stirred.

"It may be necessary to use force, but *no blood shall be shed. Not a musket shall fire!*"

Philip Minis stirred at the mention of blood. And what were they to do if indeed the British shall so much as fire at will? What was Mordechai thinking?

"I must ask you to reconsider, Mordechai. I beg your pardon, but is this entirely wise?"

Mordechai stared into Philip's eyes. He recalled Philip's dirty trousers and frightened expression that awful day in the forest. And yet here he was.

Philip carefully weighed each word: "Your call for temperance is most welcome. But let us not be innocent here, Mordechai. Musket fire may very well be directed at *us*. Are we not to defend ourselves? Shall we flee at the scent of gunpowder or return our own?"

Mordechai responded, with an immediate gush of words, clear and confident, "You know quite well, Philip, that the Sons of Liberty are not governed by cowardice. But you are correct to point out a potential danger. *Should* this discord regrettably descend into bloodshed, let not the calamity be ushered by *us*. We *will* march with guns at our sides. Their presence is sufficient. Let no man draw his weapon unless fired upon. And may it be God's will that we face no such trial!"

The men, roused with excitement that only those who had never seen battle could muster, did not take note of a thin shopkeeper, who, only moments before the rest of the motley crowd, disappeared in the direction of James Wright's stately plantation.

*

Hannah Sheftall churned the broth in her plate. Her lovely son had slept for a fortnight since he took a holiday to Charleston. And what was he brooding about, she hardly knew. But she was fixed and determined to discover the cause of his discontent. Since her husband perished (may he rest in peace!), her solace had been Levi and the grandchildren, of course. Levi, her only true living son. Those nights in the start of her marriage yielded two, yet only one remained. Yet how intemperate he could become! The rooms were darker now, and the Negro maidservants had neglected to dust the parlor and air the empty rooms. They could hardly be blamed. Levi had made it excessively difficult for them to care for certain rooms. Perhaps she *should* move to Mordechai's estate, but so long as Levi was still a bachelor, she deemed it necessary to remain at home. But of Levi, again! What is she to make of this, not coming to dinner! Hannah shifted her body from the chair, rather suddenly, and accidentally tipped the spoon; broth splattered on the wooden table. *So be it*, she thought. With a lethargic gait, she made way to Levi's room. She knocked, a gesture of respect, and was disgusted by the stale odor, mixed with unmistakable methane. Holding an oil lamp in her right hand, she walked to the desk where she found paraphernalia, a quill, ink blotted paper, and a stamped envelope. In the waste-basket she found copies of letters, crumpled and terribly blotched. She was able to discern the following:

Dear Rebecca,

I have been on the receiving end of such as I am about to impart right now, and it grieves me tremendously. But I have been deep in thought for some time now, and I have the unfortunate task of harming a wonderful soul. Will you forgive me? My heart has given me little respite since we last parted. It has come

292

as an insight, Rebecca, but I do whole-heartedly believe our union would not have been a truly prosperous one. A woman who has little trust and confidence in me cannot truly be my half-soul. I have no doubt, none whatsoever, that you will one day prove a suitable and loving wife to a deserving man, but I am sure that man is not I. I cannot express my sorrow at knowing the extent to which this letter finds you so aggrieved. Please forgive me, and let me know when happiness finds you, as it most assuredly will one day.

Levi Sheftall

Hannah Sheftall knew at once the cause of her son's discontent and wondered what would help heal his saddened state. She walked to Levi's bed and found him snoring. Beer bottles littered the bedside table, and a Bible was there too.

"Levi, son. Please wake up. I have dinner, son."

Levi's breath reeked of alcohol. He did not hear his mother.

*

James Wright dressed that morning with the same breeches he wore on the day of his inauguration. His nostrils flared at the very thought of the townspeople's *chutzpah*. The very foundations of law and government shall *not* be trampled upon, he regurgitated, time and again, in his mind. The time had come, oh indeed, it has, to show these men just who holds the reins in this town. James seized his musket and scurried over to Wright's Square, just north of the center of town. He galloped on his horse; it heaved heavily, as a woman with child. The homes, mostly merchants', were dimly lit and their curtains were drawn. Wright caught sight of a few street urchins trying to sell their wares, with the rooster's crows, with nary a buyer in sight. Fifty-four rangers were already assembled at Wright's Square, weapons at the ready. His trusted mole John Milledge was captain too, and an informant. It was at Mordechai Sheftall's home that he had discovered this capital breech of civil conduct. "Trouble" they had warned, and "trouble" they would get. Why couldn't London provide additional armed troops, as he had requested from His Majesty's government on several occasions? Why had the government so apparently disregarded his pleas? Nevertheless, armed sailors aboard *The Speedwell* augmented his own militia, one hundred in total. *That should suffice for now.*

*

Mordechai gathered his men and his musket. Wright succeeded in issuing the stamps after all. That man had the gall to do what all other governors of the thirteen colonies had not the stomach for: the blasted stamps! Dubious distinction, Mordechai believed. It was Wright's unilateral approach to governance that earned the Georgians the undeserved epithets "weak and unpatriotic." Of course the South Carolinian Sons of Liberty were keen on competing for titles of distinction. But how dare they charge the Georgians of indifference! They "refused to join in support of the fight for American freedom" the instigators declared. What *chutzpah.* Those madmen up north made true on their threat to halt all trade with Georgia and destroy all ships should they so much as attempt to set sail. Those bastards actually captured *and destroyed* two ships that had attempted to clear Charleston for Savannah. So this is domestic civil war, Mordechai thought. Or is it? Isn't it madness due to England's obdurate edicts? Surely Wright would realize the insanity of this all!

Mordechai led his assembly of armed men towards Wright's square, toward James Wright's stately manor. Surrounded by acres and acres of cotton fields and plush orchards, a few well-kept barns, stables, and coops, vagrant gardens, a statue of lions by a man-made pond, and a well-paved gravel road where two separate coaches parked neatly, side by side, Mordechai gaped at the sheer opulence of it all. Even at dawn the plantation gleamed of all its majestic beauty. The men began to jostle one another, and even James Habersham's boy, the one who had *not* previously insulted Mordechai, but rather a more rugged type, vociferously demanded, "Show yourself, Governor!" The men raised their muskets in unison. "Show yourself!" they repeated. In a heat, very much like warring barbarians for a second there it seemed,

294

the Sons of Liberty spewed their rancor on James Wright's stately door. Inside, Percy shooed the children away, insisted the mistress remain in the upstairs bedroom, best under the beds, and lock the children in the playroom. The doors were bolted, but he feared musket fire. Any one single madman could shoot and harm one of the little ones. The hens clucked, as though they feared the bullets were intended for them, and the horses shifted in their stables. Percy didn't like the sound of Habersham's boy; perfidious it seemed to him.

James Wright stood in the square and made out the noises. Why! He thought. It's as though they are right here. For goodness sake! He immediately followed the noises and found a contingent of men, the Sons of Liberty no doubt, banging his front-door, yelling, pounding, spitting, spewing, and gesticulating. He was nearly dumbstruck when he noticed Habersham's boy John among the men. James thought of his own brood stuck in the house, and nearly ran toward his own home. John Milledge, his trusted captain, and a few others in fact, hurried after him, but Wright insisted on continuing toward his own home.

"I am not intimidated, Milledge. Don't fret. Just remain behind lest I need you." John nodded in agreement. Wright made sight of the rebels and was disappointed that Mordechai should lead the men. *Ingrate*, he thought. *Dirty Jew*. Wright marched with solemn step toward his own estate, quietly as though not a single man were yelling or banging his musket on the well-paved ground. And just as he began to part the crowd, a silence fell over him. Until he reached the front stairs leading to his own home. Those nearest him backed away, and John Habersham disappeared from the head of the crowd. Mordechai removed his hat, but he was still holding his musket. A gleam of white skin, all sweat and anticipation, reflected off of Mordechai's forehead in the early morning light.

"Good morning, gentlemen!" James began. "I was able to discern from your howls, (and particularly yours, Mr. Benson, quite a stentorian voice you've got, by George), that you desire an audience with me. The mistress of this house, and I am sure she has been rudely awakened this morning (you all *do* owe her an apology for you have interrupted her toilette), requires my attendance; however, as I am sure you all well know, I am generally most receptive to such requests, as many of you (now looking at John Habersham) can attest. There is no *need* to resort to *shameful* public *exhibitions*, the current circumstances notwithstanding. So, what was it you desired to say?"

Mordechai looked around the crowd and wondered who would speak up. James had certainly disarmed them with his impeccable *British* manners, surely devised by the British, he now realized, to deflate the incivility justly caused by *their* over-reaching pride and dominance. Nevertheless, Mordechai and the crew were disarmed—save for Johnston.

"We wish to know, Sir, if the appointed Stamp Master shall remain officially now that it has been made clear just how *unpropitious* it is to retain one. Sir. What has occurred in Charleston shall not remain an anomaly. Our livelihood is at stake. We beg of you, Sir, reconsider!"

"George Angus is not welcome here! We know what he has come to do, and we will not allow it!" barked Mr. Benson. "Hear! Hear!" repeated the crowd.

James lifted his hand to silence them all. "Don't be foolish. The provisions of the Stamp Act will be observed by this colony without disruption of any sort. At present there is no one to distribute the papers. A gathering of this sort is no manner to wait upon the governor of a province! Let not the Sons of Licentiousness," staring now at Mordechai, "convince you to the contrary."

And with that, he slightly bowed and lifted his officer's cap, and marched toward the square. Percy had heard every word and wondered why the men had removed their caps as well and dispersed so suddenly.

Mordechai knew James was lying. "At present," he said which does not mean "not soon" or "in the future." That wretched George Angus will regret the day he was born to a British shrew. Mordechai barely contained his anxiety. All that preparation, and yet the devil *knew* of their plans! It was entirely clear. One hundred armed militia, and more garrisoned by Fort Halifax in the eventuality of a break-out. Well, thank God not a single shot was fired, at least. His son Sheftall was playing on the table with his toy soldiers, and his daughter with her doll, when he finally sauntered into his home. How wonderful it is to never worry, he thought. Frances served the roasted vegetables on a dinner platter, with fine Carolina rice, an expensive commodity when business was slow. The nanny fed the children and Frances held his palm.

"It will be fine, you'll see. James Wright will see reason, I assure you. No other governor could enforce these terrible tariffs, and neither will he. Not in the near future. You'll see!" Mordechai smiled at Frances, and hoped her insight into politics was accurate.

*

Damn him, thought Wright. When was the last time General Thomas Gage bothered to respond to one of his letters? The commander-in-chief of the British armed forces was detained by larger matters! The populace will nearly have him hanging by his precious gems if he doesn't find a way to control the masses. And only armed men, and many of them, could achieve that end. But where were all those trained British soldiers? James reluctantly pulled out another scrap of parchment, a quill and ink.

Frustrated, he underscored the most significant points, hoping Gage would gauge the situation in Savannah:

To the Honorable General Thomas Gage of His Majesty's Royal Armed Forces,

I regret to inform you, Sir, that the political spectrum of Savannah has diminished to all but anarchism. A true exigency exists. If you will: After much delay, the appointed stamp official (a chap by the name of George Angus) arrived in Savannah, to assume his post. He succeeded in selling a fair number of stamped papers due to perseverance on my part, which is no trifling feat, if I may say so myself. The poor chap nearly lost his bearings, and he had to seek refuge in my own home; such was the extent of concern for his very safety. At first, it appeared that tensions would soon subside. Unfortunately, that was not to be. Rabble-rousers (from South Carolina, no less) incited Georgians and mayhem ensured, quite regrettably, I assure you. Every ranger was put to good use. Disturbances ran high, exceedingly so. The poor chap shivered in his pants like a school boy, and the Sons of Liberty turned the country side into Dante's very hell. I must stress, General Thomas Gage, during these perilous days I had come to realize, with brutal lucidity, that *the very government of Georgia was in dire constrains, and even in jeopardy. Our militia is insufficient to counter civil unrest, were such attempted.* Had the revolutionaries proved successful, we could very well have been *driven out of the colony, with no impediments*!

Refusing to risk the order of this government, I hastily removed Mr. Angus from his post; he returned upon the *Speedwell*. The rabble-rousers and riffraff of this town temporarily succeeded, at best. Indeed, for I will not rest until this matter is settled.

Sir, I implore you, send reinforcements. Today perhaps the winds have calmed by the shore, but tomorrow tempests may rise. By then, it may be too late.

Signed,

James Wright
Governor,
Colony of Georgia

"May I come in?"

SAILING TOWARD HOPE

IN THOSE EARLY DAYS OF Georgia's burgeoning youth, the air surrounding the township was abundantly rife with hope. The vast expanse of the southern border housed many eager housewives hoping to churn butter for their little ones, together with the aid of Negro hands. The market place was never empty. The rice paddies were soaked shin-deep most of the year, yielding fragrant and luscious rice grains. Apothecaries traded their wares, learning a few tricks from the Indian Creeks who spoke a fair amount of English to persuade Englishmen of the potency of willow leaves and rare alligator dung. Children were reared to assist on the farm; those who could afford a governess or school-master taught their children numbers and letters. Every so often, a child was recommended for university. Perhaps Harvard, a revered institution since the days of Salem. Jews lived with their own ilk, and the folk in Ebenezer kept to themselves. Horses' hooves pounding on gravel or hard-dirt roads dispelled the calm every so often. Georgia was, compared to New York, a young colony, betrothed to England only decades ago. The earlier strife, roused by the Stamp Act and other irritating edicts by Parliament, briefly stirred the ale houses off the shores; once the act was rescinded, Georgia continued to expand its trade, build its roads, harvest its plentiful fields, and plow the promising lands. James Wright had garnered the respect of the masses once again, with jovial promises of the great benefits of standing by the King. Few had the wits to consider much of this; small day-to-day matters took precedence. If an ox should be slaughtered or sold; should a nursemaid be hired, or a school boy chastised. Yet others searched the colony for love and solitude. Many sought their fortunes in trade. Many lived as paupers, subsisting day unto day. Those who could, traveled to Northern colonies, where labor was easily found, particularly in stately homes. The Negroes, of course, could not practice much. If one escaped by way of underground means, he was lucky indeed.

The year was 1773. Seven years had passed by as swiftly as a migrating bird finds his destination in far-off continents and returns so suddenly to his home base. James Habersham's boys now *all* joined the Liberty cause, including his John, who at first had been quite the antagonist. Frances had given birth to more children and lost two infants. Hannah had grown old, and Abigail Minis had nearly become the octogenarian of Savannah proper. Hannah Minis had yet to find a gentleman worthy for matrimony; Levi *not* quite the same. James Wright sent his wife to Mother England, to sojourn there for a bit while matters in Georgia were relatively peaceful. (Ironic, no doubt.) Eddings visited Wright as usual, and Habersham dined with Wright. The *Gazette* was duly a source of endless amusement, and Johnston furtively wrote many of the incendiary articles himself. Under the placid exterior, however, lay a layer of bitter resentment. It was soon to be borne.

Mordechai lifted his eyes onto his son Sheftall Sheftall. Shefy, as he was fond of calling him, was struggling through his nightly Hebrew practice. Mordechai listened with a mixture of pride and resignation. He was very much concerned with his son's education. How difficult it was to raise his child in the ways of his ancestors in the barren landscape of America! Of course Jewish life in Europe possessed many *disadvantages*, but the old country certainly offered a solid communal infrastructure. Children as young as three attended *cheder*, a Hebrew day school, in some circles. His father had taught him Yiddish and the *niggunim*, hymns, but in Prussia Benjamin had learned such from a *melamed*, which was perhaps preferable. Many nights Mordechai had to balance his hefty books, attend meetings, and assist Frances (especially during the difficult years of her infants' sickness and subsequent death).

But now he had to be consistent—Sheftall would soon become a Bar Mitzvah, a thirteen-year-old "adult" in the eyes of the Law—and he *had* to prepare him for the readings, the Torah portions, the incantations, the prayers, and the donning of phylacteries, *tefillin*. Not to mention the dearth of Hebrew books! Translations were abominable; those that were sold in town were undoubtedly Christian texts. No right-minded Jew would so much as glance at a King James Bible. It contained the New Testament—the very source of anti-Semitism from which his father had sought refuge in America. Only translations and transliterations in Yiddish were acceptable, but Mordechai wanted his son to read in the Hebrew.

Much of the days were passed idly during the pre-harvest season. James Wright's manor provided a source of endless balls and soirées for the upper echelons of Savannah. Only Tories were invited, of course. A few merchants on the sidelines of the Whig party may have been invited, if there was ample evidence he should so much as convert, as was wisely recommended. Old party-line loyalties were not so difficult to overlook once the individual in question was more than keen to contribute to the British cause. Ample soldiers on duty in the Northern provinces were in dire need of hospitality and generosity. It wasn't unheard of British soldiers demanding lodgings, even forcing all kinds of cruel acts on the unwitting maidens of the house; too many colonists disliked the British soldiers, but those stories did not circulate amongst Wright's lot. Indeed, the Sons of Liberty spread the rumors, oftentimes unverified but still suspiciously smelly. There must be fiendish truth to the rumors, many conjectured.

Lulls in Georgia were expected. The colony was finally enjoying commercial growth of some kind. After the setbacks of the Writs and the Stamp Act, merchants were finally free to sell their wares to the northern colonies and the East Indies. During this time, Mordechai Sheftall's pecuniary worth increased; more oxen were bought, merchandise and housing depots were filled to the brim; Frances could easily afford help in the house and the cash flow was promising. Levi amassed considerable wealth too; after all, he was a single man in want of building his fortune. His luck took a turn for the better.

The West Indies provided many Jewish merchants with mercantile opportunities, and Levi was no exception. Only he did not expect a rose in the desert, so to speak. Twenty-seven and eminently available, the bachelor had few flowers to pluck in his part of the woods: Jewish women were difficult to come by. Having put women out of his mind for a while, Levi escaped to St. Croix; pangs of rejection gnawed at his soul with the persistence of a leech. Truth be told, Hannah's presence had never ceased assailing his very soul. Should he but so much as visit his brother's estate— and there she was. Should he venture to Savannah's marketplace, who should he meet but Hannah? Rebecca married within the year to a gentleman from Pennsylvania. Levi's bitterness did not cease upon hearing the good news. Quite the opposite, in fact. He had grown more morose, thinking how love eluded him while his brother, Philip Minis and his cohorts took wives. When he glimpsed at the couples, he couldn't help envy their marital bliss. And then he would grow ashamed at himself, wondering why he could not fully share in their joy.

So it was with this heavy heart that Levi settled in St. Croix for a time. (His stated reason was business, but lucrative trade was truly unassailable and it was obvious to anyone who knew the Sheftalls that they were on constant lookout for profitable trade opportunities.) The women wore woven baskets on their heads; most were black-skinned. The homes that belonged to the European settlers were clearly the stately manors by the beautiful coves, a few miles inward. Most of the inhabitants were slaves to the host empire, working the fields from a ripe age. Sugar cane and bananas, cotton and rare fruits, were cultivated by numerous human machines. If it rained at all, the inhabitants did not seek much refuge. Theirs was but to work the land, only to return to huts in the evening for a repast of coconuts and buttered biscuits, an admixture of foods reflecting the strange combination of cultures, and the clash of civilizations.

Levi did not question so much the institution of slavery, as had many during that time. But he did dislike hearing of the cruelties inflicted upon any man, woman, or child. The slave-owners argued it was the only language the Negroes understood, but Levi knew it was all lies. He himself had never had cause to strike a Negro, and his father taught him to ensure the safety of his entire household, particularly the Negro hands. After all, the Torah forbade mistreatment of Canaanite slaves, and according to the Bible, the slave-owner had to feed and clothe the slave before his very own self. So it was on the week of his arrival in the Paradise of St. Croix that he witnessed a Frenchmen beating a poor slave woman with a reed pipe. She stood five foot eight, tall for a Negro slave, and had beads webbed into her scalp. Her rags barely covered her taut body, and her legs were fiercely structured. The cause for the abuse was irrelevant and ultimately insignificant. Levi sprang from his horse, and accosted the sweaty gentleman.

"Let your hands off the woman!" Levi yelled, ready to strike the man should he persist.

The Frenchman, with a slight moustache that twirled on both edges, looked up, surprised any individual should take interest in his actions. With a heavy accent and a cock of the head, he snickered, "You know this cow? She isn't fit for a good gentleman such as yourself. Why waste your time?"

Levi looked at the woman and felt a twinge of pain for her. To be so reduced!

"Whom does she belong to?" Levi asked.

"Well, well. As of now, she belongs to the Delamottas, the rich Jews, but if they find out what she's been up to, soon enough, my friend, she will belong to no man, you can trust me."

"And what is her crime, pray?"

"The cow is guilty of stealing milk. You see here," he pointed to a spilled bucket of milk, "she milks the cows while they are out to pasture." He flicked her head for good measure and continued, "if the master gets wind of this he is likely to sell her."

"Let me speak to her, and then perhaps I can speak with her master," Levi reasoned.

The Frenchman rolled his eyes and shrugged both shoulders in succession. "Do as you please, but it is a strange custom you are beginning. I gather you are not from our parts. Here we do not consider the voices of bitches and human mules such as these."

Levi tuned out the epithets.

"Does she speak?" Levi asked, naively.

The slave woman put her head down. She whispered, "Yes, sir. I do speak."

"Very well, then. I am not in need of your services, Mr. —?"

"Francoise. I am not known by my surname."

Levi cared little for the man or his name. He took the slave woman by the side and began an inquiry.

She had delivered a babe; her milk dried from the intense heat; he was hungry, thirsty, dirty. The child, did he have a father? She pointed at Francoise. Where was the babe now? In the hut, with her other child, now seven years of age, a girl. Hungry and dirty, but yet capable. Does Master Delamotta know of this child? No. Who assists? The cows do.

Levi gathered the pail, and the slave-woman walked at a rapid pace towards the grand estate of Delamotta, a Sephardic Jew whose family settled in the West Indies after the Spanish Inquisition. The woman did not speak another word and was ashamed that a stranger learned of her shameful situation. Standing with his hat in his hand, Levi knocked on the door of the Delamottas. Levi was too focused to pay attention to the cultivated gardens, the beautiful water fountains, and the myriad flowers growing in full promise. Neither did he notice the shore on the other side of the house, and the majestic mountains overlooking the mansion on all sides. A Negro woman wearing a pinafore and a plain black dress answered the door, surprised to see Arelia standing there, all barefooted and sooty. She was supposed to be caring for the chickens and then the cows.

"Yes?"

"I must seek company with Mr. Delamotta. May I come in?"

*

It was on that day that Levi first set eyes on Ms. Delamotta. She was dark-skinned, of olive hue, and light blue eyes were of such contrast with her dark hair as to virtually draw any man's attention to her. Levi nearly forgot the cause of his visit. Mr. Delamotta was in his study, but the ravishing beauty was knitting on the divan, wearing an ivory gown with lace details; her brows were thickly set, as though still uncultivated as most women's brows were. She barely looked up from her knitting or whatever she was embroidering. He could barely tell. Her fingers were long, and her nails finely trimmed. A smallish ring bedecked her pinky finger, a pink pearl on a fine gold band. Her hair was loose, but had curls all along the edges, with a bit of reddish tint in the sunlight. Levi stared at the young woman, wondering why she did not address him; perhaps her father had many visitors. Surely with a daughter such as—

"Excuse me, Ms. —?"

"My name is Sarah," was all she proffered. She did not even look up. How frustrating!

"My father is not home. You can wait for him in his study if you wish."

"Yes, of course." He stood in the room a while longer, studying the curve of her back. He noticed the sash around her waist was finely tied into a delicate bow, with fringes of chiffon falling to the sides. The ivory complimented her.

"Would you mind to show me the way?"

Levi hoped Sarah would stand and show him to the study. He wanted to assess her height and determine her age. But she just pointed with her chin, and then with her delicate finger to the left, put her head down and assiduously continued her point work.

Levi could barely contain his agitation. The girl was asocial! So be it.

*

Sarah Delamotta suspected the man had business affairs with her father, as most men in town were wont. She had grown tired of their comings and goings and barely took note of their presence. Levi was no exception. She did not even take note that he had never been to the house, as most St. Croix merchants most certainly were well-accustomed to the mansion. Sarah was but fourteen, and while she was curious and intrigued by men, she was not overtly seeking their attention.

Levi waited for quarter of an hour before returning to the parlor where Sarah was still at work.

"I am sorry. May I request a cup of water?"

Sarah was surprised. She had forgotten about Levi! Feeling inhospitable, she rang the bell for Adele.

"May I?" Levi asked, pointing to the divan.

Sarah shrugged her shoulders.

"May I ask what you are working on, Sarah?"

Surprised the stranger called her by her name; Sarah looked up and was delighted the handsome man should ask. Most of her father's friends ignored her pursuits, only inquiring if she was healthy or otherwise feeling well, out of courtesy she believed.

"Yes, of course. I am sewing a fine collar for one of my summer dresses."

"I see you are fond of light hues, such as ivory and pink."

"Yes. And I *adore* lace. My father buys the latest designs from France, and this one here (she pointed to a yard of fine lace) is from *Paris*. Can you imagine? And this (she pointed to the threads) is fine *silk*, from *China*! It is a wonder. I am very keen, you see, to finish the collar, so I can begin working on—"

"And who is this gentleman speaking to my daughter?" Mr. Delamotta entered the room, quietly, a bit unnerved a stranger was speaking to his daughter in such an easygoing manner. Levi immediately stood erect, slightly bowed, and walked up to the master of the house.

"Levi Sheftall. Forgive me, sir. I was waiting for your eminence, and your lovely daughter was entertaining me. Pray, forgive me. But my initial desire was to speak with you, on a matter concerning your slave, Arelia."

Mr. Delamotta warped his brows, wondering what this foreign man had to do with his slave.

After much clarification, Levi was able to negotiate Arelia's release. Mr. Delamotta was no longer interested in owning a slave guilty of debauchery, although it seemed the crime was one-sided on a male counterpart, but Mr. Delamotta refused to hear reason.

As such, Levi offered to purchase Arelia, needing an extra hand himself, now that he decided to remain in St. Croix.

And so began a lengthy courtship and a fine-tuning negotiation with the master of an empire and his breathtaking daughter in the West Indies.

*

Sarah was young, but her age was not a deterrent. She instantly revived Levi; he felt, when staring at her youthful countenance, as though he had never aged since his initial days of falling in love himself, back when Hannah had captured his attention. But, as though time had turned its immovable head, Levi was free to bask in the sunlight of Sarah's youth. Her every whim was of great interest to Levi, who delighted in her innocence. She loved flowers, and spent innumerable hours by the beach, collecting all sorts of sea shells. He followed her on the many expeditions, particularly to the other side of the island, where rare birds flew above head, scouting the water for their feasts. Orange-hued pelicans dropped from meters above, only to snatch beautiful fish underwater. They had caught sight of the beauties a few times, and Sarah squealed with delight when Levi ran into the water to see the action first hand. Her dresses were light weight, and she too loved running along the water, wetting the hem of her dresses and revealing beautiful feet and ankles. The mores of the American continent were virtually non-existent in the paradise of the West Indies, and Sarah embodied the free spirits of the island.

Levi shared meals with the Delamottas, learning the master was no tyrant once promising conversations were had. Mr. Delamotta was only too glad to learn of Levi's successful tannery businesses and mansion in Savannah, which was only waiting for the right female touches. He was even gladdened to learn of Levi's relations, who had amassed considerable wealth as well, offering a buffering zone in case Levi's prospects were somehow reduced.

The question remained if Sarah was intrigued and keen on leaving the West Indies, marrying, moving away... but she felt safe with Levi and became very fond of him. Leaving the West Indies seemed like an adventure to her, and she wouldn't be lonely if she had Levi by her side. Delighted, the two married and set sail for the American heartland, shocking Mordechai and Frances with a new sister-in-law of most incredible youth and vigor.

Mordechai was a bit surprised when he considered the difference in their ages; Levi was nearly double her age! But Levi seemed to adore the girl, and she eventually proved quite capable and fertile. She busied herself round the mansion, fixing this corner with a painting, adding wallpaper to the bedroom, ordering the slaves in Creole, mixing well with her mother-in-law, who was simply enthralled Levi married at last, and to such a delightful flower! Sarah's beauty added to her fine characteristic traits; surely all who set eyes on her had to concur. Levi shielded her from the townspeople, believing he captured a rare gem on one of his expeditions. Sarah missed her family, and Levi tried as much as possible to be her companion. She fussed a bit when he went to Charleston on business matters, but did not question the necessity of such; she had grown quite used to the matter from her youthful days in Sr. Croix. Her father had absented himself for many long summer months. The weather in Savannah was warm most of the year; the shore a reminder of her home-town. The shops in Charleston were quaint, and she enjoyed Frances's wise counsel, which she was desperately in need of. Having few siblings herself, Sarah knew little of maternity and motherhood. But that soon became an occupation she excelled in. Levi had chosen well. But for a few times, it seemed, Sarah had yet to comprehend the complex world in the same vein as Levi. The maturity of ten years was not so easily overcome, but Levi had promised himself to be a patient man; after all, the benefits of a young wife far outweighed the deficiencies of adult-oriented conversations. At least in the first few years of matrimony. Eventually, motherhood and labor, child-bearing and child-rearing, matures any young woman. Even if she begins the journey at the tender age of fourteen.

And so, the years flowed nicely for Levi, who had nearly given up on hope. His children blossomed, and his mother enjoyed the little ones. Passover meals were joyous occasions, with the Sheftall clan celebrating together. Mordechai had lost children in infancy, and Levi had feared the same would occur to him. But his progeny proved sturdy, and the future seemed bright.

*

That December, a fellow by the name of Jacob Hicks ran his thick fingers across the edge of his bayonet. A redcoat, he left Georgia for Massachusetts. General Gage's orders. General Gage ordered *all* royal forces in Georgia to relocate to the North. Hicks was slightly vexed by the command, but didn't think much of it once he settled in. Georgia was boring for any soldier after a while. What passed for a monumental act of defiance in Savannah was standard daily fare up in Boston. At least in Boston there were actual *skirmishes*. No one had been killed, thankfully. But what is a soldier to do in a town like Savannah? Boston was a *city*! Swamps—nix. Wild animals—nix. Entertainment, the live sort—Yea! Besides, Hicks discovered he had an affinity for avoiding serious trouble. Too bad for Governor Wright, though. Gage ostensibly left Wright's colony naked. Rumors have it Gage ignored Wright's request for five hundred additional troops. Wright's flagging authority was now a surety.

But the best, the very best part of his new assignment was a delightful law. A law! The Quartering Act had enabled Hicks to finally *feel* flesh, *see* live women, and *breathe* and *drink* to his content. This Act was a grace of God. The colonists, by virtue of this most thoughtful law, required colonists to provide lodgings and other amenities for British soldiers!

Hicks looked up at Anne Brunswick, the luscious girl whose mansion served as his lodgings for the past fortnight. This delicacy in the fancy house turned any thoughts of ill-will toward the King into great devotion. God *bless* the King.

"Parliament did not intend for soldiers to abuse their rights, Mr. Hicks. I am not obliged to prepare a four-course meal. Mutton and cheese will have to do," Anne said.

Anne detested the man. Why wasn't her father home now?

"Now, now, pretty thing, you don't want to mistreat a senior officer. It is an offense, you know."

"I know of no such thing. What I *do* know is that my cousins in New York refuse to pay for soldiers' food and drink, so you better be grateful you get that much here!"

"Is that so?" Half-amused, Hicks stared at her lasciviously. Her gown was simple, but his mind compensated for her modesty.

Hicks stood from the table, where he cleaned his plate of mutton and fine cheese, and deliberately made way to Anne, who sat by her needlepoint, nervously stitching away. He stared at her breasts, barely able to contain himself. From above, it seemed as though he could easily take hold of her. She felt incredibly suffocated all of a sudden and felt her ears grow hot. Just as she felt he would grab her, she stood and nearly ran to the other side of the room. She rang the bell for the butler, hoping he was on hand.

Hicks, only lured by her sudden fright, followed her path, and stood half a foot away from the panting girl. "We live in treacherous times, my dearest. You should consider yourself fortunate to have a stout-hearted soldier *protecting* you, Anne."

Recoiling at his calling her by her first name, Anne turned her back, and was jerked by Hicks' strong hold of her forearm. She felt his hot breath on her neck and felt nauseous. "You may need me one day, Ms. Brunswick, in more ways than one," he said, lecherously.

Anne shoved him away, and nearly kissed her butler for intervening. He had heard the bell. And Anne would have to move to New York. This could not continue. If it did, she was sure the brute of a Brit would ravish her and destroy her prospects for eternity.

*

Undeterred, Hicks decided to take an evening stroll. During the early winter months, Massachusetts Bay was a gathering place for soldiers and laymen alike. The frigid air had not yet accosted the town, and the sun had yet to set. After dark, Hicks preferred to remain indoors, but Anne was not the most amiable tonight, and the mutton sat in his gut, refusing to be churned. He noted the curtains were drawn in most homes; certainly uninviting to British soldiers in need of temporary accommodation. God only knows Anne was an enticing and charming diversion, but she was much too chaste and hostile. The woman could send a shiver up the spine of a man desperate for a woman's touch. Perhaps the fallen women by the bayside would do for tonight. As Hicks made his way toward the not-so-secret tavern where many a bastard child found way to the church door, he heard a booming noise and then tremendous shouts. It sounded as though an entire Indian tribe had descended on the city. For a moment he had forgotten his dissolute intentions, and hurried toward the noise. Whether he wanted to or not, the soldier's instinct overwhelmed his more selfishly inclined ones. He headed towards the pier, where the noises seemed to emanate from. And then he stood transfixed.

A group of men, clearly half-drunk, painted their faces like the heathen Mohawks. Feathers and beads matched the horizon. Red and orange streaks of paint across their foreheads and cheeks, rather sloppily, creased with the splash of water: The men had seized His Majesty's ships, hoisted entire crates of tea, and dumped them all overboard. As each crate crashed into the waters below, a holler of war-sounding catcalls filled the night air. A few women were on board as well, their skirts all wet by the hem, and their hair in loose braids like the heathen women. A crowd of Bostonians gathered by the ships and urged them on.

"Good for nothing tea! Dump it all!"

"Yea!"

"Damn them all!"

Hicks began to suspect that he had better report to his superior officer.

"Looks like a British regular decided to join the party!" shouted a mysterious man by the wayside.

Hicks instinctively raised his musket, but a youth with a smirk on his face yanked it from him, nearly knocking him onto the floor.

A gang of four men, boys really, with their belligerence clearly etched on their faces, began to encircle Hicks.

The same boy who nearly knocked him down snickered, "We don't permit guns at our party. Someone might get hurt."

Hicks started to sweat. The defeaning screams of the American revelers momentarily disoriented Hicks. The crowd started to take notice of Hicks, many having recognized him from town. Many detested the man for his haughty airs and his wandering eyes. Most were still hooting for the partiers dumping all that precious tea into the Atlantic, but started to wonder what the devil the Brit was doing in their midst, ruining their party.

"Stand back!" he commanded, but the men found his tone of voice and the pathetic expression on his face amusing and encouraging. Abhorring mockery, Hicks gained his steam. He juked right, and then lunged to his left at the shortest assailant. Hicks' forearm landed square on the kid's delicate jaw, sending the rebel sprawling backwards, nearly a foot from the edge of the pier. Hicks tried to gather momentum to flee the scene, but he stumbled, and before he could run, an arm caught him round his thick waist. Hicks bit the man fiercely, as though he were a lioness. The assailant screamed, his screech blending in with the noises by the pier. Hicks for a moment felt as though he were free, and he began panting, pushing and shoving his way through the crowd. And then he felt a piercing pain on his temple. Someone clubbed the side of his head. The crowd became increasingly hazy, the sky fell to the floor, he heaved, and then three more attackers were upon him. A whoop from the crowd. Tea in the sea. And then everything went Apocalyptic black.

*

Anne sat in her room, wondering what the ruckus outdoors portended. Having lit a candle to read Samuel Richardson's epistolary novel *Pamela*, Anne was annoyed. She didn't want any more diversions. But soon there was a knock on the door, and Anne rushed down the stairs with barely a shawl covering her gossamer gown.

"Lay him on the divan, sirs. I'll fetch the apothecary," said the tall Butler, in a nightcap.

Anne couldn't believe her eyes. The devil be damned! The loathsome tenant looked badgered in such an awful way.

"Good God in heaven!" she heavily gasped. She looked round her; who could supply her with answers?

"We meant no harm. It was a form of self-defense, assuredly so! He struck Conan first. The law is on our side, surely!"

"You fiends!" Anne yelled, instinctively. "Look at the poor fellow! It is a miracle if he is breathing! This is *awful*, simply *terrible!*" She could barely understand herself. She imagined that she had hated him all this time. But it was unconscionable, to nearly kill a man!

"Get out of my house!" she ordered the miscreants and the few decent fellows who carried Hicks to her quarters.

"Be careful, Anne Brusnwick. If you shower this man with too much concern, you are liable to arouse the suspicion that you are, indeed, a Brit-lover." Anne looked at Conan, the effeminate youth whose voice croaked like a pubescent *thing* between male-ness and female-ness, and immediately retorted, "Watch your words, or the suspicion of your association with dissolute men will arouse the ire of the Church!"

*

Governor Wright slammed the door to the parlor shut, while Eddings and Habersham smoked their pipes.

"By God! Rather than quell the growing defiance, the Intolerable Acts are only further heightening the rebels! They grow more certain and assured by the hour!" he nearly spewed. That was all they ever spoke of lately. The growing resistance in the colonies and the impending doom it spelled.

"It is no coincidence the rebels donned heathen clothes during their Boston Tea Party," quipped Eddings. "They are barbarians and shall probably cast this country into civil war or worse."

"They are unlikely to stop, now that their cause has gained momentum," added Habersham. "Their aim is to de-establish and then re-establish order."

Wright stared at both Eddings and Habersham. "That damned Tea Party took place nearly a year ago, and now the First Continental Congress, held in Philadelphia no less, passed *economic sanctions* against Great Britain! The gall!"

"Well, at least Georgia failed to send a representative. All other twelve delegates obviously do not share in the political divide that is becoming clearly less divided by the hour here in Georgia," Habersham sadly noted. He hated all this talk. It reminded him of his rebel sons, who had all dishonored him and his poor wife by sympathizing with the Georgians and their cantankerous lot.

"I can guarantee you that dirty Jew Sheftall is behind a great deal of the anti-loyalist stirring. He conducts meetings, joins several committees, oversees their finances for Christ's sake, and contributes his own hefty sums to the cause. The man is a rebel indeed," Eddings added, with an air of righteous indignation. He hated those vicious Jews who capitalized on political situations for their own power and aggrandizement.

"I hear he can't convince his brother to join, no matter how persuasive he seems otherwise." Habersham said, as if an aside in a Shakespearean play, not meant to be heard.

"You mean his half-brother," clarified Wright. "He is more level-headed, from what I hear. It is the elder who is an idealistic wretch. If he only knew the type of stirrings he is devising. The fellow is in for a damned surprise." Wright sighed.

The men nodded their heads in agreement.

*

Mordechai reclined in his bed, looking at his wife who was lying on a different mattress. She covered her entire body trying to warm her frigid bones. Mordechai was tired, but distressed nevertheless. These weeks of abstinence provided opportunity to converse on matters which have long required address.

"I thought it would be different in America," he whispered.

"In which way? Mordechai? In which regard do you refer?"

"The land grant. The Commons House of Assembly. Their refusal. It just seems unjust."

Frances shifted and leaned a bit closer to her husband.

"Mordechai. You have to find a different method. You can't expect the House to agree."

"Yes. I understand. But their *reasoning* was *wrongful*. No other word will suffice."

There was a lull in the conversation for a moment. Frances was awake, but completely at a loss for words.

In his mind, Mordechai kept on re-hearing the Upper House's rejection speech: "No Person would choose to buy or rent a house whose windows overlook a Burial Ground of any kind, particularly one belonging to a People who might be presumed, from Prejudice of Education, to have imbibed Principles entirely repugnant to those of our most holy religion."

Damn their holy religion, he thought. *My people need a burial ground!* The two Jewish cemeteries in Savannah have been completely occupied since 1770. Numerous applications for a land grant to the Commons House yielded nothing. Of all people, the local gentiles, those he was *most* cordial to, opposed his petition for more land. Mordechai was just hoping no one would die in the foreseeable future, a thought which he knew was foolhardy and infantile.

"Mordechai?"

"Yes?"

"Perhaps you can devise an alternative plan, one that will not require the courtesy of those who are determined to dispute you on this matter."

"Perhaps you are right, Frances, but it is the principle of the matter that sets me at ill-ease! To think that I have dealt in business matters with these very same people, incurred financial loss in some instances just to prevent their tongues from wagging or otherwise misjudge me, and here I am, begging for a plot to bury our own kind. The last act of kindness upon a living being. And they persist to argue about the desirability of rentals! It is absurd!"

"Your anger prevents your figuring out a better solution, dear. You must understand, to the gentile, a Jew is a Jew. They may be *cordial*, but do not expect them to be *magnanimous*."

"But the obvious attack on our religion! And which principles, pray, are entirely repugnant to their religion? Most of their principles are *Jewish* ones. 'Do not unto others,' 'Respect your elders,' 'Take heed of the orphan and the poor.'"

Frances sighed. "Mordechai. Forgive me for cutting you off, but your assumptions are based on faulty premises. To a Christian, a Jew is forever the murderer of their Lord. How could you not find such an individual repugnant? And to think that education will wipe them of this inveterate miscomprehension is a lost cause, my dear. It is ingrained in them since they are but children in the schoolroom. If they do not persecute you, bless them. This is what my mother has taught me."

"But we wish to build a country that does not seek differences under the law."

"That is a fancy. If that were the case, why are few championing the cause of the Negros? I *do* enjoy the benefits of the institution, and God save me if I mistreat any one Negro man or woman, but if you speak of equality, why stop at landowners? What of women? What of children? How many champion their cause?"

Mordechai fell silent. His wife was a most astute woman. But she misunderstood one basic idea—change cannot occur on a radical level!

"Frances! What you call for is an upheaval no society is entirely ready to accept! We must work in increments; I believe we must begin with respectful relations amongst governments, religions, and people of differing opinion. And perhaps one day, the world will be ready to incur more change, as you so rightfully pointed out."

"Ach. All this tires me. People change but rarely, Mordechai. If we should experience such in our lifetime, we will have lived in a great epoch. Good night, love."

"Say no more!"

CACHE OR CASH

MORDECHAI THOUGHT OF HIS FATHER'S melancholy expression when he first learned of Mordechai's anti-loyalist leanings. Levi's condemnation of the Sons of Liberty's meetings did little to assuage his guilt. Fire burned within him. How was he to play a fiddle and sing a merry tune at once? He did not want to alienate his brother, but this was not a time for personal considerations! This was a time for a man to decide who he *was*. On this topic, the brothers could not disagree *more*. The thought of Benjamin perhaps siding with Levi augmented Mordechai's anxiety. But there had to be a way to seek reconciliation, peace, a common cause! By God, it eluded him. For a moment, Mordechai sought peace in the words of his prayers: "May G-d grant peace"; the Priestly blessings.

Levi was disappointed with his brother, but did not speak much on the matter. Today was not the most adventitious moment to discuss the muddled political scene. Mr. Samuel Cohen had just perished, and his bereaved wife, a friend of Sarah's, came knocking on the door. Weeping, her hair falling out of her bonnet in sweeps, roused the entire house. The slaves were in commotion; tea, biscuits, water, handkerchiefs, what would possibly ease this woman?

"Worst of all, Levi, there is no place for me to *bury* him! What am I to do? Wretched, wretched woman that I am. So suddenly he perished! But who is to bury him? Who is to purify his body for burial? Oh, dear, dear husband, to be so wretched in death!"

Levi's heart could not have felt more pain. He called for his coach, had Mrs. Cohen join him, and immediately took off for his brother's house, despite the proximity. This matter *had* to be settled—now.

Mordechai had slept peacefully that evening, for the first time in months. The knocks on his door at the late hour stirred his concern, and, quite irritated him too. Quickly running to his front door, with barely a cap to cover his balding head and slippers to prevent his feet from frosting, Mordechai was surprised to find his brother all amiss, with a woman crying by his side. The moonlight barely allowed for Mordechai to recognize the woman. What in heaven's name could this be? He wondered.

"Mordechai. This is too urgent to speak for long. Please. Let us solve this matter at once."

The two deliberated in the parlor as the fresh widow cried bitterly, partly for herself, partly for her sons, and of course, for her deceased husband who had much toil and few moments of pleasure.

"Then it is agreed?" She overheard.

"Yes," Mordechai answered, firmly. "It must be so," he added.

Mordechai held Mrs. Cohen's hand and whispered, "Your husband shall rest in peace in a cemetery in a designated parcel of land. You have no worries, now. Please, return to your family. My brother and I shall tend to the matter entirely."

Mrs. Cohen began to kiss Mordechai's hand, and cried tears of relief. "Bless you," she whispered, and then fell into Levi's arms, as he carried her to the coach and whisked her away to her family, now less one.

*

"Have you heard the latest development of that rabble-rousing Jew?" Eddings goaded Habersham the following afternoon. Habersham barely registered the question. His mind was too full of his son Joseph's latest escapade in falling in love with the daughter of a well-known Whig. What cares he for the Jew Eddings seems to obsess over? A fig for all he cares.

"Since your posture so demonstrates your desire to learn of the matter, I shall divest you of your suspense: he has deeded *his own land* for a Jewish burial ground! The gall! First he tries to convince the Assembly to grant Georgia land proper, and then he realizes he has enough land of his own to spare! The Shylock!

318

Always counting his own ducats, afraid to part with one, save when he is absolutely in dire need of such!"

Habersham grew tired of Eddings anti-Semitic rants. "Really, Eddings, that is a *positive* development. Are you not entirely for Jews being buried in their own land?"

Eddings found Habersham's statement *most* perturbing, and quite honestly, unexpected. "Yes, of course, but that is not the matter I am disputing here. I am enraged he did not do so without the inconvenience he posed on Christian folk, making them feel as though they should bend to his whims, just because he has ducats to defray most people's debts."

Habersham just stared coldly at Eddings. How was he to break the news to his poor wife? *Our sons are all rebels. All our hard work gone to waste.*

Sarah held Mrs. Cohen's hands as they mounted the newly designated Sheftall Cemetery. The poor body of the deceased lay in a coffin, and the grim crowd quietly looked on as the family members placed stones by the gravesite. The earth covered the coffin, slowly, slowly, and each mound of dirt thrown atop the coffin gave rise to an upheaval of tears. The children wept beside their mother, and Mordechai recalled the burial of his own infants not too long ago. It was a wretched pot of luck to have a child die, especially in infancy, when their bright faces can barely register in the memory of harsh realities and the mundane activities called life. And now this poor woman! But, in all of this evil, there was a function for the good, Mordechai was now compelled to realize: the allotment of land for the deceased, a home, an eternal resting place for those who would have remained homeless. Mordechai decided to speak for a brief moment, although such was not his custom during funerals.

"We must thank Levi and Philip for helping me. Were it not for their assistance, we would not have merited this moment. We have performed the greatest act of charity; the dead will not be able to return our deeds. May the Almighty look favorably on His children and protect us from all evil."

"Amen," they all answered, without much gusto or enthusiasm. They were spent from the day's ills.

"Bear witness!" Mordechai continued, undeterred, "I hereby dedicate this field as a cemetery for any of our brethren. Let us pray God keeps David's seed alive and well."

Sarah was amazed by the generosity of her brother-in-law. With all the criticism her husband had attributed to Mordechai's political maneuverings, it was clear his heart was in the right place. Sarah had long realized her husband's pragmatism balanced Mordechai's idealism. This time, the two collaborated, and she was proud of them both. Levi had helped purify the corpse, gather the necessary victuals for the meal following the burial, and even offered mattresses for the poor children to rest upon. Sarah thought of her own little ones back home and prayed she should never, in her lifetime, need to make use of the Sheftall Cemetery. She walked together with the crowd, towards the manor, where Frances and Hannah had prepared lentils and eggs, and stared at her husband's bent back, praying, silently, that he too shall outlive her. It was a crime, a true tragedy, to carry on in the world while loved ones lay cold in the ground.

*

Weeks since that day had passed, and the two brothers could barely see beyond their differences. Levi was bent on remaining neutral while Mordechai prophesied the absurdity of such an act. Levi believed his brother entertained Apocalyptic zeal toward the rebellion.

"We shall help create a new Zion for the masses. It is so believed."

"Yes, by *Christian* folk," Levi insisted.

"Perhaps their understanding is different from mine, but our goals are the same. America must rid itself of the Commonwealth's influence and create its own history, its own birth."

"But that influence has stood us in good stead these many years. Why alter that? Why risk near annihilation? Who is to guarantee Washington and Adams and all those enlightened men will be able to achieve such in this land? There is influence in every colony, from Catholic thought to the Protestant ideology. How can any civilization be free of its sister civilization?"

"By breaking away, for a start! Washington and Adams are far more secular than you imagine, Levi. They envision a country where there is *separation* of church and state. That is *ideal*, considering the situation in Europe, would you not agree?"

"Yes, but the moment you say there is a 'separation' you insinuate that such is probably, in all truth, no separation. Did you not mention a new Zion previously? Then you cannot say that your rebellious zeal does not emanate from a spiritual source!"

"Perhaps; however, all that you suggest is irrelevant to the cause itself."

"Yes. Most of the bitterness can be sorely pointed to one's pockets."

"It is far more complex than that. Perhaps it is expedient for you to remain aloof for financial reasons," Mordechai bitterly whispered.

"I cannot deny that I do not see it prudent as of now to abandon my business matters and my obligations to Sarah in order to risk my life for a cause I do not inherently believe in. No, Mordechai. And if I am condemned and labeled aloof, then so be it," Levi stubbornly answered, turning his back toward the door as he left Mordechai's parlor. Flabbergasted by his brother's recalcitrant stance, Levi walked on home unconsciously tearing some grass with his walking stick. It comes as no surprise, then, to note a flicker of a smile on Eddings' face as he witnessed Levi's irritation. As the old saying goes, *two Jews, three opinions.*

*

Jacob Hicks wished General Gage never re-routed his division to Massachusetts. Since the blasted Boston Tea Party, he had these irksome vertigo spells that threatened to drive him mad. Quite often enough, he had desisted from eating his supper and even, oddly, lost some of his libido. The damned rebels only grew more audacious with each passing week. That nasty boy got away with offending him and nearly killing him by virtue of his "tender years," and reparation was nonexistent. The only positive outcome from the entire event was perhaps a kind gesture from the beauty Anne, but even that was short-lived. She moved to New York. Indefinitely. The house was now quiet and all his for the taking.

Jacob heard from regulars that Governor Wright was losing ground back in Georgia, and Hicks wondered if the situation would improve at all. Tonight he would learn of General Thomas Gage's next orders, and he hoped Gage would command a return to Savannah.

"Quiet! Listen carefully as I read the latest dispatch from General Gage!"

Hicks stood a foot away from the redcoat who was known as *Bullhead*. Since the Scotsman was always red with drink, his ears looked as though someone had thrown red paint on them. Hence the appellation. *Bullhead* read,

As of April of 1775, the British armed men of Massachusetts colony must repress the militia of the American rebel forces. No soldier shall stand idly by. Permission to return fire and to shoot once provoked is now granted by the seal of the King. God bless the King.

Hicks nodded in agreement. No problem shooting. Not for him. In fact, it would be an *honor*.

Hicks followed his regiment the next morning to Concord. The weather was accommodating, and the foot soldiers were singing. The situation would not last more than a year, Hicks predicted. The country was full of women and children; there were few able-bodied men in his estimation. The colonies were separated by vast distances, and the woods offered a haven for a large corps of men. The Americans were foolish if they thought they could out-maneuver the Redcoats. *Bullhead* began to sing a jolly song and the vanguard carried the tune. Some marchers whipped out their flutes, and the younger recruits drummed away. The breeze eased Hicks' mind, and for a long time, he did not experience those dreaded vertigo spells.

As though Satan follows the beating drums and seeks to destroy the sounds, a barrage of bullets suddenly flew past Hicks' men. *Bullhead* caught sight of the rebels and began firing away. The rebels began to run off; Hicks counted their hurried legs; perhaps less than thirty men! Quickly, *Bullhead's* division followed the men and a firefight ensued. The rebels ran into a hut well-camouflaged by the thickets and the evergreens so abundant in that part of Concord. Hicks immediately returned fire, resting his musket on the plush ground as he reloaded. The Redcoats outnumbered the rebels, and Hicks believed he could at least shoot a few rebels if he tried. But just as he inserted a musket ball into the mouth of his gun, a wave of nausea filled his inner mind and he lay on the ground, cursing.

"Bloody boy, ruined my bloody life. Please Lord, let this spell pass me! I swear to uphold the holy laws, dear Jesus! But just let these spells leave me in peace!" *Bullhead* saw Hicks sprawled on the floor, groaning, and believed the worst. With the fury of a drunkard who discovered he had been fooled by his wife, *Bullhead* stormed into the hut firing his musket and tearing the flesh of any rebel who so much as stood in between him and imminent death.

When Hicks finally recovered, *Bullhead* emerged with three rebel prisoners, whom he summarily shot to death. To their great surprise, the Redcoats captured not only the men, but also a military supply depot.

The men greedily took a musket each and stuffed their leather carryalls with musket balls. It was a jolly march back to Cambridge, their next outpost. Some Redcoats undoubtedly were injured, but not so poorly. Nothing a few bandages couldn't fix. The British men were rather pleased with their quick response and the booty, which they truly needed, come to think of it. *Bullhead* indicated a respite of two hours was called for, and the men nodded in agreement. Those with leg wounds breathed a heavy sigh of relief, and the medics concurred. Hicks thought of his mother for a moment, wondering if she just knew where he was and what he was up to in the American heartland. Killing swine, that's what!

Hicks removed his carryall and began rummaging for a few biscuits he had yet left uneaten. A few of the men began to cook potatoes and corn by the fire, and *Bullhead* was on an expedition for a rabbit or other field animal. Bottles of rum passed between the men, who, having little knowledge of germs, spread theirs with great magnanimity. Hicks saw a couple of the men were eating apples and asked for a trade. Just as he was about to chew, *Bullhead* came running back with a bloody rabbit and muttering curses.

"Stand ready!"

All the men could not believe the order. But the smoke that ensued filled the lungs of every Brit for the next two hours. Rum bottles burst, men fell on their boiled potato peels, and rabbit hairs clung to wounds. The trees were not as thick in their part of the woods, and few Redcoats could find cover. The birds perched high above flew away; some got caught in the return fire. Hicks lay on the floor, holding his head, and then, despite the dizziness, the trees that were falling from the ground and the grass that was on the faces of his enemy, he managed to fire and fire and fire.

*

"The damned Johnston sounds absolutely merry in the *Gazette*! I detect such, I tell you Habersham. Here. Have a look. The world has gone mad. Absolutely mad."

James Habersham lifted his reading spectacles to his eyes, an invention of a great American inventor, Benjamin Franklin. He placed his tea saucer aside, and wiped his greasy hands with an embroidered handkerchief.

"Let me see. Yes, 'Seventy-three British soldiers are dead of rebel fire and another two hundred are unaccounted for or missing. In Concord, the Americans suffered fifty dead and thirty four are badly injured. It is believed the battle at Concord has virtually killed any hope for reconciliation.'"

"Do you not see the injustice of the *Gazette*? 'Americans "suffered," while the "seventy-three British soldiers are dead."'"

"Please, Wright. Everyone is quite aware the *Gazette* is a loyalist paper. This should come as no surprise."

"Perhaps, James, but the death of British soldiers should not be enumerated as though they are fish at sea. They are men!"

Habersham thought of his son Joseph who had absolutely broken his wife's heart. He placed his spectacles in his pocket, and leaned in towards Wright, "I would not want any man to be killed, British or loyalist. This is a grave and grim day indeed, Wright. Justly so."

Wright just listened to his friend and for once did not utter a word in agreement.

*

May of 1775 was particularly balmy. Men and women began to peel off their layered clothing earlier than usual. The women despised their petticoats, envying the heathen women with their bare legs and open-toe moccasins. Many men didn't bother with overcoats, just getting by with linen or cotton breeches and gossamer shirts, mostly white to reflect the sun's pitiless rays. Children whizzed by Tondee's Tavern, their parents preoccupied with the disturbing news: the battles at Lexington and Concord reached Savannahians' ears. (The actual event took place three weeks prior.) Conflicting rumors pinned the first shot on either side; either way, the townspeople were overwhelmed by the implications of the battles.

Mordechai Sheftall pounded the oak table in Tondee's Tavern numerous times; the hubbub in the room was just as palpable as the sweat accumulating in their underarms, chins, and countless other areas. The light was dim and the shutters were closed and the door was locked. Not a single breeze cooled the men; this was a meeting that no man outside of the Committee could attend or otherwise breach.

"Attention!" Mordechai repeated the pounding, and soon enough, the room quieted. The eyes of twenty leading Savannah patriots were glued upon Mordechai's profile. Standing as though by a podium, he nearly choked on his spittle. The irony of the situation dawned on him quite unexpectedly. How could it be a mere Jew was elected Chairman of the Georgia Parochial Committee of *Christ Church* parish, a rebel group that functioned alongside the Sons of Liberty? Had he simply lived alongside the *Christ*ians in relative safety—well, then, as is stated on Passover, "*Dayenu*"; it would have sufficed! Would he have been free to practice his religion *openly* and not *clandestinely* (as poor Nunez' family and all Sephardic Jews knew all too well during the years post Inquisition), well, then, "*Dayenu!*" But here he was, a *conspicuous* Jew who carried his Necessaire (an encasement of cutlery for kosher consumption and a koshering knife) and *kept the Sabbath*, and somehow, the Christians who had forever branded his ilk with the typecast "Jesus killer" deemed him a respectable fellow!

Joseph Habersham's doe-like eyes rested on Mordechai. Not long ago the handsome young man had been a sworn enemy of the Sons of Liberty; but just as strangely as a child becomes a man, Joseph abandoned his initial stance and soon became a staunch supporter of the cause. But the question was if he was able to see Mordechai as a rebel or as a *Jew* rebel; it was yet to be determined, Mordechai believed. Having invited them all to Tondee's Tavern, Mordechai cut to the chase:

"Gentlemen, we have all heard the alarming news. I fear the blood on the fields of Concord and Lexington presage a long carnage ahead. No war in the name of independence from such a strong force can be won in a week or a year. A conflict such as ours will test the fabric of each man. But we must not stand by idly and allow the blood of countless men to have been shed in vain. We must prepare ourselves for the war that is most assuredly coming; we must join our brothers in Massachusetts and fight tyranny and oppression."

"Hear, hear!" the crowd responded, banging their whiskey glasses on the round tables.

"It is no longer sufficient for us to express support with words alone. Decisive action must ensue. Our actions will define our commitment to the cause of liberty. With your permission, men, and if there is no dissent, I shall submit my plan, which I recommend we execute—without a moment's delay...."

*

Levi sipped his tea with Sarah nearly falling asleep by his side. Dinner had been served a bit later than usual; Levi had been to his mother's house for a brief visit. Sarah guessed it had to do with Mordechai, but she didn't want to bring up the subject; she hated to see the anxiety painted on each of Levi's features: his mouth would tighten, his jaw would lock; his eyes would dart this way and that, then settle, and the iris of his left eye became a shade more gray. The children had finally been put to sleep, having remained out doors most of the day. The house was too warm for this time of year, and the shades were all open. The slaves put the last dishes away in the cupboard, and the crickets could be overheard by the windows to her right. When they first married, Levi and Sarah would stroll by the shore, interlocking hands, regaling one another with tales of childhood and mishaps of youth. Sarah shared her account of learning of love, how oddly she happened to learn of the matter from a slave-woman who had borne a child out of wedlock. Levi's expeditions were pure fantasy to Sarah's ears, and she enjoyed learning of all the interesting ventures her husband had faced, long before he met her. But those idyllic days were long past, save for those lovely careless moments with her beautiful children. The seashore gladdened their hearts, and when the sun shone on them it seemed the world would not collapse into chaos as Levi predicted or as Mordechai envisioned. Instead, the excitement of each new passing day in the New World would hearken a banquet of unsurpassed mysterious pleasure, of newfound potential, of a glory she had never imagined possible. Here, in America, she could raise her children without the fear of the Inquisition on her back; she could raise cattle and own men and women who would release her of labor. The orchards were plush, and the ships passing by the shore offered wares from the great countries abroad; from teas, and cocoa, to French tulle—what could money not buy in this great land? When she had sojourned in St. Croix, it must have been *months* before shipments arrived, of any considerable goods, and how remote she felt! But Georgia, although young, was robust!

The colony enjoyed great benefits—and all for being *associated* with the Great Commonwealth country of Great Britain. This was her husband's stance, and of course, by proxy, hers too.

But all this has been mulled over for months, if not years. And yet, tonight her husband seemed particularly melancholy, brooding over *something* he had yet to communicate.

"I don't want you to take the children to Mordechai's house anymore, Sarah."

"Why ever not?" she answered, quite perturbed. *Why would he say something like that?*

"Because very soon, he will become a notorious man in the eyes of some very powerful men, and I don't want my children or my wife involved or even *there*. God only knows what can come of this."

"Of *what?*"

"Listen, Sarah. You must not repeat this. But Mordechai is meeting *tonight* and deciding his *fate* tonight. He's sealing it. That's it. There is little we can do. I tried. God only knows I tried. Ima tried. Poor mother! I don't know how she'll bear it; I really don't. Thank God father is no longer alive, and I can't believe I just muttered that. I can't!"

Sarah began to understand. Oh yes. So Mordechai will have decided upon an action that will forever brand him as a rebel; and God only knew what vengeance those such as Wright and Eddings and Habersham had in store for a man, let alone a dirty Jew, who commits treason against their beloved King, George the Third, may God spare Mordechai.

*

When she had consigned herself to a life of marriage, Frances imagined nights of passion and endless frolicking. Moonlight dances. Candlelight suppers. Friday nights with joyous hymns. Quiet walks on Sabbath. A breakfast of giggles. It was all child fantasy, of course. But most women eventually learn to make peace with married life and the mundane and, quite regrettably, the sorrows of childrearing. Frances had learned to expect her children fighting in the evenings, refusing to succumb to their pillows. She grew accustomed to the accordion body of womanhood, from pregnancy to postpartum to the few months of respite in between. She learned to make peace with a husband who increasingly showered the world and foreign men with attention and concern while waiting for him patiently, thinking of him in her heart. But she was not so readily going to accept *secrecy*. Nor was she going to allow her husband to even consider, for a single moment, that she was oblivious to his plans nor inconsequential in the effects of such plans. But how was she to approach him? He was infamously mulish; my god, he was as immovable as a stump of a long-dead tree.

Frances refused to go to bed until Mordechai walked through the door. The slaves were all in bed, and it would be she Mordechai would be forced to reckon with once he stepped foot in through the door.

A woman's job was but to sit and wait.

It would be some time after Frances decided to knit another yarmulke for her youngest child, and countless stitches that strained her eyes before Mordechai finally returned to his home.

He imagined the entire family asleep, so when Frances stood before him with a candle barely lit he nearly jumped in fright.

"Oh! How you *frightened me*, Frances."

"I am sorry, but I have remained awake so that I may speak to you."

"Is it urgent? I am quite tired, dearest."

"Yes, in fact it is."

Mordechai knew from the look in Frances' eyes that he had better not try to abscond or offer any pretense or other.

"I want you to tell me where you went and what you were doing. I believe as your partner in matrimony and indeed in life, I deserve to know."

Mordechai looked deeply into Frances' eyes and wondered how the years had dealt her blows on her countenance. Her eyes had a pallid hue to them; her cheeks seemed a bit more sunken than he remembered. Her hair sprouted some gray roots, intermingled with the blonde hair that had turned dark brown for lack of the sun's lightening rays. Gray circles shrouded her glowing skin, and her lips seemed thinner. Frances suddenly smiled a bit, frightening Mordechai a bit less. It was late, and she had forfeited sleep to speak to him. He must oblige, for goodness sake! She *was* his wife. And soon enough, God only knew what burden that would entail.

*

Mordechai checked his pocket-watch; fifteen after three in the morning. With nothing but the dim moonlight to guide their cautious steps, Mordechai and fifteen other men inched through the underbrush. Mordechai froze; he motioned the others to do the same. The rustle of the leather soles on the thick grass sounded as though a trumpet were blasted in their ears. Mordechai motioned for silence. He then whispered into the ear of Noble Jones, a fairly stout man in his mid years who occasionally forgot to pray the catechism, who passed the message to the man directly behind him, Joseph Habersham, who relayed the message to Philip Minis all the way down the assembly line. Each man nodded if he understood and pointed to his ear once more if he could not make out the message. This was the pre-set arrangement Mordechai devised prior to their mission. *Now, if just a dog could start barking somewhere far from here, or some other distraction, God, that would be wonderful.*

Just beyond the foliage, about ten feet ahead of Mordechai, stood the royal powder arsenal. How Mordechai learned of this was a matter of pure luck. Having wharfs on the coast of Georgia where wares of all kinds were stored and then outsourced *readily* availed him of this arsenal. *A godsend*, indeed. But Governor Wright was no fool—the area was patrolled round the clock—but lately, thanks to the battles in Concord and Lexington, more and more men were no longer stationed there. During the dreadful time of night Mordechai issued reconnaissance of the area the week prior and it was *this fateful* hour that proved the most breachable. The men stationed could not help but either doze or drink. Mordechai checked his pocket-watch. Twenty-two after three. He stepped into the clearing and scanned the road: no men on horseback as far as he could detect. Foot soldiers: absent.

Mordechai, with excess energy, waved his hand *twice.* That was the sign. Without hesitation, Noble Jones and Joseph parted the greenery and joined Mordechai. The three now stood before the small rather innocuous-looking building. Really, thought Joseph. Who would think such was a storage house? Joseph, who had grown taller and broader, handed Mordechai a pickaxe. He had taken it from Wright's own estate, without Percy noticing, of course. It would only be just, the youth believed. Taking turns, Joseph and Mordechai began chipping away at the metal bolt, trying to break through the entrance. *God, this sounds like a damn orchestra,* Joseph thought. Noble Jones began to sweat; by *Christ* it was taking *too long.* He kept his eyes on the road. Thankfully, no man still. The other men were nervously waiting for the gesture to come towards Mordechai and wondered what took so long. Mordechai took the pickaxe from Joseph one last time, and with all his might he hurled the weapon at the door. The bolt clattered to the ground, and the heavy door swung open from the force of his arm. Mordechai had to ensure safety first: he stepped into the repository, lit a candle, scanned the area quickly, and motioned for the rest to join him; they were in.

They hit the jackpot.

Without a single word, almost like ants at work, Mordechai heaved a fifty-pound crate of gunpowder and handed it to Joseph, who passed it down the line. *My God! This is heavy enough to blow up Savannah,* he mused. The men worked furiously. Philip hurled the last crate into the carriage by the clearing, the last of the load. Mordechai checked his pocket-watch once again: three-forty. In less time than it takes to boil an egg or poach a chicken, the men had managed to clear six hundred pounds of powder from the storehouse. The powder that would have blasted their roads and their homes and only God knows what else was now in *their* possession. Noble Jones detected a light in the distance. He motioned Mordechai the warning signal; "Time to disperse. Go!"

The carriage with the booty slipped off into the forest, and the men scattered about.

By the time the sentry reached the storehouse, the men were running through the forest holding lanterns like schoolchildren hiding from their parents on a beauteous night.

*

Rebecca McIntosh slammed the door on Governor Wright's Anglo profile without blinking. Served the man right, she believed. What gall! To knock on the homes of women while their husbands were clearly hard at work. And for what? To implore "all cessation of sinful and shameful activity." The absolute nerve of the man. And what makes him think her husband had what to do with the recent looting and lawlessness? And even worse, to practically beg, with such obsequiousness, to support the Royal Seat of Governance! Would that be the king in England who sits on a bedecked throne while her husband has to work until ten at night supporting his family—for the King's coffers? Is that whom she should "support"? Was it not enough her husband fought in the War of Jenkins' Ear? Or was that too long ago for anyone to remember, now that all this talk of rebellion is on everyone's mind? It was the Jew Sheftall who was undoubtedly behind the storehouse robbery. Not that she thought it a terrible idea after all, so long as all that powder doesn't end up on her front lawn, destroying all the hard work her poor husband endured all these years—and in the name of *loyalty* to the throne! Why, he could have continued his Solicitor's post, but he abandoned it all after the war! And now this James Wright comes knocking on her door! The man owns ten plantations! Ten. He has well over five hundred slaves. Of course he loves the King. Of course he's as loyal as a dog to his master. Has he ever known a day's labor?

James Wright winced as the door slammed shut. Habersham looked down; Mrs. McIntosh was not the first to disgrace the governor, but probably the first to throw around a couple of unwarranted epithets. The governor *tsk-tsk*ed his head, and continued down the road toward Broughton Street.

"You might as well turn the other way, Wright. The Jew rebel Sheftall and his co-conspirators live there. Including Johnston and McIntosh. Not much chance they'll heed your entreaties."

"We're losing them all, one by one. That damned Sheftall; he's managed to turn the entire town into Judases. It's simply unpardonable!"

Habersham's nostrils flared. He was losing his own *sons* to the damned Jew rebel. First Joseph and now the other two.

"What's simply unpardonable is their consistent *disregard* for any of your ordinances or your threats. Did you not declare a public proclamation denouncing any meeting at Tondee's? But the Jew rebel and his cronies attended nonetheless!"

"Of course, Habersham. You are only painting a grimmer picture. But what the delegates that evening adopted is by far the reason for our being treated so *indifferently* by the masses."

"Yes, but we must not overlook that the delegates adopted resolutions affirming the colonists' allegiance to the British Crown!"

"Rubbish! You call a seditious act of looting *from the Crown* 'allegiance'? They are merely playing political cat games, is what it is."

"I'm at a loss, James. The town's disloyalty is only mirrored in my own home. James, Jr., my brilliant son, serves in the revolutionary state assemblies; John, my favorite, is a prominent member of the Sons of Liberty, and Joseph, God bless the child, frequents those notorious meetings with Sheftall at Tondee's Tavern, for crying out loud!" He suddenly turned to the governor, looking all morose, "I'm a broken man, James. I'm just all torn to bits." *Just like Savannah.*

The two continued walking, headed toward the main thoroughfare. Many men saluted, others cordially removed their caps; a few slightly curtsied.

"At least they're cordial," Wright sarcastically whispered.

"Yes. The question is if they are cordial for past services or for future ones."

"Hear. Hear. They may very well intimate they will no longer require such."

The Savannah gardens did little to assuage the men. Habersham remained quiet for a good while; there was little he could think of that would not be mordant. Goodness! How the past few months had seen such a radical shift among the populace! It recalls *Julius Caesar* and Shakespeare's condemnation of the fickleness of humankind. How one wrong stroke can undo years of service and loyalty. It was as though an entire nation became Brutuses. *Et tu?* Habersham barely recognized his own sons. His own home was sharply divided over the burgeoning rebellion. At first only James, Jr. And then John seemed to follow along. Joseph had remained by his side quite the longest, until the pendulum began to swing toward the rebellion and his older brothers. Disdain for royal authority: commonplace now. Wright's inability to do anything about the situation was the silent truth Habersham dared not mention, but the townsfolk clearly realized his ineptitude. Wright may offer a fifty-pound reward, in sterling, for the identification of perpetrators, but no response seems forthcoming! Why just last February a poor customs official was tarred and feathered by a rowdy mob. But all the money in Wright's chests amounted to little in the face of the new world order. Poor Wright! The seizure of all that gunpowder was a festering wound in the half-beaten man! His offer of fifty-pound sterling found not a single man in possession of information. The men and women of Savannah became rebels, now a sizable percentage of the populace. And *that* was a grim reality Habersham and Wright could no longer deny.

Wright walked alongside James Habersham in companionate silence. The word "cordial" sent him off on a silent tirade. On the surface perhaps they were stating their loyalty and appearing cordial, but the rebels were undermining his political power at *every* opportunity. Case in point: the Parochial Committee, under the jurisprudence of the Jew Sheftall, *assumed* control of governmental functions, including granting commissions, regulating trade, and even adjudicating! The Jew has the nerve, and the Christians who put him at the vanguard of the committee are committing a crime in his opinion, to wrest control of heretofore gubernatorial powers! It was a shameful act indeed, but Wright could not figure a way to punish these perfidious men.

"Did you hear of the latest development the blasted Whigs have devised, Habersham?" Wright broke the silence with a

334

question he no doubt intended to answer. "They created a Council of Safety to enforce Savannah's adherence to the resolutions of Continental Congress. You believe? The rebel Washington now has more authority than we do. It is his cronies' resolutions they now wish to maintain."

"Yes. I hear these resolutions include the most disloyal measures—including the formation of a military force."

"How dare they impose an embargo on British goods! It is such ingratitude and absolute impudence!"

"Indeed," Habersham whispered. "Indeed it is, to support 'resistance' to 'Parliamentary oppression' is such a broad resolution. Why, any man may mistreat and abuse a British soldier for the misperceived 'oppression' no doubt enacted by Parliament. It is all absurd, and I don't see a clear way out of this imbroglio."

"By God, is that Wilson running with his hat all askew in those filthy breeches, Wright?" James Habersham pointed to Mr. Wilson's figure as it approached. The scant hair beneath his hat was replete with oil and dandruff. The two shifted uncomfortably as the man breathed heavily on them.

"Compose yourself, Mr. Wilson," said Wright. "Whatever is the matter?"

Wilson tried to catch his breath, but his fear only augmented his inability to do so.

"The weapons store was plundered, Sir. There was nothing I could do to prevent it," he quickly added.

Wright's jaw stiffened. The cache of weapons in Wilson's command was by far larger in scope than what Wright wanted to think of at that moment.

"Did you recognize the perpetrators? Tell me immediately! Who did this?"

Wright hoped he could now identify the looters. Surely these were the same brigands who raided numerous stores!

Wilson reached for a rumpled sheet of paper and handed it to the governor, now all red in the face and incredibly irate. He handed the paper to Wright and a brief moment of silence ensued.

"The audacity of these scoundrels has reached a new summit, dear Habersham. A new zenith, I tell you! A list of names! To think that they demonstrate such bravado in the face of retribution! They scoff at justice!"

"Read the names, Wright! Who are these barbarians?"

In a monotone voice, as though one defeated, Wright exclaimed, "Mordechai Sheftall [but of course]... Joseph Clay [who would have guessed]... Edward Telfair [the two-timer!]... Noble Wymberly Jones [the ingrate!]..."

"They are familiar names, all, as much as it displeasures to hear of Jones and Clay. Sheftall poses no surprise. Indeed."

"Carry on. Carry on. I should like to know who else has no fear of governance and the King's crown!"

"Joseph Habersham [so sorry good friend. This pains me too.]... Philip Minis...."

Habersham snatched the letter from Wright's hands. "Enough!" He yelled. "Enough of this downright bloody rubbish! I'll hear no more."

OASIS OF LOYALTY

COLONEL WILLIAM PRESCOTT AND TWELVE hundred patriots worked feverishly throughout the sultry night of June sixteenth of seventeen hundred and seventy-seven. Their mission: to fortify Breed's Hill and Bunker Hill, strategic positions just north of the Charles River. The Colonel, thoroughly bred for war, feared his men in arms were perhaps brimming with more bloodlust than with skill. But the planning fell on him, and the men were eager to follow orders, so there was little he could complain of. General Gage, the blasted and highly experienced British warrior, had already seized nearby Dorchester Heights, and was sure to attack the American positions before long. The Americans were compelled to secure *some* of the high ground overlooking Boston Harbor in order to wage a successful siege.

Colonel Prescott cursed the day his mother decided he was meant for arms. His hands would be filled with blood, and all the snowfall in New England will not be able to cleanse him, he was sure. But who had time or the luxury to pontificate? The heat stultified the mind; the body could but obey. Mounted on his horse, Prescott could see the advantageous position of the Brits and began to strategically plan a battle route. He charged his men to fortify the ground with cannons and explained to the men the ready positions. The cavalry would stand ready for his order; they were not to move an inch past their initial positions until commanded to do so.

"Sir. If I may have a word with you?" Captain Isaiah McBride had been pestering his superior for a consultation nearly all day. It was dire. Prescott would have to acquiesce.

"Yes. You may address the Captain."

Isaiah stood five-foot-four, quite short for an American patriot, but his mind made up for his stilted form. "Sir. Permission to speak freely."

Prescott was never too keen on that phrase. That inordinately meant *something negative* had to be stated. But it was only civil to grant the right. "Yes. Proceed."

Isaiah knocked his feet together and stated, in rapid phrases, without missing a breath, "Sir. The American army is keen on fighting the Redcoats, but we face a disadvantage that cannot be overlooked: we lack basic ammunitions, sir. Each soldier has, I say I calculated this with precision, only enough powder available to take nine shots. Nine. No strategic position could compensate for that most deleterious disadvantage, Sir!"

Prescott nodded his head and a doom began to hang over him, as though a cloud took root, one of deep despondency, over his sorry head. "You are quite right, but as I do not have word of any shipment or any reinforcement, we must be able to face our enemies with what we have. If it comes to bayonets, then we shall muster the fortitude and fight as men in Rome. Without muskets. I have no words to assuage your concerns besides for this: I have yet to encounter sheer determination in another group of fellow Americans. This strength shall serve us well, I pray." And with that, Prescott dismissed poor Isaiah, who decided perhaps it was best to recalculate the powder/shot ratio; perhaps he erred in his calculations.

Prescott knew Isaiah was right; the math was not adding up favorably on their side. But the evening was coming to a close, and the positions were not yet formed. Some soldiers bathed by the river to cool off; the rest were readying the battlefield for carnage and war. Men could only plan with what they had at their disposal.

The Continental Army could not offer much financial compensation to these patriots; so merely their presence seemed to calm Prescott's nerves. He had been in the army long enough to know that men of will are far better suited for warfare than men of opportunity.

Prescott began to settle in his tent, tired from the sun's relentless rays, when a carriage pulled up with five patriots smiling from ear to ear. The moon had yet to shine, and the stars were still not visible in the sky; the twilight hour descended on the American encampment, and the night activity was disturbed by the horse's hoofs and the clattering of the carriage.

"Sir! Please see this!"

Isaiah stood with his comrades, optimistically standing by the horse's hind legs. He opened the doors and led Prescott to the interior of the carriage.

"What are these crates?" Prescott inquired.

"These crates contain nearly *three hundred* pounds of gunpowder, Sir!"

"How did they arrive here?"

"They were clandestinely ferried across the river and delivered, Sir!'

"Whoever from? I was not expecting any such delivery!"

At first Isaiah himself did not know of the answer to Prescott's inquiry. It was all a mystery. As the men began to unload the crates, one found a note nailed to the side of one of them, "From your devoted friends in Savannah."

Isaiah ran and delivered the note to Prescott. Prescott read the names again and again, "Who is Mordechai Sheftall? And a series here of names listed, why, I have never heard of them!"

Isaiah turned to Prescott and whispered, "They say God works in mysterious ways, Sir."

*

That evening Prescott was able to rest his heat-exhausted head with more ease than he had anticipated. Their ammunition was still short, even with the surprise supplement. But the mood! How it shifted! It now took on an air of confidence and camaraderie. To think that *Georgia*, the scorned *thirteenth colony*, previously *irrelevant* in Continental affairs, had made such a contribution! Isaiah calculated the powder could increase each man's efficiency by twenty-two percent, if used wisely. The men of Prescott's army were filled with a renewed sense of hope; perhaps the Americans *can* withstand the upcoming assault. The unity amongst the nation that night was palpable on Breed's Hill—and many knew, that if they shall fail, the fight for Independence shall succeed if the will of the nation so wills it into being.

British naval fire began at sunrise, setting buildings ablaze and filling the air with black soot and smoke. Evacuations took place the evening before, and many men cursed the King. Eight hours later, 2,400 Redcoats landed under the black cover of smoke and brimstone; they attempted a rear assault on Breed's Hill. Prescott's men did not anticipate such; but the entire first column of Redcoats was decimated by militiamen from Connecticut and New Hampshire. A lengthy stone rampart served as a firing ground, and the Redcoats fell like weak branches in a hailstorm. General Gage recalled his men and decided to regroup. Perched on his steed, Prescott could see Gage point to the front of the hill, and assumed an attack would ensue from there. Indeed, Gage stormed the front of the hill—twice. The Americans were quick: they swiftly repelled the advance of red men whose bodies fell by the dozens under the torrent of American bullet fire. Cries of wounded men filled the air of Bunker Hill, chilling the blood of those fortunate to still be among the living. Cries for water and mother, for Christ and lovers, polluted the dank air. Muddy faces and half carcasses littered the hill; men lay on the dead; the air stank of guts.

General Gage began to fear the worst. His men were flies in a hornet's nest, and worse. But suddenly, the firing ceased. Quiet filled the air; the silence of the purity found in nature's best reserves. *Is this some kind of ploy Prescott has taught his bloody men?* Isaiah stood on the fortified hill and counted fifty-nine.

"There is no more," he whispered, suddenly afraid to die.

The patriots had run out of gunpowder.

General Gage quickly scanned the field with his telescope. He could not believe his eyes! The Americans were furiously attaching bayonets to their muskets, ready to charge!

"Charge!" General Gage roared. "Charge! Charge!"

The British charged Breed's Hill from three sides, bayonets glistening. The Redcoats, renewed with blood lust at the sight of their brethren's fallen bodies and mutilated torsos, gritted their teeth in determination. The rebels! They had no more gunpowder!

Isaiah unleashed his fury and charged at any redcoat as though he were an enemy of deepest ill regard. These were the men who fought for a king who abused his rights; these were the men who would rape their women; these were the men who would plunder a home at will in the name of their superior rights over man; these were the men, if not killed, would kill him.

The hand-to-hand combat was bloody; and the Redcoats were by far better trained for this kind of battle.

Prescott saw his men tottering; more and more fell to the sword, as the British warriors began mutilating his men. It was a sight Prescott had little stomach for. "Retreat!" He hollered. "Retreat!"

Again and again, Prescott galloped across Breed's Hill yelling the order to find safety in Bunker Hill. Gage overheard the order and sighed a deep breath of relief. He did not see it fit to pursue the damned rebels. Shocked by the losses—over 1000 casualties and counting—Gage was glad to call the battle over and perhaps won; a retreat, in the name of war, can be deemed a victory; but the price!

Prescott, with half as many soldiers and fewer supplies by far, lost over 400 men to death, injury, or even capture.

Prescott later saw Isaiah tending to the wounded with scars all across his forehead and a bleeding tunic. The heat dried the blood on his face, and his bayonet was black with blood. The men gathered the dead once the British gathered their own and began to write the hateful letters home.

There would be another letter he would have to write; to Mordechai Sheftall; without his aid, the American resistance could not have succeeded to the extent that it did. Amidst the carnage, Prescott realized, as did many colonists, that, despite losing strategic ground, the Americans proved they could indeed war against the mightiest soldiers in the world.

General Gage, though daunted by the rebels, had ultimately achieved his objective—to retain certain strongholds. The fight for independence was now a reality no man could dream to deny.

And the cost for that dream would now be auctioned to the highest bidder.

*

Throughout the country, fathers and sons, husbands and wives, family and friends sat by firesides and contemplated the implications of Breed's Hill. Stout and well-established men refused to take arms; impetuous youths eager for bits of "experience" placed their apprenticeships aside in favor of liberty. Placards "Join or Die" littered every tavern, every town square, inducing hundreds to succumb to public pressure. Men of all breeds, even Natives and Negroes, considered joining the cause. The Redcoats were formidable, but not, perhaps, insurmountable was the underlying message most gleaned from the Battle at Bunker Hill. The Sheftall Household was no different in that regard; Mordechai convened his family for an "emergency session"; Levi begrudgingly attended. Sarah feared her husband would be swayed by his persuasive brother. Frances was a fraction of her usual self; nerves ate away at her nails, and her skin was sallow. The same controversy would reverberate throughout colonial homes, including the elite Habershams, who, having sons, would have to part with them one way or another. Independents and the impoverished considered the militia too—Percy, the black butler whose eyes opened in the last years, fell into that group.

This was a week that would determine the history of a nation.

*

Mordechai leaned on his chair uncomfortably, restless and agitated. What was taking Levi so long? Frances was ordering the Negro hands to hurry with the refreshments, and the little ones kept peering down the stairs. It wasn't every day their father paced the house with such consternation. Something was amiss. Sheftall Sheftall was ordered to put the kids to bed, but that was more of a wish than a command; he, too, was aglow with curiosity. He had a strong feeling it had to do with the latest news from Boston. The

Gazette littered his town, and he read the paper with the same curiosity adolescents page through erotica or romantic novels (depending on the gender, no doubt). Mother was obviously nervous; when was the last time she yelled at the kids to hurry to bed? That was the job of their governess, and when she was absent, as today, the duties of Sheftall Sheftall.

Levi finally sauntered in, most conspicuously uptight. Sarah wistfully gathered her skirts, kissing the *mezuzah* as she followed behind her husband. The two now seemed ages apart; Levi's beard was still dark, but his hair turned gray and even white by the temples. Sarah's beautiful locks, though covered, were still visible beneath the bonnet; hers was all ebony yet. Frances kissed her sister-in-law on both cheeks as was their custom, barely putting much emotion into the act; both were preoccupied with much thought.

"Let us sit in the parlor," Mordechai said, as he shook Levi's hand and patted his brother's shoulder.

The party summarily sat, each wife sitting beside her spouse. Frances ordered the maids to pour the lemonade, and the meeting had officially commenced.

"I do not doubt you have all heard the latest developments. They are quite dire," Mordechai began.

Levi nodded his head, staring at his fingers. Sarah shifted a bit, finding a comfortable position.

"This portends a war, no doubt, of immense proportions. I am most sure an outright Revolution will be declared at any moment."

Levi interrupted his brother, "It will be bloody, no doubt. Just this one battle claimed over 1400 hundred lives, on both sides."

Frances and Sarah's eyes widened. Blood and lives—they were not familiar with the ugly kind. How frightening it all sounded!

"Indeed," said Mordechai. "The battle proved the British monarchy will not easily relinquish control in America. King George will battle us to the core, I am sure. And for that reason, I must now announce, (and Frances, hold strong, because this means you must bear quite the brunt of it all), I mean to enlist and fight the Redcoats. This is a war a man *must* engage in."

Frances gasped, "Must! Must a man lose his life when there are so many others who may do so in his stead! Must! And 'must' you not tend to your family? Is it not enough you support the cause, that you've enlisted as a committee member? Must you also risk your very life?"

Levi joined in, "Mordechai! *Must* you carry arms and brand yourself a rebel in the very truest sense! The British will have your neck and hang you in Wright's square if you are caught and the war is lost! In a moment, you will have lost your life! And for what? For a cause! Is life so bad that you must die for an idea?"

"'Nonsense!" Mordechai retorted, disappointed his wife was not immediately backing him up. "The Revolution is not an idea, Levi, as you put it! It is the key for a future! Don't you see? The Americans want to create a *democracy*, where *religion* is not grounds for *impediments*. They want to create a *free society*, where a man may be his *own* master! In such a society, *Inquisitions* cannot occur! Expulsions will not be *legal*; indeed, such will be against the grain of the country's very establishment! Complete liberation from the British Crown will enable America to finally break loose from Europe's antiquated ways and usher in a new world! It is a *mitzvah* to fight in this war, to end the tyranny!"

Levi was flabbergasted; a *mitzvah? A holy deed? Has his brother completely lost his senses?*

"How dare you enlist our holy religion and deign to believe fighting in a war is a good deed, worthy of God's blessing? You have no right to assert such a thing, Mordechai!"

"Yes, indeed I do!" Mordechai retorted. "Has it ever occurred to you that perhaps it is God's will America should come into being, that it should be a haven for people from all over the world who seek a new life, a new chance to live once again?"

"And how are you to know, with all certainty, (as you most assuredly speak as though you knew the very thoughts of God Himself), that America will *not* one day become just as corrupt and vile a country as Great Britain, with all its unjust taxation, wars fought for gain, political alliances for aggrandizement and all other evils all great countries eventually are guilty of?"

"I cannot predict the future in that regard, Levi. But the country's leading men, (I am sure you've heard of Jefferson, Adams, Franklin, and Washington) are erudite men who will lead the country and draft laws to ensure the prosperity and fairness of the political system, I am sure."

"No human mind is free of error. One wrong word in their documents may spell doom in the future. For all that, you, Mordechai Sheftall, are willing *today* to risk your life, and the comfort of your home, the esteem of your wife!"

Frances placed her hand on her husband's thigh, and whispered, "Perhaps with such a vision, Mordechai, perhaps I must let you go. I esteem you *more*, not *less*, dear husband, for your conviction, which only time will unfold its truth. How it pains me! My first instinct is to hold on to you, but when I hear you speak, and I sense your passion, how can I hold you back?" And with that, the poor woman began to shed immense tears, quieting Levi and Mordechai.

Sheftall Sheftall overheard the conversation and couldn't believe his mother's words. This means she will have to care for the house and the estate, and doubtless many other responsibilities! Could she manage on her own?

"I want to join too, father."

All eyes turned to Sheftall Sheftall, and Frances stopped crying for a moment. "What? Have you gone mad? You are but a child!"

"No! I am not, mother. You yourself told me I became a man at my bar mitzvah, did you not? These were your very words mother: 'Now that you are thirteen, you are lawfully considered a man, Shefy.'"

Frances began to cry once more. If the father was a stubborn man, the child was even more so.

"I will not let you!" cried Frances, looking pleadingly at her husband.

"Mordechai, you can't possibly let your son—" Sarah began, but Mordechai simply stated, above her tone, "we can discuss this at a later time."

Sheftall Sheftall did not stir. He remained at the entrance.

"But it is you, Levi, who have not stated whether or not—"

"It is out of the question, Mordechai. I will support the committee, as I have done in the past, but I refuse to put my blood on the line! With all this talk of liberty, the warring may end and amount to nothing but imprisonment or worse! I will not risk it!"

Sarah breathed in deeply. Her husband was far more level-headed than his idealistic brother, and she thanked God for her good luck. How was she to ever care for a family all on her own, as now Frances must do? Sarah pitied her sister-in-law and wondered how Hannah would digest the latest desires of her adopted son.

Mordechai said nothing. Inside, he was seething, suspicious his brother was speaking from cowardice more than conviction, but he did not want to belittle him before his wife, which was doubtless a sin by every measure.

"What has befallen us?" Levi said, nearly a tear falling from his eye. *In all my life, I have never felt so estranged.*

*

July 1775: Dearest Catherine:

As I sail the *Liberty*, keeping a keen eye for a most conspicuous cargo ship bound for Georgia, my thoughts settle on you. When I consider how wonderful it is to bask in your love, I am no longer so warmed by the Savannah sun, as profound as it may be. The situation has progressed, my love, from most serious to most dire; if I fail in my mission, Savannah and many rebel posts may be in danger of attack or worse. Pray for my success, and I hope by the time I deliver this letter, my initial trepidation will be transmuted to glee.

With undying love,
Joseph H.

Joseph Habersham looked up from his note and admired the coast of Tybee as he penned a letter to his newfound sweetheart. The girl, Catherine Willoughby, was very much like him: the daughter of an aristocrat with fervor for adventure and rebellion. The two had chanced upon one another by Providential interference, but the matter was barred from her loyalist family—for now. He sealed the letter with a Habersham insignia, and placed it in his military pouch; he'll deliver it once he's docked safely closer inland. For now, his main priority was sailing the *Liberty* and keeping watch for British naval ships.

Not far from Habersham, and in fact right off the bend, lay Captain Richard Maitland, of the British merchant ship *Phillipa*. He was rather fond of his pipe and preferred to inhale its contents to eating the cooks' less than delectable meals. His forehead, the color of persimmon, reflected the strong rays of Georgia's July sun. The breeze, quite gentle, hardly stirred the gray plumes, surrounding Maitland with a halo of self-initiated smog. Maitland, who had been Captain of the seas longer than he'd like to recall (and no doubt lost much love to his labors at sea) was in the habit of musing out loud. His audience, a black slave, was of no particular interest to Maitland, but nevertheless, the only human being available for repartee:

"You know, I've been thinking, Lennox. This is as good a life as one can conceive. I'm sure of it."

Lennox barely registered the Captain's deep thoughts. His were quite removed; who thought of luxury? His poor back, scorched from hours on deck, suffered all the more for the incessant scrubbing, as he was not unoccupied.

"I tell you, Lennox," Maitland continued, "the earls and dukes back home believe their fancy castles and their dallying with their fine mistresses is the greatest pinnacle of life, but they are much deceived. It is here—out at sea. Wouldn't you say?"

Lennox grumbled some response along the lines of "Yes, Sir. 'Tis hard to disagree," for he was convinced had he remained silent, Maitland would be wont to muse aloud all the more.

Lennox's aspirations were far meeker than Maitland could comprehend—his desire was far more elementary: *he* wished to reunite with his wife and four children back in Africa—the country he had been stripped from like an animal in the night and forever banished from, guiltless of any crime save for his strength and muscular appearance: six foot two with an exceedingly sculptured back and torso, frightening any white man into becoming his absolute master. Where he had first fought like a caged panther marked the brutal markings of his initiation into servitude: his back was laced with markings of the lash.

The *Phillipa* drifted off the coast of Tybee with Maitland ignoring the nearly inaudible response of the slave, saying thus:

"This ship carries cargo of such import; I cannot say the Americans will be glad of it. It's for the British, mind you. Those damned Americans have been riling things up in the colonies—and I need not tell you the King will not have any insurgencies in his colonies. We mean to put an end to that—and that's where the Indian heathens come in, Lennox. You see, we mean to bribe them; the Americans have made enemies of the Cherokee and Creeks too, not only their host, the King Himself. Fools all!"

Lennox was out of ear-shot most of the time, but that did not deter Maitland. Off he continued in his way.

The ship continued down the Savannah River, and Maitland, who rested on deck, stood by and peered around. "Why! There isn't a single British ship in sight! Perhaps that Governor James Wright was in earnest when he wrote 'Georgia remains an oasis of loyalty to the Crown!'"

*

"Fire!" Joseph Habersham yelled, squinting for a moment as the sun penetrated his vision.

A horde of young Americans sprung to action aboard the *Liberty*, and six of its ten cannons were summarily aimed directly at Maitland's *Phillipa*. Maitland froze. His pipe long forgotten. His reveries long shot down. Before the British captain could lend a voice to command the men below deck, two cannons erupted with force in the crisp air.

"Jesus!" Maitland cried; automatically, he lay flat on deck, covering his head with his tobacco-stained fingers. Mayhem ensued below deck, with massive hysteria breaking loose.

One cannon whizzed by—fifty feet off target. The other— failed to make contact as well. Maitland, thinking of all his cargo, quickly ran to the mast, yelled for support, and desperately tried to maneuver the ship around.

But it was too late.

The breeze increased suddenly, and the *Phillipa* was too heavy to circumnavigate the Savannah back toward the sea. "Lennox!" He called. "Men! The sails!"

The *Phillipa* came to a standstill. Now all Maitland could do was sit—and wait.

Joseph observed Maitland's crew with binoculars, a gift from his brother James, Jr. It was clear the British captain had not foreseen the eventuality of cannon fire. A black slave with a massive and muscular back managed to control the ship's masts and movements, with the captain by the ship's wheel. Joseph made note the captain by the helm had the forehead most resembling that of a drunken Irishman, nervously bellowing orders, and spewing all this yellow spit on his crew.

Joseph ordered the *Liberty* to advance on the *Phillipa*. Within twenty feet of each other, Joseph stepped forward with an intense and audacious tone:

"'By order of the Georgia Provincial Congress, identify yourselves."

Maitland stared at the young man, a boy really. How old was this man? He thought. Twenty? That he should order *me* about?

"I know of no such organization!" he responded.

"'I find that difficult to believe, Captain. Either you are a flagrant liar or an ignoramus! The Georgia Provincial Congress is the acting government of Georgia! By their direct order, no ship shall sail past these waters or engage in commerce without authorization."

"Really now! And what does James Wright, Governor of Georgia last I heard, say on this matter?"

Joseph half-smiled and nearly chuckled. "James Wright has little say on any matter, Captain. Now, Identify yourselves! State your business."

Disgruntled, Maitland feared a reprisal. The men on board the *Liberty* far outnumbered his own, and the cannons shot only fifty feet off target were less likely to do so once again. Had the brazen man's cannons hit the target, an entire eruption would have incinerated him. The damn navy wasn't worth his behind on a grilling pad, he reasoned.

"Captain Richard Maitland of the *Phillipa*," he acquiesced. "We come to deliver goods before departing for Florida. Our will is to disturb no one."

Joseph turned to his men and pointed to the *Phillipa*. *This is the very ship!* "We shall inspect your ship before you are permitted to continue, Captain," Habersham stated, rather matter-of-factly.

"That's absurd!" Maitland retorted, quite indignant.

"Nonsense! What will be absurd is a sunken *Phillipa* on the Savannah shores. If you wish, my co-captain Oliver Bowen may relieve you of your command—*if* that is your desire, Captain."

Maitland wondered how the boy could disregard his own youth and speak to *him* in such a manner! He gritted his teeth. The damned Americans. Who were they to tell a British naval officer what to do?

"That will not be necessary," he managed to state.

The two vessels sailed up the Savannah River and anchored at Cockspur Island. Three hundred men were patiently waiting to inspect the British naval ship. Maitland would do nothing but watch as hundreds of men littered his vessel. Joseph ordered the gangplank lowered, serving as a bridge between the two. Maitland's ire increased dramatically as he witnessed Joseph placing an "American Liberty" flag on the *Phillipa's* masthead. (What audacity, the British officer thought.) From his corner, Lennox was astounded at the sight of it all and he stared, very much in disbelief, as Joseph handed Maitland a document bearing the official seal of the Parochial Committee.

"And who the bloody hell is Mordechai Sheftall?" Maitland asked, ready to pounce on Habersham for his gall. Is this Mordechai a Jew? Which gentile is named Mordechai? Is he upstaged by a renegade Jew? Bloody Mary! Maitland thought. What is this world coming to? So *this* is America!

Livid, Maitland wanted nothing more to do with the fiasco. He blamed James Wright for not warning him appropriately, and for not protecting his rights to sail in American seas unmolested.

Joseph, of course, was jubilant. All that gunpowder! All thirteen *thousand* pounds! *He* couldn't wait to boast of this great victory to all the Sons of Liberty back at Tondee's. The unloading of the merchant ship was smooth; his men lugged the barrels of powder in the July mid-afternoon with nary a complaint— the *Liberty* was now filled to its very capacity with the bounty of British goods, just as they liked. The rebel ships from South Carolina joined in the plunder. Today, thought Joseph, there is ample booty to loot.

Joseph found it wise to allow the emasculated Maitland to uncover his shame to James Wright himself, absolving Joseph from writing to Johnston in the *Gazette* and perhaps riling his father more than was necessary. Joseph was sure Wright would be able to figure out just who had intercepted Wright's urgent request for naval support for the *Phillipa* weeks ago, and instead, wrote to the London Government: "Georgia remains an oasis of loyalty to the Crown." (Good Percy! What would the Sons of Liberty have done without his most crucial meddling?!)

As the final transfer was complete, Habersham inspected the boat one last time. Some ammunition they left on board, but it was just as bare as one of the Creeks. As he was about to disembark, a dark shadow emerged from the corner and tapped Joseph on the shoulder. If the tap had not been so gentle, Joseph surely would have removed his pistol.

"Take me with you, I beseech you sir!" A black man stood, towered in fact, above Joseph—the very same who had managed the sails and cleaned the deck. Habersham, startled and quite surprised, responded, "I beg your pardon?"

Lennox started at his bare feet, blackened, coarsened, and calloused. "I beg you," he repeated, "I'll do any labor. I'll—"

"But you already have a master!" Joseph insisted, disliking the idea of a turncoat.

"Please sir. I am a slave. Seize me as you have seized the cargo. I am strong!"

For heaven's sake! What is a man to say to such a pathetic creature! Habersham wondered what the slave had to gain by asking for another master.

"Very well," Joseph acceded. "We'll find something for you. God only knows we need as many men as possible. Do you know how to shoot?"

*

James Habersham considered the luck he had now to face—all three sons rebels! Outcasts! And he, the great right-hand man of the Governor of the town! How it reflected ill! He sipped more and more bourbon as the hours whiled away and the grandfather clock ticked. Eddings was railing against him, behind his back, of course, questioning *his* loyalties. What pull does a father have on independently minded sons? So this was the price a man must pay for being a *public* man—having no say in his *private* matters! How could Joseph do this to him?

Joseph, his beloved son, the one with the luscious ringlets and eyes of a doe. How he doted on him as a child! How his poor wife wept when he had been born a boy but then delighted in his every gesture! How could he so debase a British naval officer? Every slave on Wright's *hundreds* of plantations was whispering about that blasted Percy, turncoat Negro! How could he so deceive his master? And to think that it was his son who convinced the slave to intercept letters, steal the waste basket and bring its contents to Joseph, eavesdrop on Eddings—it was monstrous! And now rumor has it he has persuaded the daughter of Willoughby to elope! How could he bear the indignity?

When Wright went on sabbatical following that terrible year of the Stamp Act and all its political implications, it had been James Habersham who had led the governor's position. Who did not know of James Habersham? And James, Jr., with all his political debates *supporting* the rebel cause! How could he have raised such ingrates?

Habersham cursed the bourbon; it wasn't nearly as strong as he recalled. Where was that whiskey? The July heat should deter his drinking; God only knew he sweated all the more after drinking. But what else was a man to do? How could he face Wright? The man was *reduced*! And that bloody Jew, Mordechai Sheftall, now *headed* the Parochial Committee and had *considerable* pull in the Provincial Congress; the blasted man! Judas' very like! Who was it granted him all those wharfs off Savannah coast? Who granted him the very ability to do trade? Was it not Wright! Of *that* the long-nosed Jew made quite his fortune! And now to mistreat and debase Wright! To turn Wright's government into a child's play put for his nanny's amusement; to scorn the mouth that feeds, that's what. Most detestable!

And as James Habersham was pondering all the ills of his son and his failures, pouring his ire and misery on bottles of whiskey and old rum, banging his fist on this oak table and that precious porcelain bowl, throwing pillows across the room, a shooting pain like no other and a dull throbbing numbness corroding his arteries rattled every bone in his body; he suddenly began to shiver, he felt the floor turn, and the room began to spin. Images of Joseph as a child spinning his top on Christmas Eve filled James' third eye, and the ballroom where he had first danced with his wife whirled into view.

And then he fell to the floor.

*

James Wright ruminated, sadly considering his luck. *I had been knighted by the King's court Sir James Wright, yet I cannot control the very province named after the King's late father! I had garnered and gleaned more acres of land in this colony, more plantations and prestige, yet all that amounts to nothing! Absolutely nothing! The summer had been a fiasco for me; first the brat Habersham and then all that talk of joining the rebellion. Plundering of merchant ships! And all under the aegis of Mordechai Sheftall! The man who has made his fortune thanks to me! To me! And now I wait in my estate for a good word from Eddings from Parliament—but so far, nothing. Nil from London. How many times did I beg for support? Reinforcements! That's all. Left with one hundred men, and then Gage decides to deploy them all to Massachusetts to quell the mess*

Thomas Hutchinson couldn't cope with. And now Habersham, the only fellow who could possibly commiserate with me, is dead.

Such and such were the musings of James Wright during the long winter of January 1776, a year Wright felt most bereft of loyalties amongst the provinces of his rule.

But perhaps worst of all, considering the mere status of the man in question, was the perfidy of the black slave, who, having been discovered, escaped. The man had deceived him in a manner most odious to consider! James Habersham probably still knocked his head underground each time his spirit contemplated the backstabbing child of his persuading Percy to stick a knife in his master's back; yet Percy must be held *most* accountable! If he should so much as find the man!

Seething in this manner, Wright sat at his desk and noticed three correspondences; one was most certainly from Parliament. Well! Wasn't it about time!

Dear Sir:

We hereby inform you of the presence, shortly, of two British war ships now setting sail from Charleston toward Savannah. The ships carry cargo of ammunitions, arms, and well-trained men. The provisions and presence of military officers are at your disposal once setting foot in Savannah.

James was able to sigh and relax just a bit in his chair. So now that the mole Percy was not interfering with the mail, and the bastard son of his good friend was no longer signing letters with his seal, Parliament had finally responded. After all that pleading, perhaps those in power realized those in power were powerless unless fortified by *armed* men.

We'll see just how far Mordechai Sheftall's scheming can affect the situation now, James thought.

*

Joseph sat in Tondee's bar shivering from the breeze, but nevertheless warmed by the whiskey now in hand. The moment of his greatest achievement thus far in the rebellion had produced his greatest pain: his father died of a stroke, and his mother blamed *him*, her youngest child. Over the grave, with his father's heavy body still recognizable, she seethed like a crazed woman let loose from an asylum. His brothers stood erect; neither James, Jr., nor John came to his defense. *But they're rebels too.* The blame fell on him, and the scratches on his face attested to that for some time. Joseph thought his joy after his success at sea could not be matched, but discovered his bereavement certainly fell on the other side of the spectrum. Indeed. The entire winter had been a quiet one for him, his main post by Tondee's and the pictures of fallen women serving as his meditation background. But tonight at Tondee's Tavern the Council of Safety decided to assemble there. They termed it an "emergency meeting." Joseph was in no mood for rambunctious men; he hoped they would leave the tavern soon after they arrived. Tondee placed the podium by the far side of his pub, waiting for the president, the pompous but well-respected George Walton to take the stand. The room started to fill in, and Joseph was surprised to see the constituents who comprised the support: wealthy aristocrats (all of course recognized him despite his bushy beard and unkempt attire), land laborers (those that protected Percy and fed him with Joseph's stipend), family men (even those who have settled in Georgia for less than a year), wild youths (a few of *terrible* repute), Christians, Jews with their black eyes and protruding profiles, and even a couple of avowed atheists (they refused to recognize the Pope or God).

In America, thought Joseph, a motley crowd such as this is necessary if the colonies are to achieve independence.

His father would never have deigned sit in a room with *lower classmen*. And Jews? Since he was a child, he heard nothing but of Jews plundering the state, forming conspiracies, hiding jewels in their fringed garments, the backward ways of the Catholics with their *rites* and *saints*. Not to mention the diseases of the laborers, those who never bathed save for Christmas or the eve of their wedding. It was dull to him, especially now when he considered how wrong he had been about Mordechai Sheftall, the one Jew Eddings probably cursed as much as Haman cursed the original man of the same name during the reign of exotic kings in ancient Persia.

But now with his father gone, truly, Joseph reasoned, his presence in Tondee's can serve no ill, can cause no *shame*. It had been Mordechai after all who appointed him the captain of the *Liberty* and delegated responsibilities to him, unlike his father who had, for years, either coddled him or assumed he would take to the law. It had been Mordechai who demonstrated that a son *could in fact* participate *alongside* the father—did he not even transfer some responsibility to his son, Sheftall Sheftall, who, only of late, was perhaps growing a hair on his white chin and a few inches above that of a young girl?

President George Walton's voice forced Joseph out of his mind's expanse and into the sphere of Tondee's. The matter tonight was the imminent confrontation, no doubt, between the British war ships headed for Savannah and the inhabitants of the city itself. (My goodness, I can't hear a thing; won't those two stop jabbering?) What's that? That's right! Georgia plans on enforcing the Continental Congress law of non-exportation—which stipulates that no American supplier can export to the British. The council's members had now to deliberate. What to do? If the British are refused, will they use force? The noise in the bar reached incredible levels, but from what Joseph could gather, most of the men (who had certainly disagreed on many matters before) seemed to be in agreement. Walton pounded the podium with a half-filled whiskey bottle. (By God, he should be wary! Lest it crack!)

"I have received a unanimous voice from the Council: we hereby *affirm* our commitment to the non-exportation agreement!"

"Hear! Hear!" the crowd bellowed.

Joseph swallowed the last bit of whiskey left in his glass and made way for Mordechai Sheftall, who, having agreed to meet at Tondee's, nevertheless refused to drink with his compatriots.

*

"You see, Frances, Wright *deliberately* chose Noble Jones and Joseph Clay for the meeting because they are gentiles."

"You are wrong. He chose them because they had previously shown sympathies to the loyalists, whereas *you* have *always* remained steadfast in rebellion."

Mordechai knew his wife's intuition was on target, but still felt slighted by Wright's *obvious* disregard for his *superior* position. For a moment consider: when seeking to address an organization, does not one invite the President before his inferiors? To wit: does not one first speak to a father before a son? The reasoning is simple! Yet his wife's coherent response to his suspicions somewhat eased his mind. Somewhat.

The British naval ships have arrived, and now Wright was trying to maneuver his way about the non-exportation agreement by *backhand* dealings.

"You need not worry, Mordechai. Noble Jones is one stubborn fellow who will not allow Wright to convince him to behave in opposition to the Council of Safety."

"Yes. But if I know Wright, he'll offer some type of generous plan for their loyalty. It will not be the first time he utilized this tactic, Frances."

Frances sat silently pondering what Noble Jones would do in that case.

*

Noble Jones and Joseph Clay knew Mordechai would want a repeat of the conversation verbatim. Uneasy, the two followed the new black butler into Wright's grand parlor, noticing they were not chaperoned by Eddings, the detestable prig who spread rumors that Mordechai poisoned Habersham. Only a fool such as Eddings even considered the possibility—since Mordechai was most conspicuously in Charleston that day.

"Please, take a seat gentleman," Wright began, removing a pipe and inserting tobacco with his thumb and forefinger. "I pray you don't mind, this habit has begun to increase in both intensity and duration."

Both men nodded their heads; *on with it.*

"Allow me to share with you a development of which you may or may not be fully aware: three warships have joined the *Tarmar* at Tybee. One of these vessels (named the *Raven*, a most glorious title for a British ship, I believe) shall be stationed in Savannah for the duration. The other ships wish to purchase supplies and provisions, after which they will be on their way."

"Pardon me for interrupting," said Noble Jones (clearing his throat), "But I am afraid these vessels will find not a single Georgian will engage in trade. The embargo is still in force."

"As I am aware." Wright couldn't suppress his resentment, "Your bravado is quite impressive, Noble Jones, if I might so say. The embargo is *illegal* and therefore *unenforceable*. According to *your* law, the Jew you report to must first authorize the presence of ships in Savannah's seaports! Has it occurred to you, Mr. Jones, that the ships now docked in Savannah have *no intention* of departing without supplies?"

Noticing Noble Jones' countenance deeply sour and Joseph Clay's legs beginning to shift rapidly, Wright softened his tone: "I have been assured, numerous times, gentlemen, that their intentions are *most* peaceable. They wish to pay fair market price for their purchases. They will pay in sterling if you so desire. Think of the opportunity to the colony sirs! Most assuredly, if citizens of Savannah comply with these wishes, all will be well. No doubt. But note: I cannot ensure that the warships will not use coercion. They have the capability to take what they desire by force, and if circumstances lead to it, they may very well—"

"I thank you for your diligence, Governor Wright," Joseph Clay suddenly said, addressing James and looking at Noble Jones. Jones, understanding the situation, immediately rose to his feet and stated, "We shall deliver your message to the Council of Safety." (*You mean the Jew,* thought Wright.)

"Yes. Do that. Make sure they are aware, particularly the President of the Parochial Committee (who I have heard decided to enlist his *child* in his most obstinate rebellion) that Georgia is, and yet remains, a loyal English province. He should be aware of that, as his father most certainly was."

The two men slightly nodded, curtsied out of duty more than respect, and turned their backs to Wright's slight smirk, which he permitted himself feeling somewhat vindicated after the shame of the last months.

I choose you, Joseph, because you have the temerity and the courage; I choose you because only you can carry your pistol like a weapon of war and not flinch; do not despair of your father; his unhealthy lifestyle hastened his death. Right now you must put your heart aside and think with your head! The cause needs you. Desist not.

These were his words to me that evening. These were the words that finally settled the whiskey and turned me sober. *Only history will dictate who is to live in infamy and who in glory.* Another line to ease the throbbing pain in his heart. Despite his origins, the committee of Christ Church was wise in choosing Mordechai; he knew how to speak to men. Some cynically believed he was posted for the position because of his well-known generosity. It was common knowledge the man donated large sums to the cause, with a rare purity, shushing all mouths that accused the Jew Sheftall of avarice. Others theorized the man was elected in case of defeat—to have a Jew serve as scapegoat was quite convenient. Joseph didn't want to believe these vicious rumors and maintained merit was the chief basis of Mordechai's ascendency, and if it was not believed by the anti-Semites of the town, then perhaps some truths will always be denied.

"We must not waste a single moment," Joseph turned to Noble Jones. The two quietly continued down the street holding a piece of paper only the two had read and then burned.

*

Wright took his breakfast that morning with his family in a rare moment of domestic serenity. The biscuits were deliciously warm and the butter melted evenly across the thin crusted layer. The new cook was astonishingly skilled; the butter was churned quite well. The mornings still quite chilly, his family preferred tea and strong coffee to warm their bones. The latest velvet waistcoats were fashioned for all the males; and the females donned burgundy cloaks from the same Parisian garment houses the French aristocracy was known to frequent. Wright read the headlines from the *Gazette* with his usual indignation, this time smoking bits of his pipe between turning the pages. Johnston was fond of reprinting papers penned by those who attend the Continental Congress in Philadelphia, the same men who should be hanged for treason according to most British statesmen. Johnston even printed a very controversial opinion piece, purportedly written by a woman, supporting abolition—the cessation of slavery in America. *That* was the *most* preposterous idea Wright had read throughout his years in Georgia, and by George he read *many* a foolish op-ed. Liberals littered every country, and America had its fair share.

The butler announced the delegation of loyalists now arrived for a session in his grand estate. His wife and children were to be occupied elsewhere; the grounds were extensive. The remaining staff attended to the men: removed coats, straightened lapels, gathered paraphernalia, and ushered them into the parlor. Five rows of six chairs faced the portrait of King George the Third, the latest rendition of the Regent in all his glory. Commissioned by Sir James Wright upon his knighthood, the painting hung with the same gravity as its subject; the fixtures of light illuminated the luminous wig of the Regent and reflected the red coat of its bearer with a grandeur few words could describe. The men sat patiently before Sir James Wright took to his seat; the butler was stoking the fire across the room, and the mantelpiece boasted another portrait—of Queen Anne—that caught the eye of many loyalists as well.

Just as Wright walked in, this time with a grandiose wig fashioned in Paris but designed specifically in London to match his bright red waistcoat (resembling the hue of the painting), Joseph Habersham and a few riffraff from the Sons of Liberty shuffled in and burst on the crowd. Joseph ran to Sir Wright and pointed his rifle directly at the governor's left heart chamber.

The crowd froze; mouths were agape; the men were aghast.

"You are now a prisoner, Sir James. You no longer have jurisdiction over these men!"

"My word, Joseph! You must be mad! Put that pistol down this *instant!*" Flabbergasted and entirely perplexed, James could not believe his long-time friend and the son whom he helped raise could point a weapon of war at a representative of the King!

"I daren't."

Noble Jones pointed his finger at Wright, "Make no sudden movements, sir. The Council of Safety voted (unanimously) and agreed—you are to be placed under house arrest, effective now."

The crowd began murmuring, afraid of making sudden movements. Joseph, afraid of mayhem, pointed the pistol at the crowd. "Silence! This is the law in Savannah!"

"Law!" Wright spewed, nearly laughing in hysteria. "Law? It is high treason! Point that gun down, boy I say!"

"No, Sir. I will not. You are prisoner of Georgia now and I am its soldier." James simply could not make sense of the moment. Could it be? Could it be the world has simply gone mad and he was the only one who realized it? This boy, this *lad,* had been but a child a few years prior, listening to him *rail* on the *expanse* of rights provided to *ordinary* men who *happen* to own land in America, and any man, if he is so assiduous and painstaking may do so after some time (granted he was not a slave, which would be impossible anyway). And this is what came of those hours of instruction and indoctrination? A *soldier* of some "Safety Council"? Damned these men and that bloody Jew Sheftall! He was behind this all, he *knew* he was. How could the child of James Habersham, the most blaringly loyal former deputy of the colony of Georgia, commit this, this? This monstrosity!

"Joseph," he said bitterly, "you will hang for this."

Joseph, suddenly envisioning his father's deep disappointment in him, stated, "The Council has agreed to grant you and your royal councilmen paroles of honor, but under two conditions, sir. First, you are forbidden to leave the city, (apologies) and second, to likewise contact the ships in the harbor."

So this was the way the "Safety Council" solved their most trying issues—they simply forced compliance from those already in power! What was this if not a coup? But how could he resist? With the pistol pointing in his face and his family stowed somewhere in his mansion, Wright began to feel as though his feet were perhaps too minute to stand upon.

"Do you accept the conditions of the parole?" Joseph asked, almost in a whisper.

James could not utter a sound. He simply sat in the chair, legs apart, chin down and nodded his head.

So this was how Sheftall wanted it all, thought James. The colony of Georgia, once an oasis of loyalty to the British crown, was now a desert boon for the Whig party.

Wait on the Lord.

SAFELY STOWED

CATHERINE WILLOUGHBY STROKED HER LONG, auburn hair with a comb fashioned from boar hair. She was grateful she had no sisters to compare herself to, for she was most certainly the jealous type. Her green eyes sparkled with newfound passion in the looking glass as her handmaid, a Jamaican slave, looked on waiting for Catherine to issue an order. Catherine usually preferred hair styles that displayed her long neck, but today she was fond of all her hair and preferred to brush each strand at least a dozen times. The winter months were a bore, but she hardly felt it since her romance with Joseph sprouted. How she loved the chiseled features of his jaw! All her friends, those who knew of the liaison, were simply roasting with envy. Her mother and father, of course, were ignorant of the matter; it *must* be kept that way Joseph warned. His involvement in the rebellion stoked all the wrong responses in Tories and loyalists such as her father. *She* could hardly muster a thought on the subject. What did she care for politics? Catherine stood and straightened her linen gown, donned a heavy woolen shawl and dismissed her maidservant, tired of her glaring eyes boring into her back. She daintily walked to her oak bed, lifted the mattress just a bit, and removed the latest letter from Joseph, whom she hadn't seen since the late fall, after his father's most *inconvenient* death.

Dearest, loveliest Catherine,

How I long for our reunion! Your every feature is ingrained in my soul, and I can only sleep at night when contemplating your extraordinary grace. But this letter finds me most worrisome for your safety, dearest. Therefore, be patient, for I must apprise you of the situation in Savannah and abstain, if just for once, in enumerating your every perfection.

The British refuse to depart Savannah and a confrontation, I fear, is imminent. If it were simply a matter of tit for tat I would not issue a warning as I am wont. But hear me: The Council of Safety (which I am privy to their intentions) and the noble Whig landowners (those that are *most* influential, I assure you) passed a resolution to *burn* Savannah to the very ground rather than to let it fall into British hands.

I am now under the command of a most capable man, Mordechai Sheftall, who is stationed under the command of the notable Archibald Bulloch. We await orders any day—but my love! Flee northward if you can! Devise some plan with family or friends. Depart, my love, depart from this town! I shall not bear the thought of harm reaching your quarters or an inch of your radiant self so much as besmirched by the British onslaught, should it indeed come your way.

My divine sprite! Heed my words and simply disappear from Savannah.

I shall send word to you, my most exquisite fairy as soon as circumstances permit.

With my undying love,
Joseph H.

Catherine wondered just how she was going to convince her mother she had to visit her aunt in New York in February, when doubtless it was colder and more dangerous to travel in the North.

*

Levi gathered his trunks and his most precious property in the main quarters of his estate. The Negroes were to carry the loads onto the carriages at any moment. He glanced at his pocket watch—it was still early morning. Sarah ordered every housemaid about, forgetting to eat breakfast or taking to her toilette. The children were well-behaved, sensing the anxiety slowly building in the house. Levi stroked his beard, wondering if he had forgotten any important article behind. He ensued with a mental checklist: prayer-books, prayers-shawls, jewels, coins, portraits, journals, business-related paraphernalia, and clothing as well as provisions, of course. (The latter was his wife's main concern, but he reminded her of such as well.) His hair on his forehead was now mostly white, and he wondered how his brother's was still dark, even though Mordechai was both older and under just as much anxiety, be it against Levi's political stance notwithstanding. He motioned for his butler to begin the arduous task of loading the carriages. The rooms were locked; the beds covered with linens; the furniture dusted and overturned, the closets emptied, and the pantry locked. The slaves that could not escape were welcome to remain, but the house was ostensibly under lock and key. Levi held the key to his plantation in his hand, and decided it was time to speak to Sarah and the kids— the time had come.

*

Frances, not far from the scene, remained at her Broughton home. Incapable of disappearing and desiring to be of support to Mordechai, she prevailed to rely on an ancient text to relieve the angst building in her stomach: the Book of Psalms, which she referred to as *Tehillim*. Oh God! How King David's words seemed to prophesy the siege of these British war ships on Savannah! Frances read:

> *Though an army may encamp against me,*
> *My heart shall not fear;*
> *Though war may rise against me,*
> *In this I will be confident.*

An exuberant declaration of faith will serve me well now, she believed. She nearly began to cry when she recited, "Do not hide your face from me!" Continuing in this very fashion, Frances began to rock and sway, fearing and imagining the very worst. Suddenly, as though the spirit of the ancient king descended upon her, Frances felt an overwhelming calm fill her being. She then placidly stated, as though one who has overcome the greatest obstacle and climbed the pinnacle of a vast mountain:

Wait on the LORD;
Be of good courage,
And He shall strengthen your heart;
Wait, I say, on the LORD!

Frances read the entire book of Psalms that morning, as her husband took to his position in Colonel McIntosh's regiment overlooking the approach from Tybee. The children, wondering where mother had gone off to, sat beside her as she concluded her prayers with a heartfelt desire to donate more funds to the orphanage her husband supported, another sure way to win succor in the eyes of the Lord, as it is stated, "Repentance, Prayer, and Charity shall annul an evil decree."

Frances believed it was her duty to shield her husband from all evil and fervently beseeched the Lord, the Compassionate One, to accept her supplication on her husband's behalf. The one consolation she took was her successful attempt at shielding Sheftall from *this* particular battle. How long her protestations will last was uncertain, but in the least, she thanked God for the blessing of her eldest child, securing her household and her heart.

*

Mordechai pondered the mystery: no one knew just *quite* how he did it, but the scoundrel succeeded either way. Rumors had it the scene went as such:

James Wright had shrewdly requested his wife and family depart for the North to ease their sickly spirits; visitations to family members would cure their ills. The house arrest, of course, was primarily the governor's lot, so Mordechai and his compatriots saw no point in detaining Wright's "frail and most delicate wife," as he so aptly put it…. But that surely should have forewarned them! Alas, it did not. Wright played the jailed prisoner to perfection: he "succumbed" to the brunt of the shameful arrest with the grace of a true dignitary, placing all the jailors at ease.

3 A.M. it must have been…. James Wright, in the dead of the night, crept out of his palace. The jailors (boys really) were not only asleep, but drunk and heavily burdened with alcoholic stupor. (As the saying goes, if an invasion of Visigoths hit the shores, they would have walked into an Eden of a battle.) Through the same marshlands and backwoods Mordechai utilized for his own "misdemeanors" and "illegal activities," the aristocrat and statesman, very much like the fugitive, followed a clearing with a torch or without—no one really knew. How wretchedly bitter and cold was the eve, no doubt prevented even a heathen Cherokee or Creek from encountering the renegade governor.

Before dawn, very much like a rat seeking refuge, James Wright sighted the British warship Scarborough, *the greatest sight James had yet sensed since his arrival in Savannah as governor general. The flag upon the mast, even in dim light, filled his heart with a sense of utmost security and pride.* At last. *There, he chanced upon some British warmonger no doubt, who assisted the humiliated ex-governor (by ruling of the Council of Safety) into safe grounds—aboard the* Scarborough.

Captain Barkley, the pock-marked sailor with the scruples of a pimp, it was presumed greeted Wright with the full honors befitting a man of honor and rank. Safely stowed.

Mordechai simply *detested* the standoff. For two months ships laden with all kinds of goods lay motionless, and the British soldiers and their large fleet menacing the town did not make matters any better. The question was—when would the Savannahians give in to the Brits? For weeks now his wife barely slept at night, pacing the hallways, shifting her position in bed, rousing him time and again. Her family had lived in prosperity, and the notion of warfare frightened her beyond measure.

The standoff cost the town in pence, but the merchants (in possession of the goods) were loath to sell their goods to the fractious Brits. The sense of confrontation, however, was mostly military, not domestic—but that did not deter his brother from fleeing town, at least for now.

The man in charge was now General Lachlan McIntosh. Few recalled the man who had fought valiantly in Bloody Marsh with Oglethorpe back when Georgia was a burgeoning colony. Mordechai recalled his father Benjamin fought alongside the man when he was a chap fresh from England. At the time, of course, his loyalties were with the Brits. Time has changed all that; perhaps his wife's most obvious scorn for Wright and his ilk fomented McIntosh's animosity all the more. It was difficult to know. Most importantly, not everyone in Georgia deemed him fit for duty. He was an older gentleman, so that either spelled his doom or his mark of glory. Others were certainly up for the job, but McIntosh was promoted by the end of the day. Mordechai wondered if the compromise choice of McIntosh was wise; many suspected he was not up for the battle. His feet were too "frigid" as the rumors went. He was appointed Colonel of the Georgia Continental Brigade (GCB), but many stipulated that perhaps Button Gwinnett (the strapping man, a well-known brutish sort) were not a better choice after all, while the moderate Whigs preferred Samuel Elbert, an ingratiating prig by many accounts. Mordechai didn't see the point of division within the ranks—they had to channel their energies to wage war against the Redcoats—a goal McIntosh as well as every Georgian man or woman was keen on, regardless of political leanings. In the least, McIntosh had seen battle, and perhaps had grown wiser with age.

Joseph was busy composing another correspondence to his sweetheart, and Noble Jones, an unattractive youth with an acne-ridden T-zone, cleaned the chamber of his rifle once again. The lads, young men really, joined GCB out of sheer ideology. No one could assume, even for a moment, that the two were interested for any monetary gain—there was little to be had in the armed forces, and the two had plenty of financial resources of their own. Despite their rebellious natures, the families did not entirely disown either one. Remarkably, even local fighters were serving largely on good faith, the general economic hardships being what they were—little money coming in, trade at a standstill, families fleeing, and the threat of war. This was exacerbated by Georgia's issue of new currency; it was not often honored elsewhere. Consequently, the

Provincial Congress (in lieu of Wright's assembly) could offer little incentive to outsiders to join the militia. What would a South Carolinian do with the new Georgian currency? A soldier's wife would have him hanging by the ears if that were his pay!

Mordechai, hoping to bolster the value of the new coinage, had begun dealing almost *exclusively* in it. Frances warned him, as did his solicitor, that perhaps this was not the wisest use of his funds. Nevertheless, Mordechai deemed it just; furthermore (and this truly irked Levi), he loaned substantial amounts (in sterling) to the Provincial Congress—much of which Mordechai was glad to learn defrayed the costs of the war (particularly the soldiers' fees, which he waived). A shrewd investment it most certainly was *not*; indeed, if the Provincial Congress so much as collapsed, if the war was all but lost, every last shilling would be lost to him forever. *But I am investing in the rights of man! Who can put a price tag on such a priceless gift? I am willing to incur the reward at great personal risk.*

Mordechai unwrapped his phylacteries, the specialized leather encasements (boxes really) containing specific portions of the Holy *Torah* or Bible, round his left forearm and center skull. The sun firmly in the horizon, Mordechai deemed it time to recite his early morning prayers. Lennox, Percy, Jones and Joseph (his crew of men) observed the Jew proclaim the oneness of his Lord: "Hear O Israel! The Lord our God, the Lord is One." He slowly whispered the prayer, meditating on the meaning of each word, cognizant it may be his very last time declaring the *Shema* prayer, God's authority over the Universe, as well as his personal obligations toward his Host. Savannah's future, the impending battle, all was momentarily suspended—and the supplication of centuries of wandering Jews was his entire focus. His mind entertained no else.

Joseph Habersham thought the phylacteries lent Mordechai an authoritative air and was momentarily at peace when Mordechai donned them. *Maybe his Lord will protect us. We could use all the help we can get*, he mused. The black slaves simply looked on with curiosity, the rest of the regiment thought him quite peculiar and perhaps even queer. But the men were busy conversing on the merits of McIntosh and the shortage of men to concentrate too long on Mordechai's strange habits.

Noble Jones cleaned his rifle one more time and stated, utterly discouraged, "Very nice of the South Carolinians to join (granted they won't gain much but shooting some Redcoats), one hundred in all, but that won't solidify our defense."

The men concurred. Spitting tobacco leaves behind him, Joseph piqued, "We could use some aid from our Bostonian brothers; they have more experience in battle than we."

"Well, then General George Washington would have deployed them, Joe." Noble Jones answered, picking a pimple on his temple.

"Stop, Jones. You'll make it worse," Joseph pleaded, completely disgusted.

Easy for you to say, pretty boy. Jones thought for a moment there.

"Well, General Washington sends his good wishes, and that's all we have for now—is our prayers," Mordechai said, wrapping his phylacteries sounding nonplussed.

Silence filled the encampment for a while. The men ceased pacing; they devoured their breakfast of quick beans and biscuits, grilled what they could find in the market (pork mostly), and drank their cider or rum. Mordechai decided to find a private place to empty his bowels, and the rest of the crew began to play dice. Scoffing a bit of biscuit and left-over pork loin, the men continued in this aimless manner. By mid-day, Noble Jones restlessly flung the dice and sighed, "How long are we to wait?" to no one in particular. His brows began to itch him, and the acne scars began to bleed. Joseph turned his face the other way, thinking of Catherine's clear and resplendent complexion. Mordechai's sigh surpassed Jones's, "It is hard to know. It all depends on Captain Barkley. He's running the show, no doubt."

"That abominable Brit has been prolonging this standoff for months! Why won't he just sail off?" Joseph asked, entirely perturbed the captain could not get a hint.

"The damned Brit wants his supplies—and he requests only that. But we refuse to sell to vermin—so why can't he go elsewhere?" Joseph reasoned.

"Because the damned Brit wants *our* rice and *our* goods—the avaricious beasts won't have it any other way," Jones answered, a tone of bitterness clinging to his tongue.

"Well, Captain Barkley can go to hell first—we're not selling a grain of cocker-spaniel's droppings to the man!" Joseph retorted, angry at the gall of the British Captain. The men all laughed heartily, enjoying the imagery of Captain Barkley eating shit. As the guffaws died down and slight smirks settled in their place, a loud tone roused the camp; someone sounded the alarm!

The men quickly gathered their belongings, wondering what the alarm portended. A messenger on horseback galloped towards Mordechai's group, shouting repeatedly, "The British have captured the rice boats! All men report to Colonel Bulloch!"

Mordechai and his crew began marching toward Bulloch's camp, about one hundred fifty yards to the east. Their captain had left them waiting like sitting toads in a pond for long enough; they wondered: what would his orders be?

Captain Bulloch, tall, lean, and by every measure exceedingly handsome, mounted his steed to witness the rice boats and their captives. Damn! He thought. *Just Damn!* All those dozens of ships, with *thousands* of pounds of rice, maize, sugar, flour, and other key supplies had been confined to port, and the men who *should* have been stationed round the boatyard (*protecting* the provisions) have been deployed elsewhere! (McIntosh's fatal error!) And how in bloody hell's name did those cock-eyed, lousy-teeth British soldiers maneuver past the channel *undetected?* Just *what* were his men doing all this time?! This spelled overt provocation! That bloody fellow James Wright surely conspired with Barkley! If the governor could escape his own enslavement in that fancy plantation of his, there was *no* doubt he could orchestrate this plunder! They mean to take over the city, if not the colony. This is a wrestle for control.

Bulloch wondered what he was going to command his men. Feeling entirely helpless, he decided it best to pump their spirits with rancor. Good old malice toward all.

Beyond that, he had to await orders himself. From McIntosh—the general who had few experiences in battle save for the war of Jenkins' Ear *years* ago with the founder James Oglethorpe—a point he was fond of reiterating and relying upon when making judgments or amusing dinner guests. God save us all, Bulloch thought as he caught sight of Noble Jones picking another pimple—this time on his long and wide nostril.

Colonel McIntosh desired, above all, to avoid a full-fledged battle with the superior naval warships under Barkley. War was bloody hell, he knew. But now, despite it all, Barkley and his men *impelled* McIntosh to do precisely what he hoped to avoid: attack. Having to first explain himself to his joint forces and his greatest critics, McIntosh called for a briefing. Button Gwinnett, his rival and a favorite among the merchant class, scowled at McIntosh (revealing rotted teeth)—*he* too doubted McIntosh's abilities to command. *We'll see about that,* McIntosh thought.

In a clipped tone, McIntosh (whose beard was overgrown and whose eyes were masked by protruding brows, his hair no longer the strawberry blonde of his youth) stated:

"Men. To my greatest disappointment the British warships *Hinchinbrook* and *St. John* snuck through our defenses. (A failure I am most ashamed to admit.) They anchored at Tybee without our notice and commandeered several merchant ships. The captain and his crew, Joseph Rice, was taken prisoner. They did not detect the enemy in time, supposedly under orders to remove riggings—it's not entirely clear at this moment. This development was only brought to our immediate attention by two American sailors who managed to desert the British."

Gwinnett listened intently, as did Bulloch and the others. The failure of McIntosh's militia was gross. (Who else were they to blame?) *Never under my watch,* Gwinnett begrudgingly believed. *He should be court-marshaled,* Bulloch reflected, noticing McIntosh stated "several ships" were confiscated, when in truth, the numbers were well above a dozen. Livid, the colonels could not comprehend how tens of vessels could sail undetected past rebel boats. It was beyond inexcusable in their estimation. *Absurd!* Sensing the frustration building amongst the ranks, McIntosh continued, with a graver tone:

"At ten this morning I had sent First Lieutenant Roberts and Captain Demere to demand the release of our men. They failed in their mission: contrary to the principles that guide civilized men, the Redcoats now hold them prisoners as well."

"That's *outrageous* McIntosh! And why are we standing here deliberating?! This is outright war! I say we sound the alarm and shoot the hell out of those British provocateurs—including Wright—down to hell I say!"

McIntosh nodded, "Just so, Bulloch. Just so. It's war."

"Fire!"

Battle of the Boats

Horses galloped across marshlands, between positions. Cannons were stuffed, men running close to shore behind makeshift ramparts, ready to fire. Veins pumping blood back to their livid and excitable hearts, Bulloch, Gwinnett, and McIntosh rapidly dispersed, ordering their ranks into various firing positions. Mordechai kissed his phylacteries, Joseph a portrait of lovely Catherine, and Jones his King James Bible. They awaited final orders from Bulloch, their superior commanding officer. The breeze from the shore dried the sweat building on their brows; it was warm for March.

On horseback, with expensive and indispensable binoculars, Bulloch surveyed the battle front: the open sea. He silently prayed, readied his men, listened carefully for the alarm, and yelled, "Fire at will! Fire at will!"

Immediately responding to Bulloch, Mordechai leaned on his knee, placed the musket comfortably, and took aim at the first Brit he could easily identify. The Redcoats were truly easy to detect with the glaring hue of their waistcoats—a source of pride, but also an obvious sighting hazard. Cannon fire erupted from the *Hinchinbrook* and *St. John* in rapid succession. The reverberations of the balls could be heard as far as Charleston some said days later. Mordechai's heart skipped a beat as the cannons landed only yards away. "Jesus!" yelled Jones. A few men fell; wounded by shrapnel. Dust filled the air, and Mordechai had to bury his face in the dirt. Between attacks, Mordechai took aim, wondering if the man who fell was due to his shots. The fighting continued in this manner for hours; eruptions from the Americans failed to hit the boats, and the fleet of British soldiers began boarding their ships, under orders to fire from a safer distance. Bullet fire harmed the British divisions, but not as significantly as McIntosh desired.

Joseph began yelling in the heat of battle, pointing at the vessels—"They're retreating!"

Mordechai ceased filling his musket with bullets and took note. Indeed! The British were content to depart Savannah, but just like that?

The Americans didn't suffer many casualties thus far, and the British only a few. But still! The battle was over? So soon?

"Something must be amiss," Mordechai stated. "They wouldn't just depart before the battle has been declared won or lost!"

Joseph yanked Mordechai to his side. "They are escaping with merchant boats—I *know* it! Why else would they flee? They *cannot* escape with all those pounds of provisions!"

Lennox and Percy were utterly confused. If no blood was shed, wasn't that preferable?

Utter mayhem ensued. Joseph was prepared to swim and burn British boats all on his own. Ranting and flailing his arms, Joseph cursed McIntosh for allowing the Brits to retreat. Mordechai tried to calm him down. Percy and Lennox stood, awaiting orders.

Bulloch began galloping toward his men. "Hold fire!" he hollered. "We are to await the orders from the Council of Safety."

"What? Damn this! I'm going," Joseph said, brushing Mordechai aside.

"Nonsense! We must wait!" Mordechai said, catching up with Joseph.

His face all sooty and his breeches torn by the knees, Joseph barely looked back at Mordechai.

"For what?" He mumbled. Realizing Joseph would not be restrained or persuaded otherwise, Mordechai followed the lad through the battlefield, hoping to avert a major catastrophe, fearing his impetuosity.

Like a blindox ready to gore at any provocation, Joseph began preparing a small boat. He ran to the ammunitions depot. *Where's all that gunpowder?* Hurrying along and glad Mordechai chose to join him, Joseph barely noticed two horses galloping passed him toward Bulloch with a parchment of paper. Bulloch read the letter, nodded, and sent for Captain Oliver Bowen, Joseph's co-captain of the infamous *Liberty*. Bowen, long loyal to Joseph, caught sight of his friend with the Jew preparing a boat for departure. *It's time to take action,* Bulloch thought, *and I know just the right men to accomplish this,* he mused.

Oliver Bowen pulled Mordechai and Joseph aside, "Come with me! I need your help!"

Joseph, entirely bent on his own plans, was at first quite loath to abandon them.

"Trust me!" Oliver said, looking Joseph straight in the eye. With little time to question his friend, Joseph followed Oliver in the *Liberty* toward the *Inverness*, a merchant ship. The plank was lowered from the *Liberty* onto the *Inverness*.

"Take this!" Bowen ordered. Mordechai, Jones, Percy, and Lennox held torches in their hands, yet unsure of their use. Bowen began to throw petrol across the planks and stern of the *Inverness*.

"What the hell are you doing?" Joseph asked, aghast. "This boat contains thousands of pounds worth of deerskins and rice. This is madness! Utter madness!"

"These are our orders, Joseph. You have to trust me." He repeated once again.

Mordechai and the men began to set the *Inverness* ablaze; rice and provision, hide and barrels of cotton all meant for exportation burst into an inferno. Oliver hastily sent the vessel drifting toward the commandeered rice boats, the *St. John* and the *Hinchinbrook*. The wind at first carried the burning *Inverness* towards the confiscated vessels.

James Wright, atop the British warship, stationed and buoyed about twenty yards away, stared in amazement as *the Inverness'* sails began maneuvering the boat toward the, as of yet, untouched rice boats. Barkley, hearing his name in frantic succession, ran to the helm and grabbed Wright's binoculars.

"By God, they're mad! The *Inverness* is worth thousands of pounds in cargo! And to set it ablaze! Your Savannah men are mad, I tell you!"

Wright suddenly realized the purpose of the conflagration. "They are no fools, Barkley. They mean for the *Inverness* to serve as a weapon, Captain. See—how it sails toward the *Hinchinbrook* and *St. John*!"

Horror-struck, Captain Barkley now understood what Wright meant when he said the rebellion has cost the Americans their minds and their sanity. How wealthy were these merchants and how sincere in their rebellion? It was now becoming clear.

Citizens of Savannah began to crowd around the bay, watching in the early twilight hours as the fireball of a vessel sailed toward Tybee and the confiscated rice boats. The stench of rotted wood and the billowing smoke filled the lungs of Joseph and his crew aboard the *Liberty*. Even Frances on Broughton Street left her home—what *was* that stench? Neighbors, Negroes, Church members, and those who had not abandoned their homes began marching toward the shore. Hannah Minis and her siblings, glad Phillip did not battle, Sheftall Sheftall, Rebecca McIntosh, and Johnston (eager for an eye-witness account of the Battle of the Rice Boats) and any curios onlooker—all flocked to Savannah Bay. The *Inverness*, heavy and rapidly deteriorating, suddenly veered off to the side, the sails having been burned and the breeze having died down. It ran aground. The Savannahians were terribly crestfallen. All that deerskin gone to waste; all that for nothing.

Wright and Barkley sighed in relief, as the burning boat harmlessly consumed itself.

"Damn! We should have set the boat ablaze after some time! That was an error, Bowen. We should have—"

"Listen," Mordechai interrupted. "We have no time to find fault. Let the *Inverness* serve as our cover. Let us burn the *St. John* whilst we can!"

The men aboard the *Liberty* quickly prepared a smaller ship, more of a paddle boat, and filled it with gunpowder.

"We must work rapidly; the boats are retreating at a faster pace than we initially presumed," Mordechai whispered. *We're running out of time.*

Frances held her hands by her mouth. Hannah Minis was crying. *Where was Mordechai? Is he dead? Is he hurt?* Frances, unafraid to express her fear, cringed at the sight of the fireball in the bay. "My God! Oh God! Where is Mordechai in all this?" Just as she felt no longer comfortable watching the horrific scene before her, particularly the smoldering *Inverness* now a globe of flames, Bulloch's men came rushing through on horseback, "Stand Back! This is a battleground! Return to your homes at once!"

Frightened, Frances rushed back home with Sheftall in tow. *Hashem,* the lad prayed, *watch over Aba! Protect him. Send Angels to safeguard his every step. Please Hashem! Have pity on my poor mother!*

*

Captain Barkley and James Wright witnessed the botched plan from the safety of their vessel. Wright, exhausted and tired of being confined with British soldiers, gazed at the burning boat with an overwhelming sense of numbness and loss. The boat had somehow gained more symbolic meaning than he had anticipated. All those years in Savannah—were they too gone to waste like the rice and deerskins board the *Inverness?* Had he too amassed hundreds of acres and black hands to watch it all burn? Is one's labor all for the sake of oblivion?

"Retreat!" Broken for a minute from his self-pity, Captain Barkley overwhelmed his crew with the command to disappear from Georgians' sight. "Retreat! Not a minute more am I to remain docked anywhere near those ruffians and madmen of yours, Wright." He continued, hollering between his thick hands, "All commandeered rice boats and British warships under my command are to begin sailing North immediately! (Sound the alarm, Wright.) Retreat!"

James listlessly wrung the alarm, moving about in a daze.

"We're done here," Barkley said, witnessing James barely registered his words. "We have all we wanted. We waited for

378

those Georgians of yours to open trade with us—having denied the British Crown, we've simply garnered what was truly ours by maritime law. They were forced to succumb....."

Mordechai waited for the boat to near the *St. John*, a massive boat, slightly wider than the *Inverness* reputed to be worth thousands of pounds in sterling. Its breadth was immense, and the sails were all down. The men atop the vessel were downing the sails, and the co-captain by the helm was commanding his men about. Sailing on the small paddle boat was Mordechai alone—Joseph and the crew remained on the *Liberty*. Confident the water would quickly maneuver his small boat in the right direction and with the proper speed, Mordechai dusted the boat's interior with gunpowder and petrol. He ordered the men to shoot the torches onto the boat. He jumped into the frigid water just in time; the small ship was now ablaze and completely camouflaged by the *Inverness*. Lennox, with his mighty strength and strident arm, hurled the torches repeatedly hitting the stern of the paddle boat, now a sailing weapon. Mordechai felt his limbs freeze; the Atlantic waters still cool from the winter. Joseph grabbed Mordechai, and the men hurled him on board. Percy quickly covered him with warm blankets and helped him undress and don a clean and dry uniform. Bowen rowed the *Liberty*, together with Joseph at the helm.

Just as the Redcoats aboard the *St. John* were mocking the Americans and their folly, the burning paddle boat crashed into the *St. John*, exploding into a great ball of fiery smoke. "That's all the gunpowder put to good use, Joseph," Mordechai whispered, fairly warmed up. "Tis a miracle!" Lennox exclaimed.

The *St. John*, heavily laden with the confiscated goods as well as tons of ammunitions, gunpowder, British goods, and, most importantly, *Redcoats*, began to explode. At first, the rear, and then the fire spread to the cabins below. British soldiers stuck below deck began clamoring up, forgetting their belongings or friends. Pushing, shoving, yelling, men afire, piss on the floor and mayhem all commenced. Soldiers, some half-burning, began to jump overboard in a haze of hellfire and smoke. Many passed out from inhalation, and refuge was found for those lucky enough to escape.

"Fire!" Bulloch yelled, off his horse and by the very shore. Mordechai, now warmed and energized by the success of his mission, didn't miss a beat. Safely docked, the men returned to their stations and resumed musket fire. Mordechai aimed his musket, as did Jones, Percy and Lennox (not to mention Joseph who was firing before them all) at the beleaguered Brits. Hundreds of American soldiers aimed at the drowning men, annoyed many of them were out of firing range. Undaunted, Joseph once again boarded a paddle boat, and began to set sail toward the Brits, shooting them, yelling, "Down you go! You damn British fiends! Down you go! To Hell you go!"

American soldiers, those who realized their muskets could do little harm once the Brits waded toward the safety of their fleet, jeered at the dazed Redcoats as others cheered the burning boat, rice provisions, contraband and all.

The fire amid the *St. John* swiftly spread to the *Hinchinbrook*. "Cut the lines! Cut the lines!" yelled those aboard the *Hinchinbrook*. But it was too late. In the pandemonium, the sea officer failed to disconnect the thick tethers connecting the vessels—both the warships and the stolen merchant ships. The towing line connecting the boats was now an incredible hazard. The fire travelled quickly; the flames amidst the rice boat traveled so rapidly that yet *another* ship began to catch fire. The sky, long darkened by the black night, detonated with light as more and more rice boats began to catch fire and blow up in smoldering flames.

Four burning ships drifted back and forth in the Savannah seascape. A light show and a ballistic fire explosion lit the night's sky. Many Americans witnessed the flashes and orange sparks, awed by the majestic gusts of white light in the dark expanse.

Captain Barkley, sensing the Americans were unfamiliar with their own terrain, began sailing through a back channel with ten unscathed and unaccounted for rice boats—the remaining plunder. Surreptitiously, Wright set sail with Barkley that evening, as Barkley noted, "Let them rejoice over their spoils," a line of animosity covering his darkened face.

"They destroyed their own goods, for Pete's sake. They rejoice in defeating our purposes, Captain," Wright exclaimed.

"Rubbish. We've captured sixteen hundred pounds of rice— enough to feed my men until the upcoming winter! We've left them markedly poorer than when we first docked months ago."

"Is it all about your rice? Are you a fool? They have ousted their government!"

Wright barely comprehended Barkley's glee. To Barkley, barrels of rice was worth the wounded and dying men and the countless hours of confrontation. Wright, while escaping via the back channels of Tybee (and wondering just how McIntosh and his militia did not keep an eye out for their escape), bemoaned the loss of authority, the loss of his duties to the Crown:

Savannah is now free to do as she pleases, which she craved all along. I have failed the King! Oh! To consider I returned after that awful Stamp Act fiasco to restore order only to run off like a frightened slave in the dead of night. The Whigs will claim victory; McIntosh's ragged militia, Sheftall (that damned Jew, may God smite him!) defended Savannah after all. They are now an independent colony—they've freed themselves from my clutches.

What shall I say to Parliament?

*

General McIntosh shook hands with Bulloch and Gwinnett. The rounds of rum were freely dispensed that evening. Sheftall and Joseph claimed the honors that evening, warming the hearts of the locals, not to mention Frances and Sheftall Sheftall, who praised God for answering their prayers. Percy and Lennox were not invited to Tondee's to share in the toasts, but they too felt pride in defending the colony.

The air of success was tempered by the escape of the ten remaining rice boats, and the detained soldiers still aboard the British prison, a boat of treachery. The matter had yet to be deliberated, specifically the escape route of Wright and Barkley, the scoundrels who started the mess to begin with.

The wounded American soldiers were hailed as heroes, as everyone pondered the future of the colony. Joseph, exhausted, mustered the energy to pen a letter, and Mordechai mused aloud, cleaning his face with a bit of water, "The coward escaped to Boston, leaving his men to wallow in shame. Wright was wrong again—his colony was not defeated as he had envisioned." He sighed and kissed his phylacteries, noticing they were clean and ready to be worn on the morrow. "Goodnight men. I am most tired and eager to return home. God bless you all."

Frances gathered Mordechai in her arms that night—as Wright wrote in his journal: *This chapter in my life is firmly at an end. Georgia is now in Continental hands. God spare them all!*

DECLARE AND PREPARE!

"I'LL HAVE TO TELL THEM, you know."

Joseph held Catherine a bit longer. "You can wait, until the war is over. By then, your father would be more than willing, I am sure."

Catherine hoped Joseph was right, but she was afraid he was too optimistic. Her father maligned anyone associated with the rebellion, and her brother enlisted after the battle for Boston. Tensions ran high in her home, and the romance, as sweet as it was, ignited Catherine's anxiety. *What will I do if Father finds out?*

In a remote forest midway between Charleston and Savannah, Catherine and Joseph met after a long separation. Savannah now free of Wright's control was still mightily fortified and teeming with soldiers—the kind her father detested. But Joseph's embrace seemed to melt away any second thoughts or doubts, and she basked in his love. She threw her bonnet aside, too hot for layers on her head. The breeze was slight, but enough to momentarily soothe her.

"Let's cool off by the stream, Joseph. I'm just too hot!" Catherine suggested, aware of the indecency of her proposal. He lifted his brow. "How would we manage *that*?" She began to walk toward a brook and Joseph followed, eager to see how this fine lady would manage to lift her skirts high enough to wade in water and "cool off" as she so aptly put it. Amused, he began to chase her and she squealed, until she beckoned him to "turn around!" pulling off her pantaloons and splashing in the water, glad for the reprieve. Unabashed, he removed his breeches and waist shirt. He jumped in the water and began chasing her once again. Flipping her hands and screeching, Catherine tried to run away from Joseph, only to trip on a stone and cry out as she stubbed her toe. Joseph began laughing, holding his belly. What a sight! The girl's locks were all loose, her dress mostly wet, and her face the exquisite picture of sweet agony. "Let me see, darling, let me see…." Catherine didn't resist, her toe all red just where she put the most pressure with each step. He kissed her toe and she breathed in for a moment. "All better, no?" Joseph asked, with a glimmer of mischief in his eye. *How will I let father know of this?*

*

August was a steaming hot month that year. Tenants returned to their homes after the battle, only to settle outdoors most of the day. Children cooled off by the shore, and men and women congregated by the taverns near the bay. Tondee's was a favorite and always very busy. Archibald Bulloch headed there late in the evening, after the sun's glow faded considerably, allowing for some much-needed respite. His feet no longer burned in the intense heat at that hour, and the sounds of crashing waves calmed his nerves. Now the President of the Council of Safety, Bulloch enjoyed the authority he desired since the near botched campaign during March. Bulloch knew McIntosh's failures nearly cost the city its future, and he saw the effects on the economy. The confiscated rice boats, and the burned ones too, cost the city dearly. The army relied heavily now on private donators, especially the Jew Mordechai, who, despite rumors his estate was waning, donated hefty sums. Well, today he did not contemplate too heavily on the matter of the militia—he was too giddy with the scent of freedom. A parade of men followed behind him, the entourage eagerly anticipating a word from the President. Standing by the liberty pole opposite the tavern, Bulloch faced the crowd that gathered there that night. The bay splashed with awesome waves, and the ships docked by the bay offered protection from some of the stronger waves. The sky, midnight blue, was illumined by the yellow of the lamplights. He raised his hand, signaling for quiet, when the crowd began to cheer boisterously. He held in his hand a parchment, and it seemed to delight the crowd. Bulloch smiled and raised his other hand instead. The crowd was familiar with the routine—this would be his third time reading the parchment. Silence filled the vicinity, and he began:

"When in the course of human events, it becomes necessary for one people to dissolve the political hands which have connected with another, and to assume among the Powers of the earth, the separate and equal station to which the Laws of Nature and of Nature's God entitle them, a decent respect to the opinions of mankind requires that they should declare the causes which impel them to the separation."

The crowd began to hoot. Whistles and loud banging of jugs on walls and on the tables nearly drowned Bulloch's voice. Mordechai joined the men at this point, and heard the following words:

"We hold these truths to be self-evident, that all men are created equal, that they are endowed by their Creator with certain inalienable Rights, that among these are Life, Liberty, and the pursuit of Happiness."

Mordechai paused and tears filled his eyes. *To think that the world has finally learned the lessons of the Torah! The Holy Book espouses men treat one another as equals, even granting the Canaanite slave certain liberties. How the word of God has been delivered through this great Declaration! What I behold today will be for generations to come an inspiration for all mankind! How God ordained I should be privy to this great epoch in history. It is by far a great privilege. My heart swells with praise to the Lord! How America should come into being, but with the Divine Cause behind it all; it is willed by God. "Endowed by their Creator" such are the immortal words to be reckoned with by godless despots for eternity! How Mighty are Thy ways. As King David has stated, "This is the day God has brought into being, Let us Rejoice in this moment!"*

Bulloch noted Mordechai was in the crowd and moved toward the warrior. Mordechai Sheftall was esteemed by the armed men after his heroics. "Please read the rest, Mr. Sheftall." Bulloch moved a bit from the post and allowed Mordechai to resume Jefferson's words. Mordechai was suddenly overwhelmed by the honor and held Bulloch by the shoulder, whispering, "Thank you very much."

With gusto and with accompanied silence, Mordechai read the remaining charter. Women cried on each other's shoulders, wondering what the Declaration had in store for them all. While Mordechai read the famed words, the armed men knew their liberty would come at a high cost. The British garrison in East Florida threatened the safety of Georgia and the Carolinas. The Continental Congress issued a campaign for early September 1776, to outflank and destroy the small British force protecting East Florida—a mere one hundred and fifty men. Mordechai's calming words echoed in their ears, and the dancing in the streets lasted throughout the day, with cannons blasting well past midnight.

They were rebels all now.

*

Sheftall leafed through Johnston's *Gazette* one more time that evening. His father spoke of nothing but the Declaration of Independence for the past fortnight. Philip Minis, his father's trusted friend and comrade, spoke of much the same. The Congregation, which his father hosted under the aegis of "Mickve Israel" debated the implications of "pursuit of happiness." Will that include less governmental authority or more? What entails liberty? How will a new government be formed, once Britain succumbs, of course. *Will* America defeat the British powers—with Washington's army hanging by a thread, with men abandoning their posts? Unconsciously, they all realized the Declaration was an act of egregious *chutzpah*. What did this spell for the Jews? Will they be able to continue practicing? Will laws grant them their right to circumcision and the *kashrut* rituals? Philip argued the Declaration was not legally binding, that the Continental Congress ought to consider concrete laws; it was more of a statement. Few disagreed, save for Levi who believed the entire country was bound by the ethos of the Declaration, which is by far greater than law: it was an ideology. Supportive of the cause, Levi was encouraged by Minis and the others to join the armed forces, but he continued to decline. Sheftall wondered if he was playing it safe with the British authorities, but then again, few remained in power in Georgia. Philip opined that may be the case for the time being, but ultimately, Levi was more of the prudential kind; not all men were willing to bind themselves on the altar of liberty. Philip would have resigned to that stance as well had he heeded his wife's fears and paranoia. But Sheftall's father had long recruited many men, and among them one more he probably did not intend—his son. The *Gazette* featured articles and essays describing the battles, and Sheftall continued to read them. They all seemed immensely exciting in Sheftall's estimation. His father managed to dissuade him from battle, but Sheftall swore to himself it wouldn't happen again. Boys his age were enlisting—and why shouldn't they?

The Congregation of Jews was a potpourri of all sorts; most of the boys his age were forbidden from joining. Indeed, Sheftall realized his father was the anomaly amongst the Jews: most were willing to contribute with their wallets, but few with their lives. Many were older gentlemen, truth be told. But able-bodied men were fearful of the British authorities, having accustomed themselves to being subservient to great political powers. Those who emigrated from Holland were in the habit of obedience to all authority; who dreamed of bearing arms? Political leanings and preferences were topics of conversation, especially on the Sabbath during the festive *Kiddush* meal—the lunch after services. But who in Heaven's name considered loading cannons and muskets? A credo, a silent one, echoed silently amongst the crowd: observe in silence. See but remain unseen. The British were not famous for their clemency or their charity for rebels. Beheadings were not uncommon in London for nary a mischief-maker—what would be done to a rebel?

Sheftall absorbed all the *schmoozing*. But he knew his father subscribed to a different philosophy. Mordechai undoubtedly viewed the Cause as his moral duty; so Sheftall saw it fit to learn a few tricks from Joseph Habersham. It didn't seem too difficult to shoot a musket once Joseph demonstrated such on a lame duck in the forest. Joseph warned him though, "One wrong move, and you could end up like the farmer's son who ploughs with three missing fingers. You don't want that, take it from me. No girl wants a broken man, if you know what I mean."

Practicing by the forest became his new hobby—and his mother believed he had been learning Talmud with Philip, a fabrication Sheftall felt guilty of, but could not help himself nevertheless. It was a messy, dangerous business. But thrilling. He just felt bad for all those dead forest animals. *There must be a better way to practice on a moving target*, he thought.

*

Joseph rolled his sleeves and knocked on Mordechai's door. He was ushered into the parlor where, as on any typical Saturday morning, services were being held. Mordechai's house served as the epicenter of Congregation "Mickve Israel," and the prayers were coming to a close. Joseph naturally would have preferred visiting on a different occasion—but circumstances seemed to place his preferences aside; he didn't really enjoy considering the *Jewishness* of his friend. He wasn't entirely comfortable with the religion; after all, he *was* raised to believe certain prejudices, specifically the "blood-stained Jew." But the war had placed everyone's differences aside; all that mattered was their common goal: defeating the British. A year had passed since they battled Barkley's ships. The excitement of the rebellion waned with discouraging tales of defeats in the North. The British down South were a menace, and the Council of Safety—the interim government—was a mess. The men in power could not agree on important matters, and politics littered their advancement. The winter was harsh, and Catherine had been absent during the duration. Rumors James Wright was headed back didn't delight a single fellow, and fears the rebellion would fail sparked controversy even amongst the most enthusiastic. He fantasized about proposing to Catherine and not waiting for the end of the war. His gut told him it would protract. And now the latest news. Maybe Mordechai could shed light on its significance. God only knew he was at a loss.

Mordechai was praying at the dais and a commotion ensued. General Robert Howe, Continental Commander for the Southern Department, General Lachlan McIntosh, and Brigade General Samuel Elbert sauntered in. The doors remained open, and their carriages (most spectacular and driven by war horses of the most exquisite pedigree) were neatly parked by the entrance of the estate. Joseph recalled Mordechai requested his presence on this day and wondered how he had forgotten. A waft of some type of meat dish filled the air every so often; it smelled strongly of spiced beef or bean stew. Mordechai's children, dressed in white linen to match the spring's gossamer blossoms, walked between the men. His youngest held Mordechai by the shins, hugging him. The boy's curls reminded Joseph of Catherine's ringlets. The scrolls of the Torah were softly displayed on the front altar, and Mordechai commenced to roll them, very gently, back into their casings. Joseph knew the scrolls, made of deer-skin parchment, took many laborious hours to properly prepare. It contained all five books of Moses in ancient Hebrew text.

The prayers ensued and the Jews in the Congregation varied in their intonation. Some men originated from the Spanish towns, and their Hebrew had a Middle-Eastern inflection. Mordechai's enunciation of the prayer and of the reading had a German-sounding twist. Joseph was surprised Mordechai could issue such noises; he otherwise had no detectable accent in English. It was all strange, but quite, quite interesting. The few times Joseph tried to broach the subject of Jews and their ways with Catherine he was summarily requested to speak little of a godless people.

Robert Howe didn't intend to interrupt the services, but he was by far respected by Georgians as well as most North Carolinians. *What is he doing here?* Joseph wondered. The Jews shifted seats, honoring the men with ever-so slight bows to the head. In the shul, bows were reserved for the Lord. Howe removed his hat and patted one of Mordechai's children on the head. McIntosh sat beside Howe and bowed his head in reverence. Before long, the men concluded their prayers. Joseph noticed Philip Minis kissed the fringes of his shawl and folded it neatly before placing it in a beautifully stitched casing, undoubtedly his wife's needlework. Sheftall remained by his father's side, attending to the prayer books, kissing each one before returning them to the oak carved shelves. One man, a da Costa, kept handing the children sweets, and the women, who were separated from the men by an Oriental panel with lace screens, tsk-tsked the generous man.

Mordechai served as the first President of the Savannah's congregation and thus began addressing the crowd. "Evening services will commence at six in the afternoon. *Tehillim* reading in the house of Abigail Minis will ensue at four in the afternoon, and the Sabbath ends at seven twenty-four. I would like to call upon Major General Robert Howe of North Carolina, the honorable general who has serviced our country with fortitude to speak to the Congregation today in lieu of our usual sermon. Your attention please."

The crowd stood in honor of the general. Howe stood before the men and noticed the paint on the walls was beginning to peel away. The women removed the screen and Mrs. Sheftall held the hand of her youngest child. Howe felt his stomach grumble; it must have been that faint smell of bean stew.

He cleared his throat and began, "Ladies and Gentlemen. Thank you for opening your doors to my men—may we share many occasions together in peace and prosperity."

"Amen!" they answered, eager for a blessing from a gentile.

"Your humble host, I see, has neglected to mention a very significant commission (turning to Mordechai), as I see you are all in absolute befuddlement as to my being here. You can sigh freely; my men do not intend to baptize you all (laughter) or convert (more peals). I hereby announce, and it is my honor to do so, the appointment of Mordechai Sheftall as Deputy Commissary General of Issues to the Continental Troops in South Carolina and Georgia."

The crowd was stunned. A general in the army? Mordechai? Did they understand Howe? Frances burst into tears and the women began to comfort her. Her mother-in-law was shocked as well. Why had he not mentioned a thing to her? Were Frances's tears ones of joy or trepidation? Her husband had been serving all this time, how much of a difference would this make at the end of the day? Sarah hugged Frances and whispered, "We're so proud of Mordechai! This is a great honor!" Frances nodded, "Of course! I am just *overwhelmed*, that's all."

Mordechai noticed his wife was emotional and knew it probably had to do with their conversation the previous evening. She begged him to reconsider battling in Howe's army and to join her brother Joshua in Charleston where the situation was safer. He remained silent the entire evening, listening to her implore him over and over. *So this is why he was reticent! How can he refuse this now? The honor of serving was an ideal of his; it now came to full fruition. Oh! What's to become of the children, of me?*

After a brief moment of silence, the crowd clapped their hands and crowded round Mordechai, shaking his hands and wishing him much success or *hatzlacha*. Mordechai gestured with a wide hand, "Please! Ladies and Gentleman, join us for a celebratory lunch! The *Kiddush* and *cholent* will surely suffice for such a pleasant crowd!"

Frances had the Negro women prepare more platters of fruit and pickled meats. The men filed into the next room, blessed the wine, and ate a few pastries before heading home; their wives cooked fine meals and would be unhappy if their husbands did not partake heartily of their own cooking. General Howe remained as well as McIntosh and Elbert, curious as to what "kosher" food tasted like. Joseph remained as well, entirely floored Mordechai should keep the promotion a secret. He was also a bit famished.

"Mordechai! How the deuce did you keep this from me! What a momentous occasion! What do you people say?"

"Mazel tov—we say 'Good luck' like everyone else!"

Mordechai poured Joseph a cup of fresh cider and patted Joseph's shoulder. "I reckon you'll have to await orders now, son. No matter how impetuous you may feel, eh?"

Joseph nodded, smiling. *He's referring to the battle of the Inverness. Truly Mordechai steered us well that night. He deserves the post.*

Sheftall walked up to Joseph and whispered in his ear, "I shot three field rats dead the other day. That makes for twenty kills in three weeks. What do you say?"

Delighted, Joseph smiled and winked, "I say you're on a roll for an excellent position in the army; hopefully, your father will see to that."

Mordechai only overheard the latter half of the conversation and said, "What's that?"

*

Robert Howe surveyed the room and noticed Mordechai's estate was orderly. The room was grand without any ostentation. Howe's men were stationed in Habersham's estate, Wright's late go-to fellow. Habersham's estate was just as grand, but far more European in style. Mordechai's taste was similar to his personality—strong, but subdued. The walls were painted a plain ivory white, and few paintings pictured females draped or nudes, as Wright's estate surely had. His wife covered her hair with a bonnet that was rather simple, and the children were clean but not over-dressed, even for a Saturday. Howe noticed the Negro maidservants were calm and good-natured, a sign they were not mistreated. Frances encouraged the Negroes to eat first and then to continue working, a custom Howe believed dated from the time of the Talmud, if his studies were still fresh in his mind. She was not thin, but she was also not very heavy. Her features were not as Semitic as he imagined them to be; Mordechai's smallish eyes and elongated nose were far more Semitic in his estimation. Mordechai's half-brother was in attendance too—the fellow was tall, but with a bent back. He too contributed to the cause, but was known to purchase goods and sell wares to merchants regardless of their political affiliations. Not every rebel American read good into Levi's actions, but that did not deter the man. He was wealthy, and wealth came at a cost. *His* wife was young, with Spanish beauty. *These Jews don't all have similar features! It's as though you can find all kinds of beauties in one people, a product of their long Diaspora, I imagine.* Hungry, Howe decided to taste the warm *cholent*, a concoction of beans, beef, potatoes, barley and undoubtedly some other Jewish ingredients. He poured the *cholent* with a ladle into a wooden bowl and blew the hot vapor away, enjoying the rich aroma. "Sumptuous!" he stated, rather suddenly, to no one in particular. McIntosh overheard and decided to sample the ethnic dish. Mordechai took note the gentiles were eating from the special *Shabbos* meal and delighted in explaining its origin.

"I see you enjoy the *cholent!*"

"Indeed!" the men stated. (Joseph now gathered round and stole a few bites himself.)

"How is it prepared?" Howe inquired, forgetting his manners for a minute and chewing with his mouth open to let out the steam.

"The exact preparation is unbeknownst to me, gentleman. It is my wife's secret dish. However, suffice it to say that the pot remains over a low flame over night, from sunset until lunch."

"Why ever so?"

"Cooking is forbidden," Sheftall chimed in, desiring to be part of the adult conversation.

"Is that so?" McIntosh said, flabbergasted. *What is forbidden in cooking? Strange laws, but better not to wonder too much. It won't make much sense, no matter the reasoning.*

"How about sampling the roasted chicken? This dish *I* prepared!" Mordechai said.

After lunch, Howe raised his glass and toasted Mordechai, with Frances standing by her husband's side.

"Today we celebrate Mordechai's achievements and contributions, but few, I am sure, truly know the extent of his civic contributions. Let me say today, and let it be known, that Mordechai himself personally saw to it that our men never lacked the supplies they required, often at his own expense. Whole brigades have been clothed and fed—because of his generosity. He has even dissolved his personal assets for the noble purpose of investing in Georgia's new currency. For every transaction, Mordechai *insists* on collecting a receipt. This is to insure against any misuse of public funds or corruption. You have gained my gratitude, and I know the new position of Colonel will further recommend you to all mankind. A special toast to Frances as well, your most devoted wife (turning to Frances). By George! She can cook a hearty meal!"

"Hear! Hear!"

Mordechai's cheeks colored, and not only due to the

consumption of wine. Most of his family members were completely unaware of his financial business or private transactions. The crowd, particularly his son Sheftall, whose eyes radiated a glow of admiration, and Joseph Habersham, whom Mordechai endeavored to influence, were eager to hear a word from him. *So be it.*

"First, I must thank you for your kind words, General Howe. However, I do believe this excessive adulation is uncalled for. While it is true I have dedicated my very soul to the struggle of independence, I do not believe this is so extraordinary. The Jewish people have, for generations, lived under the crucible of despotic rule, both cruel and unusual. For centuries, we've succumbed to the will of numerous Kings bent on demoralizing us. Forbidding us from exercising our freedoms, we were forced (and my brethren surely still face this existence) to limit our liberty. Yet here, in the future that we are all building today, in America, one may freely pray to one's god without fear of persecution. One may own land and enjoy its bounty. I am grateful for all America has offered me, and I am prepared to risk everything I own to secure that prospect for future Americans— regardless of creed. I am grateful for the warm welcome of my gentile friends (turning to Wereat, who nodded his head in agreement) and neighbors. May we succeed in our mission and spread the wings of freedom to all people. Surely God will bless us all with His great beneficence if we share in our joy! Amen."

General Howe had to suppress a tear, in spite of himself, and McIntosh stood to shake Mordechai's hand.

Frances looked on and smiled bittersweetly. *How can I not rejoice? Look at the Grace God has bestowed on my husband. No matter what new responsibility this position now entails, my sole endeavor is to support Mordechai. There is little left for me but to ensure the happiness of my home. May God grant me strength!*

*

The Generals left after some time, but Joseph remained behind. He did not forget his initial purpose in calling on Mordechai. He just had to discover the truth, and he thought perhaps Mordechai might shed light on the mystery eating away at the heart of Georgian politics:

The death of Archibald Bulloch.

STONES OF RANCOR

JOSEPH MARCHED FIFTEEN STEPS. He placed a white stone where his feet stood moments before. He then marched another fifteen steps. Another stone. *This is where the men will battle their way to justice.* It was decided: a duel would determine the fate of the accused.

It was a bloody mess. McIntosh accused Gwinnett of murdering Bulloch—so he could gain the coveted post of acting governor of Georgia, Wright's American replacement. Most Georgians respected Governor Bulloch, but the man had mysteriously died one night, dead in his bed. Even a popular figure has his enemies, Joseph knew. Bulloch was too young to die from stroke; foul play was immediately suspected. Mordechai refused to take sides in all this, but McIntosh had a way of recruiting members; Joseph found himself embroiled in the mess, partly because he didn't really stomach Gwinnett; the man was arrogant with an all-too insatiable drive for power; the more he had the more he craved, very much like the gigolo. Gwinnett knew McIntosh could stir trouble, having a backing of his own, so he arrested McIntosh's brother under the charge of "treason" as a guarantee McIntosh wouldn't stir up too much trouble. *In all this damn mess, the British are mocking us in Parliament—internecine warfare will wipe out America they predict. If these political bickerings continue, then perhaps their predictions are correct.*

But Gwinnett was embroiled in his own campaign to destroy McIntosh. May was a horrendous month, Joseph recalled.

"Relinquish command, General. Your men failed three times to take Florida from the British. Do you think your pathetic army of Jews and Negroes will succeed under your abysmal command? I say, Relinquish!"

McIntosh glared at Gwinnett, full of loathing for the governor who assumed the role of commander-in-chief. Was it also McIntosh's fault the British infiltrated their intelligence and learned of the planned raid? Perhaps there were moles in the Continental Congress! Was he to blame for the misinformation as well? Weren't only 150 men garrisoned in East Florida? Many more bombarded their men, to be sure!

"You scoundrel. I refuse to step down. I am the General and I shall lead this expedition."

"If you think your men will follow a half-blind man into battle, you are highly mistaken. Your expertise in battle is appalling—"

McIntosh's nostrils flared, revealing dark hairs. "May I remind you, Gwinnett, that while you were sucking your sore thumb in the cradle, I was in Bloody March, fighting alongside James Oglethorpe!"

Gwinnett chuckled. "How many times do you plan on falling back on that pathetic glorified nothing of a battle, sir?" Gwinnett turned around and raised his head, his nose high in the air.

Joseph remembered the gnawing heat of those May mornings, waiting for orders. But the two men, with their coat of arms and fancy sabers, could not agree on a single damn thing. Each man refused to step down, despite the growing agitation on the battlefront. Joseph once again reminisced, as he counted the steps between the stones. One. Two.

"Attack!" Finally, the Council of Safety appointed Samuel Elbert in command, and his booming voice filled the void. Joseph's party, which included his superior Mordechai and Percy, Lennox, and Philip Minis, as well as Noble Jones, all responded to Elbert's final word. Muskets fired, and bullets penetrated their limbs almost simultaneously. Joseph never looked too deeply at the British soldiers he battled; to him, it was kill or be killed. Mordechai targeted each soldier as though he were the only enemy in sight. The others pretty much fended for themselves. Percy took a few shots to his upper arms without letting it stop him. The British swarmed at their company. But Mordechai's men were unprepared for the terrain.

"God damn it! My foot! My foot!" Jones yelled. Stuck in mud, through the thick marshlands of the Florida swamps, Jones's ankle twisted hideously. Crying suddenly, Jones froze, unable to muster the strength to remove his leg from the painful position. Mordechai ran to the lad, handing his musket to Percy.

"Take my shoulder and squeeze as much as you need to. When I count to three, I want you to breathe in deeply!"

Mordechai counted to three, and on that count, he lifted the disabled foot from the mud. Noble Jones screeched and jerked, squeezed and squirmed as though a child was born from his nether regions. "Jesus! Jesus!"

His ankle was twisted, and he was faint from pain.

*

Joseph recalled the endless marching, supporting Noble Jones with Mordechai, for days and days. Florida was mostly uninhabited, and the mosquitoes were enemies of greater danger than bullets at rapid speed. Men fell to fatigue; water was at short supply. Their mouths filled with sores, and soon no one had the energy or the strength, the morale or the drive to carry Jones. Useless, the man was carted on a wagon reserved for the dead or dying. Disease struck the American camps, as it did the British, no doubt. Men were collapsing in bogs swarming with alligator dung. If the thorns did not penetrate their dry skin, the alligator's thick hide grazed their legs and threatened their very lives. Joseph recalled his vision blurring and Mordechai's chanting to his God to save his soul and preserve his family from a similar fate in the hands of the cursed British. Mordechai could have sworn they were marching in circles, stuck in a labyrinth without end. After weeks of battling fatigue and near starvation and dehydration, Elbert could still not find his destination—the Promised Land: "St. Augustine."

Elbert called off the British invasion, and the men returned home, bruised, diseased, and defeated.

Gwinnett lost his title during the upcoming election—and he blamed it on McIntosh. *If the son of a Manchester hag had relinquished control, this whole mess with Elbert would never had ensued! The man was an inept fool who couldn't read a compass even if Newton himself instructed the man. Elbert was nothing but a neophyte in arms, without any suitable training, besides for a charming smile that won the hearts of all those Council of Safety buffoons!*

Mordechai returned to his post dejected at the abysmal lack of foresight of the city's main administrators. On more than one occasion, he had realized men lost their lives for no good purpose. *This war is claiming more lives to disease than to musket fire! How could this occur?*

So that's why, Joseph reasoned, Mordechai wouldn't involve himself in the duel: he detested them all. *Well! So do I, which is why I want to see them battle it out.*

After the botched invasion, John Treutlen decided to call Gwinnett and McIntosh to task for the embarrassing and highly debilitating fiasco. The courtroom was filled with soldiers, some who had defected and secretly attended (well-camouflaged by the mass of men and women); Georgians were eager to see the new government at work. What would the outcome be? Would these big shots be fined? Would soldiers receive compensation for their losses? Would McIntosh or Gwinnett pay widows their husbands' debts? What would the new acting Governor arbitrate?

Mordechai, Sheftall, and Frances sat in the front row. Mordechai's cheeks were burnished red from the intense sun on those senseless marshes. *Compass, Map, and Foresight. Why were they lacking? Who will pay for Jones' long rehabilitation?*

Treutlen, a forbearing man with a respectable-looking beard, a formidable belly, and a sonorous voice, began, after adjusting his white wig with stiff curls:

"Let us begin with a few questions for General McIntosh. Sir, if you will."

McIntosh rose, and silence filled the courtroom.

Treutlen cleared his throat, "Is it true you failed to take the British garrison in East Florida three times in a row, prior to the failed expedition?"

McIntosh was riled. *What the hell has that got to do with anything?* "Yes, Sir. But if I may—"

"I am afraid, General, you may answer questions, not pose any of your own."

McIntosh nodded, humiliated for a moment.

"Is it true the then-acting Governor, Button Gwinnett of honorable mention, *insisted* you relinquish your rank and allow him to oversee the mission?"

McIntosh nodded. "Please respond, so our courier can chronicle the hearing."

"Yes!" McIntosh muttered, annoyed and suddenly riled. *Why am I on trial here?*

"Then let us establish this once again: you were busy refusing to step down and neglected to plan the invasion properly! Is this not so, General?"

McIntosh pointed an accusatory finger at Gwinnett and erupted, "You lying, scheming scoundrel! You left me little room to maneuver, and supplanted my position with the dimwit Elbert! Who's to blame?"

Mordechai was stunned at McIntosh's outburst. *I've never seen the man lose his temper. Perhaps there was truth to his accusation.* Gwinnett sat quietly, tickled by McIntosh's pathetic display of weakness. Everyone knows a dying rooster crows loudest, he mused.

The judge, Treutlen, began pounding the wooden desk, begging for order.

But it was too late. McIntosh stormed out of the crowded room, leaving all the widows with the same empty stomachs and vapid promises.

*

Joseph awaited their arrival. After the fiasco and all that animus building between the previous governor and general of Georgia, *there was only one way.* Joseph begged Mordechai to attend—most soldiers enervated and devastated by the senseless expedition were in attendance. Noble Jones with his crutches and Percy with his healing bullet wounds were there before McIntosh's company. Joseph would mediate the duel. *It had to be.*

But what did Mordechai argue? "Nonsense. These two men have undoubtedly caused more harm to this fledging colony than

I can enumerate. And you now want me to witness their mutual manslaughter? It would be far better if the two could speak to one another as two *humane* individuals. What would they gain by this infantile display of fortitude? Who shall shoot the other first? Should it be McIntosh? And then what? Will he surely feel at ease, now that his enemy is completely destroyed? And is this truly justice for all that we've suffered? Would it not be better if the two collected funds, perhaps from their own coffers, and relegated them to the public? I had nearly lost my wits on that march—and now I see why: our leaders cannot see eye to eye, nor can they lead this colony. *Imagine I ask a child to arbitrate between two infantile adults? What would the result be?"*

Such was Mordechai's comparison to Elbert's taking over the command from either the egomaniacal Gwinnett or the inflated McIntosh.

Joseph wanted to witness whose bubble would be burst that morning.

I counted the fifteen steps. That should suffice. Now all I must attend to is the muskets. I must ensure there will be no foul play.

General Lachlan McIntosh did not ask his wife or children if they deemed his judgment fit; indeed, he invited Gwinnett to the challenge, and the latter had agreed. McIntosh sat in his horse-led carriage recalling the insults and the humiliations of the past days—all due to Gwinnett no doubt. The townspeople no longer revered him as they had once, particularly since Bulloch died. *If only I had witnesses! I am certain Gwinnett poisoned the man; if I shall kill him today, I do so for Bulloch. For justice.*

Gwinnett purposefully delayed his arrival. *Let him wait.* Gwinnett kissed his poor wife, who had refused to kiss him back, too angry at her husband for neglecting to ask her opinion on the entire matter. "Who cares about this dead-beat general? Is it worth it all?" She muttered to herself, enraged her husband should pretend her existence did not depend on his; were they not one flesh?

Gwinnett arrived and noticed Joseph Habersham without the Jew beside him. Only those loyal slaves, the ones who never seemed to miss a battle scene, even when the Brits were not the ones threatened with being blown to bits. A crowd gathered round McIntosh—his few supporters. *There aren't many in Georgia. Most are probably here to support me, of course.*

"Do you think he is a good shot, Dr. Wells?"

Gwinnett winced when he considered the possibility of being wounded, or worse. His aide, who carried a satchel with a surgeon's knife, bandages, and some kind of opiate from the Creeks, wasn't really sure how to respond. "I should hope not, for your wife's sake."

"Ah yes. She would be most perturbed, I should imagine. What do you say, Sir? Should she be most dejected?"

"Aye," he answered, wondering if Gwinnett was making light of the situation, or perhaps beginning to understand its import.

McIntosh let out a brief guffaw, albeit delicately. *The pansy brings a doctor with him; he's petrified! The woman never saw a battle, and yet he accuses me! The blimp!*

Joseph placed each gentleman by the proper marker. For each man, a white stone marked his placement.

"Let us proceed with the inspection!" Gwinnett insisted, eager to finish with the entire debacle.

"Certainly!" Joseph stated. Wells and Habersham exchanged pistols. The physician was well-accustomed to all sorts from his youth hunting in England's great wilderness. Joseph noticed Gwinnet's forehead was profusely dripping. His hands were shaking. *Can he be afraid? The man who always seems fearless?*

"We may begin!" Joseph stated, with a tone of authority.

Both men shook hands, scoffed at one another, and began marching. "One!" Joseph bellowed. "Two!"

The crowd counted their steps in unison, a stentorian echo resounding in the forest. Each man's heart beat together with his pounding boots; will this be the day I die? They wondered.

"Fire!"

The two men fired well before they faced each other completely. Pistols burned through flesh at a rapid pace, simultaneously. The silence that filled the void penetrated each man's heart. The crowd did not feel any joy, nor did they see the bullets grazing the victims. Both men were hit.

McIntosh wondered why this one bullet was more painful than all the shrapnel and artillery bits that penetrated his skin in years past. It was as if Gwinnet's loathing carried a poisonous thread that knotted each synapse with a vigorous bout of intense pain. For a few seconds, McIntosh lost his vision. His every fiber was focused on the wound hiding in his pants. *Stand. Don't let them see you fall.*

Gwinnett felt as though his thigh were burning in hell's inferno. *I'm hit! I'm hit!* He thought, hysterically repeating those words in his mind. Blood spurted; the bullet penetrated an artery. Incapable of withstanding the torture of the bullet's stabbing sensation, Gwinnett collapsed.

McIntosh's aim was rife with rancor, and it festered in Gwinnet's thigh.

Dr. Wells ran to his patient, entirely shocked by the rapidity of the duel's end. Gwinnett lay on the ground. His leg was twisted, as though a knotted branch after a terrible storm. His femur was protruding. The bone was white, with the muscles surrounding it pink and bloody. Joseph stared at the gaping wound; the horror of it all struck him suddenly, and he envied Mordechai for remaining at home.

I don't feel any more. I thought this would ingratiate me, vindicate my suffering, but I can only stare at the bone of that blasted man.

Dr. Wells muttered, "He is suffering from a fractured knee."

Perhaps that will end the matter, he hoped. But McIntosh wasn't entirely satisfied.

"Let the man stand and have another shot! This is no way to settle a duel!"

Joseph riled at the suggestion. "Was not enough blood spilled? Do not deceive us, General. You suffer as well. Let us end this duel, before even more blood is shed. Should we lose all our American men to war and venom? Shall the Devil claim more men?"

The crowd bowed their heads; their pleasures have been one of blood-lust; and now that it was satiated, they seemed oddly ashamed. McIntosh felt his knee weaken. "Very well," he agreed. "It ends here. Right now."

McIntosh leaned over the physician, who was mending the bone. Gwinnett, hazy from the intensity of his pain, barely noticed McIntosh sweep an arm in support of his leg. The Negro men aided the physician, and Gwinnett was whisked away, crying, begging for mercy from God.

God was silent that night, and three days later, after begging for water and begging for more opiates, Gwinnett died in his bed.

McIntosh was accused of murder.

*

Mordechai stood in his bedchamber, hot and agitated. He wanted to sleep outdoors, but the pests and mosquitoes robbed him of sleep, more than the heat at times. But tonight, he realized he must attend the trial, just to see if justice would be served. He was dejected by the previous proceedings, noting the new ranking governor played an uneven hand with McIntosh, despite the general's many flaws. He flocked to the trial, which was held when the heat was less intense.

By the time Mordechai reached the court, the final verdict was announced:

Not Guilty.

McIntosh breathed a sigh of relief. Dr. Wells had treated his patient incompetently. So stated the expert witness. So concurred the wife! She too complained of Dr. Wells' inadequacies.

Mordechai marched back home, wondering what history would make of the man who killed a figure whose name appears on the Declaration of Independence, and why, when they had the chance, the court demonstrated mercy, and when they had the opportunity, they had vied on the side of injustice.

DIVIDE AND CONQUER

FRANCES COUNTED AGAIN. COULD IT be? She counted again. Yes. It was late. Fifteen days late. At her age? Expecting a child! Another one! And with her husband constantly fighting battles, commanding officers her son's age. How would she do it? The past year saw more and more bloodshed than Mordechai anticipated. Always at battle; fear gnawed at her heart until all that was left was a gaping wound fearful of being filled. Howe chose wisely; her husband was utterly devoted to the cause. They now celebrated Sabbaths alone with the Minises. Father was away at war. It was the way of life now. Sheftall became her husband's clone both in ardor and commitment. Mordechai had little choice he insisted. So now Frances' eldest son held the title of "Assistant Deputy Commissary of Issues for the State of Georgia." He too disappeared from her life. Her fear increased twofold each time they battled together or heaved bullets past enemy lines. Mothers everywhere mourned their dead sons, lost in battle or wounded beyond recognition. Frances withered away a little bit more each time she considered, "Perhaps it will be me one day?" Madness raged in those men ravaged by the North's bitter winter, losing limbs and their minds to the winds of war. The cause became less and less coherent, less and less tangible as the war protracted. Frances read in the papers, now she too was addicted to the news, how American soldiers were in dire need of assistance. But who detested the British enough to send their sons to war? Who would choose to fight another man's battle? American men fought valiantly, but the riches and the hefty coffers were in enemy hands; the British soldiers rarely suffered the starvation and deprivation of the poor American lads. And the war thus claimed more lives. And in all this, Frances was to nourish an unborn child. Would the child have a home?

Months of labor at home passed the time for Frances, and before she could count her expectant days, her time had come. But then so had Savannah's: the British were on the attack! News got way—the British were coming with a fleet to demolish the Savannahians who dared govern their own people. Wright would reclaim his position; the Redcoats were back, with a vengeance, bitter and blood hungry. McIntosh headed for George Washington's northern positions, leaving Georgia all shamefaced. General Howe urged families to flee; "Search for refuge; British reprisals will be severe." Such were his words, and Mordechai's heart entangled itself—his wife, his children, his unborn child! Before December of 1778 could wreak more havoc in the vicinity, Mordechai sent them all away to Charleston—Joshua Hart's home was less vulnerable, and there she could deliver the child.

There was no choice. He had to battle the war alone.

Separated from his wife by even greater distances, Mordechai had to tend to his son and his commission without losing focus. The men were in need of more training; funds were running low, and his estate was not producing much in the cold winter of '78. He had to reduce the hands in service; his business was suffering from his lack of investment. The war had taken precedence, and the war effort suffered financially as a result.

Christmas that year was quiet. The front preparing for imminent invasion, few had the opportunity to celebrate with family. Mordechai lit his Hanukkah lights with his son wearing a cocked hat, off to the side like the wild youths, somehow still practicing their Jewish traditions under threat of extinction. This year his children would not recite with jollity the hymns; his wife would not offer him oil-rich delicacies, his beloved wife would not rejoice by the candles.

This year, the lights might be lit one last time.

How Mordechai prayed, silently, watching each candle burn, night after night, in anticipation of death or the beginning of immortality.

May this year merit a miracle! Good Lord! Let our men, who are few and devoted to a greater cause than ourselves, surmount the odds so heavily weighted against us. Let another miracle ensue this year: let our numbered bullets suffice to capture the British throngs, the Hessian warriors whose blood-lust is greater than the waters that drench the earth. May it be your will, Good God of Abraham, Isaac, and Jacob to grant the Americans their desired freedom, so Jews the world over may come hither to practice the Laws of Your Torah in peace and solitude. Do not, Good God, abandon your people in their time of need—protect us from the wrath of our enemies as you did so for the Hasmoneans of years past. Amen.

*

Joseph departed from his unit and galloped to Catherine's. *I'll propose. We'll have a secret engagement. I cannot continue like a dead animal anymore. I am barely half a person. This war has robbed me of my chances to live a life of bliss with my woman.* Marching along the snow-trodden path, Joseph mustered the courage to knock on the door. *Enough with the concealment. It must be known. I can no longer hide.* The threat of death on the battlefield deadened his anxiety. *I am a man now.*

He knocked again. The merriment in the house was audible. The gaiety was clear; Catherine's family lived in prosperity despite the starvation of Americans next door, the poor soldiers, friends of Joseph's certainly, who withered away by the end of December. Joseph's knuckles ached. Muskets stuck during battle took a toll on his hands. Red, dry, and scaly, his hands were no longer the soft gentleman's hands Catherine often dreamed of. Joseph's beard was mostly grown in—a source of warmth during the cold winter mornings of the North. Joseph walked toward a window and peered through. The Venetian curtains were slightly drawn; he was able to catch a glimpse. So that was her father: stout, jolly, with fat cheeks and a sagging neck. But it was a thick neck, and Joseph had not seen a waistcoat of such fine embroidery since his father's better days in Wright's estate. His breeches were finely starched; he donned a redcoat's attire, stating his political leanings with pride. *This is a Loyalist household.* But where was Catherine? Freezing, and feeling the sudden urge to relieve himself, Joseph tried to make out Catherine's profile. Who was that man, standing by her side? Was that Catherine? His Catherine, or perhaps a sibling? After a moment or more, she turned, and Joseph stared at her. Yes. It was she. Her gown, a Christmas green, was cut low by the décolletage. Joseph's body warmed. Her skin gleamed, and her hair fell slightly on the back of her neck, where a large cross hung. A peacock feather graced her hair, pinned nicely with an expert hand Joseph knew Catherine loved. But then that gentleman was sitting so close to her! Who was he? Joseph could not get a full angle through the narrow window; the darkness of the outdoors prevented him from escaping complete detection if he were to light a fire himself. This was driving him mad. Joseph did not recognize the man, but he was most certainly a soldier of high rank. On his lapel he wore a few stars, a sign of valor in battle. His hair was still full by the sides as well as thick and healthy. Cheeks were ruddy, and his legs were in full display in his military boots. And how his redcoat gleamed in the glow of the night! Joseph's heart was filled with rage. *How many of my men did this man butcher with his blasted bullets? How many Noble Joneses out there are suffering with limps and malaise, shock and utter hunger because of his ilk?* Joseph's heart filled with disgust as he witnessed the man kiss Catherine's hand in greasy adoration. Catherine giggled, the same way she had with him! She lifted her leg ever so slightly when the cold-eyed bastard looked up, the very same foot he had once kissed in utter delight! The shame and humiliation, the betrayal he felt so utterly in his heart swelled and he let out a howl, a cry so primal it frightened him. *Who am I?*

Catherine and the men heard Joseph's war call above the din and immediately set for the outdoors. Catherine's heart raced. What was that noise? Why did she sense, somewhere deep down, that it presaged doom? It was not an animal's cry. All the horses were stowed, too cold for even a man to be out in such a night.

Jacob Hicks held Catherine's hand. "Do not fear. Your father and I shall see to the matter at once." He bowed, learning a thing or two from his superiors and American ladies in general, and held his musket in his hand. Mr. Willoughby searched the vicinity and could find nary a soul.

Joseph ran like a hunted and wounded animal through the underbrush of Catherine's estate. But unfamiliar with it entirely, he stumbled on a cart and let out another yell. All at once, Hicks and Catherine's hefty father were upon him, lifting him from his collar like a diseased dog, ready for the shoot. Catherine ran behind Hicks, curious, fearful and secretly excited.

"Father! No! Don't harm that man! He's harmless."

Samuel Willoughby stared at his daughter, moving his lantern to study her features. "You know this man?"

Joseph's eyes seared into Catherine's. His nostrils flared. Suddenly, Catherine no longer recognized Joseph Habersham, the man who promised her love and ecstasy. Instead, she saw a dying animal, hungry, resentful, and entirely gaunt. His jaw, the chiseled jowl she had so much loved, was no longer detectable under all that hair. His hands were grimy, his pant legs each with layers of filth. His eyes no longer shone. He was foreign to her.

"No father, I have never seen this man before, but he seems like a hungry ruffian. Let us feed him some, and let him on his way. He meant no harm."

"He meant no harm!" He shook Joseph, "Why did you yell like a hound in the night? What is your business here?"

Joseph saw the look in Catherine's eye and he knew he no longer had a single chance. "Like your daughter says, Sir. I am nothing but a hungry dog out in the night."

Jacob Hicks whispered into Willoughby's ear. "This man tells me you look like a wounded battle soldier. He says he's seen hundreds of you while waging war. Is that true? Are you a rebel? Admit at once!"

"Father! Let him go! You heard what he admitted. Let him off, Father, please! I beg of you."

"You seem awfully interested in his well-being, Catherine. Is there something I am not detecting, daughter? Is there something I should know?"

Suddenly overwhelmed, remembering all the love letters and the delicate fantasies she replayed in her mind, the look of her father's remonstrance, and the guilt suddenly gnawing at her soul, Catherine let out a cry, bitter and long, and ran into her home, straight past the guests, and into her room, where she locked herself in, opened the mattress and burned each letter in the fireplace, crying, tears falling and watching her lost love burn into ashes.

Joseph glared at the man who raised Catherine all these years without detecting a thing of her mind.

Jacob Hicks, after years at battle, could detect an America rebel. It occurred to him that perhaps *this* one was nothing but a man who reached farther than permitted for jewels not for his taking.

"Bring the man into the house. Perhaps we should question him a bit, Mr. Willoughby."

Catherine's father was too angry at his daughter to care much about Joseph. He dragged him into his parlor and yelled for his daughter. The two would explain this to him.

Catherine knew her father would want a full explanation. There was no escaping his eye. Not since a child, could she hide from him, save for her heart. But it was too late now! Oh! Why had Joseph come! She could have told him of her Hicks, if he only gave her the time!

"I see you remain silent, even as I ask you to answer this question one more time. In what capacity do you know my daughter?"

Joseph sat in the grand parlor with arms folded inward; *I prefer to stare at my stained boots than to answer your inquiries, you loyalist cur.* He spit on the carpet. "Let your daughter answer that question, Sir."

With a glance that spoke all his mind was seething, Joseph glared at Catherine, who sat with her hands folded in her lap.

"Answer!"

The penetrating sound frightened Catherine again, and she began to sob.

"Father! I knew him once before the war. That's all. I have not seen him since Tom went to war, Father. I swear it!"

Joseph nodded his head in disbelief. *So that's how she figures me. As an acquaintance from before the damn war! Hell to her!*

"Do you deny this? What did you say your name is?"

"Samson White."

Catherine cried when she heard his alias. *He's lost.*

"Yes, sir. Your daughter is telling the utter truth. I have been acquainted with her from before the war. And as she intimated, *I was hungry*, and chanced upon your house. A morsel of food, *and I'll be gone forever.*"

Catherine cried a bit more, shedding tears as Jacob Hicks looked on with suspicion.

Glad to have solved the matter, Catherine's father ordered the slaves to prepare a linen bag with victuals for the hungry man. Catherine sat in the room, staring at the floor.

"This is my daughter's fiancé, Samson. Perhaps you've heard of his success in battle. Jacob Hicks."

Joseph stood, shook the man's hand, and mustered all the strength not to vomit, cry, or yell once again.

To him, the war was lost the minute Jacob Hicks sneered ever so slightly and said, "A pleasure."

*

Mordechai wondered what got into Joseph since Christmas. He was drinking too much, cursing even more, and raw tempered. In his drunken stupor he cursed women, and repeated, "Frailty! Thy name is Woman, thy name is *Catherine.*" At that point, the man would sob, drink, and collapse. With the British invasion threatening to engulf Savannah at any day, Mordechai could not have his soldier behave such. But he guessed as to the cause, and felt compassion for Joseph—how he pinned his future on that woman! All those warnings from well-meaning friends went unheeded. In his blindness, he imagined the love he felt for that daughter of a loyalist would overshadow the tsunami of war.

Bitter and even gaunter, Joseph took to his musket and prepared himself for battle. *One last battle. To hell with this bloody war! What have I not already lost?*

Recalling his own betrayal to his father's cause, Joseph's guilty conscience suddenly rose and a voice resounded in his ears: *you deserve this, you profligate and rebellious son!*

The tranquility of the outdoors belied the tension within Mordechai's ranks. Everyone hoped for a repeat of the previous month, but Mordechai wasn't as hopeful. The snow covered the fields. White filled the earth.

Standing by the fire, the unit warmed their limbs. Sheftall was now in tow, and greedily partook of the conversation.

"Maybe John McIntosh will come up with another catchphrase to entice the British warmongers. And then, we'll stand firmly, as we did in Fort Morris," Sheftall said, eagerly awaiting a response.

Noble Jones looked up at Sheftall and wondered when the child's naivety will be lost.

"It's true—John McIntosh was able to defend our key fortress in Fort Morris, but don't think it didn't come at a hefty price, catchphrase or no."

Sheftall blinked. *Why is Noble Jones so negative?* Sheftall wondered. "I thought McIntosh's reply to Fuser's ultimatum was gutsy, and very courageous."

Joseph overheard the conversation and knew Sheftall was on to something. Where the uncle Lachlan McIntosh showed ill-resolve, his nephew John demonstrated quite the opposite. What did he tell that Lieutenant Colonel Fuser, the squinted-eyed British commander who could think of nothing but sauntering into Georgian territory and demanding a full surrender? What did John McIntosh respond? Ah. Yes. "Come and take it!"

The British were not so enthused by the epithets. But they outranked the Americans 500 to 200, and thought better of losing their men to another bloody battle. Instead, the madman burned as many Georgian fields as he could along his march.

More Brits would have to come, in order to "Come and take it."

"Well," Joseph chimed, spitting tobacco on the ground, warming his hands by the fire and cursing the cold front, "They're back now. And I can guarantee you it won't be just five hundred Redcoats. This time, we're expecting those Hessian beasts. I heard they could saber off a man's head and half his torso in one deft maneuver, like this!"

Frightened, Sheftall winced at Joseph's gesture, and Joseph just laughed, amused by Sheftall's innocence.

"Don't worry. Your father will speak to them in his German and maybe they'll share a strudel," Jones joked, perturbing the lad even more.

Mordechai pretended he did not overhear the conversation. *These men have been long at battle. He knew. The more tension they relieve prior to battle, the better. Sheftall will just have to grow before his time.*

"Where are all those northern troops?" Jones asked, on edge and angry. *Why are Georgians left to battle the Brits without reinforcements, for Christ's sake?*

Mordechai left his unit to survey the outskirts of Savannah. His horse served to add height to his reconnaissance, and he took careful note of a lone soldier on the high ground of Brewton Hill. *Our numbers are so few.* Mordechai was not satisfied with that lone soldier standing vigil. The Hill was the most practicable landing spot on the Savannah River—not to mention an *easily* defensible high ground between the River and the city. General Howe was relying on messengers to relay an advance warning of a British landing. *This is what we have. But we're opening ourselves to risk!* His men were rubbing off on him, increasing his anxiety. Since the upset of previous battles, particularly the disaster at the Florida marshlands, Mordechai had a sense that as much as he was permitted to take command of his unit, he was defenseless in the face of greater powers. Lachlan McIntosh disappointed Mordechai, and the Council of Safety did not always provide the "safety" Mordechai would have desired for his people, his family and his unit. The war tore apart his community too; the shul was disbanded, temporarily. Mordechai wondered if it could all be blamed on the British; perhaps they too were guilty in fomenting the mess they now found themselves in? Mordechai wondered if Wright heard from his own sources of the political mess in Georgia, if he found the botched duel between two staunch rebels at all amusing. Gwinnett may have been a polarizing figure, Mordechai knew, but he was generally considered an able-bodied man. But he was replaceable, Mordechai figured. And now, John McIntosh seemed valorous in battle, adding confidence to the insecure American troops fearful of Hessian beasts and British militia, trained in battle from youth, with monies from home to add fuel to their bodies. *While we suffer from burned fields and colonels who cannot agree on who should take lead of expeditions.* There was no doubt the British were veteran warmongers, while the Americans were fighting tooth and nail, with inefficient weapons, half-musty and broken. Mordechai witnessed a few lads shot to death, between the eyes, or straight through the chest because a musket was stuck. One lad blew his own face off before even a single British soldier fired. Every kind of wound found its way into being on the battlefront, and Mordechai had to stomach it all. *He* could show no weakness, or his men would fall behind. Lose a limb, fall in battle.

And now the Creeks. Mordechai didn't know if the Indians north of Savannah were acting alone, or in tandem with the Brits. Perhaps they were blackmailed, paid off, or simply getting back at perceived injustices. No one knew.

Mordechai galloped back toward his men and noticed Percy standing alone, barely covered properly for that time of year. Although Percy fought alongside Mordechai from the very start, the two never truly conversed. Mordechai tipped his hat. Percy helped Mordecai dismount from the steed.

The breeze picked up, and Mordechai lent Percy a blanket stored in the steed's saddle bag.

"They're coming, Sir. I sense them." Percy said, sighing and thanking Mordechai for the warmth.

"Indeed."

"Should we win the war, I shall seek my family."

"You are free to go now, Percy. Why battle? You have been a slave for the British long before this day. Your freedom you earned; You have repaid your debt."

Percy looked at Mordechai thorough his ebony eyes, matching the blackness of his skin. "Yes. Perhaps you are right, but I wish to fight beside your people, Sir. I had been snatched from my family in Africa years ago, and not until fighting beside you have I enjoyed a meaningful existence. The British destroyed me for years. I wish to take revenge on the people who took me captive. Wright's people, the very ones who limited my chances in life."

Astonished the man should be so eloquent, Mordechai inquired if he received an education.

"Yes Sir, the very finest. From my matron, and from the great Bible. I respect your people, sir. The Hebrews were God's chosen nation."

"Certainly. And we were slaves as well, thousands of years ago. And we must never forget the bondage and suffering of our ancestors." Percy bent his head, wondering if his people will ever enjoy the luxury of prestige and the power of the white man in the country that enslaved his own kind.

"Lennox is eager to travel to Africa too, I've understood." Mordechai continued.

"Yes, sir. He was kidnapped as an adult. I have been lost to my family from infancy. His calling is far greater than mine. He, after all, has a wife and child back home, far away in Africa."

After a pause, Percy could not help but inquire, 'What happened to your slaves, Mordechai? Do you uphold abolition?'

"Ach. I sold them all along with nearly all my property, Percy. The war effort. All my money I lent to the new government… and abolition, perhaps, will occur eventually. But I don't know if Americans are prepared… to lose…."

Percy understood. *If Americans are prepared to lose their source of income.*

"If you decide to remain in America, Percy, I wish to assist you in any way possible. Perhaps to find you gainful employment…."

Percy nodded, glad to have spoken to his commander.

"Thank you, Sir." Percy shook hands with Mordechai. "It was a pleasure serving with you."

Embarrassed, Mordechai nodded his head, and said, "Likewise. Likewise."

Miles from Brewton Hill sailed the seventy-first Regiment of Highlanders under Colonel Archibald Campbell. He was to send word to James Wright upon the success of his mission. The former statesman was nervously awaiting word, wondering how long the battle would last, who should be sacrificed for King George. Would the colony be restored?

James Wright had long suspected the Georgian colonists of making fools of themselves once he was no longer in the position to set the colony on a rightful course. It came to him as no surprise, as well, to learn of the advancement of that wealthy Jew, Sheftall. General Howe had the audacity to promote a non-Christian. The very thought brought shivers down his English spine. So what would be next? A Negro official, a female politician? A plebian member of Parliament? Who could withstand such a social blunder? Social classes befuddled in such a manner! Jews remained merchants in London, and enjoyed their mansions *without* trying to meddle in politics, thank you very much. The gall! A commanding officer in the British Army was only and *only* the son of an Earl or Baron. Who ever heard of a British soldier taking orders from a mere merchant, and a *Jewish* one! America threatened the very *British* lifestyle Wright was accustomed to from birth, and to which he subscribed. The cause must be squashed. Hopefully, Colonel Campbell would see to that.

Indeed, Campbell had received intelligence long before he set sail—the colony was in a chaotic state of affairs to put it mildly. News of Gwinnet's murder and Archibald Bulloch's mysterious death reached the Thames soon enough. Parliament scoffed at the notion that Georgia was a formidable foe; the battle of the boats a thing of the past. New governors were constantly elected—three in a matter of a few years. Commanders could not take initiative, and the one asked to replace so-called competent men was the *most* incompetent of the bunch. New currency was slowly losing its weight in sterling, and men were absconding from the colony, particularly the wealthy loyalists who supported the Crown in the past. They remained in Virginia or Philadelphia. Some fled to Charleston; the militia was broken and suffering from disease. During the summer months, countless soldiers perished without so much as a British saber glinting in the fields. Nature seemed to be on their side this time of year as well. December was uncharacteristically frigid; vegetables froze before properly gleaned from the fields; farmers had little chance to retrieve their goods before the winter storms bombarded their planes—all without the firing of a cannon. Of course they had to battle the guerillas in the forests—a detestable form of warfare in Campbell's estimation. But now with the Hessians on board, the Americans stood little chance, and Campbell was hoping Providence would continue to benefit his people. The Americans were an ungrateful lot, and they should learn their place before all peoples of all breeds begin to forget their placement in this world. The world would return to its initial pandemonium—the very work of Lucifer Himself!

Dawn soon broke the calm in Campbell's regiment. Thirty-five hundred men slept in his vessels, ready to stretch their muscles and commit to their word. The sun appeared on the horizon, and Campbell was able to detect the marshlands surrounding the Savannah River; he could spot a hill very much suitable for landing. It seemed free of any American fortification, an oddity in his estimation. The city lay not far from the hill. Campbell checked his map—his compass seemed to corroborate Wright's suggestion, "land on Brewton Hill." Indeed! The actual terrain may prove somewhat difficult, but the safety of landing unperturbed could not be ignored. On December 29, 1778, Campbell's regiment disembarked after a long voyage in the cold seas. His men were well-fed, well-clothed, and well-trained. It would be a piece of English pie.

Mordechai awoke that morning and donned his phylacteries as usual. His son followed his father's incantations and wore the black leather boxes in similar positions—on his forehead and forearm. This was the custom of his people and the greatness of the American Land—they did not fear persecution as his grandfather had in Prussia. Indeed! The very men who had executed countless Jews, or at least believed Jews were blood-sucking critters who drank their children's blood every Passover Eve, would now combat them. Heaven protect them! Sheftall read in his Talmud that the phylacteries would protect them; in ancient Israel the holy men wore their phylacteries all day. Perhaps he should keep his on?

Mordechai pointed to the *siddur*, or prayer-book. His son was losing his concentration again. *Shema Israel!* His father pointed to the most significant prayer. Sheftall drew inspiration from his father. He thoroughly disliked disappointing him. *Concentrate. This may be your last chance to pray openly as a Jew.*

Lennox and Percy exchanged muskets, hoping each other's luck would prevail. Joseph chewed his tobacco and wondered how long Catherine would remain married *happily* to a fellow such as Hicks. He had done his own research and was astonished as to the man's brutality. Rumor has it he sees to the murder of prisoners of war. That's how he earned those stars—he never set loose a single prisoner in his term. Joseph spit. Good luck to them all. This bloody mess destroyed all decency, especially women's. Ha! She gave her heart to him, and soon her body to the bloody Brit. A betrayer.

"You're ready?" Jones said, a piece of hard bread stuck in his rotted teeth.

Joseph muttered something unintelligible and marched toward Mordechai's tent. The commander was beseeching his God as he did every morning. *When will he give up?* Joseph wondered.

"The British landed this morning, men. Eight hundred yards separate us from their current position." Mordechai related the news to his men, dejected Howe had not sent proper reinforcements overnight to protect the hill. "A narrow catwalk runs the length of the quagmires between our positions. News of this development reached Howe's ears this morning."

"But it's too late, isn't it, Sir?" Percy said, unafraid for once to state his opinion.

Livid, Jones yelled, "And why the hell should they *not* march across that damned marshland unopposed! Of course! We're all sitting ducks. I say let's retreat now, while our necks are still a part of our bodies."

Mordechai lifted his hand. "I won't stand between a man and his life. If you so decide to forfeit your gun, do so now. The rest of you, follow me. There is little time to lose. We must prepare our firing positions immediately!"

The men of Mordechai's unit, which included lads of all ages, more Negroes without names, and a few regulars all looked askance. Who would defect at a time like this? Mordechai began to pace briskly toward the main garrison. He had to give his men the best chances he could; the walls and the low-lands would give them cover for now. All they could do was wait.

Samuel Elbert had joined their group; indeed, he had been a fellow in arms despite his initial ineptitude. Rubbing his hands together, he made contact with Philip Minis, and Jones. These men were loyal to Mordechai and stood silently. Mordechai observed their hardened faces—his son, the only one wide-eyed and pure, never killed a man. Mordechai's unit stood wait by the outskirts of Savannah. Their hastily formed unit joined seventy other men ready to combat. Mordechai and Sheftall were among those in the front line. Sheftall's cocked hat was visible from yards away. It would be the first sight of a British soldier ready to maim and murder in the name of his King.

"Why do we suffer this ragtag defense line! The damn British are advancing—"

"Shut up Jones." Joseph said, suddenly completely agitated his friend should even wonder at the absurdity. "Just *shut up.*"

Mordechai sensed the anxiety. He checked his pocket watch. Two thirty-five.

Sheftall glanced at his father, suddenly afraid to die. "Is it true, father? Are they far greater in number?"

Mordechai's jaw dropped a bit, but he then whispered, "Listen to me, son. Nothing is beyond His glory. The outcome of this war will be determined by our actions, and by God's grace. If He so wills it, thousands of men cannot withstand His mighty arm."

"Yes, I understand, but by what measure may we determine that God will protect us?"

Mordechai sighed. "I do not know, son. Such knowledge is reserved for God Himself. We can only muster our belief. We must be brave and trust that whatever shall transpire shall be God's perfect will."

"Even if we shall perish."

Mordechai sighed again. *If it were my own body and soul I should not weep bitterly. But my son! How do I say this to my son? Oh my poor wife! To bear another child all alone, after having raised this one with all her tears.*

"To death. Let us recite *viddui* whilst we still can, while all is still quiet on the northern front."

Mordechai recited the Hebrew words of atonement, the confessional prayer recited by Jews on the Day of Atonement, *Yom Kippur.* The prayer was reserved for those who were lucky enough to beg forgiveness of past sins before departing for the World of Justice and Truth. Philip Minis joined their prayers, and all whispered, "*Shema Yisrael, Hashem Elokenu, Hashem Echad.*"

Mordechai glanced once again at his pocket watch. Three fifty-seven.

A wave of British soldiers appeared at the edge of the bluff several hundred yards away. *By God! They're marching like a damned parade!* Jones nearly blurted out loud. *Judith, pray God is with you and the dear little ones!* Philip thought, suddenly glad his wife took refuge.

"Hold fire!" Mordechai ordered. *Let us wait until our bullets can penetrate, while they are close in range. God only knows these muskets are not as accurate as those precious rifles we've been hammering for.*

Samuel Elbert was the first to fire, screaming for those around him to do the same. Like a wildfire spreading throughout a dense forest, the Americans began to shoot wildly. A handful of Redcoats fell, including the captain of the regiment. Loose parts exploded into the air; a series of tremendous booming sounds and several cannon balls rocketed the American position. Legs, arms, bowels, and ears rained from the sky and landed near Mordechai's unit. Sheftall, suddenly horrified by dismembered body parts began vomiting on the side. Joseph ran to the lad, reloaded Sheftall's gun. "Fire! Vomit later!" As the Americans reloaded, frantically jamming their muskets, the advancing British returned a torrent of bullets. "Stay low!" Mordechai commanded, afraid his men would be turned to bits before aiming once again. Percy noticed Sheftall's gun was stuck, and he ran to assist Sheftall. Sweating, Sheftall began crying. *My musket. Why is it stuck!?* Just then, Sheftall felt a huge body fall on him. It was Percy—with a gaping hole where his eye once stood. Stunned, Sheftall realized the *goy* had saved his life. He ran to gather Percy's musket, and glanced at the dead man one last time. Cannon fire erupted again, this time splitting the American encampment. Samuel Elbert began hollering, "It's done for! Flee to the forest! We're outnumbered, God damn it! We're outflanked!" Mordechai concurred and gathered his men. *The British have come in droves. This is no battle to be won.* Mordechai grabbed Sheftall and followed Joseph through the woods. Scampering, they noticed Lennox was carrying Percy's body on his back. "Hurry!" Jones yelled. *What the bloody hell is he doing?* Jones thought. Mordechai turned to his men and ordered they reload muskets before the opportunity for their use presented itself.

They continued to flee. Savannah was burning.

*

Archibald Campbell nodded his head in agreement. He surveyed the grounds prior to the attack and discovered a neglected path that circled the city. His scouts did a fine job of sketching the city's outskirts, and now that he was in the midst of the battle, he knew just what to do. *Divide and conquer.*

"I want half the forces, the Hessians preferably, to advance toward Howe's main defense, up north, in that direction. And I want James Baird's light infantry to detour through one of these swamps, here. Take this map with you, it should ease your way. This defector here, a black slave familiar with the terrain, will lead the secondary brigade behind enemy lines. Godspeed!"

The commanders set out dutiful of Campbell's every word.

*

420

Mordechai's men, in the interim, caught up with Howe's forces, emerging from the forest with multiple thorns stuck in their skin and blistering skin from dry bark scraping their bodies. Lennox finally placed Percy down near a pile of dead bodies. He closed his good eye. *Farewell.*

General Howe remained on his steed, with an expression of confusion clouding his brow. *The emergency war council elected to hold our ground, rather than retreat to South Carolina, but this is suicide! My men numbered seven hundred a few hours ago. Now, God only knows how many remain. We're reeling.*

Mordechai recognized that expression. It mirrored his own.

Campbell caught up, and he witnessed Howe's steed neighing as British soldiers pounded the Americans. "Fire!" he ordered, this time hoping the tidal wave of "Brown Bess" muskets would hail down and decimate the remaining rebels. The onslaught was intense. Those who escaped the first volley hardly recuperated before another torrent ensured. The Americans fell back. Mordechai fell to the floor, covering his son. "Down!" Jones yelled. Joseph could barely hear; his ear was ringing from the cannon fire. "Flee!" Joseph yelled, unaware he was so loud. Mordechai grabbed his son again, began commanding the retreat of his unit and nearly fell to another torrent of bullet fire. "God damn them! They're firing from the rear!" Jones yelled, taking a bullet to the thigh. *Bastards!*

Campbell observed the panic on the American patriots. It engulfed each one, without a victim senseless to its claws. "Hessians!" he hollered, "Attack!"

Mordechai froze. *Did I hear correctly? Hessians?* The Prussian soldiers with their brown skin and curling, long mustaches barked a primeval battle cry that caused all the patriots to freeze for a moment as well. Sheftall felt a warm liquid fall between his legs. *Hessians.*

With the brutality of butchers, the Hessians marched on Mordechai's unit slashing any half-fallen man with their bayonets. Entrails ripped out of victims, some still alive, yelling for their mothers. Mordechai held Sheftall for a moment longer. *This is our end.* Sheftall was too stunned to cry. In shock, they witnessed

Lennox ripped from head down to shoulder, now lying motionless on his back, all torn, his innards the color of black beets.

Joseph suddenly grabbed Mordechai. "Mordechai! We must escape! To Musgrove Creek! Quickly!"

Dashing once again, this time blindly following Joseph, Mordechai and Sheftall aimed their guns behind them. *Why can't my legs carry me faster! God! Help us!* Mordechai prayed, shoving his son to jump higher, run faster, hurdle and dash. Bullets grazed the trees around them, but they did not dodge or stoop or seek cover. Baird's light infantry chased them like a wild hunt. Heavy gunfire exploded around them. "We must seek cover!" Jones yelled. "No!" Mordechai commanded. "We must escape to South Carolina! We must cross Musgrove Creek and find sanctuary!"

The fleeing Georgians barely numbered a third of their initial force. The rest remained behind—the dead and wounded. The British—a total of twenty six casualties were their lucky numbers for the day.

Scampering and out of breath, Mordechai and Elbert's group finally reached the creek.

"Where the bloody hell is the bridge?" Jones asked, irate and nearly spent. *To get this far!*

Joseph and Elbert had presumed a bridge had been erected in case of a retreat. It had not.

And the waters were high. Frigid. And deep.

Dozens of men jumped into the raging waters. They attempted to swim across. The water was not placid, causing some men to drown in the process.

"Let's go!" Sheftall yelled, ready to swim than to face the onslaught of British infantry men no less brutal and cruel than the Hessians. Mordechai was prepared, but he froze for a moment.

"I cannot son. I never taught you to swim. How can I save myself and leave my son behind?"

"Go, father!" urged Sheftall. "There is still time! Please! Father!"

"No. I cannot."

"I'll try father to swim. It doesn't look so hard," he lied.

"Please father! They'll kill us both, this way at least we have a chance."

This is not the Red Sea. And I am not Moses. The waters will not part because of my faith in God.

Mordechai watched helplessly as his comrades struggled to swim across. Some lucky and brawny swimmers made it to safety, including General Howe and several officers. Most of the patriots soon desisted, resigned to their fate. The waters submerged them, never to be seen again.

Colonel Elbert raised a white flag. It was time to give up.

Joseph fell to the floor. *So this is it.* Naked fear replaced the brazen fearlessness he demonstrated only hours ago. Mordechai concurred. He raised his white flag too. Sheftall fell near Joseph, confused and dazed. *What will happen now?*

Baird's infantrymen charged upon the defeated patriots minutes later. Wounded Americans lay on the ground, whimpering in pain. Bodies floated in the creek, head down like children playing dead in a pond. White flags blew in the wind, and the white path was littered with vomit and tears.

"Hold your fire!" Baird ordered.

Savannah fell, and the patriots were now in enemy hands.

"Leave this man to me."

Extended Grace

THE COURTHOUSE SUFFOCATED THE PRISONERS. It was sweltering. Rebels were sentenced to hang. Others to hard labor. The patriots were packed tightly, squeezing one another. High-ranking officials were thrown together with their inferiors. To the British, soldiers were all the same—rotten scoundrels. Mordechai sat between Jones and his son. *They'll discover my exploits, and make me pay.* But the Brits were in no rush. They figured they'll make them wait. Hours passed, and the men could not move nor eat, piss nor communicate with their fellow inmates. Mordechai glanced at his pocket watch, now stained with blood, grime, sweat and tears. Three hours gone, and yet silence reigns. Sheftall glanced at his father and knew he was in pain. During the battle, Mordechai's legs were punctured by dry and splintery branches, protruding like tentacles of a great octopus. The British were in no hurry—they were busy plundering the captives. They had the town to secure from rebels—the women and children. Their officials were doubtless appropriating the most spacious and beautiful quarters for themselves; *perhaps my estate is now in their blood-soaked hands*, Mordechai mourned. He imagined brutish soldiers sitting on his wife's bed, sipping London ale, or an official conducting business where he had, not long ago, convened with his men, and his blood riled. *How did we let this happen? How!* Sheftall placed his hand by his father's shoulders. "Father, they called your name. Father?"

The door had swung open and a British officer with valorous pins on his lapel strutted into the main chamber. He held a hand-kerchief to his nose.

"Mordechai Sheftall! Identify yourself!"

So they had learned he was in custody. Mordechai felt his knees buckle. *God, be on my side.*

"It is I," he answered, staring into the eyes of a cool-headed soldier.

Joseph immediately recognized the man. "My God!" he whispered. It was Jacob Hicks.

Hicks stood, and summoned Mordechai. "Come with me."

"Father! Should I come too?" *What if I don't see him again?*

"No! Remain here. You are a child. What would they want with you? Stay with Jones or Joseph."

Mordechai winced; his wounds began to form pus. He tucked his blanket and spare shirt under his arm: his remaining belongings. His horse, and the saddlebags which contained kosher food, the Necessaire, spare clothes, and not to mention his phylacteries, were all confiscated. Mordechai kissed his son's forehead, roused himself and followed the distinguished-looking officer out of the courthouse. By God, he needed to relieve himself.

Mordechai glanced at the soldier and wondered if the man had shown mercy to a single individual in his life. Lines of cruelty etched his face, particularly his mouth, which was thinly veiled with malice. He held Mordechai as though he were a caged beast, squeezing his forearm.

"Where are you taking me, soldier?" Mordechai inquired.

Hicks raised his brow. "You shall find out sure enough. Remain silent, until addressed!"

Mordechai suddenly realized the officer would not speak. He continued to march. The courthouse now in the distance, Mordechai saw a blackened prison door with a sentry guarding its gates. His steps began to slow; was he to remain in the guardhouse? Rapists and scoundrels of all kinds have been imprisoned there since Savannah's birth! And is he to remain there now? *Better than a hanging.* Mordechai glanced at his boots, caked with mud and dried guts. The war now came at another price, if not his life, then what will it be? Hicks suddenly snapped to attention. A tall, elegant military man was approaching them. His uniform was bedecked; he carried a saber of the most elaborate nature by his left hip. It was very clean. His hair was speckled with bits of gray, and his demeanor of a refined English kind. He stopped.

"Hicks—is this the prisoner we were looking for?"

"Yes, General."

Colonel Archibald Campbell glanced at Mordechai with a mixture of disdain and reprehension. His hand, ever so slightly, grazed his sword, stuck in its hilt. He held his nose just a bit, and moved a step back. The sweat off of Mordechai was overwhelming, dried and all. Campbell for a moment wondered how a middle-aged man with a non-threatening physique could be the cause of such outstanding damage. This was the "Jew Sheftall" Wright had described as influential and most treacherous. This was the warrior who nearly drowned Wright's vessel? His legs were bloodied, his back bent. His long, Jewish nose was soiled, his face all discolored. His hands were torn. His grayish eyes were blood-shot red. This was he? To Campbell, Mordechai resembled a beggar on Fleet Street, not the man Wright had portrayed. The portrait of Mordechai, as Campbell now witnessed, was most pathetic. But his reputation! Wright had initiated strict instructions to guard him, and ensure his capture. *Appearances may deceive. Be not deceived.*

"Guard this man, Hicks. He is a very great rebel. See to it that he is secured in the guardhouse!"

Hicks nodded, saluted, and continued his march. The gates to the prison door were sealed. *I am now to be confined.*

Hicks escorted Mordechai past the sentry and into the dungeons below ground. The stench of years' old piss and human waste clung to the ceiling, the walls, the very floor. With bayonet in hand, Hicks shoved Mordechai to the floor. He fell on both knees and cried out. His wounds re-opened and began to bleed. Hicks suppressed a snicker. It was all ironic now, to see the man who killed his comrades like a dog begging on his knees. Hicks slammed the iron gate shut, and turned his attention to the sentry. "Keep your eyes on that bastard Jew. He's a great rebel."

The sentry nodded. A Jew. A faithless Jew.

Mordechai suppressed his urge to hurl. The men around him were indifferent to the stench, but how could they be? Buckets of human waste overflowed in every corner, and moist piss stained the walls like age-old water beds gone dry. Mordechai began to shed some tears, and then some more. *I am a Jew dog now, a rebel. They will do with me as they please.*

At least I have my blanket, Mordechai thought. And I still need to relieve myself. What difference does it make—if I add to the filth of this place?

Just as he finished, trying not to disturb the prisoners, the ugly sentry opened the gate.

"Leave your belongings, filthy Jew. Follow me."

Wearily, Mordechai followed him. *What do they want now? Perhaps they wish to beat me? Maybe they'll set me free?*

Mordechai was glad to leave his cell. The sentry guided him, with a bayonet's edge on his back, to another flight of stairs. The officer finally opened a door and there stood a bespectacled man. He was not overwhelmingly tall, as was Campbell, but the scorn on his revolting face, menacing and frightful, intimidated Mordechai. The sentry whispered, spitting into Mordechai's ear, "This is Mr. Gild Busler. He's *our* commissary-general. Better behave, or he'll have your behind on a nice salver for supper."

"You may leave, Christie. Take your bayonet with you. Leave this man to me."

He then turned to Mordechai. He did not speak. Not for the first three minutes. Instead, he paced around the room, glancing at Mordechai from different angles. *Let him feel uncomfortable. Let him fear the Crown, for once!* Busler shifted papers on his desk. Mordechai was still staring at him, waiting for a word. *The Jew does not move; he is not bothered in the least!* Busler realized.

"You and I have something in common, Mr. Sheftall. You may wonder what that is." He paused. Mordechai wondered why the man was fond of tormenting his prisoners. What does a man gain? He pondered. *Out with it!*

"I too am, well, you *were*, and I *still* am, commissary general. Of course, you are defeated. But from what I understand, you are familiar with the stores and reserves of ammunitions and supplies. Since you are *no longer* the commissary general, and very much vanquished by our superior forces, you are obliged to accompany me, the current commissary general of His Highness, to the secret locations of your supplies."

"For what purpose, may I inquire?"

"To feed your starving men! They have not eaten in three days."

"That is impossible. I victualed them all this morning, sir."

"Very well. Since I see you are a persistent man, I will implore you, and I say this kindly, to tell me precisely who are all those prisoners sitting in the courthouse. I want a list. Now."

"That is out of the question, sir. I must refuse your requests. All of them."

That unflinching dog of a Jew! How dare he? Does he not realize the noose around his very neck?

"I will implore you this one last time. I require a complete accounting of your current stores, what you have issued and to which location. You *will* provide this information, posthaste."

"Absolutely not. I will not comply."

Busler began to pace around the room. Rage filled his belly, and the contempt in his heart consumed him. "Might I remind you, you senseless and ungrateful cur—you are a prisoner of war!" he bellowed. He grabbed the paperweight on his desk and hurled it across the room, "You will do as you are told!"

Mordechai felt the room spin. Vertigo held him bound. *Why is the room suddenly spinning? What is that noise in my head? Cannon fire erupted, yells for water! More water! Where's the medic! God damn it! Help! Filled his ear. Percy on the floor, his blood spilling to the floor. Where are the banners!? Raise the banners high, mount them on the hills. Do not let them take our land.*

"Did you hear me, you maggot? I said you are a prisoner! Comply!"

Mordechai whispered grimly, "I must decline."

"Oh! Suffer you will!" Busler roared. He seized Mordechai and threw him to the floor. He opened the door, called for the sentry and ordered him, "Confine this man with the Negroes and madmen. That is where he belongs." Busler's rage cooled for a moment; he sneered, wondering if the dirty Jew just knew what awaited him in the dungeons of hell.

*

So this is where they imprisoned those escaped Negroes, and all these years I have never known of this place... Mordechai wondered how long it would be before death would eat away at his soul. How long had it been since he last consumed a morsel of food? His mouth was parched, his legs all pussy and sore, and his mind loud with the noise of war. What the dungeons of madmen could do to a man! *Do not stare.* But how could he not? Two men were climbing on the walls, beating the stains. Yelling all kinds of hideous words. The Negroes somehow slept through the din, but the eyes of the insane bored through Mordechai's. *Do not look.* Finally, the two banged their heads on the walls, filling them with blood, and fell into a temporary coma. Their hands were black, but Mordechai could not detect the filth on his own palms. Only a thin shaft of moonlight filtered into the dungeon, cold and below Savannah's lush grounds. Through a crack in the roof, Mordechai could detect a bit of moonlight. *The heavens have not been silenced.* Mordechai winced as he reached into his trousers for his watch, the only family heirloom now in his possession. And then, before he could tell the time, his eyes filled with tears as he last recalled his wife's expression as she had so long ago provided him with this gift—his pocket watch. What difference can it make now, if it is two past midnight or three? How long should I contort my body in an unsuccessful attempt to check the time?

Oh! Frances! God should keep you safe from these treacherous men!

Memories of Sabbath nights filled his heart. Those joyous days when love bloomed, and the threat of blood so far in the distance. The birth of his son, and the expression of his mother when he called him Sheftall Sheftall—the cheer the child filled his father's heart warmed Mordechai in his confined cell. Sumptuous dinners. How he craved a touch of challah dipped in honey! Curled into a fetal position, Mordechai recalled his youth with Hannah Minis and Philip, running around Savannah, finding a peach tree and sucking the juices out of its abundance. He thought of Levi, how he had been spared this fortune, the child of prudence.

Mordechai drifted, slowly succumbing to sleep.

*

"Where is the Jew?" the voice was subdued, quiet almost, but filled with menace. The sentry pointed to Mordechai, sleeping with his head wrapped around a sorry-looking blanket. A large form filled the doorway, momentarily blocking the light. Hicks held out a lamp and made out Mordechai's silhouette. *That's the dog.*

"I hunt dogs like you."

Mordechai shrank back. *By God! Is this my end?* Hicks stood with a bayonet in hand, ready to puncture Mordechai in the heart, as he's done to countless rebels in the night. *For my fallen comrades in Boston, for my fallen comrades in New York, for my King, for the safety of the girl I love!* Hicks pounced on Mordechai, but the bayonet struck the ground. *Bloody Jew!* He scampered to the wall, where Mordechai hid amongst the insane men. *Where the hell is he?* Hicks grabbed his lantern and tried to make out Mordechai's face. Again, Mordechai dashed to the other side of the cell, where the negroes lay like sacks of rice awaiting shipment. Sweat and pure fear gripped Mordechai. *Is Fannie to become my widow?* He closed his eyes. Pray to Hashem, he implored himself. Hicks cursed the Negroes; their black skin made it impossible to detect the Jew! Finally, he was able to distinguish Mordechai, and he burst on Mordechai once again.

But an arm held him back.

"Lower your weapon, Hicks!" It was Sergeant Campbell, a man who did not bear relation to the general himself, but who was loyal to the general as a son. "I warned you! Campbell wants him alive. He is not to be harmed! Put your weapon *down.*"

Hicks pushed the sergeant away. "Don't you dare speak to me in that tone; I am your superior!"

Campbell reeled back, afraid Hicks would take him out too. *His exploits at night are concealed, but well-known.* Hicks glared at Mordechai. "Don't think I'm done with you." And he shoved Mordechai onto the floor, rousing the Negro into a rage, and a senseless beating.

Before Mordechai could count his luck, Hicks was back to finish him off. But yet again, Sergeant Campbell, this youthful officer who transformed into an Angel, prevented Hicks. Before dawn, Hicks sought him out once last time, nearly stabbed him, only to be prevented once again.

Mordechai wondered how many times he could confront death without losing his wits. The men around him did not commiserate with him. Indeed! The blows he received that night from the ruffians and madmen, fueled by their distress and annoyed by the disturbance to their fitful sleep, certainly soothed the Devil's bloodlust that night.

By the dawn's light, Mordechai's head was gashed, his body bruised, and his spirit waiting to exhale.

*

Journal for the month of January:

January 1, 1779:

A Jew who goes by the name of Mordechai Sheftall is now serving in the prison guardhouse with all the Negro mongrels and debauched men, drunken and vile from insanity. The man refused to assist the war effort and was notably disciplined by Busler—the dungeons of Hades. That is the appellation it deserves, as those who enter never return. Last month, three dead Negroes were found alongside the madmen; their flesh was missing considerable weight. I begged my superior, Jacob Hicks, an inferior man with the polished exterior of a "gentleman" to feed the hungry beasts, but he refused. He said they'll live longer that way. The frigid air freezes some of them at night, those without a blanket. A

431

terrible brawl erupted the night before Christmas—the cold air ignited their madness, and two more Negro men were found dead, their bodies bereft of clothing; those who had fought them off were wearing them. I again begged my superior, by post since he had attended a soiree for Christmas (supposedly wooing a wealthy landowner's daughter) for blankets and other victuals. He said, and I quote, "Why hasten their death to the spring? Bodies smell in the heat, don't you say?" In all my school years, I have been taught the English are superior and genteel, the "huns" the beasts of the wild, our ancestors the great Germanic tribes of senselessly cruel warriors. I see the British have not dissolved their Anglo-Saxon ancestry after all. Some of Hicks' compatriots insist he was simply a soldier of duty before the war, but a terrible blow to the head altered his demeanor; it happened in Boston they said. I can't tell, and I don't know. But something had to be done about those prisoners.

When I overheard Sheftall praising his Lord in a German tongue, he began in a Hebrew one but then went on a mad tirade in Prussian, I could no longer remain silent. I began to converse with him in German, and although I detected an accent, it wasn't long before I learned of his father's hometown, not far from mine in fact, and the long voyage to this country years ago. He said his son speaks a tad of German too, and that his children and wife do not know of his whereabouts. His eyes were red, his face, not very German, but similar to the peddler Jews' I've seen selling wares by the wayside of the Vistula, was caked with what looked like dried blood. His brows were black, but not from the hairs. No; I believe he is nightly accosted and beaten by the madmen in the cave of Dante's imagining. By Jesus, although this man is a Jew, and I know they delay the Second Coming, as I firmly believe He shall one day appear, I could not help but feel pity for the man. In all his misery, he asked after my health. He wanted to know if I had children, if I fought as a Hessian warrior for monetary gain; if I was in dire need for a living. He offered suggestions! He said, "better to eat bitter leaves with a loving wife than to have blood on one's hand." He seemed to pity himself as he spoke these words; he is losing his wits, I remember thinking. I immediately brought him to my quarters, where I offered him to *wash up, drink some cider and ale, and beloved jam on day-old bread. The man was crying, blessing me with old age and prosperity throughout each bite of bread. He nearly hugged me, and wanted to know how he could repay me. After the war, after the war, he kept on repeating, I want you to write to me. I wish to repay you. I hurried him back to his cellar, before Hicks could get word of my doing.*

He wrote a letter in my chambers to a matriarch by the name of Abigail Minis. The woman came to my door a few good hours later with a rucksack filled with food, drink, and a fresh change of clothes. Her back was bent, and she wore a bonnet on her head that reminded me of my own grandmamma. "Let him see his child," she insisted, "it will do him good." The woman blessed me, and offered sterling as a token of her thanks. I accepted the money; the British government had not always paid us hired soldiers on time. She told me something more I will never forget, "The man served out of duty; he lost much of his worth. He fought so men like you can be free in this country. We do not wish to kill for the sake of killing. Please forgive him; forgive us all, Zaltman. God bless."

I permitted him to see Sheftall, glad Hicks was no longer in the vicinity to offer resistance. Sergeant Campbell had him shifted back to the front; his blood lust must be utilized well. I eventually allowed father and son to share my quarters. It was a heartbreaking scene— how the father shed tears over his son! "Eat my son! Eat!" but the father was gaunt. It was then the son implored his father, "Father! You must eat! Eat father!"

The son came to me and nearly kissed my hands. "You saved my father's life. Look! Had he remained there a day longer, he would have perished by their hands. May God bless your family with a long life; May God repay your kindness."

The son walked to his father and kissed his father's hand. He was no older than sixteen years of age—the age I had lost my own papa.

January 2:

The new year knows no mercy for those who have been cursed by Christmas Eve to a year of doom. The Jew Sheftall had been resting in my quarters. It was his Sabbath, and I was honored to allow the man to sleep peacefully. He recited his prayers by heart, holding his son's hand through the service. Tears filled his eyes, and he sang the hymns until late in the evening. A small piece of challah was covered, a gift from the kind old lady Abigail, and some cider served as wine. The child cried; he missed his mother and siblings it seemed. How it reminded me all of home! Before Mordechai culminated his morning services, again, amazingly by memory, an orderly (the young Sergeant Campbell) ordered Mordechai and Sheftall to accompany him. Fearful, Mordechai grabbed my hands, shook them with renewed vigor, and tearfully thanked me once again. "Captain Stanhope has some questions for Mordechai Sheftall," Campbell whispered. I feared for him then too; the captain of the war ship the Raven *is not particularly known for his kind words or gracious ways. Few have been questioned and later released. Hangings occurred by the wayside, near a tavern that goes by the name "Tondee's." Stanhope receives word from the former governor of Georgia, a fine gentleman by the name of James Wright. Rumor has it the man was inefficient and incapable. Those men I dread—for they yearn to establish their manhood before all men.*

I said goodbye to Sheftall and his son. He praised his Lord, and said, "For You have sent me an Angel. Zaltman." I am ashamed; for how many men lie cold in the ground who could have called me "Angel"? It is a sad truth—that the tongue I found most familiar to my own roused the humanity within my soul.

Sergeant Campbell led Mordechai and Sheftall through Savannah's occupied streets. Where once stood Patriot sentries now stood British Redcoats, drinking ale and forcing themselves on women. Mordechai forced his son to look the other way; the town had transformed. Where women once stood selling their wares stood buckets of waste; it was as though all forms of civilization came to a halt. The cold air did not seem to prevent the Redcoats from their lusty ways; the women did not charge a fee, they joked. *Thank God my girls and my wife are not here!* Sheftall hung to his father, his body aching from the cold. The one blanket they had in possession had remained by the kindly gentile Zaltman. Sergeant Campbell marched them across town. In every home now resided a redcoat, debasing the men and lusting after their buxom daughters. Finally, they reached the home of Joseph's father—James Habersham. The estate was now occupied; long ago it ceased to be a home for the loyal man, who had died before the war. How would Joseph take to this? Mordechai wondered, knowing just how hotheaded the youth had been, but perhaps had become less so since the end of December. Captain Stanhope stood where Joseph would rant and wave his hands about, where he had whispered his secrets to Jones, and where his brothers swore allegiance to the American cause. The surrender of Savannah became all too real for Mordechai at the moment Stanhope walked across the front lawn, saluted to the youthful sergeant, and spat in Mordechai's wizened face. "Despicable wretch. You're lucky to be alive. If it weren't for direct orders from Colonel Archibald Campbell himself, you would be in a ditch with no markings, I can assure you. Bring him in!"

Mordechai glanced at his son; *why does God test me in this manner?* Sheftall looked down. *I don't know if I can see my father treated in this way.*

They continued to the front door, where the two were ordered to lift their hands. Stanhope's men groped Mordechai, as though he had a weapon concealed. Stanhope nodded his head. They were alone.

"Your crimes are foul. You malevolent Jew! You are a shame to all that is civil! Is it true you are a Jew? A *Jewish* rebel!"

Mordecai stood ramrod, his face red. He stared back at Captain Stanhope, wondering what type of terrible mother he must have had to mistreat another in such a manner. "Have I been summoned in this dreadful, bitter cold to be thus accosted? To listen to your insults?"

Stanhope smacked Mordechai, hard. He went reeling. But he held himself. *Cannon shots filled the air again. Help! My damn musket again. It's stuck. Joseph! Help! Cannon fire.*

"Do not open your smutty mouth to me, Jew. Your arrogance is only second to your iniquity. How dare you! You refused to supply the King's ships with provisions; you shut down the church door—you conniving Jew! You rebelled against God and Crown. You revolting dog." Stanhope began to kick Mordechai in the shins, sending him to the floor.

Sheftall began to cry.

Swim across the creek, Mordechai. What are you waiting for! Cannon fire. Swim! The British are coming, this is our last chance. The Carolinas! Sanctuary! But my son!

Mordechai's head still stung, and now his legs ached. *Oh! My God. Give me the strength.*

Mordechai held Sheftall's arm, supported by his scrawny shoulders. "Your accusations are false. I have never closed the church door; that was not my decision. I was one of many committee members. And I had not refused to provide provisions. One man alone does not supply a King."

"I see your Jewish arse has an answer for every inquiry. You are a liar, a distorter of truth."

Stanhope began to seethe, grapping Mordechai by the collar, and then added in a chillingly quiet tone that frightened Sheftall all the more. "I see you are determined to live the lie of every Jesus-killer—distorting the truth of Christ for your own money-making schemes. Just how much money did you make out of this rebellion of yours, you filthy dog? Do you think we are blind or dumb! You scheming—"

"You speak of shameful deeds? And if the King were standing right here, right now, would he not be shamed by your maltreatment of His Majesty's prisoners?"

Stanhope released Mordechai. About to strike him, and Sheftall recoiling, Stanhope abruptly stepped away. His face, which was flushed with ire, stiffened, and he was without expression for a moment.

Mordechai took a good look at the Captain. He could not have been older than fifty. His stout frame, with a large midsection, revealed his ungoverned appetite. Mordechai suddenly did not like the way he stared at his son; there was a tinge of lust in his eye. *God spare my very soul. I swear to uphold every mitzvah I can, but spare my son good God in Heaven and Earth!*

"I summoned you for your own benefit, seeking to extend my grace. You obviously do not deserve such compassion. It is our custom to offer a general pardon to the prisoners in exchange for an oath of allegiance to the Crown. In addition, we will permit those pardoned to retain full ownership of their property. Most of the rebels who have been graced by this offer wisely accepted."

Sheftall caught his breath. *This is most excellent! He thought! We can go back to Ima! We can live in our house again! We can be free of these madmen and this lunacy if we but swear allegiance to the British Regent! Oh! How great is God's grace!*

Am I mad to accept or rational to refuse? How can I stand by my son and permit myself to lie this treacherous falsehood? And can he be believed? To allow a man all his freedoms for a mere few words of lies? How can I stand now and balk from all that I've held sacred, for a pardon, for perfidy. What will I teach my son, if I were to accept his offer? To live a life of convenience? And what about my principles? Are they too to be surrendered to their Crown? Good Heavens! But what about Frances and the children, the child I had not yet held. Should I allow them to suffer for a mere formality, a few vaporous words, senseless and untruthfully said?

Stanhope paced the room, staring at Mordechai's son, "What have you to say?"

Mordechai spoke, and the captain turned to face him. "So?"

"I refuse to swear falsely. I cannot align myself with tyranny. I am American, and I will not swear allegiance to the king who wages war with his own kind."

Stanhope simply did not respond. Instead, he turned to Sheftall and addressed him, "If you swear allegiance to the Crown, pretty boy, you will escape punishment. You need not imitate your father's ways." *How I yearn to escape this punishment he speaks of and smiles in anticipation of my pain. Hashem in Heaven, Lord of Hosts, have my father change his mind so I can live.*

Sheftall glanced at his father; Mordechai did not seem to blink. He had prepared himself for this moment. But he did not pressure his son. *So I am to become a man again today.*

Sheftall cocked his hat, which he generally wore a bit tilted anyway, and stated: "I shall, in all ways, follow in my father's footsteps. I shall not swear a false oath."

Stanhope spit on the ground by Sheftall's feet. "Treacherous Jews; impudent rebels both!"

He turned to the orderly and spat, "To the prison ship immediately. Keep them both under secure surveillance at all times; they shall not remain under the aegis of the King any longer."

The sentry glanced at Mordechai and wondered what danger such a pathetic looking man with an elongated nose and smallish eyes could possibly pose; the child was scrawny with large, frightened eyes, the expression of a doe afraid of a hunt.

Sheftall held back his tears; *I am no longer a child.* Stanhope shoved them both toward the sentry.

"God will not forgive you so readily for this," Mordechai whispered, glaring at Stanhope one last time before departing from the Habersham home, *finally* an oasis of loyalty to the King, may He live long, and prosper.

OF HAM AND FOIE GRAS

FROM THE WRITINGS OF FRANCES Sheftall, February 1799:

When I first learned of the fall of Savannah, I had immediately taken ill. My newborn child had not yet learned how to suckle, and I had become an invalid. Joshua revived my spirits days later, when he discovered from refugees that Mordechai was among those who surrendered. My spirits revived, I was able to tend to the babe once again. Delivering the infant without Mordechai by my side, I believed, would be the greatest ordeal of this terrible time. But I was most egregiously wrong in my assessment—it is this waiting. The lack of knowledge, the feeling of living in a purgatory of knowledge and sheer ignorance is more than I can bear. If my brother had not been a near-father to my children, I know not what recourse I would have had. Since my youth, Mordechai has been a bastion of hope, a rock for the ages I suppose. He wooed me, won my heart, consumed my soul and possessed my whole self, in a way only a woman desires from her soul mate. But with him no longer around, indeed absent from my life, I feel an abyss awakening within me that is simply worse than a thirst that can never be quenched. To learn of the capture of my dearest was bittersweet—he is alive! Yet what may they do with him, now that he is in their possession. News of hanging and beatings travelled quickly. Joshua endeavored to shield me of this terrible news, but I overheard such from the Negro hands; many of them lost sons to the war. Some fought for the British, hoping to gain their freedom. They died too. Others, like Wright's butler, served alongside Mordechai. I wonder what happened to him.

Word from Mordechai! It is not to be believed! This morning Joshua knocked on my door with this gentle insistence. He knew I was nursing the child, but could not wait a minute longer. A courier arrived with a letter; he had the good sense and forbearance to refrain from tearing the letter apart. It was a strange envelope; not a single return address was evident. I tore the letter open; a small sheet of paper dropped into my lap. How strange it was to read his print!

It read:

Dearest Frances,

As you are most surely aware, the battle for Savannah did not end in our favor. Indeed, I now inform you of my being a prisoner in the white guard house where I am treated as well as could be expected. As it is the duty of every honest man to give praise where it is due, I must acknowledge that I have met with genteel treatment from officers I was formerly led to believe were brutish and entirely cruel. Our son Sheftall, thanks be to God, has escaped unscathed, and is with me. We are reduced to the clothes on our backs, and when we shall be transferred from this place, God above only knows.

I beseech you, darling Frances, to remain steadfast in caring for our children. I am deeply indebted to you, and I pray you are well. Endeavor to keep up the strength, for the sake of our children. Do not fear—I will not forsake our son Sheftall, while there is still breath in me.

I have met with the kindest treatment from Abigail Minis, for which I will be forever grateful. I yearn to see you and the dearest ones! But when I may see you again, Heaven only can say! Therefore, I beg you, dearest wife of mine, to keep your spirits high, as I and our son do ours, and wish and pray, fervently as I know you are wont, that the Great Disposer of compassion should continue to shower us all with His immediate protection.

Your ever-loving Husband,
Mordechai

I must say, his excessive praise worries me; how I fear he is hiding the truth! If I know Mordechai, he is protecting me. But he says he has met with civility. In prison, can such a thing be? How grateful to Heaven I am that our son lives and is unbroken. They are well; they receive proper treatment. Perhaps we will be soon reunited? What can these British soldiers have with my husband? He mostly saw to financial matters, had he not? Such are my thoughts. I must tend to my infant; it is time for another feeding.

April 1779:

Not a word from Mordechai in all these months! It is just maddening— for I only recently discovered Mordechai has not been detained in the guardhouse he spoke of for longer than a week! A week! Good Levi discovered the truth—my poor husband languishes in a prison ship! Those are notorious throughout this blood-stained continent! What am I to do? Whom do I reach out to? John Wereat no longer holds power in the Georgian political arena; most of the members of the parochial committee are nowhere to be found. The war dispersed us all. Oh! Whomever shall I write to? Levi proposed I write a letter to General Howe—after all, he had promoted Mordechai to the position of commanding officer; he bears some responsibility for Mordechai, does he not? Perhaps Levi is right. For now, I shall beseech the General. What else can I do for my poor husband, God spare him!

I finally received a correspondence. Howe mentions the loss of his commanding officer as a great disappointment. But he is power-less at this point. He is waging war in battles words are senseless to describe. Write to a Mr. Lincoln. Perhaps he can be of help. Wishing luck, and that was all. I shall write directly. Not a moment to lose in this battle for my husband's return.

*

Levi Sheftall wondered how his life would have turned out if he had succumbed to Mordechai's persuasions. *Mordechai languishes in some British ship, a prison.* The British separated poor Mordechai from his son, and Levi shuddered at the prospect of never seeing his brother again. Knowing his older sibling, Mordechai would not curry favor with his captors, nor was he likely to sit back and receive verbal abuse. He was the proverbial stiff-necked Jew, and Levi worried it would cost him. Feeling entirely helpless, Levi suddenly felt a torrent of guilt raining down on him. He had escaped to Charleston with Sarah and the kids, together with Frances and all of Mordechai's children. He had played it safe, while Mordechai risked it all. He even increased his wealth deposits. Charleston was safe, for now. But was that all that really mattered? Up until now, Levi had not considered different options. Perhaps he relied on Mordechai to be the hero. He could protect his assets, and his family, while Mordechai saw to the hungry soldiers, the torn clothes, the victuals, the half-broken muskets, and the entrails of Negroes caught in barrels of cannon fire. It was convenient, and Levi was suddenly ashamed of himself. His brother lived by a code word that Levi wasn't so sure was as expansive as Mordechai most clearly believed. And that word, in a nut-shell, was duty. From duty to God, to fellow-man, to country, Mordechai didn't draw the line, not for family and not for his own pocket. This sacrifice cannot be undone by capture; Levi realized he must lift the torch from his brother's fallen hand; he *had* to do something.

Levi tried to suppress his tears; his guilt would not offer him respite. *You pay for Frances' every expense. You have not abandoned your brother's wife, his very flesh. You have helped the cause as well, in many ways. Just with prudence, and restraint. Mordechai's methods have always been filled with ardor and chutzpah. You did not escape Savannah's fires out of cowardice, but out of sheer instinct. The British consider you a traitor, just as they do Sheftall and Mordechai. To them you are the same—so why should you so berate yourself? Be honest! You do not regret limiting your role in this bloody revolution....*

It's just that things now have changed, he said aloud. But what does that mean for him? He continued walking home toward Frances' abode, wondering if she heard from her husband, if her son would be reunited with his father. *Try not to imagine what he's experiencing. Just don't.*

*

Mordechai held the mop in his hand, and silently cursed the heat. With his left sleeve, he wiped the sweat off his brow. This must have been the third time he cleaned the deck of the ever-filthy *Nancy.* A fancy name for a dirty ship. And it would not mark the last time. Before dusk, the crazed soldier from the guard house, magically reappearing as though summoned by Satan Himself to torment him, was recalled from the battlefield with a case of vertigo so powerful, so perturbing, that he could do nothing but whip prisoners aboard prison ships. Jacob Hicks didn't deserve the appellation "Jacob"—for he was anything but the compassionate leader of many men, or the descendent of a great man such as Abraham had been. When it dawned on Mordechai that Hicks learned that torture is far more sustaining than a moment-of-a-hunt-and-kill, was the very moment Mordechai's imprisonment took a turn for the worse. "But he must be kept alive," the latest orders from Governor Wright himself, who would have Mordechai alive and a near-slave than dead and all his worries dead as well. It was Wright who issued the command for Mordechai's ultimate imprisonment, after all—for how would have Colonel Campbell heard of him altogether? It was obvious; from the day Sheftall took the reins of Georgia's council Wright had it out for him. Hicks was the perfect liaison in this case, and today was just another day of misery amongst the many he had endured thus far. And when will it come to an end? *Let me just be with my son, and then I will worry entirely for myself.*

"Sheftall, your lunch is served."

"I shall desist once again. You know why, Sir *Jacob* Hicks."

"Plenty of men on this prison ship would battle for your serving."

"There is no point in tormenting me thus. As you know, pork is anathema to me."

"Yes. But it has been days since you last ate. Do you really think I will offer you a morsel of bread before you succumb?" Hicks tasted a piece of pork, chewed it deliberately, and smiled. "Delicious."

It had become routine. Since his arrival, Hicks had *insisted* on serving him pork. But Mordechai could not eat the meat, and not because he had lost his appetite; he was famished. He just couldn't muster the will to place a fork-full of food that he had been taught from infancy to abhor, or in the least to reject. Hogs filled his barn; but he had never consumed them. Indeed! The animal represented so much more than just a pink slab of otherwise sumptuous meat. If the Torah had not somehow called it impure, it would have been easier. But it was, wasn't it. That's what his parents taught him, his dear father, and the mother whom had never known him. It was too much to bear. *Why is my Jewishness such an effrontery to this man?* How could Hicks not overlook his religion—after all, he was born into this religion. Just as Hicks was undoubtedly born into his. Should he harbor hatred in his heart on that account? Mordechai sighed.

He was famished. And Hicks kept on chewing. He had put up resistance for months now. He was sick to his stomach. But he was hungry.

"In the name of the merciful Lord, I beg you to *please* provide me with a different meal."

"Dinner won't be served for another six hours. You need your strength, Sheftall."

And with that, Hicks turned around, marched off and limped out of Mordechai's sight.

Mordechai breathed in a deep breath of humid and hot air. If he focused on his chores, the gnawing pain in his stomach would somehow disappear. If he tried hard enough, surely.

Letters to influential men had helped in the past. Mordechai wiped the floors and kept composing letters in his head.

"Dear Sir, It is my ill luck to be thus imprisoned. I beseech you to find a method by which to release me...."

"Dear Samuel Elbert: I have landed at Sanbury and cannot learn whether my son is to be permitted to come here or no.... Whatever may be said of me, he was taken in the line of his duty as every other officer was; therefore, it is astonishing to me why he should be pointed at in so particular a manner. You must suppose that is very grievous to me to have the lad kept from me in the manner that he is. Therefore, I must request of you and Major Habersham to use what interest you may have to get him on his parole to this place. It will be laying me under a lasting obligation to you both, never to be forgotten."

By the time Mordechai had to eat his dinner, he was faint. Hicks came once again with the same ham meal. They went through the usual routine: Mordechai begged for another meal, and Hicks mentioned the next, breakfast this time. Twelve hours hence. Mordechai breathed in, and struck his fork against the edge of the pork. He slid the pink slab neatly between the slits in the fork. He closed his eyes. *God forgive me my sins.*

Mordechai couldn't believe his own response. And for years he was ashamed to admit, that truly, it tasted like heaven.

*

James Wright was glad to be home once again. Campbell did a superb job of securing the city. Savannah was under Wright's control once again. Robert Howe proved a weak opponent to Campbell, and now those who were haughty enough to wrestle his own colony out of his imperial-kissed hands now lay either in prison or in ditches. Joseph Habersham and that pock-marked faced Jones were yet in the guardhouse; Sheftall was duly separated from his son and undoubtedly suffered imprisonment upon the *Nancy*, the awful ship now docked in Sanbury, not too far off, in fact. It was precisely as he wished ever since his banishment, that awful time. Parliament rebuked him, and that was far more than Wright could have borne without the promise of one day proving all those politicians *wrong.*

The estate was not in order, well, not since Percy had defected to the patriots. Much good it served him. Wright heard, from reliable sources, of course, that the man died an ignominious death on the battlefield. British mortar fire killed him off, of course. The Negro barely stood a chance, so he was told. But his main obsession was not his butler, but the Jew. At first, Wright thought to have him executed for treason. But then his wife had said, "Don't you know it is worse to suffer than to die?" And it dawned on him that the Jew had better suffer than cease to be altogether. The first step, of course, was to ensure that a man who could see to the job was placed with the duty to torment the man. Rumor had it a New York soldier with the reputation of a butcher at night, who also served in Boston, was perfect for the position. The soldier was glad to comply, glad to be off the battlefield. And even more glad to be a tormenter. It was truly what was called a mutual arrangement.

But pressures mounted for clemency; the Jew had his talons in every influential corner. "Let the son join the father, what harm would it cause." After much deliberation, Wright had to acquiesce; after all, what difference did it make if the son was tormented *with* the father or *without* the father? Wright smoked his reed pipe with a mixture of satisfaction and downright comfort. He was finally in his own home, and was putting every last detail back in order.

*

Joseph grabbed the sentry's arm while Jones slaughtered him. It was two hours before sunrise, and the guard had been asleep. The two had worked together, managing their slick maneuver between the bars of their cell. Tomorrow was execution day; this was their last chance. Joseph used the edge of the bayonet to reach the keys. After much effort, he managed to unlock his cell. Jones quickly tore off the soldier's clothes and donned them. Joseph grabbed the musket and headed out. There would be more men to kill before they could breathe the outdoors.

Quickly marching through the dungeons, Joseph and Jones ambushed one sleeping sentry after another. Now they both dressed like Redcoats, only their faces were marked by the suffering of the prisoners. *We have to hurry!* Once past the last gendarme, Joseph and Jones began to flee toward the swamps. A siren blasted just as they began to hurdle past the debris from the war and the homeless women and children who escaped their homes and the debauched soldiers who occupied what was once their homes.

"I can't see a damn thing, Joseph! Where are we going?"

"I don't know! Into the forest! Where else? Just run!"

"Let's think this through. Why don't we hide and pretend to be Redcoats?"

"We don't have a damn British accent! We don't know the names of our superiors, and we look like damn prisoners of war! Stop thinking, Jones." And with that, Joseph began to sprint across the dark forest, falling over, and suddenly realized he was alone. "Jones! Jones! Where are you *damn it!*"

Joseph continued to run; Jones had remained. Perhaps he was hiding. God only knew what the boy had in mind.

And then a gunshot. And then more. And then none.

Joseph's heart beat, so loudly he did not detect the sweat on his brow or his bowels aching for relief. His nerves were shot. *Where was Jones?*

In the morning, Joseph found Jones's body covered with leaves, mud, and a few good caterpillars crawling between his torn boots. His eyes were open, and his chest was caked with dried blood. Jones was outsmarted in the end, Joseph thought, and he cried like a baby.

*

September rolled in and the British were triumphant at almost every turn. New York fell. Other cities were at risk. The continentals were poorly prepared for battle. The Brits were simply superior, particularly in morale. The Americans suffered tremendous losses everywhere. But Savannah had yet to succumb to the full-fledged control of the British.

The continentals wanted their city back. And they knew just the man to turn to.

Comte Charles Henri d'Estaing. The Frenchman had earned numerous feathers, which marked his conquests, and he wore his cap with the air of a peacock. His men were in fine spirits. In September, Henri realized, Beaulieu, a nice shore-town just south of Savannah, was perfect for campfires and some pretty ladies. His tent was occupied with a beautiful southern belle; he had first pickings, an honorary gesture. An American mongrel, but a beauty nonetheless. The men passed along some fine slices of fresh meat and fresh-baked bread. This was the first decent meal, and

Henri filled his belly before turning to his tent. They joked about the British, even when they tried, they couldn't seduce a woman. It was their teeth. No. It was their manners; women like to be wooed, not lectured over cups of tepid tea. Henri ate amongst his men, only his white breeches slightly browned by the knee caps—the rest of his attire was crisp and quite clean.

Admiral of the seas, captain of his regal Frenchmen, Henri did not hesitate to lift his finger and remove a piece of meat stuck between his teeth. The Admiral oversaw a fleet of four thousand men. *Of course* the women would be eager, but he had to be slightly presentable.

"Admiral. There are Americans who insist on delivering a letter to you in person. Should I let them through?"

Henri did not stir. He simply held out his palm. *What can they request now?* His men played it safe, when they could. His interest was to gain as many feathers, and not to endanger French boys needlessly. The guard handed him a letter and Henri placed it aside. *After my fine dining, well, then I shall read this urgent letter.*

*

After dawn, and after a full night of pleasures, Henri once again read the letter. Of course.

It was *another* request:

To the Honorable Comte Henri d'Estaing:

We have received notice that you decline our request to assist in the recapture of Savannah. You had done so, personally, and rejected General Benjamin Lincoln and Governor Rutledge, twice. We cannot emphasize our dire situation and the necessity of your assistance in our future campaign. There is not a single man whom we are aware of who has vanquished our mutual foe. We plead, we beg, for your assistance. We are quite aware you desire to return to France; perhaps you can do so after another victory.

Please consider our appeal,
The French Consul in Charleston

Henri sat back and thought for a minute. Perhaps one more battle would do him more good than harm. Perhaps this was his last calling before setting sail. He would just need a bit of help from the regulars or the inhabitants of this city Savannah. He was completely unfamiliar with the terrain. He *never* fought a battle without proper intelligence. Now where was that Jewish merchant he chanced in Charleston on his way to church? He must find him and meet with him at once! He was the only man he had met in this American continent that both spoke some Creole/French, and knew Savannah's ins and outs.

*

Wright sauntered around his town and wondered where all the British regulars were. Of course it was still quite warm outdoors, so many were occupied by the bay, but how many were armed and standing by their posts? Needless to say, the men had to be well-fed and otherwise tended to, but that should not prevent them from their duties. Wright wondered if the rumors from his moles were accurate—were the Americans planning a reprisal? Should Wright prepare the militia for an attack? How significant was Savannah, anyway? Didn't the American rebels have other cities to secure, to recapture—how about New York? God the rebellion was bloody. Even in London Wright heard of Bunker Hill and the slaughter of his men. Granted the patriots suffered losses too, but when would it all end? Wright recalled Habersham's sons—where were they now? John was imprisoned, but Wright ordered he should not be executed. He couldn't do that to his old, albeit deceased, friend. But Joseph was another matter. He had fought alongside the *Jew.* As far as Wright was concerned, that placed him in a similar category. He placed Joseph squarely in the hands of the court. *They* sentenced him to death. But, by George! The scum escaped! A warrant was out for his arrest, but by now, the traitor was probably in South Carolina or some other patriot stronghold. *Perhaps it is best; maybe James would have wanted him to live too, despite his treachery.* Better leave justice to fate, for now. Wright had bigger fish to fry, and Savannah, above all, must not fall into patriot hands.

*

"Admiral, an American visitor wishes to meet with you. He says you called for him."

449

"Yes! Yes! Bring him here. Take this lady with you, and place her in another tent for now, will you? Bring him in once she's stowed."

The messenger tipped his cravat and returned moments after. In the interim, Henri cleared his desk, set his bed as quickly as possible, and removed all evidence of his lady's existence.

"Good evening, Admiral."

Levi Sheftall bowed his head slightly and nodded. "Welcome, Mr. Sheftall. I hope you are prepared for a long evening."

"Yes. And I have brought along a friend who can serve as a scout as well, when the time comes."

"Is he to be trusted?" The Admiral feared for a moment.

"Have no fear, Admiral. Philip Minis fought and killed for the cause. He is only glad to assist."

"Then let us work at once. There is no time to lose—*oui*?"

*

Henri summoned Levi Sheftall one last time. A detour road had to be mapped out with precision, and it was the Jew's expertise he sought. The Americans were only a bit more tolerable than their British woes. How Henri detested the pompous Brits! But the Americans had a *way to go* before they could reach the sophistication of *his French* ancestry. How could one compare this fledging country with his hometown, with *Paris*? But time, Henri knew, may alter that. Besides, it wasn't his business to oversee the cultural development of the Americans, only the sustenance of its future. The success of his mission was dependent on *his* bravura on the battlefield, and of course, his superior judgment.

Some assistance was needed, of course. The plan called for the aid of General Benjamin Lincoln's Continental forces; they had yet to arrive. Four days had passed since the General's promise to join forces. But how could one just sit while a city lay defenseless! Savannah was less than a few good miles away—why delay the siege? Why wait for a single day of rainy weather to forestall the inevitable? Henri was not a patient man. It was time to march onto Savannah and retake the young city from its barbarian occupiers, the British *courads*, or cowards.

*

Wright ambled around town on foot, leaving his steed at home. He did not like the general atmosphere of the town; it was *too* serene. Taverns remained opened into the early morning hours, and the men of the town were still asleep. He peeped at his pocket watch—seven. Where were all the sentries? A few guards stood to attention as he passed them, but not nearly enough. Perhaps he should call upon General Augustine Prevost—the man on call for mortal combat. Perhaps *he* would have an explanation.

Wright found Prevost's occupied home. It once belonged to a friend of the Jew. No longer. They all escaped to Charleston. *We'll see how long they'll hold onto their fancy homes there. Soon it will capitulate too; it's all a matter of time.* Come to think of the Jew, rumor has it his brother was a traitor of the most vile nature, assisting in the war effort. *Just give them a chance, and they'll stab you all in the back.* Nothing surprised James Wright anymore. Not a single man of civility in this whole colony. Not a single man to uphold, to revere. Loyalty to fealty was a lost ideal. But they would learn, these Americans. Just as insurgents of all kinds throughout history learned.

With these rambling thoughts, Wright knocked on Prevost's door. A Negro woman with a dirty apron opened the door. She ushered him into the General's chamber. "He's ill." *Of course. That explains a great deal.* And why had he not been informed. "And since when has he become an invalid, may I inquire?" "Mm. I ain't sure, sir." *Of course.* Wright climbed the flight of stairs to the general's private quarters. He knocked on the door. Someone groaned inside. Perhaps it was the drinking water. Those who had not lived in Savannah from youth had a difficult time adjusting to the water. Some complained of watery stools, others of food-borne illness. Whatever the case, the General held a letter in his hand and tried to stand for the governor. Prevost's face was pallid, and his eyes yellowish. His silk pajamas were all crinkled, and the room had a dank, musty odor.

"Forgive me," he muttered, his face all contorted and his beard all white. "I was not expecting your arrival, particularly this early in the morning. You'll have to excuse me, Sir."

Wright nodded, removing his hat. His own hairs have not been as dark as he would have preferred, and Wright wondered if he too would one day appear so aged and tired.

"You must read this letter, Wright. It is good that you arrived when you did. It is Providence, I tell you!"

"What does it contain?" Wright asked, as he quickly read the letter aloud.

"Honorable Foe: (who writes so strangely?)

The one who conquered Grenada now surrounds your city on all sides (who is this pompous fool?). Your defeat is assured (what effrontery!). In the name of his most Christian majesty (is he finding fault with the Anglican Church? The nerve!), King Louis XVI of the great nation of France (oh! The despicable French with their airs!), I demand immediate surrender of the town. (What!) Let not gunshots be fired. Should you thereby delay the inevitable, the crime will fall squarely on your shoulders.

Most cordially,
Comte Charles Henri d'Estaing"

"I received the letter this morning. It is dated 16 September, as you can see."

Wright did not respond. He was enraged. Who did this Frenchman suppose he was writing to? And with such an ultimatum?

"What shall we do?" Prevost asked, coughing up phlegm. Wright did not respond again. He sat on the General's bed and contemplated the question. *What shall we do?*

*

Henri smiled. So this would be a bloodless battle. The retiring general asked for twenty-four hours to prepare the official terms of the surrender. Superb! *Parfait!* He would claim victory, set sail, lay siege and never fire a bullet. This was a night to celebrate in momentous fashion. Where was that beautiful mademoiselle? In France, the ladies would sing lovely songs for the soldiers, entertaining them with tales of love and *histoire d'amour,* histories of love. But where were they now?

The Jew encamped with them, and he seemed a bit out of sorts. He didn't eat the *jambon* (ham). Of course! Well, some mutton would have to be fetched, but that proved useless, since the man had to slaughter the *mouton* (sheep) himself, with a specialized slaughtering knife. Well, some cheese and good French bread should suffice, but the cheese he turned down too! Henri felt a bit sorry for the man as he chewed the day-old bread. Henri realized his religion did not prevent him from enjoying any food. He reminisced for a moment. Turtle soup, frog soufflé, Lobster au Gratin. What else? Of course, foie gras and confits. Did that have to be kosher too? So what did these Jews eat? Levi said, "Beef, lamb, mutton, fish. Just certain kinds, and not sea food." Oh well. He then realized few restrictions were forced upon him. The Jew seemed to have all kinds. "No femme?" Henri pointed to the makeshift harem, where soldiers were seen entering every few hours. "I have a beautiful wife." "So?" Henri joked. Levi did not join him. Instead, he glanced at his watch and bowed, wished Henri a good night and went to his tent. That was all.

Henri thought of the priest of his hometown. He had promised that if Henri just provided the poor parish with alms, then his sins would be forgiven. Yes. In his religion, Jesus died for the sins of man. Henri wondered what the Jew believed.

*

By daybreak two days later, Henri awoke to the sound of a horse's hoofs. Perhaps this is the final surrender, he thought. They are late by twenty-four hours, but I shall forgive the British just this once if I may set sail this morning. Henri quickly pushed his femme out his tent, and received the corporal. He read the correspondence, and then he cursed Prevost's English mother and all British femmes.

He kept on rereading the letter from the two-faced Prevost: "We prefer to retain the city. Your generous proposal is thus refused."

I have been fooled. They utilized these twenty-four hours to fortify the city, while I woo my woman and dream of foie gras. This is war!

SIEGE OF SAVANNAH

CANNON FIRE! HOLD ONTO ME, we'll swim past the crocodiles. Hold on to me. But I can't swim father. Hurry! What's taking you so long? Go Samuel! Leave us here. Cannon!

Mordechai held onto his head. It was Hicks again, pounding away at his skull, and Sheftall was cringing in the corner, too scared to cry out. *Please God in Heaven! Take this man from me; Spare me!* At last, Hicks kicked Mordechai in the gut one last time and left.

"Father?" Sheftall held his father's skullcap. It was dirty and torn. Why did I have my son brought here to witness this, Mordechai wondered.

"Thank you, son. Can you fetch me some water?"

Sheftall was scared of the sentry. He was an Indian, and battle scars were etched on his brow, hind legs, and his forearm. The man donned strange-looking animal bones across his neck, and his hair was long, tied with a red band. A tomahawk was stowed in his breeches, which were made of deer skin. The fringes only momentarily covered the scars on his legs. This was the new guard: *Destroyer.* Sheftall knew from the poor wretch next door, Thomas Gibbons, a lad from his father's unit, that the Indian wasn't hesitant to make good use of the tomahawk. "They just throw the bodies overboard, Shef. Do you hear it, in the morning? I did. It sounded like a dunk in the water, you know? They rid the boat of the Negro prisoners first. I heard the Irish are next. My gut says the Jews will follow. Sorry, boy, 'tis the ugly truth." Sheftall buried Gibbons' words. He didn't tell his father. Perhaps he already knew.

Sheftall had to beg for water. It was for his father. But why would the Indian acquiesce? As he headed toward *Destroyer,* Sheftall overheard Hicks: "When do I leave?... So soon? Are there no men in the battalions?... If it was a personal request, I cannot back down... better. The vertigo isn't as bad as it once was…. Thank you."

Forgetting his errand for a moment, Sheftall ran to his father. He had good news to report.

"Then a battle must be imminent," Sheftall realized.

"Is that good for us, Abba?"

"I don't know. It depends on the outcome, son. But if he is no longer to torment us, then perhaps already our salvation has arrived. But we must be diligent. I don't know how much longer we can remain on this blasted boat. The men are starved, beaten. *Ravaged.* I don't know, son. I've heard the cries of the men. Some while dying, I'm sure. And the diseases on board will fester soon; how they increase in such circumstances. We must be very watchful."

"What do you propose father? You swore that you would not directly, or indirectly, serve against His Majesty. What if you were to violate the terms of you parole? Would they still permit a prisoner exchange? Perhaps they *know* you will violate the terms, and they therefore have a greater punishment in store!"

"I know one thing, son. The longer we remain imprisoned with these barbarian Indian allies, these Tory irregulars and all the Jacob Hicks in existence we are in jeopardy. The math is that simple."

Sheftall nodded, and went to fetch the water. He had to trust his father's instincts. He had few of his own to rely on.

*

Joseph held Jones's letter. It was the last one he wrote to his family—the one that Joseph would mail, *just in case.* He had to mail it. But most importantly, .he had to join the Continentals. Word had reached him—the Americans were going to lay siege on Savannah, and Joseph wanted to become a part of the final battle for his hometown. He marched toward General Benjamin Lincoln's position. But it would be fraught with danger—he had to cross enemy lines before presenting himself to his American compatriots.

October was just round the corner; this was a good time to fight. It was the time Sheftall once said the Lord judges countries and men of all creeds. Joseph wondered what God would decree for the year to come—the Jewish year, that is. Will God sign his death warrant, his life certificate? Will there be defeat or a victorious retreat of occupiers? Will Savannah fall to Wright's ilk for good, or will the siege prove successful? Joseph sighed. He was tired of the war. Where had all his ideals gone? If he was keen on killing, it was to avenge Jones. He was murdered like a hog in the slaughterhouse. Why did he hide? Didn't he realize the gendarmes would be searching for Redcoats—after all, they left the British sentries with only their undergarments still attached to their dead bodies. What had happened to his friend, always so astute, so wise, so critical? Perhaps it was the starvation. It numbed his mind. Joseph recalled Jones's pock-marked and frenzied expression as they hurried past the sentries. Something was missing in his eyes. It was as though he had lost his friend before the bullet claimed his life. It was an emptiness that Joseph feared. It was the emptiness of death.

"George Washington's vineyard is Mary's, and he permits entry to those who don't pick his cherry tree." Joseph whispered to the American sentry at post.

"What the Devil is this? Identify yourself!" The sentry froze. The man wore a redcoat, displayed the secret code of entry, and yet had the haggard look of a half-dead man. His accent was not by any means British, or Hessian he thought. What should I make of him?

"Joseph Habersham, brother of Major John Habersham. I'm here to lay siege on James Wright, and my hometown, Savannah. Please allow my entry, Sir."

*

For three long months, the *Nancy* had imprisoned Mordechai's body and chained his soul. The Tory irregulars and their Indian allies proved worse than Hicks. *How could such a thing be*? Mordechai wondered. To throw day-old excrement on prisoners, to force them to clean the filth, to chain them, and worst of all, to slash them. Days would go without a morsel. Men died. The fleas aboard the ship had much to feast on. Sheftall was slowly wasting away. He began to chant, but then received a beating. He then began to sway. The British regulars at Sanbury, as terrible as they had mistreated them all, had not been as harsh as the *Destroyer*. When his tomahawk unleashed itself, a prisoner would soon be heard begging for his mother's mercy. Sheftall stopped crying. And Mordechai felt entirely at a loss.

This time, their new captors violated the terms of the parole Mordechai had sworn to uphold. But if he were to remain true to his part of the bargain, soon, they would all be denizens of the ocean floor. Something had to be done. Mordechai realized his son would not survive that much longer. And this, above all, frightened him most. The war had taken a toll on many a soldier, but the harsh, brutal treatment on the prison boat was far worse. The heat. Oh! Just the heat in those cramped quarters. And the stench. Mordechai could not believe his body could accumulate so much dirt. The curse of washing the decks proved a blessing in one regard—he secretly washed his face with the filthy waters. It helped, momentarily. If Frances just saw him now. How repelled she would be. The mice scavenged away and the lice ate away at his thinning scalp. Sheftall's scalp was ridden, and the scabs on his beautiful head marked the hours of deep discomfort. At night, when Mordechai dreamed of unperturbed sleep, his feet would itch incredibly, and his head would ache. The heat! He was afraid to sleep without his clothes, lest the lice should travel to his entire body; after all, his body was not hairless. Sheftall's was past his early boyhood years; he too suffered a similar fate. On Rosh Hashanah, what Mordechai was most certain according to his calculations, he prayed for salvation, peace, and a return to sanity. Fasting on Yom Kippur was facilitated by the Indians—they refused to feed the inmates on occasion, and that was one such instance. It was only the following morning that Mordechai tasted the concoction of a slop that induced vomiting in all the prisoners, but was forced down with sheer determination. Survival. Mordechai had yet to see his unborn babe. His wife surely delivered, and he was yet a father to six children. His daughter, Perla. The daughter whose soul flourished like a petal of a rose, inspiring him more as she matured. His lost child he no longer recalled; the infant disappeared together with all his lost memories. He held onto wondrous nights when his were unbearable, and he then swore to aid himself, and not to wait for salvation to come from men who could not imagine his misery nor suffered his torments.

*

"My men are dying! The siege continues and my men fall like flies—without a single battle yet fought! My victuals are waning by the hour, and you expect me to remain like a muted frog?"

Henri was infuriated. The siege on the city of Savannah was not meant to kill off his poor men! It would be one thing to wait indefinitely, but to suffer such losses to the terrible diseases lurking in the waters of this God-forsaken town. How many more men are to fall ill to disease? The humidity did not give way, and yet there were fears of hurricanes pounding the city's fortresses. And they were all docked by the bay—the *most* vulnerable position. It was a waste and a terrible misfortune; to lose his men ere a battle had been won. Henri's fury was directed at the American General, a tall man with a beard and the name of an ancient Hebrew, very biblical. Benjamin. His surname American, difficult to pronounce: Lincoln. He stared at his maps over his large, Grecian nose. His brows sweat-ridden and his boots buckled, the man did not respond quickly to Henri's complaints. He had grown accustomed to setbacks. After a momentary lull in Henri's diatribe, Lincoln turned to him and said, "Permit me to remind you, good sir: the best opportunity to overtake the city belonged to you. You had been duped into a truce. And we now all suffer the consequences of your ill judgment."

Henri could not believe he was being accused of killing his own men. "I sought a peaceful solution and followed established protocols of war. I hoped to avoid needless bloodshed. Perhaps we could have accomplished that—had you not delayed for so long!"

Lincoln nearly rolled his eyes at the Frenchman, admiral and feathers and all. "We must prepare for the upcoming battle, may I remind you once again, Admiral, to ensure that the defenses General Prevost surely prepared will cause *minimal* damage and suffering."

Henri unconsciously clenched his fists. Yes. The Americans were quick to place the blame on his "pompous pageantry," as Lincoln accused him of. But they needed him, and what remained of his men. The sun ignited Henri's temper all the more, and the humidity bore through him like a butcher's knife. He could no longer remain silent.

"I will not remain here a single day more. I will set sail tomorrow. This cannot last."

Lincoln's blue piercing eyes stole a deep and ruminating glance at the French Admiral. *He means what he says. I cannot lose this ally.*

"So be it. We will proceed with the bombardment before dawn." Lincoln nodded his head, and no longer took note of Henri's impatient gestures.

"I will send out the orders at once." Henri responded, but Lincoln was busy staring at the maps again and did not see his ally out the tent. He hoped General Lachlan McIntosh would come through in time with the South Carolina Continentals. They were going to need as many men as they could find.

*

The morning hours are upon us, Henri thought. *God preserve my men,* he prayed. It was the fourth of October, an auspicious day, he hoped. Be it what it may. They had all played their parts, the Jew, the scouts, the cooks, the ladies. Now it was time.

On his steed, Henri spoke to his Frenchmen and his orderlies and sergeants awaited his words. In clear and plain-spoken French, he addressed his men:

"*Mon frère!* We fight this morning with the intent to decimate our mutual enemy. We have fallen ill, yet we are strong. The men who lay behind these walls are *couards*! They have reigned over these poor Americans with a tyrannical hand, and they have decimated their *own* countrymen! Do not be fooled! They will not rest until they have destroyed this country and its innocent men. We've all seen them in battle, how they slash our men like beasts

459

upon their prey. We must not forget the shame they have made us all suffer in years past; it is time to uplift our great King's chin with pride once again. For King Louis!"

"Long live the King!" they yelled, suddenly eager to wage war against the detestable British warmongers they have been raised to despise. For them, this was a call of revenge. To avenge their lost comrades. The men crossed their hearts, muttered a quick prayer to Mother Mary, some kissed pendants of saints, and some simply hoped Jesus would see to their safety.

Henri gave his men a minute to gather their thoughts. And he then yelled the command: "Fire!"

The shelling began. Savannah was bombarded with heavy artillery, as dew so often watered the tall trees in the forests. The women and the children, those Prevost requested be peaceably removed to safety ships in the Savannah River had remained behind. Henri refused Prevost's request—he feared it was another delaying tactic. And so the artillery reduced homes to rubble, claiming all the lives inside, innocent children and the sleeping mothers alongside their newborn babes. Streets pummeled, and it rained gunfire hell and brimstone. Thousands of shells forced residents to take shelter in makeshift bunkers. Mayhem reigned, and Governor Wright awoke that morning to great hellfire. His nightmares could not have evoked such terror in his heart. His house shook from the massive artillery fire, and the barns outdoors were up in flames. The horses screeched in sheer fright, and their masters lay burning to death by their posts. Hurrying to his wife and children, who were frantic in their nightgowns, Wright quickly gathered them all and ran toward the British infantry. This was the safest corner. Most of the officers' wives and children were there, sitting on the grasslands. They all escaped. They were untouched. *Thank God. Please! Watch over them, dear Jesus.* Wright ran down Broughton Street and saw countless animals running about. A man held his dying child, yelling for a physician. Most sought shelter in the cellars. Negro hands, white landowners, artisans, and drunks huddled around one another, hoping for the shell fire to cease. It was their own kind! Most of those in hiding, most of the victims, Wright realized, were patriot supporters! This was chaos. Utter pandemonium! Where would they seek refuge? He realized many townspeople were running toward the northern end of the city, out of the shell fire's range. They were headed to the frontier home of Moses Nunez! The son of the famed doctor who long ago helped save the city—so he too saves the children of this town, Wright thought as he wandered his town, now burning and covered in ash. *My* estate, does it burn? He ran toward his home and stared in astonishment as fire consumed the barns and began to consume the gates surrounding the massive structure that was his beautiful home. Standing in his pajamas, his body all sooty and sore from his escape through the burning city, Wright fell to the floor in utter despair: flames engulfed every corner of his estate, and his precious paintings, and all its grandeur. His head began to spin; the heat from the inferno began to eat away at his skin.

"Governor Wright! We've come! We've come with water, sir!"

The town's firemen began to sprinkle his home with water, but after hours of their heroic efforts, little remained of the home but the skeleton of its frame.

*

The French did not cease. All throughout the day, Savannah was besieged with fire and long-rage artillery. As though the hurricane they had anticipated finally came—in the disguise of fire. The town's firemen could not stand by and let their city burn. The heat of the summer still lingering in the early October air would carry the blaze from house to house. And so they began their efforts. Children were carried out of homes, some badly burnt, others clinging for a bit of air. Houses were doused with water as fire rained from above. All of Savannah was under the mercy of the French guns.

And when they had imagined the fire would end, and the bitter rains of conflagration cease, the French once again opened a barrage of bombs. Those stuck in the gutters and cellars perished from inhalation, dehydration, or pure bad luck: a shell landed while scavenging for water and food.

The siege on Savannah may have lasted a month—but the shower of hellfire lasted for four days, an eternity in the eyes of Wright, the victims, and the many orphans who now littered the town.

And then the French army charged toward the city, ready to take down Prevost's defenses.

The advance toward Savannah had begun.

Henri d'Estaing, on his fair steed, galloped toward Spring Hill, a favorite summer spot of many a Savannah housewife. The Negroes would carry the linens and baskets up the hill, and festivities would certainly ensue. Spring Hill, especially in early October, was fantastically breezy; just the right amount of air would cool off the children, and some would fly kites. The River was certainly visible, and lovers would embrace under the foliage. But not today, thought Joseph. Not today. *Today we're assailing these British, destroying our own damn town just so that we can reclaim it and live as we had.* Joseph marched with Benjamin Lincoln's men, thirty-five hundred in total. The French led the way. South Carolina Continentals were directly behind Lincoln's men. This time, Savannah would be won with men to support her fortresses.

Admiral d'Estaing marched, at the very front of his battalion, finally off his steed. Galvanizing his men, he fought to stick to his battle plan: March in the hours of darkness, right before dawn, toward the Spring Hill, a key British defensive position. It was only eight miles from Savannah. Once the dawn's early light hit the hill, he would attack. That simple. It was Philip Minis and Levi Sheftall who mapped out the outlying marshlands for the invading forces. But there was one catch in all this plan. Key players had to distract the British from this secret advance.

And there was no way to communicate with them.

Isaac Hunger was sent with troops from the east; Arthur Dillon's from the west. Both divisions had to wade in dirt-sodden waters and marshlands. Would they manage to distract the main British defenses? Would they indeed get bogged down?

Henri hoped for the best. But he hoped in vain.

Henri was completely unaware Hunger and Dillon both failed. The men collapsed in flooded rice fields, and the British, sensing the commotion, opened fire. The Frenchmen under Hunger's commission began rumbling into the mud. Retreating toward their initial position, the men tumbled, drowning in bullets and their own blood. Pellets of gunfire bore through the Frenchmen, sending rice and massive waters spraying into the air. Cannon fire erupted, and the men could no longer detect the white fields of the water—it was all red by daybreak.

*

Dillon's men scouted their area prior to the attack; but it didn't help. They still lost their way in the darkness and slush. They eventually realized their error and found the way. But it was broad daylight, and the Brits gunned them down, sending them scampering into the forest, cursing their luck. Both side's parties should have occupied the British resistance; they were meant to lessen the assault on Henri's men. But now the Continental forces would have to meet with full force.

Henri's men marched toward the main British garrison expecting Dillon and Hunger's divisions to lessen their load. Such was their every anticipation. Henri had predicted their success, especially after all that scouting. But he soon realized he had raised the bar of hope too high for the bogs of Savannah and the deep woods of its environs; it was a country that consumed its inhabitants.

The thrill of war yet in his veins and with the ignorance of his failed plans, Henri waved his musket and shouted, "Open fire! Open fire!" The cannons erupted and the hill shook from the blasts. The men loaded the cannons with the precision of restless ants: for an entire hour, the British ground was pulverized, the men crushed by the weight of each flying ball. Hands and legs littered the battlefield; dazed men began to search for their lost limbs, only to die of mortar fire. Ears throbbed; torn arteries pulsated and watered the earth. Chunks of Savannah's moist mud clung to open wounds. Heaps of dung from denizens of the hills infested the wounds; not a single man's mind did not throb with the threat of death. It was everywhere.

Henri's men could only take the hill if they raced to the top, mauling Redcoats, and taking heavy losses. Henri witnessed his men fall with each British round of bullet fire. But the men would have to lie on the grounds; their comrades continued to charge, as though the bodies had not fallen in succession, very much like waves at the sea—they simply keep inundating the shore. Bodies writhed on the floor, but Henri's eyes were focused on the top of the hill—the gate to the fortification was now less than three hundred feet away.

"Ready for close combat!" he ordered. *It's time to fight like a true Roman warrior now. I must take that man. He seems oblivious. What's this jagged stone! Ah!* Before Henri could hop around the boulder blocking his way, a bullet struck his right arm. In an instant, Henri crumbled to the floor, dropping his unsheathed sword to the floor. As he hit the ground, he nearly impaled himself. Pain erupted, but his mind was elsewhere. *What! Victory almost at hand—but to be thus debilitated! No!* He immediately stood, but fell to the ground. The pain was unbearable. "Help!" Comrades came to his assistance. Bullets whizzed. "Get down!" he urged, biting his lips. And with that, two Frenchmen hobbled back down the hill for treatment. "General, we saw what happened. The boulder saved your life. The bullet could have struck your chest. Today is your lucky day, sir." Henri looked back and tried to remember the face of his assailant. He was tall, with a cruel expression. He recalled one mark of distinction: he had many stars of valor on his lapel. *Like me.*

*

Lieutenant Colonel John Maitland fought for the British army for quite some time. His eight hundred men of British reserves were planning on assisting the sickly Prevost and hard-working Governor Wright. It was only a matter of time. But it seemed the siege prolonged itself just for his purpose. "Continue! March." He demanded. His men were tired, but their assistance was most necessary. Rumor has it the Americans plan on a vicious attack. Yes, theirs would be a trek, with Beaufort thirty miles away from the battlefront. But it would be well done, he was sure. "March," he yelled. Only time would tell.

With the battle far from over, Joseph followed General Lachlan McIntosh's brigade of South Carolinian continentals up the hill. The French had done most of the hard work. *We're the first to reach the hill. Now we just need to decimate them.* McIntosh ordered the boys to shoot, even from close range. He was not fond of the close-combat slaughter that d'Estaing seemed to prefer when battles raged with such intense proximity. The fortifications of the hill were exceedingly difficult to break through, even with all that musket fire and cannon eruptions. Yet there *was* a narrow entrance, filled with rubble, but an entrance nonetheless. Joseph witnessed his comrade Captain Thomas Tawse, a staunch South Carolinian loyalist make way for the entrance. In the month that Joseph had remained with the Carolinian loyalists, he had learned a thing or two about each warrior. Thomas' story was simple— he had lost his father and brothers at Bunker Hill, and he now planned on avenging their blood. He was only seventeen. Joseph wondered how long Thomas would wait just to the right of the entrance with his sword at the ready. The first two that had already darted for the same entrance lay dead; they were slain almost upon entry. Thomas didn't hesitate a moment longer: he thrust his sword into his victim. His victim writhed in pain, but did not die so easily. He was fat, and Thomas' sword was stuck in his massive entrails. Joseph ran to Thomas and helped extract the sword. *Run up the hill!* Joseph didn't turn back. Six Americans made it past the entrance before Thomas fell—a Brit fired at point blank range— Thomas collapsed with his sword in midair.

Joseph suddenly froze. *Could it be?* He was staring at the gunman, and it was he—Jacob Hicks. Enraged, Joseph charged at Hicks with his bayonet. *Forget the musket.* Livid and blinded by his hatred, Joseph missed Hicks as the British warrior dashed to the right. Bullets flew in the air and men were falling at every instant. Hicks realized Joseph was stunned, and he prepared his musket. Joseph charged again, his saliva falling out of his mouth. Yelling and seething in rage, Joseph's bayonet slit through Hicks's lower abdomen. Joseph kicked Hicks in the shin, felling him to the ground. But Hicks was superbly built, and he managed to punch Joseph in the face, hard. Hicks's musket lay on the ground, only a few feet away. Joseph knew the man could not shoot at him; it was a matter of wills now. Hicks picked himself from the floor and searched for his musket. He found a sword filled with blood instead. Joseph knew what the man had in mind, and steadied for close combat. Holding his wound with his right hand, Hicks steadied the bloodstained sword with his left. *My weaker hand, but the boy doesn't know.* Joseph felt his knees weaken. He suddenly feared for his life. The expression in Hicks's cold eyes frightened him, and then he wondered, "How could she leave me, for *him*?"

"She never loved you," Hicks suddenly yelled, foaming in the mouth. Joseph had spoken his thoughts aloud. Joseph couldn't believe a word Hicks blurted, and with renewed ire he ran toward his opponent and slashed his arm, but fell to the ground as he felt his sword cut through flesh. *I'm wounded.* His left leg was torn, by the thick flesh of his upper thigh. Hicks smiled a strange, cruel smile. "She never groaned as much as she—"

Joseph could no longer hear a word from Hicks. He jumped and rolled behind Hicks and slaughtered him, just as he finished his final words, "had when she was with me." But blood filled his mouth, as his lungs filled with blood. His face buried in guts and blood and all the mud of Savannah's Spring Hill, Hicks struggled to breathe. Joseph stood above his body, yelled a primordial battle cry, and slashed his skull one last time, before he took a bullet and fell to the floor beside Hicks.

Just as Joseph's body hit the ground, two flag-bearers emerged atop the rampart. They plunged their flags into the bloodstained earth atop the hill. One was a jolly Frenchman, the other an American patriot. Both were not yet twenty and both were shot just as the flags were safely thrust into the wet American soil. The American boy was known as Will Jasper, the law student. He saw Lieutenant John Bush scramble up the hill. "Hurry!" He yelled. He was shot in the chest. Bush was shot too, but in the legs. Both were sputtering blood all over the flag, but they did not let go. Jasper and Bush were later found on the flag; each succumbed to his wounds embracing a pole with stripes and stars. South Carolina's flag. Theirs was a twin death.

The battle for Spring Hill ensued. Smoke filled the air and cannon fire continued to erupt. And then a steady battle cry of horses, men at arms, and musket fire spurted forth. Heavy British fire caught the French and American forces completely by surprise. *Another battalion!?* From the forests, Lieutenant Colonel John Maitland's men counterattacked with brutal force, sprung to life after their long trek from Beaufort. Their bayonets were extended, their boots caked with the mud of the forests. It was as if they had been plagued with one terrible blow only to face another. The Americans could barely respond in time. Slaughter ensued: the Brits split open Frenchmen together with the patriots in one fell swoop. In the time it took for a patriot to load his musket. By then, he was dead, slit in half by expert hands. The patriots began escaping the hill, back across the narrow entrance that had been the way in. Now they all wanted out of the trap. British regulars continued to march through the forest, slaying men and maiming them beyond repair. "Retreat! Leave! Get out!" The Americans were frantic. Hysteria mounted, and the men tripped and fell over their comrades, hands caught in entrails, feet stuck in body parts. It was utter hell. The narrow gate was jammed—troops mauled one another as they desperately tried to escape the Redcoats' bloodbath. "Move! Make way! Out!" Some never made it—they were trampled to death or an easy target for a Brit, firing from less than ten feet away. The precision of their shots increased the mayhem. The patriots began climbing over the fortification, jumping to their deaths. Few succeeded to maneuver past the bloody bodies now clogging the only exit. "Get out! Get out!" The South Carolinians were not entirely familiar with that area. Some men began to scramble for cover in ditches atop the hill. Patriots fearful of the bayonets down below began to follow the soldiers who took cover by the ditches. And then the hell of sheer fire and brimstone spewed from the sky. It was artillery fire. Men danced their last dance as bullets tore through their bodies. Men screamed their last screams for their poor mothers and wives back home. The British massacred them all. The ditch was just another swamp, and the men floated atop the muck that covered the hill. The Brits captured the American and French flags only moments after they had been raised. The hill was no longer in patriot hands.

In the midst of the carnage and mayhem, Admiral d'Estaing suddenly appeared, as though a ghost warrior. His shoulder was wrapped in a large bandage. It was stained a deep red, but he paid no favor to his wound. With his feathers waving atop his head, Henri D'Estaing led a desperate charge against Maitland. *His men must pay*! The French admiral joined General Lincoln in a deep trench just outside the main fortification. From where they both stood, the scenes of carnage were piercingly visible. Lincoln's brows were heavily weighted with despair and worry. "Fire!" He kept shouting at the cannon men. Lincoln's attempt at sniping proved unsuccessful. Maitland's men continued to slaughter his men. He stood, hoping the winds of war would change for his men, stuck in a ditch and caught in a terrible trap. *Damn them!*

"We cannot continue in this way!" shouted Henri, desperately raising his voice over the din of booming cannons. "Our men are dying! Like flies!"

Lincoln knew his tactics were not prevailing. Sighing deeply, he responded, "Perhaps it is time to pull back and fight another day!"

D'Estaing shook his head in disagreement. "No! It is too soon to admit defeat. Now is our chance to take the city. We must do it today!"

Lincoln thought the Frenchman was mad. But perhaps he was onto something. *We must rally the men. It is do, or die.*

"Continue to hold fire, Lincoln! I will charge with my remaining men around the side of the hill—you see! From there. Like this." He pointed to the maps Lincoln had spread across his steed, and explained their last attempt would include a charge around the side of Spring Hill. They will sandwich their defenders, and entrap them!

Lincoln concurred. D'Estaing marched swiftly, ignoring the pain in his arm. His white breeches stained black and brown, with small pieces of human flesh stuck to its thinning threads. His men were haggard, yet focused. Their admiral led them, and they encountered little opposition. They must not let their fallen comrades die for naught. As they approached the rear of Maitland's forces, the French Admiral and his concentrated force of men began to shoot with abandon.

Maitland's forces had been focused on the northern side of the hill—where the slaughter of patriots was consuming his men's attention. *What in heaven's name?* "French regulars! Aim! Fire!" he began to order his artillery forces to pound them down, this time maneuvering toward the other end of the hill. But his men had been slow to respond. And then, fire erupted from the sea.

All men stared out into the horizon and stared for a moment at the beautiful sea. The Hill, after all, was right by the bayside. *Could it be?* A British naval ship arrived and had now begun firing random volleys in the direction of the advancing Frenchmen. Henri did not look back once he understood the ship was another source of enemy fire. "Continue, march!" he hollered. Like automatons, his men advanced toward Maitland's troops under a barrage from the British naval ship. Some fell, but many succeeded to the top of the hill. The carnage escaped their notice—the only focus was the human targets with muskets and bayonets geared toward their slaughter. The British soldiers were at an advantage, after all. They were on higher ground. D'Estaing's men were easily picked off; their attackers began a full-fledged defense. Frenchmen fell in the dozens.

The desperate charge was too little, too late.

D'Estaing did not despair. His men fell atop one another, forming mountains of dead and dying. The groans in the battlefield were nearly soundless in the beating and rushing thoughts of each man. *My men fight valiantly. I must continue!* And then Henri yelled out in pain. *I'm shot!* He fell to the ground. *My leg. My right leg!* He staggered back, quickly trying to stand on his good leg. The pain from his arm now forgotten, Henri could feel nothing but knives and shooting nerves screaming from sheer torment in his leg. *The battle is lost! The battle is lost!* His men reeling, Henri suddenly lost his cool level-headedness and began screeching, "Retreat! Retreat!" *How I detest those words!* Vertigo spells began to accost him. "Retreat!" he continued to yell, dizzy from his wounds, dizzy from the chaos, and dizzy from the bloodbath atop the hill. "Men! Follow me!"

And then he collapsed. His men saw their admiral all bloodied and dirtied. "He's down! He's down! A gunshot to the leg!" Once again, his men ran to his aid and carried him back to safety.

"This way!" ordered one of the men, his face all soaked with his own blood. A gash to the forehead nearly blinded him, but he saw the way to safety.

"I know this path! There is a Jewish cemetery here, far from artillery fire! Follow me!"

The Frenchmen placed their wounded admiral behind the walls of Sheftall's cemetery. They passed Perla's grave, little Sheffy's, and all the Jewish congregants who had died since Savannah's inception in 1733. There lay the Admiral, numb and dumb to defeat.

*

"It's over. Tell our men we are pulling back. I've seen enough bloodshed today." General Lincoln's men pulled back, stopping their cannon fire. His eyes had seen what he would not, indeed, could not forget. *This is the bloodiest battle of the bloody revolution, by God.* The landscape was a mass graveyard. Bodies littered the hilltop, from its lowest points to its apex. Piles of dead men, torn into bits and pieces, were placed like logs by a fireside. Already the flies and pests were at the fresh flesh. Skulls battered and crushed were no longer recognizable. Only the uniforms identified the men. In death, they had suddenly gained a certain brotherhood of sorts.

Over a thousand bodies served to fortify the earth of Spring Hill—and it was renamed by those who survived—Death's Hill.

Lincoln and Prevost both agreed to a truce—they had to bury their respective dead.

Each side claimed victory in a manner most confusing to the inhabitants. Governor James Wright declared a holiday upon the successful battle at Spring Hill. Yet the Continental Congress proposed a holiday as well! A truce had come to play, in a most strange manner.

Henri could not believe the carnage Savannah had suffered due to the siege. Upon his recovery, he had met the fathers of the poor children who had died. The firemen who doused homes saw to his wounds and waves of guilt consumed him. Sleep would not come, and the pain in his legs a reminder of his own ghosts. Orphans offered him water, and a few kindly women changed the bandages binding his leg. Something had to be done. These people, he thought, never meant me any harm. In a desperate attempt to cleanse himself, Henri wrote an apologetic letter begging Prevost to forgive his "callous refusal of the insurgent people" to allow innocent women and children to seek safety in the Savannah River, on boats, far from the scene of fire and fury. Henri could not forgive himself; he had been too eager to set sail, too eager to end the siege, begin the battle and end the entire standoff. And now I'm stuck here, waiting to heal, he realized.

General Lincoln heard of the French admiral's transformation and was truly irate the man should apologize to Prevost. But soon worries flooded his camp in Charleston, where the British were soon planning on seizing with swift military might: smallpox infested his camps, and the disease further decimated his fledging forces.

What man would not devise, nature had intended, he realized. Charleston was now defended by less and less capable men. Most of his valiant soldiers lay underground. Indeed. He tore the correspondence detailing Henri's penitent ways, and began to drink heavily into the night.

*

Henri thanked his physician, and boarded his fleet. Ailing, and dejected, the admiral finally set sail to France, his beloved country. *My fleet is much lighter. The best I left behind.*

UNBOUND AND REBOUND

"Hold my hand!" Mordechai whispered. Sheftall held tightly. The plank was loosely bound, and Sheftall had to jump across the *Nancy*, the she-killer of a boat, and board the small American schooner, *Betsy*. The sun had not cracked through the horizon just yet. A cadre of American officers jumped aboard. The Captain, a bold man who heard of the prisoners' travails aboard the British ship out of *The Inferno* was headed to Charleston when he decided, quite last minute, to help those poor patriots seek sanctuary. The American brigantine neared the ship, and now, right before the Tory irregulars and their mad Indian allies could detect, Samuel witnessed as scores of broken men sought refuge. A young man, a boy by every measure, gaunt and sickly-looking with a blank stare most disturbing to the captain, held what appeared to be his father's hand and nearly tripped. His legs were weak, by the knees. His father's firm grasp eased the boy's fall. "Quickly! There's no time!" The men jumped, assisting one another. One at a time.

"Father! What if they find us!" the boy asked his father, apprehensive and frightened.

The father did not respond. He just held his son and whispered an odd-sounding prayer. His beard was riddled with specks of white hair, and the dirt on his face made his eyes appear smaller. His cheekbones jutted, lending his profile an asymmetric appearance: his nose was extraordinarily long for his face. His hair-line receding, he appeared to be the child's grandfather, but his strength was still visible, despite the starvation he had no doubt suffered aboard the deathly prison ship. Captain Samuel Spencer thought he recognized the man, but he was not sure.

"You seem oddly familiar, Sir. I'm the commanding officer of this boat. Captain Spencer."

Mordechai glanced at the captain and wondered what he must have thought of him. Ashamed of his appearance, he muttered his name.

"Well! I am glad to see they did not have your neck on some noose, sir! I'm sure you've heard—many patriots were last seen hanging by the post near Tondee's tavern, you know, I'm sure, the very sight of many clandestine meetings...." The captain realized Mordechai did not have the stomach to grasp the information; he appeared to be lost in his thoughts. *Perhaps this is too much for him, poor fellow.* Captain Spencer tipped his cap and ordered his men to see to the needs of the prisoners. Food, water, and a good wash. These men were ridden with lice for Christ's sake!

"The ship moves slowly, father." Sheftall whispered. "Shh. Rest son. You need your rest." Mordechai said, nearly choking on the thought *soon we shall be free from these monsters.*

*

Levi returned to Charleston dejected; his efforts amounted to senseless deaths and defeats. The men were shot in the paddies of rice, contaminating the source of the colony's main income during the war. And how they floated! Rumors reached his ears of the battle's impending doom, and he fled under the burning sky. He had personally led the men through the thickets, the underbrush, the massive boulders, and the infested bogs during the lull before the bloody battle—how he sketched the way for them! It was a sure-all, he believed. But like my brother, he realized, my efforts did not bear fruit. The rebellion failed. Crestfallen, Levi marched toward his house afraid of his own estate burning down, like all those beautiful homes back in Savannah. The British were sure to overtake the Carolinian city too. It was only a matter of time. What will help turn the tide of war? He wondered. *And what, above all, will I tell Frances?* With her husband languishing day by day, what comfort could he possibly offer?

As Levi walked toward the Hart household, he noticed the streets were quiet and empty. Few horses galloped in the roads, and even the bakery doors were shut with a sign "out for the day," hanging lopsided, slightly swaying. Levi noticed a horse tied to the gates. *Who does it belong to?*

The housemaid let him in and greeted him cordially. He removed his riding cap, his buckled shoes and waistcoat. It was a long ride home.

"Joshua?" he inquired.

But the house was eerily silent. Levi walked past the parlor and up the stairs, to where he heard muffled noises. Frances was crying, delicately wiping her nose. Her children were all quarantined into the room. A physician with a black briefcase was whispering into Frances' ear. Joshua was in the corner, holding a candle. "It may be a mild case, but you cannot be too careful. They seemed to have contracted the disease from one another. I advise you keep the youngest one as far away from them as possible—the infant is quite vulnerable, as I'm sure you are aware, Mrs. Sheftall." The physician spoke calmly, but firmly. He had seen too many patients die young.

They left the room and bumped into Levi standing, eavesdropping. "Levi!" Frances whispered, relieved to see he had survived the terrible siege on her beloved hometown. "My God! It is a blessing to see you! But you should go to Sarah! She is over her head, Levi. It's the children—they all have the smallpox!" Crying again, she whispered, not wanting to frighten the kids who could overhear, "It is ravaging the town, Levi. There isn't a single household without a poor child suffering. It is simply awful, but the apothecary seems hopeful. He says it may prove a weak epidemic, as such there are at times." Her voice trailed, and the two climbed down the stairs, with Joshua just steps behind, and the three quickly blessed one another, hoped for better tidings, and wondered just how those on the prison boat fared, if the smallpox claimed them too.

*

Sheftall sighed heavily. He kept expecting to see *Destroyer* marching by with his tomahawk. He kept vigil each night, making sure he was not a target. *Destroyer's* rage would accumulate at a certain hour of the night, and it must have been about now, Sheftall assumed, that the barbarian attacked Gibbons. *Stop! For the sake of mother Mary! Ach! No! No!* Those were the only sounds in Sheftall's ears. He did not hear the curling waves, the gulls, the lapping waters. No. He only heard Gibbons. *Dunk.* "Sleep son!" Mordechai placed the warm blanket across his son's frail body, wondering just when his child became a man and when he had become a child again. How his eyes seem to speak words of an aged man! Mordechai thought, as the sounds of cannon fire erupted every now and then. They were nearing Charleston. Perhaps the British were assaulting the town? The prison boat shook during the siege. Mordechai and Sheftall heard the cannon fire—it must have been for nearly four days, perhaps more. Even from so far away, the winds carried the cries of the fallen soldiers. The gulls were cantankerous at night, as though murmuring the curses of the impaled and the wounded. *I can't swim father, but go! Carry me!*

Sleep eluded Mordechai.

Captain Spencer handed the sails to his junior officer and decided to sleep in his cabin for the evening. It had been a long, arduous day. The prisoners needed much tending to, and it was his sole desire to ensure their recovery. How blighted their spirits! How dampened their mood! By God it was difficult to imagine what they had endured. One prisoner ate his portion like a hungry wolf, licking his dirty fingers and crying with pleasure. Another ate until his vomit later served to sully the deck. Most bathed with buckets of sea water, finally appearing somewhat human. His seamen gladly lent articles of clothing, helping the poor men with their laundry. At night, when the air was frigid, once again, his seamen aided the men—most were covered with thin layers of flesh, so they shivered far more than his healthy men. It was a matter of course. The Jew and his son ate their dinner, even though there was some unkosher foodstuff in the recipe. They had seemed dumb to detecting such. The father kept prying the son with food, and the son kept offering his meal to his aging father. They were mostly silent. By midmorning, most of the prisoners were asleep, except for the boy. He seemed far away, looking over the horizon. Waiting for someone or something, it wasn't clear. *Let sleep settle my stomach; I have seen enough for one day.*

Mordechai Sheftall. I am providing you with a choice. Swear allegiance to His Majesty—and you are free. Refuse and you shall perish by your own hands. Swear! I cannot. I am an American, and I refuse. Comply! I refuse! Jump! Jump! The Creek will lead to safety! Father! My musket! It's stuck! Shoot! Aim! Fire! Cannons! Lay down low! Fire! Help! Cannon fire!

"Father! Father! Wake up! They are taking us back! Father! They found us out!" Sheftall's eyes appeared larger, the hysteria in his voice rising and drowning the cannon fire resounding in Mordechai's aching head. *It was a nightmare?*

"Father! Look!" Sheftall ran out of the cabin and pointed to *Guadeloupe*.

"Father in Heaven! It's a British frigate!" Mordechai whispered, dumfounded and aghast.

"What shall we do now?" Sheftall said, suddenly crying.

The British did not waste their time. They fired cannon rounds, frightening all the prisoners and Captain Spencer into quick submission. *The loads of gunpowder on this boat will decimate us all if a cannon ball shall so much as land on my precious vessel.* Running with muskets and polished boots, the British held their muskets high, pointing their guns at each man they could, pathetic patriot prisoner or healthy American sailor. To them, this was a battle. With the swift movement of his hand, the captain of the *Guadeloupe* ordered his men to empty the boat of prisoners of war. Sheftall froze and shivered. The image of the Indian terrorized him.

"Come on! Let's go boy. Don't make this far more difficult than it has to be." But he could not budge. It was his knees. Or his legs. Mordechai whispered into his ears, "Do not fear. Son. Do not fear." Together they boarded the British frigate, utterly dumb and shocked. *Freedom had nearly been ours. It's gone now.* Captain Spencer sat in his cabin, holding his heavy head in his hands. The eyes of the Jewish boy blazed his memory, and only a bottle of rum could undo the torment of its glare.

*

The *Guadeloupe* sailed. It sailed for days. The British men aboard the ship did not pay much attention to the sleeping prisoners. They fed them when their bellies were already full, and they didn't torment them. They just sat, spat, played their cards. Cursed the war and blessed their king. And then, finally, the boat docked on a British Island—St. John's in Antigua. Black slaves littered the shore, and Negro children hung to their mother's long hemlines. The sun's rays are far stronger here, Mordechai realized. His skin itched and burned. Most of the men held their shackled hands by their eyes, endeavoring to block the lethal rays. It was futile; the fetters weighed too heavily; they could not lift their wrists. The British marched and the prisoners followed in a line, slow paced in the blistering sun. The Negroes wondered who the white men were, and if they too would be sold in the American continent. Their brothers and sons were sold many a time; their homes were raided, their ladies ravaged, their children no longer theirs. But these were mostly white men; would they sell their own kind? Did they speak their language, or did they speak the language of the white man? They seemed weak for labor—why would they be bought at all? The Negroes were mostly strong, with muscles of great steeds, of arms of massive beasts. Their labor was a commodity—but these pitiable creatures? What good could they possibly provide?

Mordechai was cramped into a cell with four other men, including Sheftall, whom he refused to depart from. The chains on their legs and wrists frayed their skin, and they desired to be released from the constraints. But the British left them rotting in their dirty clothing, without a morsel, with their hands tied and their every physical need neglected until the evening, when sentries came with slop, keys to unchain them, and chamber pots—the latter which was no longer necessary in some cases.

Mordechai nearly forgot to bless his food; his mind was in another world. *I need a pen. I need paper. I must send appeals to everyone and anyone I know may be of help. I must make a mental list. Here, we will remain for eternity if I shall not endeavor to liberate myself and my suffering son. Oh! God of my fathers, let your people go! Let us breathe free!*

*

Levi turned to his wife and kissed her gently. "All the men are escaping to Virginia, love. I hate to leave you behind, but it's safer this way."

"How am I to learn of your return? When shall we see you again?"

Sarah was unnerved. The British were only hours away from taking over the government of Charleston. Her husband had already become notorious. The women and children the British left alone, but the men they imprisoned, or worse. With the smallpox raging yet, Sarah felt at a loss. *Is this what Frances feels?* Having wed Levi in her late teens, Sarah could not recall a moment without her husband. She had developed into his third arm, learning from Levi how to live her life. He had been patient and loving, and most of all, understanding. He did not abandon her for a cause, like Mordechai. Instead, he remained by her side. Except for now. Since his brother's capture, Levi had become a man changed by circumstance; it was as though he lived a half-life, in the name of a ghost, filling in its shoes. He tried, desperately, to do so. And now he had to pay the price—and so did she. Sarah hugged him and began kissing him fondly. She knew he was right; he had to go.

She prepared a few good meals for him, mostly sandwiches with cold turkey. He packed his prayer shawl and *siddur*. "Please write as soon as you arrive in Virginia, Levi. I will anticipate the letter and relate all that is occurring here." He nodded and hugged her. "Depart from the children, Levi. They will miss you terribly."

Levi knew his wife was right; her intuition was usually correct. His children cried, begging him to remain. Their cries and small arms binding him so close to their poor pocked faces tore him to bits inside. He would have preferred to steal out at night, but he could not become a thief in the night. He barely recognized their beautiful faces, but their voices were engrained in his mind.

The carriages were waiting, and the roads fraught with danger. Sarah began hugging him again, clinging very much like the children, holding his head. "Hurry home, Levi! I love you, dearest."

*

From the Journal of Frances Sheftall:

December 1779:

This year, the goyim celebrated Christmas with British guns and artillery fire instead of their lights. Hanukkah was dimmed by the sadness in our hearts. The children barely recovering from the smallpox (although I must admit, Perla did not suffer as much as the others, with barely thirty pox covering her entire form), we opened the gift boxes with a mixture of joy and sadness. Sarah's poor child does not fare well; the pox ravaged his poor little body. We all prepared potato fritters, well, that is I did. I no longer have much help. My poor husband sold all my Negro housemaids to fund the war! Truth be told, I was very unhappy with his choice. After all, since our marriage I have grown accustomed to both a nurse and a few good housemaids. My Negro staff did not want to leave; they said other masters would not let them take the Sabbath or rest even on a Saturday afternoon. They were afraid of beatings, and their children being taken terrible advantage of by the males in the homes. I need not detail the horror stories we've all heard. There was Betsy. She tried to ward off her master, but she never did succeed. They say her three children are his. Their skin is not as dark. Perhaps the rumors are true. I fear to learn. And there was Collette. She was truly a darling girl. Only twelve. The pregnancy was too much for her small frame. The master did not bury her in the Negro burial ground. It was as if she had never existed. He just asked the shipmasters to dispose of her body, together with the fetus, still stuck inside, in the great Atlantic. And now I must tend to the housework myself, and yet I wonder if Mordechai shall ever return, if I can find my previous handmaids again, if their cruel masters (or indifferent at best) will release them for purchase. Perhaps it is better this way, to some extent. My children have learned to assist in all the duties of the house; the girls learn to mend, sew, bake, and cook. The boys too! Although they are young, they know how to prepare a chicken for Shabbos dinner, and they chop the wood nicely, for such small hands!

But now the British are in Charleston and I hear of more abuse. Women rarely leave their homes without male chaperones. But who will see to the Negroes? The poor women are enslaved by their new British masters with pitiless barbarity. They slay them, once they're done with them. This has been the spiteful and terribly vicious revenge they seek on the American housewives. These Negro women run into abandoned cottages, waiting for the blood lust of the captors to subside. I have placed two in the cellar. Their eyes are filled with an august fear. I feed them daily, until they shall be able to escape perhaps. They shall suffer from their American owners too, once they return. No woman likes to be left without her hands, and the patriots, as much as they are keen on their own liberty, do not extend that freedom, of course. The slaves shall remain bonded, but at least they can escape with their lives. The children are not any safer. A girl of nine, especially a developed one, is in jeopardy as well. So I have heard. There is no end to the malice of our captors.

And now I think of Mordechai. How he must endure the cold, ruthless hand of his captors! He does not describe his every suffering moment, but I cannot imagine their treatment of prisoners of war as humane. I have opened my eyes, and cannot pretend he is away and in good favor. I have sent appeals to many influential men; and Mordechai has written as well. Our dual maneuver should, with God's grace, prove somewhat successful, I'm sure. He's in touch with Wereat, and a business acquaintance, a one William Bingham. But the anti-Semitic Governor of Antigua seems recalcitrant: he refuses to hear Mordechai's case for a prisoner exchange. I am convinced governor Wright, the ex officio judge and jury, curries favor wih the anti-Semite and thereby persuades him to ignore my husband's pleas. Thus, I have failed to ameliorate his situation, and so has my poor husband. I can only surmise as to his lassitude. What can expedite his transfer, or better yet, his exchange? I shall write another letter to the Continental Congress—they cannot flout her request. Surely they will prove equitable, after all Mordechai had sacrificed for the cause! They can influence Wright to grant amnesty, if they would but ingratiate themselves to the man. As much as Wright believes he has full autonomy in Georgia, he does not. He must answer to men like Hamilton and Adams. We'll see what these letters produce; for now, I must open my psalms and pray.

February 1780:

How these British men transgress all laws of decency and compassion! They forbid my sending any articles for the relief of my son and spouse! They are terribly distressed, and I am hampered from assisting them. What heinous occupiers, most odious! I now share the animosity of all American men and women for our captors; the British heart is cold, and it knows no sympathy. Their soul most retrograde. They pillage our town, debase our women, and desecrate our people's every right. The patriots are all the more eager for restitution, and they desire full disconnection from the Majesty's throne. They foment the war, and disseminate hatred in the minds of man. They shall not defeat us—God will see to that.

Summer 1780:

I must inform Mordechai that our Savannah estate no longer belongs to us. How he will sadden to learn this news. But it had been forfeited to Wright's government. The British troops now reside there, enjoying the bounty of my husband's labor. Many of our people retired to Charleston to escape the siege, and I am glad for it. The Minises too, God be blessed. We few Jews have escaped unscathed, and must be forever grateful. How frightful was the siege! Every woman I know was frightened of the men's talons and their lust. How it hailed. It was as though the cannon balls flew like hail in the heavens. I had to hire a house at the rate of fifty pounds sterling a year, eventually. How will I let him learn of my financial difficulties? Nothing but hard money goes here, and that, I must assure him, is hard enough to be got.

Of course I have not been without resources. I must let him learn of that too. After all, I don't want him to be overly worried. I will let him know that I was obliged to take in needle work to make a living for our family. I will leave him to judge what a living that just may be. The few Negroes that I managed to procure after some financial success have been at the point of death for many weeks. All are, thanks be to God, getting better. Except for Billey. Poor child died of the yellow fever on the 3rd of July....

I need him to return; how much longer can I postpone paying the doctor's bill and house rent? I will hint to the financial difficulties, knowing that he will be able to sympathize and perhaps hurry his own release.

Levi tore his shirt and wailed incessantly. *I must sit shiva for my son, I must mourn for seven days.* How can I sit here in this warm parlor in Virginia while my wife buries our child all alone, despondent and disconsolate? Oh my Lord in Heaven, is this the very end of the road? How could my child disappear from my grasp; am I no longer to hold him? He cried such and thought bitter thoughts for much of the evening. He held the letter detailing the terrible misfortune of his son, now blotted by tears and phlegm.

Levi, my husband,

Please sit down as you read this letter, for it bears news of the most terrible nature. The smallpox has claimed the life of our youngest son, and his illness is now finally at an end. He did not mutter a single cry; he was simply cold in my hands, as I rubbed him again and again. He did say he loved his Abba, and that he was sure to see you again in heaven. He bore his disease with such dignity, and with such humility, that I am most proud to have borne his lofty soul. His voice filled the air, right before his last breath, and he prayed to God the Oath of the *Shema* with fervent faith in His Judgment and Compassion. He then ceased breathing and fell into a serenity he had not known since the early winter. *Baruch Dayan Emet,* May God blessed be, even during our time of misery.

Sarah

Levi ached to return to Charleston. This was no time to be hiding away. The British cannot hold onto their territorial gains for that much longer. Defeat was imminent. Such were the rumors circulating in town. I must take advantage of the one offer left at my disposal, and the one deed that will prove my undoing—but I cannot weigh my own honor against the family I am duty bound to protect in this time of dire need! He thought. Levi gathered his letters, belongings, and all odds and ends and hurried to the office of the British commanding officers. He raced to the busy court, past the blooming fields and the budding tree; little evidence remained of the blizzards and terrible storms of Virginia's harsh winters. Women sold their wares, and he bought a few loaves of bread, lettuce, and some jam. This would have to suffice for my journey, he believed. Without a single delay, he marched to the front doors, demanded to sign the oath—the one method of amnesty to fools of the revolution and perfidious traitors to the Crown—and swear his Allegiance to the most Kind Crown, the Glory of America and England.

His final and single act of desperation.

He exhaled as he signed under the petition:

I, Levi Sheftall, shall not endeavor to partake in any activity to imperil the sovereignty of his Majesty King George the Third, and do solemnly swear to uphold the British Crown above all. I thus swear my Allegiance to the Throne of His Majesty King George the Third upon this notarized document.

Signed,
Levi Sheftall
Colony of Virginia, 1780

Levi could now return home, and the Disqualifying Acts were thus officially void—he can now be his own master again. No law would steal away his own estate and lands.

His wife shall not suffer alone. For him, the war was over.

*

Governor Wright smoked a fine cigar and sauntered around Habersham's estate of old. His own house in ruins, Wright now took residence there. Granted he had many more plantations, but it was a useful and most practical arrangement. The main officers remained in Habersham's eerie home, and the papers were in order. Wright's oak desk was brimming with correspondence, from abroad and from domestic sources. Finally, General Lincoln removed all his Continental troops from Georgia! He reflected. He and his French madmen nearly destroyed the city during the siege. Well, *his* forces took revenge on Charleston. It hailed balls of cannon fire soon enough in Charleston's roads. After a relentless assault and pandemonium, the patriots thought better than to wrestle for control. They surrendered in May. It was a beautiful morning for the Tories. A holiday ensued for their households, and the whiskey glasses clanged throughout the night. But a chaotic spring followed the May holidays. The Tories and the Georgia militia had it out for one another. Savannah was spared, somewhat, and Wright believed he had only his own wits to thank. But rumors spread of British soldiers defecting, of Hessian warriors complaining of the mad heat. Wright thus opened the pubs for the Germanic men, and ensured their most generous welcome to his town. Women were at their beck and call, and the soldiers were occupied for most of the summer and hopefully into the autumn.

His cigar had a funny taste today; the humidity in the air lent a musty scent to the tobacco. He placed it in a crystal bowl and rang for his butler. "Clear this from here, will you." The Negro nodded and summarily left. "Now it's time for the latest correspondence." He rummaged through his letters. *How did I miss this one? It's from Antigua.* Dated April! He removed the red seal and began reading,

Honorable Governor of Georgia, Sir James Wright,

Your foresight is most acute, sir. The island proved beneficial in one regard: the captives have no hope of escape. But they have recourse to the post, and one such captive has made ample use of his influential powers with the continental

484

government. As directed by your honorable orders, I have remained averse to exchanging prisoners of war. However, behind my very back, indeed without my knowledge, the Continental Congress has allowed the traitor Mordechai Sheftall to sign yet another parole. My hands are bound in this regard, as you can imagine. There are plenty of our men in the hands of the detestable patriot foes. One lucky man shall find refuge amongst our ranks if this detestable man is to be exchanged. Sir, Sheftall was authorized to proceed to New York and from there to Philadelphia. He is no longer in my possession. Indeed, soon an honorable fellow, Jacob Jarvis, will be unfettered. That is my only consolation, and perhaps should be yours as well.

Forgive me this failure. As I mentioned earlier, I was given little choice in the matter. It seems this man is a great rebel indeed.

Signed,
Governor of Antigua
April 1780

And how long did this letter sit on his desk? He wondered. He is free! And I now learn of the man's devious behind-hand manner of escape—all legally now. No midnight foils with Hicks. No boarding frigates in the early morning hours. No. This time through his cronies in Philadelphia—those he bought out, most *certainly!* Wright cursed the man. So he is free, after all.

"Curse him!" he yelled, throwing the letter into an ash heap and calling for the butler once again.

*

Mordechai and Sheftall shaved their beard aboard the vessel. Soon they'll visit the colony of New York where many Jews will certainly take care of their needs. Soon I'll pray again in a shul, he realized, eager for a new life. Sheftall had grown taller, despite the lack of nutrition in their diets. *Soon I'll be with Frances and the children. I'll have recourse to kosher food, and begin my life anew.* He did not know how, but he was determined to rebuild his assets. He had nothing but the dirty shirt on his back and his son by his side. All his possessions were gone, forever. His wife, thanks be to God, cared for the children, and that was his greatest reward. *They tried to break me, but they failed. I thought I would perish, but I survived. I am alive.*

Sheftall smiled at his father. He looked younger now without all those white hairs sprouting from his cheeks. The New York harbor was slowly coming into view. He cocked his hat. Maybe he'll meet a nice young lady now that he was free. The Continental Congress came through; they didn't abandon his father in his time of need. God had sent the proper messengers—and they were liberated! Two years of filth and torture—were they truly a thing of the past? These weeks aboard the vessel have been a dream, he suddenly ruminated. The men on board were jolly, telling merry tales and drinking ale most nights. Their jokes about the ladies weren't decent, but they were humane. There was no rancor on deck. No Indian with tomahawks, no *dunks* of dead men beaten by merciless beasts in the silent hours of the night. In New York, his father promised him, were *Jews*. Men and boys like him, with a circumcision, who read the portion of the Torah, who were free to practice the Sabbath rituals, the dictates of their ancient religion. He had not been a very good Jew for these past two years, he soberly realized. At first he did not eat the pork. But he was starving, and even his father eventually gave in. At first he prayed with his father, word for word. But then, while in prison, there were some days that seemed like one long, endless night. He neither spoke nor prayed; he neither stood nor sat. Like a dormant slave, afraid of his overlords, Sheftall just dreamed of his childhood, of playing with his younger sister, Perla. Of jumping through the waves of Savannah's shore, of his kindly nurses, with their black skin. In his mind, he heard the flutes of the Creeks meandering through the thick forests—the very ones he was forbidden to roam. He imagined dining with his favorite friends, the Minises, and the kind face of Abigail, the matron who had saved his father's life. He recalled the smiling embraces of his dear grandmother, Hannah, and his father's half-brother, Levi, his beautiful and exotic wife and their sweet children. His practice of Judaism wasn't what it should have been, he sadly noted. He didn't *really* bother to bless the food, because it had no taste. It wasn't *really* food. He was cursed like the primordial serpent—everything he ate tasted like dust. And then he thought of the cinders of all those dead men, and his appetite would evaporate. But that would change now, his father assured him. The war yet raged, but the British could not possibly win God's succor after all their crimes. No. They had harvested God's wrath. His father and Sheftall were testimony of all that one man could endure and yet survive to tell the tale. God alone would see to Justice, his father swore. He would not abandon the poor patriots who lay cold and battered, interred in the muddy grounds of the American landscape. No, the war was not over. There was still Joseph and Jones. They would fight their battles. They had not perished in the battle that claimed his father's sovereignty. No, they would avenge Percy, poor Percy who died for his freedom. The black man who hardly spoke a word to him; God's messengers would be avenged. So it is believed. So his father said.

In New York, his father promised, they could buy *challah*. And there they could begin to rebuild their lives.

TEARS OF GLORY

1782: THE TIDES OF WAR had finally begun to swing in America's favor and Washington's men began to wage war against a failing army. The situation in Georgia was no less dire for Wright's ilk, and he was withering away in Habersham's estate, afraid of what would happen next. Hessians had enough of Savannah's pubs. After a bit, not even the women could distract them from the intense humidity, the extreme heat, and the blood-sucking insects that killed off their Prussian men with ease. The Creeks contaminated the waters, and the Prussians were ailing with dysentery. The Savannah swamps backed up in the springs months into the River, and the entire town stunk. And how was one to dispose of waste without a proper sewerage system? The dirty British did not seem to care, and those that remained in the city had no power to change their own circumstances. Savannah's heat that April of 1782 was brutish, and long-lasting. Without respite at hand, the Hessians simply gathered their rucksacks and made sail. Zaltman was one of the few that defected the previous summer. Working for the British, many realized, was a dirty business.

The time had come, and Governor Wright could not believe the details of the latest orders from the new British commander in North America, Sir Guy Carleton: evacuate. *Evacuate.*

General Washington's men devastated British ranks. The French were valiant, plundering the troops. Nothing was left in their hands, save for Savannah. *And now that too is gone, without so much as a drop of damn blood to soak up the earth.* Wright stared into the silent abyss of his falling and failing universe and wondered how he was going to break the news to his wife.

The keys to the city no longer belong to me.

∗

Mordechai's keys to his estate were lost as well. Indeed, he was a destitute fellow now. *A pauper.* But his wife was healthy, and their children were still alive. Many men and women were not as fortunate. Many widows littered the towns. Mordechai promised he would never forget the emptiness in his heart and the starvation of his soul during those two years of hell. No. He was not alone to suffer from the blight of the British. His brother now suffered as well. Levi was coldly treated by all who had met him, calling him a traitor. He had sworn allegiance for convenience, many said. They accused him of being a Tory, and Levi now had to pay the price for being loyal to his family, and not considering the larger sentiments of Duty and Honor. Mordechai wasn't proud of his thoughts; it barely suited him to be so pessimistic. Levi suffered because of his judgment, and so had he, come to think of it. Both had been faced with the same choice—and yet both suffered as a result as well. Just differently, but somehow the same.

He replayed his moments of secret joy with his wife for months, to keep his spirits high. She had done a fine job of building a home for their children, on the small income that she had managed to accrue. She had tended to the children, but he had yet to meet his youngest son—a sheer image of the little child he had lost years ago, Frances was most certain. His voice reminded her of Sheffy, and Frances' youthful tone returned to her letters. Shabbos meals will not be as grand as they once had been, but there will be warmth. The war had reminded him of what was truly most significant in his life—and he wanted to give back. He wanted to give back to his people—*a synagogue must be built to serve as a stronghold in the new country of the free and the brave!* That would be his undying commitment from this day hence, he decided.

Philadelphia was not Savannah in many, many ways—but it boasted a thriving Jewish community. After his long exile in

Antigua, Mordechai began to embrace the notion of community living all the more. It was vital—to create a bastion of like-mindedness and friendship in a vast, and only getting larger, country. Here, the homes were more colonial in style and packed closer together. The streets were filled with traffic all hours of the day. It was bustling with life, and Philadelphians were involved in their neighbor's lives. Tonight he would attend to this desire of his, to once again contribute to his people. A meeting was scheduled for members of the Philadelphia Jewish community, and a *shul* was the main concern on the table.

Many important figures sauntered into the parlor of a wealthy community member, a one Mr. Choen. The rooms boasted of fine porcelain vases, beautiful portraits of the ladies and children of the house, Dutch-looking in their beauty and other wonders of the civilized world. The walls were ensconced with elegant candle lights, and a crystal chandelier of well-lit candles illuminated the wainscoting on the walls. The carpets covering the wooden floors were in excellent taste, Mordechai noted. And the paint freshly layered with an expert eye; French or Italian molding (he wasn't sure) techniques were utilized throughout the ceiling, and it was high. The blue paint was reminiscent of the Savannah River's hue in late spring. By the hearth, a Menorah of sterling was evidence of the religion practiced in the home. Otherwise, it appeared in every continental fashion of the time. Few slaves worked in Philadelphia. The ladies in waiting were indigent, but properly dressed. They were most certainly the revolution's orphans and destitute. At least they are gainfully employed, Mordechai thought. He thought of his savior, Zaltman. The Prussian, Mordechai hoped, thrived in his hometown. Not everyone was so lucky, he sadly mused.

The meeting proceeded. The owner, Mr. Choen, began to solicit the necessary funds to begin construction. The ladies in black gowns and white pinafores, their hair neatly tucked in white bonnets, offered refreshments. Mordechai uncrossed his legs and reached for a *rugelach*. He had not eaten one since his wife departed for Charleston. Mordechai sighed. His dream, years prior, and eons before the revolution wreaked havoc on his life, was to build a synagogue in Savannah too. He raised his hand, "I offer three pounds." That was all he could afford, and he wished to suppress his shame. *I had once the sum of King Solomon.* Most of the congregants clapped their hands. They knew three pounds for the destitute refugee from Georgia was a paltry sum given with great sacrifice.

After the bids and the promises, Mordechai was eager to leave. This place was not for him. He was no longer the high roller he had once been. Dejected, he gathered his hat and thanked Mr. Choen. It was time to head out, he thought.

A short, elegantly dressed man appeared beside Mordechai, right before his planned exit. "I overheard the announcement of your donation and simply *had* to introduce myself."

Please leave me alone. Please just let me go back to my quarters.

The man was quite verbose. He did not let Mordechai slip in a word. His velveteen waistcoat was combed so perfectly, Mordechai wondered how many brushstrokes succeeded in achieving that end.

"Haym Salomon. It's a great honor to meet you."

Mordechai was stunned. *This is the man?* He was short, and his warmth was palpable. He continued, "I have heard of your heroic feats. It is an honor. An honor." He shook Mordechai's hand and did not let go. Mordechai's spirits rose.

"It is an honor too. I have heard half the Continental Army is in your debt for their wages and outfitting," Mordechai retorted, knowing what may be meaningful to the man. Salomon's boisterous laugh caused many heads to turn. "Quite the exaggeration, I assure you. My monetary investment shrinks in comparison to yours. I have heard you lent vast sums to the Continental Congress, am I correct?"

Mordechai nodded his head. "Yes. But I am no longer the same man, Haym. I am destitute. I expected Congress to repay, at least some, of my loans. But they have remained silent to my pleas. My predicament, unfortunately, does not merit their attention."

Salomon's eyebrows moved closer and closer as Mordechai related the extent of his poverty and his deep disappointment with the Continental Congress. What disturbed him most, he confessed, through tears, was the disagreeable fashion with which the men he had so much honored and revered turned a cold shoulder to his dilemma. Mr. Hamilton, he admitted, responded in a decent manner, but many others left him simply heartbroken. To be thus abandoned, in his time of need.

Haym Salomon knew of Mordechai's travails, he said, hoping to comfort the broken man. He too advanced a colossal sum—a total of $650,000. He too has yet to receive a cent in return. And he is not optimistic. What was a loan may have been, at the end of the day, a large donation.

"But let not your sprits sink you in a quagmire, my friend. The trees of tomorrow sprout from the toil of men, today. Our children, the generation of men and women to come, surely, will eat the fruits. Of that, I have a guarantee." Salomon patted Mordechai on the back, offering him a ride, blessing his generosity, and shaking his hand once again.

Mordechai ruminated on Salomon's words. He knew he was right. He invested everything he owned, even his own flesh and blood, his own sanity and waning strength, his every penny and his every ounce of freedom. But it was a small price, after all. He realized it was not necessarily his lost funds that ached at his soul—but the neglect from Congress at his hour of need. He felt abandoned, lost. Suddenly, he felt as he had years ago, when his father passed on. It was that dreadful abandonment all over again. Rolling over in his dry and rigid cot, he cried like a baby. He cried now as he had not allowed himself to cry when in custody, when in the midst of fighting for his life, when the claws of Hicks were at his neck, when the *Destroyer* came for him one night, and the watch that he had bribed him with saved his sorry life. Now he cried, suddenly a child again, whose mother lay cold in the ground, and he sucking his thumb wondering when she would stand and sing to him his favorite lullaby, when she would hold him and take him to the beautiful sand to play. All those tears that he held back came down pouring out of his soul. He had fought for a country that helped him in his time of need, when he was young and building his vast wealth. It was American land that had served as his father's refuge, and the land that he had sacrificed for. It was Savannah's heartland that blessed him, and it was for Savannah and its mighty men that he had fought for. Rolling over, his cot now wet from his tears, and his back aching from all those nights of beatings and sleeping on cold floors, Mordechai wept some more. He had escaped with his life, and now he was half-dead. But he must not despair. God had not abandoned Him, and he suddenly recalled the kind face of Hannah Solomon, his adopted mother, kissing his full cheeks and promising to be kind. She had renewed his life with a sense of love and wonder, and she had helped him regain his trust in man. It was her face that suddenly appeared to him, very much in a wakeful dream, promising him good fortune, if he were to just think of all the joy in his life, past and present, and certainly future. With tears in his eyes, he rolled over once again, and this time heard his father's voice, singing in the Yiddish of his ancestors, "*Modeh Ani*. I am grateful. Be grateful my son. God basks yet in your glorious deeds. You have honored Heaven's name. Be not eager for glory, for God glorifies in the deeds of the meek. Seek love and peace, a place for his Glory to Shine. Do not despair, my son. My *mamaleh*." And then he most certainly heard his lovely mother's voice, dear Perla. Singing, "My *yiddishe kinderlach. Mameh* loves you, dear. *Mameh loves you*. Wake to glory, my son. Your wife heads to you; Your son now sails toward your shores. Fannie and the children await your joyous embrace. Awake, my son. Awake to glory."

And when the bright morning sun did awaken him, Mordechai's heart ached, for it knew of no greater glory than the love in his heart for his country, his family, and his Lord.

POSTSCRIPT

THE CONTRIBUTION OF THE PEOPLE of Savannah to the Revolution against the British led to Georgia joining the Union as the last of the initial thirteen colonies. But the spirit of hope and freedom that prevailed among the people in the early days of Georgia's history did not last. The establishment of the Ku Klux Klan in 1866 ushered in a period of racial discrimination against blacks, Jews, and Native Americans that ran entirely contrary to the original spirit of the early settlers of Savannah.

MORDECAI SHEFTALL

Mordecai Sheftall (1735-1797) was born in Savannah Georgia: "The Rebel of Savannah" and ardent patriot, a freedom fighter, a generous philanthropist, and a great humanist. He was elected Chairman of the Revolutionary Committee (1776). In 1777, he was appointed Commissary General of Purchases and Issues to the Georgia Militia and was responsible for supplying the colony's soldiers with food, clothing, and material. Sheftall often reached into his own pocket to purchase supplies for the volunteers.

A great American.

TEMPLE EMANU-EL
HaSifriyah
Haverhill, MA 01830

Made in the USA
San Bernardino, CA
30 June 2014